ROMAN

Innerworld Affairs Series

Book Six

Marilyn Campbell

Cover and Book design by eBook Prep
www.ebookprep.com

May, 2015
ISBN: 978-1-61417-751-7

ePublishing Works!
www.epublishingworks.com

PROLOGUE

Katy, Texas, 2064 A.D.

As a uniformed police officer enters a convenience store, he slowly scans the interior, apparently looking for someone in particular. A middle-aged man is behind the counter, handling a sale to an elderly woman with an oversized purse. He waves at the officer but receives no acknowledgment.

Only one other customer—a young, fairly attractive woman—is in the store. She chooses a six-pack of beer and heads for the counter. The way the officer watches her suggests she is the one he's looking for.

He waits until the old lady turns to leave with her little paper bag. He removes his gun from its holster, shoots the clerk and two customers in their heads, then, placing the weapon's muzzle in his own mouth, pulls the trigger one more time.

Adam Sirilovich opened his eyes and studied the expressionless face of the woman seated on the other side of his desk. He had invited her to his office in downtown San Antonio based on an underling's mediocre recommendation. But clearly that one had no idea how talented she was. "Very impressive. On a conscious level, I knew you were planting the scene in my head, yet I didn't sense an intrusion. The scene felt like a clear memory to me, as though I personally witnessed a real crime."

"That's because you did."

When she said nothing more, he was too curious not to prod, even though it revealed more interest than he normally would during an interview. "Explain."

She exhaled audibly, as though she were running out of patience. "Mr. Siril—"

"Stop. Do not speak that name ever again. Do not even think it. From this moment on you will think of me only as Adam. Is that understood?"

"Of course...*Adam*. I was told you were looking for someone who, for the right reward, would be willing to ignore a few, uh, legal restrictions, and was capable of distant mind manipulation. Although I might be the only person on the planet who meets both those requirements, I still thought I would show you an extreme of what I can do using my skill."

This time, he simply raised one brow and waited.

"The officer in the scene gave me a speeding ticket as I was driving through Katy on my way here this morning. Because he handled my license, registration and the ticket, I was able to maintain a connection with him as long as I continued holding those items." She lifted her hand so he could see she was still holding the documents then tucked them away in her purse. "Long-term control requires that I have handled and retained possession of something of their physical body, like hair or a nail clipping...or blood." She paused for him to confirm his understanding of how her skill worked, then continued.

"When you asked for a demonstration, I simply sent the officer to the nearest convenience store and planted a scenario in his mind. He instantly recognized the three people inside as the cold-blooded murderers of his wife and children. He fully believed he had been given orders to shoot to kill on sight. The suicide was just for my own…entertainment."

"When did this happen?"

"You were watching the events as they occurred. It can be confirmed by the news in a minute or two. And by the way, the reason you could tell I was in your head was because I allowed it."

Adam felt his pulse quicken with excitement. Was she the one he'd been waiting for? The female whose gifts would complement his own? The yin to his yang? "I heard no sound. Why is that?"

She shrugged. "I don't know. But I've never put any energy into it either. As long as I have visual, audio is an unnecessary accessory for what I do."

He gave her a nod of understanding. Physically, she was rather plain, but not completely unappealing. On the surface, he was only average-looking himself. With medium height, weight and coloring, he was generally overlooked in a crowd. His exceptional traits lay hidden inside. Like him, she was clearly ruthless, calculating, intelligent and self-confident. And she appeared to be in good health, something he could confirm in time. He ceased his analysis when he saw her glance at the clock on the wall.

There was so much he wanted to discuss with her, but he knew there would be time for all of that later. For now, he simply had to secure her commitment to be part of The Eden Experiment. "So far, I have located two others who are capable of mind control but neither has the ability…nor the conviction…necessary to force a law-abiding person to commit murder, let alone suicide."

"Obviously their talents are inferior to mine."

He smirked. "Or they are not quite as conscienceless. I've been looking for someone for a very special assignment. You can obviously plant information into someone else's unexpanded mind without them being aware, and you said you *allowed* me to know you were in my head. Are you also able to read a person's thoughts?"

"Unfortunately, no. Apparently, I can send but not receive."

"I see." Adam took a moment to categorize that information before continuing his interview. "That would have been helpful...but not totally necessary under the circumstances. What is more important is whether you can prevent someone with telepathic abilities from reading *your* thoughts."

She tilted her head to one side then the other. "I really don't know. I've never had the opportunity to test that possibility. Is that your gift?"

"Unfortunately, no," Adam replied, purposely repeating her choice of words. He touched a button on his intercom. "Join us please."

Seconds later, a ten-year old boy rushed into Adam's office. "This is Cain. He's the most gifted mind-reader I've discovered. Cain, this is...no, wait, let's make this a game. Can you tell me her name?"

The boy rolled his eyes in disbelief at such a simple challenge, but as he stared into the woman's eyes his expression changed to confusion. "She's not playing fair," he complained to Adam. "It's like she's hiding, but I don't see any way to look for her. Is this the kind of game where I have to do something else to earn a key in order to see the secret door?"

"I'll explain later, Cain. You can get back to your studies now."

As soon as Cain left, Adam smiled broadly at his guest. "Apparently, you have the ability to block a powerful intrusion. That is excellent. How do you feel about taking the name Eve from now on?"

"She was the one who disobeyed God's orders, right?" She waited for him to nod then gave him his answer. "That would be acceptable...*if* I decide to join your merry little band of mutants."

Adam's cheek twitched at the insult on top of the suggestion that she might refuse his offer, but he responded in a calm, controlled tone. "We are not mutants or deviants. We have simply experienced an awakening of the dormant parts of our brains—an evolutionary progression predicted by many brilliant minds, including the enlightened Doctor Kanji Cho. You really should read his latest book to fully understand what has happened to you. As to The Eden Experiment, I told you as much as I can at this point. I thought you understood—"

She cut him off simply by holding up her index finger. "There are two important details you omitted. Exactly what is the special assignment you have in mind for me?"

For a millisecond, Adam wondered if she had used her skill to stop him from talking, but his desire to enlist her assistance was stronger than his suspicion. "A special task force will soon be created to figure out what my *merry little band*, is working on. I need someone to keep me apprised of their actions."

"Aah, you want me to be your spy. Why can't the wonderkid just read their minds and tell you what you need to know?"

He shook his head. "His gift is formidable, but only works if he's within a few feet of his target and looking in the person's eyes. Also, like most boys his age, his attention span is limited. Besides, I must assume most, if not all, of the members will have psychic gifts, so they might pick up on someone...less experienced...trying to invade their minds."

"And someone might try to get into mine to find

you," she added. "Which is why you wanted to make sure I could recognize and block a mental intrusion?"

"Correct."

Eve granted him a half-smile. "All right. I'm not completely bored. I'm assuming the task force you want me to spy on is not one I can just sign up for. So tell me how my skill could benefit your plans?"

Adam rubbed his jaw. "I had something in mind, but now that I've witnessed the extent of your ability, I'd like to hear how you would go about it."

Over the next hour, Adam told her what he knew about the task force and she offered suggestions of how she could infiltrate it. When there was nothing more to be gained by further discussion, Adam asked, "I believe you said you had two questions for me. Your assignment was one. What was the other?"

She paused, leaned forward and gave him an unmistakably seductive smile. "What special talent do you bring to the band?"

He leaned back in his chair and intertwined his fingers behind his head, purposely opening himself to her visual inspection. "Professionally, I am a successful architect and civil engineer, which, when added to my genius I.Q., goes a long way toward my being a master strategist and facilitator."

Eve narrowed her eyes at him. "I don't believe you've answered my question."

"Actually, all of that is accurate and comes in handy, but you are correct. I do have an extrasensory ability as well." He decided the woman he had chosen to be his Eve should rightfully be the first person to know his secret. "I can see the future."

CHAPTER 1

Washington, D.C., Six Months Later

Roman Locke leaned casually against a back wall of the Oval Office. So far, he had gleaned nothing worthy of his special gifts or his skill as a tracker.

Outerworld Monitor Control had only been able to discover the time and location of this impromptu meeting. As a transient emissary of Innerworld, Roman's current assignment was simply to observe and report back on the proceedings.

The President of the North American States remained stone-faced throughout the brief reports from the Directors of the FBI, CIA, Armed Services and Homeland Security. They all assured her nothing unexpected or out of the ordinary was going on anywhere in the world. There were only two people left to contribute information, a big man and a beautiful woman. They made everyone wait while they exchanged whispers.

Roman had recognized the man immediately, more by the uniform than his stature and weathered features. He was Chief Mike Friedrich, head of all the Texas Rangers. The instant Roman had seen him enter the room, he'd decided to add that man's attire to his Outerworld collection of clothing styles.

The black shirt and black denim pants weren't unusual but the calf-length duster coat, well-worn snakeskin boots and black felt cowboy hat were rarely seen outside the New Republic of Texas. Roman especially admired the low-slung, two-holstered gun belt on which the Chief's golden Lone Star badge was clipped. He bet the empty holsters usually held old-fashioned six-shooters rather than high-tech laser pistols. Though he didn't have the man's heft, he felt he had the height and shoulders to pull off the whole old-time cowboy look.

The Chief's position in the New Republic of Texas was equivalent to the combined responsibilities of the four Directors sitting around him.

"Madam President, Directors, Ah'd first like to thank you for respondin' so quickly to my request for a sit-down."

Friedrich's dialect was new to Roman's ear but he found that noteworthy as well. He imagined that the meanest threat could be disguised by such a lazy-sounding delivery.

"Ah must respectfully dispute y'all's insistence that there's nothin' out of the ordinary goin' on anywhere. Now y'all know very well how we Texans prefer to handle problems in the New Republic by ourselves. But recently we've had a whole passel of unexplained incidents reported—people doin' things against their nature, misdemeanors and petty crimes bein' committed by upstandin' citizens who have no idea why they did what they did and burglaries with no physical evidence of an intruder. Ah'm very reluctant to say this, but there's a growin' consensus that there's somethin' paranormal or maybe even *alien* goin' on down there. An' Ah don't mean the illegal human sort. At any rate, Ah felt it was time for us to compare notes."

Roman noticed how President Kriss Callahan's head moved ever so slightly at the word *alien*. She was one of a select group of Terran officials who knew of the existence of Innerworld, the Noronian mining colony in the center of the planet where Roman had been born and raised. But even the leader of the largest country on Terra was unaware of the Innerworld emissaries unobtrusively stationed throughout Outerworld.

Callahan cleared her throat and the others turned their heads toward her. "These incidents you mentioned, are they at all focused?"

The Chief shook his head. "We can't be sure of when it actually started—like Ah said, the incidents themselves were unremarkable and unrelated—but we picked up on it as some sort of growin' trend in San Antone around four months ago. Since then, we've had scattered, but similar, reports from all over the Republic. And before y'all ask, there's no pattern that we've deduced. Plus, there've been a couple days where several things happened as far as six hundred miles apart at precisely the same time."

As Friedrich gave specific examples of incidents and locations, Roman studied the woman at the imposing man's side. She'd been formally introduced to everyone by the Chief, which suggested it was her first time being included in this esteemed group. Despite that, Dr. Erin Breswell appeared calm and confident. Either she believed she could handle whatever they tossed at her or she was as talented an actress as his Aunt Cherry.

It was obvious to Roman that he wasn't the only one in the room who found the lady intriguing. CIA Director Donald Najinski and the President had both been sneaking glances at her shapely calves, possibly because so few professional American women wore skirts that stopped above the knee. Callahan and FBI Director Latisha Garrison were more typical in their loose-fitting trousers.

His gaze, on the other hand, was focused above Breswell's shoulders. Her hair was the color of rich burgundy wine, pulled away from her face and tightly twisted and clamped at the back of her head. A creamy complexion and rose-tinted lips perfectly contrasted the darkness of her hair and brows, but her eyes were what intrigued Roman the most. They were golden-brown, or brownish-gold, or brown with gold flecks—the hue seemed to change with the light—and they sparkled with intelligence.

He couldn't resist getting a closer look. The instant he neared the circle of chairs, however, her nose twitched, as though an offensive odor has just wafted by, then those fascinating eyes shifted and peered directly into the space he was occupying.

It had to be a coincidence, of course. There was no way she could see him standing there…at least not in his present state. At the moment, he was invisible.

His unique ability to disappear at will ensured that *no one* in the room would be aware of his presence. Invisibility was the reason he was given such a high-level, sensitive assignment. It was imperative that none of these authorities discover that a representative of a non-Terran civilization was spying on them.

As long as his bare flesh didn't make contact with anything solid, everything around him remained visible and appeared perfectly normal to a viewer. Besides that precaution, he was very careful never to wear any product that emitted a scent. Thus, whatever Erin Breswell had smelled couldn't possibly be emanating from him. That had to be a coincidence also. But two coincidences were one too many in his mind.

Both Roman and the object of his curiosity returned their attention to Friedrich as he said her name.

"From time to time, the Rangers hire civilian consultants, like Doctor Breswell here, to take a look at a case from a, uh, less grounded point of view. We've mostly used her skills as a psychological profiler but occasionally we've had success by tappin' into some of her, uh, less academic trainin'."

His vague reference immediately raised questions, but he sidestepped them before they were vocalized. "If y'all don't mind, Doctor Breswell can explain what she does better than Ah can. But Ah want y'all to know she has the complete trust of the Texas Rangers, so Ah suggest you take what she has to say quite seriously."

"Thank you, Chief," Dr. Breswell said quickly taking over. "Gentlemen, my doctorate is in parapsychology. Through my research and my work as a criminal profiler, I have occasionally found an individual with verifiable extrasensory perception, or expanded mental abilities, of one form or another. However, more often than not, the *gift* a person seems to have is based on excellent deductive reasoning and a willingness to trust one's first impressions or gut instinct. I have a series of tests that help me determine the difference."

"And you, Doctor Breswell? Are you...*psychic*?" asked Garrison in a tone that implied she would need solid proof if Breswell said yes.

"Not at all. My professional success is attributed to education, experience and a very high intelligence quotient."

"Plus..." She hesitated for a beat. "I have a working knowledge of ancient metaphysical tools, like astrology, numerology, runes and tarot." She smiled at the range of expressions those words elicited.

Roman noted how her reference to people with expanded abilities barely raised an eyebrow, but referring to tools of divination created obvious tension. Such things had been banned in various parts of the North American States during the years of realignment. Although the Third World War had ended with the China Compromise six years ago, there were still plenty of people looking for answers or reassurance. The rational reasoning for the bans had been that too many innocents had been taken advantage of by charlatans. The irrational conviction came from those who had turned to ultra-conservative religion as their anchor. They believed such devices came from the devil.

Roman had no idea if any of the people in this room believed the latter, but he didn't care what the others thought of Dr. Breswell. He was intrigued before she smiled. Now he was enchanted.

"Skepticism is a justifiable reaction," she told them with another understanding smile. "Public trust in those tools has fluctuated throughout recorded history, but they have always had supporters in certain respectable private and scholarly sectors. The truth is, I was once a hardened skeptic myself, but real life experiences opened my mind. And that is all I'm asking of you today. Have an open mind about what I have concluded."

Roman gave her points for presentation. She knew exactly when to pause for effect. She glanced at Chief, he nodded and she delivered their message.

"My conclusion is that there is more than one individual using mental telepathy to control the minds of unsuspecting citizens. I'm certain these events are more organized than they appear to be and the person behind these events is a male, Earth-born human. I can also tell you that he is shrouded in darkness and his intent is far from benign. Yet the reported incidents have been relatively harmless, suggesting he may be in some sort of testing stage."

Garrison's expression remained doubtful and the Armed Services Director frowned, but neither commented.

"I've seen enough to know that mind-reading and telepathy are possible," interjected Najinski. "But the only mind *control* I've come across involved long-term brain-washing and chemicals. However, I'm willing to keep an open mind, as you requested. But what do you mean by a 'testing stage'? Like, for something bigger?"

From Homeland Security came, "Could we be looking at a new type of terrorism?"

"*Psychic terrorism?*" President Callahan questioned in a hushed voice.

The Chief took those questions. "Possibly. If Doctor Breswell's interpretations are right—*which they usually are*—messin' with people's behavior and committin' misdemeanors could certainly be practice for somethin' much bigger in scope, or possibly somethin' more subversive." He shrugged and shook his head. "On the other hand, until we have hard evidence to support her conclusions, we have to go with the possibility that this could just be some kid who hit puberty and got super powers along with his underarm hair and he's been experimentin' with his new toys. We don't have enough facts to predict anythin' with complete accuracy yet. But if y'all start pickin' up on similar reports we'd sure like to add that information to our findin's."

"Also," Dr. Breswell said clearly then paused and glanced toward where Roman stood before meeting each of the group's eyes. "I'm putting a task force together—another parapsychologist and a few of those truly gifted individuals I mentioned. I would welcome a qualified representative or two from the North American States."

As the meeting shifted to allow questions and answers, Roman noticed a fine sheen of perspiration appear on Dr. Breswell's upper lip. Was her cool confidence an act after all? A feigned cough gave her an excuse to cover her mouth and dab away the evidence of imperfection.

But when he saw her cheekbones flush and a hint of panic flash in her unusual eyes, he wondered if she was suffering from something worse than a case of nerves. Before he could draw any other conclusion, everyone's attention was drawn to an opening door where one of the President's aides appeared and gave her a hand signal.

The meeting inside the Oval Office ended abruptly, but the attendees continued their discussion in the hallway.

Najinski immediately maneuvered himself into position beside Breswell. Roman felt an inappropriate sense of protectiveness as he saw the man touch her hand as he spoke.

"As I'm sure you're aware, my agency has a division that specifically devotes itself to following up leads related to extrasensory perception. Perhaps you and I could—"

"Excuse me," she interrupted and took a step back from him. "I don't mean to be rude but I really need a bathroom break. I promise to be right back."

The others returned to their conversation as Dr. Breswell headed away. Roman couldn't help but wonder if she really needed the restroom or just space from the attentive spook. His instincts told him to follow her, so he did.

She took a few steps, stopped and turned around. Her gaze slowly scanned the seemingly empty hallway before she resumed her walk. A moment later, a young woman exited an office and smiled as she passed. The doctor stopped again, this time sniffing the air as she visually examined the space around her.

Roman took several steps back, just in case she was actually picking up a scent from him. He watched her shake her head then continue on her way.

When she finally entered the ladies room, he programmed his Innerworld ring to transmigrate him back home. His parents weren't expecting him but he had no doubt they would make time to hear his report.

Innerworld

Co-Governors Romulus and Aster Locke greeted Roman as though he'd been gone a year rather than a week. But their smiles vanished as he related everything he'd heard in the Oval Office.

"Could an Illusian be involved?" Aster asked. "I remember how they were able to deceive everyone when Gallant kidnapped Cherry."

Rom shook his head. "Not a chance. Anyway their abilities were limited to creating believable *visual* illusions. They were never able to manipulate behavior. And whenever they used their skills, one of our emissaries picked up the surge of psychic energy. No one has reported anything like that to date."

"Well," Roman continued, "the Chief of the Texas Rangers and Doctor Breswell are convinced something extrasensory is going on and I'm inclined to believe them despite all the others' reports to the contrary. So far it sounds like San Antonio could be the source site and that's where Doctor Breswell is basing her team. I plan on setting up there myself to keep tabs on their progress, but you know a psychic tsunami could pass over me and I wouldn't know it. I'd suggest you alert the emissary in the Texas Republic to put feelers out for any special visitors who shouldn't be on the surface of the planet. Same goes for any unusual energy waves, no matter how minimal."

"Agreed," Romulus and Aster said together.

Roman could tell they'd been communicating telepathically during his report—an ability that followed their formal joining ceremony. He waited to see which would pose the question they were discussing. When his mother spoke, he knew it would be of a more personal nature.

"Will it be necessary for you to remain invisible on this assignment?"

"I'm not sure. It's why I got the job of course. But I'll establish an Outerworld bio before I go back, just in case I need to actually converse with someone."

"And make sure you check in with Medical before you leave."

Roman reacted to her mothering with an eye roll and a half-smile. "You know I always do, though it's only to calm your worrying. None of my systems have ever had the tiniest blip, visible or invisible."

"Now tell us what you didn't say about Doctor Breswell."

Romulus smothered a chuckle and Roman lowered his gaze. Although his hair was dark like his father's, his eye color was midnight blue like his mother's. The irises didn't change with his emotional state as his father's and his sister Shara's did, yet his mother had looked into his eyes and saw...*something*. Since he abided by the Noronian code of honesty when he was in Innerworld, he answered with the truth. "I found her quite attractive."

"And?"

"Intelligent."

"And?"

"The most likely Terran to get to the bottom of whatever might be going on." He decided not to relate how Dr. Breswell seemed to be aware of his presence. Omission with a valid reason was permitted under the code and his mother being made to unnecessarily fret over him was reason enough.

"That's it?" Aster prodded. "No anxiety? Itching? Rise in body temperature?"

Both Roman and his father laughed aloud at her blatant hope that Roman had encountered his soul's mate.

Aster smirked at them. "Go ahead and laugh now. But you need to be attentive to the signs. The Noronian mating fever hit your sister at a younger age than you are now, but she was fully prepared and didn't waste any time once she met Gabriel."

"Unlike the two of you," Roman teased.

"Our situation—" began Romulus.

"—was very unusual," finished Aster.

Roman, and every other Noronian in Innerworld, knew exactly how unusual his parents' joining had been. Because of his father's political endeavors, Outerworld Terrans who were accidentally transported into Innerworld—as his mother and her companions had been—were assimilated into the society. There were only two freedoms withheld from them: no Terran was permitted to return to Outerworld and Terrans and Noronians were forbidden to join. Aster had defied both those laws. And although she and Romulus had set a precedent that could possibly lead to another transplanted Terran and full-blooded Noronian formally bonding, it hadn't happened since.

Rather than repeat a conversation they'd had numerous times, Roman excused himself to go take care of the list of details required for his new mission. What he kept to himself was that he *was* feeling something unusual—he felt tired, as though he hadn't slept in days, though that wasn't the case. He decided he was simply in dire need of a little relaxation before heading back out to the planet's surface.

Roman had barely entered the Indulgence Center when he was lifted off his feet and swung in a circle by a gray-skinned, ten-foot tall octoman with a bulbous head, four legs and four tentacle-like arms protruding from the sides of his torso.

"Where the drek have you been Norona or Outerworld again was it a new mission?" The giant stopped spinning and held his suspended friend at arm's length. "Have you had dinner I would be happy to treat for a story or two."

Roman laughed at the exuberant Farcutian, whose voice sounded like he was blowing bubbles with each purposefully formed word. He had always refused to use a universal translator in order to be clearly understood, because he thought it took the fun away from speaking. Unfortunately, he had never mastered the ability to insert pauses between questions or thoughts. "Hello to you too, Prince. I accept your offer…as long as you let me walk to the restaurant on my own."

The octoman's wide mouth curved into a semblance of a grin as he set Roman back on his feet. As they made their way toward the restaurant that best accommodated Prince's size and nutritional preferences, Roman encouraged him to talk about his week.

"They only needed me to do the weekly cargo run to and from Norona but I brought back three new volterrin miners and their families one of them had two children and they allowed them to play games with me."

Roman couldn't help but smile as Prince went on about the youngsters. The Farcutian was a humble being of enormous physical strength, endless enthusiasm and unlimited generosity but, like others of his kind, his intellect was childlike compared to a Noronian.

Fortunately, the Farcutians possessed an innate navigational talent that made them welcome members of advanced civilizations. While the flight from Innerworld to Norona had previously taken six days, once Prince was approved to pilot, the trip time was cut in half. Though he couldn't explain how his shortcut-finding ability worked, Prince could locate and use spatial wormholes as easily as other pilots followed maps through charted territory. Of secondary importance was that his elongated, multiple limbs made it possible for him to control every station of the helm without additional crew members if the need arose.

Few Farcutians ever left their home planet, however, and Prince was the only one of his kind in Innerworld.

Their relationship seemed peculiar to some, but Roman felt they had more in common than most friends. As a small child, Roman's mixed heritage had made him just as much a target for teasing as Prince was for his physical and mental differences. Thus, they had become friends in their first year of primary school. Because his birth name was so long and hard to pronounce, Roman dubbed him Prince, which was actually his true title on his home planet.

While Roman was the son of the formidable Co-Governors of Innerworld, Prince was one of a very large brood borne to the royal family of Farcu, a very small Confederation planet in the same galaxy as Norona. He was just a baby when his parents and most of his siblings were murdered by an opposing family. A Noronian couple in diplomatic service on Farcu rescued the three surviving children and relocated to Innerworld shortly afterward. Years later, when they moved back to Norona, Prince had chosen to remain in the colony—mainly because of his friendship with Roman—and Roman made sure he never regretted that decision.

"…and I named him Roman so even when you are away—"

"What?" Roman cut in when Prince said his name. "I'm sorry. Who did you name Roman?"

Prince laughed aloud. "Which was it this time daydreaming or did a pretty girl catch your eye?"

Instantly, Erin's image flashed in Roman's mind and he shook his head to send it away. "Sorry. It's been a very long day and I'm starving."

"Me too but we are here now."

Roman was a bit surprised that they had walked past the long row of shops and restaurants without his noticing any of them. Nor had a single *pretty girl* caught his eye, truly a rare occurrence for him. Was he really that tired and hungry? Or was something else bothering him…something about the mission that was just beyond his consciousness?

Once they placed their order, Roman asked Prince to repeat what he had said about someone named Roman.

"The Feinsteins ordered him from Outerworld and gave him to me as an early birthday gift they said he is called a mastiff and a long time ago the Outerworld Romans used them in battle which really makes his name even better and they gave me an Outerworld book about dogs too." Prince took a breath then continued. "He is little now but they said it will not be long before he will be a giant like me well maybe not as big as me but big for a dog."

Roman had to restrain himself from voicing the concerns that immediately popped into his head. However, if his mother's elderly friends had decided it was a good idea to give Prince a pet to take care of and keep him company, it was undoubtedly thought through completely.

"Congratulations! I can't wait to meet my namesake."

Prince's black eyes brightened. "You do not have to wait you can come by my place after dinner."

Roman hated to disappoint him but he had no choice. "Sorry. Too much to do tonight. But I can tell you a little about my mission while we eat. Would you like to hear where I'm going tomorrow?"

Prince's expression went from frown to avid interest in a blink.

"Texas."

"Where the cowboys live?"

"Yep. And today I was actually in the same room with a real one." For the next half hour, he entertained Prince with descriptions and imitations of Chief Friedrich, without actually revealing anything specific about where he had been or why. Against his will, thoughts of that man's burgundy-haired associate kept tugging at his attention.

"Did you have to—" Prince glanced from side to side then continued as quietly as he could manage, which was not really quiet at all. "You know what?"

Roman nodded. Prince was one of the few people

who knew what he could do, mainly because he'd been standing next to him when he had once vanished by accident. "But the oddest thing happened. There was a female who seemed to know I was there."

Prince's eyes narrowed. "Maybe she has super hearing and could hear you breathing or she has telepathy and heard your thoughts or she picked up your energy signal I remember you telling me how your trainer Falcon can do that." The octoman's shoulders slumped slightly. "I cannot do any of those things."

"No, you can just find your way through space with a blindfold on and have fifty times the strength of us little people." He waited for Prince to grin then got back to talking about Doctor Breswell. "I can't be sure but I think she *smelled* me."

Prince leaned forward to take a sniff of Roman. "I do not smell anything but I guess that could be a super power too was she pretty?"

Roman chuckled. "Yes."

"Are you going to play with her?"

"Absolutely not," he replied quickly. "Playing with Terran females can get too…complicated. Besides, when I'm out there, I'm working, not playing. I'll stick with the pleasure companions and entertainers who work here for that."

Saying it aloud cemented his decision to have a little fun before he took care of business. It might also be exactly what he needed to stop thinking about the Terran. As soon as he and Prince parted company, he headed for the Indulgence Center's Fantasy World.

Though he knew exactly what he wanted to experience, he perused the entire selection of enactments available in combination with a one-on-one full sexual encounter and release with a single human female. He finally purchased one of his favorites, the standard "American Wild West" production in which he would be the sheriff of a small town whose bank gets robbed by an uncivilized, gun-toting gang.

He had no trouble describing his costume and the female he desired. As he left the dressing area in the same attire as Chief Friedrich had worn, he received enough appreciative comments to feel great about his choice. And the holographic enactment chamber had been perfectly transformed into an American Wild West town.

But when the schoolmarm approached him on the planked walkway and shyly smiled up at him, he felt as though a puff of air had been let out of his fantasy balloon. The young woman's hair was closer to orange than red and her eyes were pale blue and they didn't sparkle with an inner light.

As he did with every role he played, whether in a reenactment chamber or for an assignment, Roman immersed himself in the part and enjoyed every moment of the realistic action. There was a traditional shoot-out, during which he eliminated several of the gang and would have been shot himself if it were not for his superb agility and physical conditioning.

Just when it appeared he was winning the skirmish, the gang's leader grabbed the red-headed schoolmarm, who the sheriff was "sweet on", and rode off with her. The heroic sheriff pursued and rescued her from the bad guys. For which, of course, she was ever-so-grateful to him.

The pretty actress expertly performed the transition from prim schoolmarm to playful sex kitten and the physical release was satisfactory.

Unfortunately, none of it ejected Erin Breswell from his thoughts.

He told himself it was simply the mystery of her

that enthralled him. Otherwise, she was just another beautiful, intelligent *Terran*.

He repeated the words he had told Prince—that relationships with Terran females were complicated and he would be in Outerworld to work, not play. Mixing the two did not bode well for anyone. In reality, Roman was well aware that a relationship with any species of female was complicated.

However, just in case the temptation to unravel her mystery became too great, he would maintain invisibility whenever he was around her…for both their sakes.

Roman delivered his report and discussed his mission agenda with his handler at Outerworld Monitor Control. Together, they arranged for the appropriate forms of identification and a profile that would hold up under moderate scrutiny by most Outerworld agencies. Plus, there was an established Innerworld emissary in the Ranger's Houston office who would confirm his legitimacy if necessary. Once the details were set, Roman picked up a new wardrobe and props to support his chosen cover as a Texas Ranger. And finally, since he'd promised his mother, he checked in at Medical, even though he saw it as a waste of time.

Twenty-four hours later, he was ready to get to work.

Yeehaw.

CHAPTER 2

New Braunfels, Texas, 2064 A.D.

"I am strong. I am healthy. I am successful in my work. I am..." Erin Breswell frowned at the face staring back at her in the mirror of the private bathroom attached to her office. She tried to voice the other two affirmations that usually followed—*I am calm and I am very happy with my life*—but the lies refused to form aloud.

Three days ago, those words flowed easily from her mouth...because they were true. Three days ago, she *had* been calm and happy. Three days ago, all of the anxieties, insecurities and obsessive behaviors that had made her early life miserable were still under lock and key in a tiny corner of her mind...as they had been for the last nine years.

Two days ago, something happened to her peace of mind. She just didn't know what that *something* was. On her way to the White House, she had been filled with positive energy and looking forward to being part of such an important meeting. As she sat in the Oval Office however, she started feeling nervous and had the sensation of being watched, not on a security camera but by someone in that room. The thought that she was being paranoid, stabbed her with a fear she hadn't felt in years. She had managed to maintain her professional cool despite her body temperature rising by the second. Even that discomfort might have been possible to ignore, but the sudden sexual demand pulsing between her crossed thighs was unlike anything in her experience.

Today marked the beginning of the interviews she would conduct to choose her psych team and she needed every bit of her exceptional intelligence and intuition to be focused.

Terrified that she was backsliding, she'd confided in her mother, who diagnosed the symptoms as early onset menopause and gave her an herbal tea remedy. However, with so much at stake in the coming weeks, she also paid a visit to her doctor, who prescribed an anxiety-suppression medication.

In her formerly unbalanced life, plenty of medications had been prescribed for her. Although one or two had helped quiet "the crazy", as she'd called her collective neuroses, they all had undesirable side effects of one sort or another. Thus, she had no intention of taking the new pills sitting in her cabinet. She had only needed them as a mental safety net...just in case the odd symptoms turned into a full-blown relapse.

CHAPTER 3

Norona (Terra Date 2353 A.D.)

It was almost over. Terra's sun and its surrounding system would soon be a black hole in space. Nothing left to do but say goodbye to the planet that had played an important role in Norona's history and development for thousands of years. A tiny spark of light amidst the dense smoke suggested there were still one or two powerful flares left in the dying sun.

Not that it made any difference. All life on the surface of Terra had been obliterated months ago. The unexpected, massive impacts of deadly solar flares had at least been somewhat merciful in that respect. The fate of the thousands trapped in Innerworld was not known. Had the assault on the planet proven instantly lethal to them as well? Or would they be forced to experience the final stage, the total implosion of the planet?

Catastrophic Science Director Cattar waved her hand through the holographic display, turning off the image being relayed across two galaxies. There had been forecasts, of course, but none had come close to predicting how imminent the danger was. A dozen times each day she turned on the broadcast, illogically hoping it had all been a nightmare or that a miracle had occurred and the dust cloud had blown away, leaving Terra damaged but reparable.

She slowly rose, walked out onto the veranda bordering her spacious office and took a deep breath. A cool breeze lifted and swirled the colorful caftan around her plump figure but her mind refused to clear enough to acknowledge how lovely the day was.

Her doctor had ordered that she shed some of her excess bulk the hard way, by eating less, exercising more and getting some fresh air every day. She took another deep breath and walked back to her desk, deciding that counted for two of the three directives. Besides, it seemed wrong to enjoy the beauty of the bright Noronian day when Terra's sun was dying.

"Johann," she said aloud and the hologram of a young, fair-haired man appeared before her. "Has there been any change at all?"

"That's a rather challenging question," Johann replied. "Considering we are hoping that a particular man in the year 2064, temporarily located on Outerworld Terra, receives the message you sent back to him using unproven technology in a volatile environment and, given the theory that if he *had* acted on that message, we would not necessarily know that something had changed in the present time from what it was before the message was sent—"

"*Johann, please!* I know you comprehend what I'm asking. Is there any indication that the cryptodrone landed on Outerworld? Has a mention of it appeared in Terra's historical records?" She ordered herself to be patient with the computer's analytically driven limitations.

"I apologize, Madam. As you requested, I have been continuously searching for such mentions and would have alerted you immediately had I found any.

Nothing has shown up in the historical records to indicate the people of Terra received the warning yet chose not to act. Nor is there any notation that a strange decahedron of an alien substance was found and locked up in a museum without anyone ever figuring out what the object was for. The only answer I am able to deduce with some certainty is that it appears the cryptodrone has not reached its intended destination."

"*Yet*," Cattar added firmly. "It has not *yet* reached its destination. We knew there was a possibility that the unstable atmospheric conditions could affect the trajectory of the delivery capsule. And we must keep in mind how faulty the tempometer was when it was employed ten years ago. The arrival time could be off by an hour or a year. And if it's the latter, Roman Locke may no longer be anywhere near that location."

Cattar sighed and rubbed her temples. After considerable research, she had chosen to use a device long ago relegated to the archival vaults. Technology and mental enhancements had made the cryptodrone obsolete. But it was the perfect vehicle for her plan. By taking the drone to the Intergalactic Space Station closest to Terra's solar system, sending it back in time, then physically through space to an Outerworld location where Roman's activity log showed him to be during a specific period, the chances of the drone remaining intact were promising. Unfortunately, the chances of overall success were still poor. With time travel being outlawed for all sentient beings regardless of the reason, and without the ability to enter Terra's solar system in the present, jettisoning the cryptodrone back through time and space was the only option, regardless of the odds of success.

Encoding the drone to open only in the hands of Roman Locke, or a very close DNA relative of his, was done to guarantee that no unqualified person would receive the message and discard or ignore it. The only additional safeguard they'd been able to manage was to add a subtle energy signal to the delivery capsule. In the event the timing or guidance mechanisms were off and Roman was nowhere nearby when it landed, the hope was that someone associated with Outerworld Monitor Control would detect the signal and retrieve the drone. As long as whoever found it could interpret the ancient Noronian language on the exterior, it would eventually be delivered to Roman or a member of his immediate family.

According to historical records, Roman's assignment had placed him at the epicenter of a series of events that would negatively alter the future of the Terrans and, subsequently, Innerworlders. It was the point in time that came to be marked as the beginning of the end for that civilization, but only a minute faction of Noronians believed that interference was justified at the time. Although that opinion was eventually accepted by the majority, it was too late for subtle interference.

She and her cohorts had come up with this plan and, though it was not sanctioned by the Noronian Tribunal, they believed it was worth the sacrifice of their careers if it failed.

As long as the cryptodrone reached Roman in time for him to act, Cattar had faith that he would believe the explanation she wrote about how she had met his family two hundred ninety-eight years ago. Then surely he would heed the encrypted warning and attend to what needed doing.

She could only pray that Roman had matured into the man he was meant to be before his fate was altered by his sister's use—and abuse—of a time-travel device.

CHAPTER 4

New Braunfels, Texas, 2064 A.D.

"Oh, dear God! He shot them! They never had a chance."

Erin covered Vicky's hand with her own and squeezed. "Close the curtain, Vicky. You're safe, here in my office." A tear ran down the middle-aged woman's cheek. She trembled so badly, Erin hated to upset her further but it was imperative Vicky relate what she had just visualized while it was fresh. She handed Vicky a tissue as she gently prodded. "I need you to tell me everything you saw...before it fades."

Without opening her eyes, Vicky slowly related the scene as it had appeared in her mind. "A policeman, in uniform. All black or dark blue, I think. He...he walked into a small store, like a grocery or rest stop. The clerk was a man...I couldn't see him clearly. There was an elderly woman in front of the counter...with a big purse...and a young woman...I think she was buying beer...He didn't warn them...just shot all three, then killed himself." She sniffed and wiped the tears from her face.

"Did you recognize any of the people?" Vicky

shook her head. "How about the location? Anything familiar about that?" Again Vicky indicated in the negative. "Can you see the outside? Maybe a sign?"

Vicky pursed her lips and wrinkled her forehead. "There are shelves blocking the windows. The officer is in front of the door...I think there's a parking lot. Some vehicles. A police unit."

"That's good. Try looking around the store inside. Maybe there's something..."

Vicky opened her eyes. "It's gone. I'm sorry, Erin. It was really fast. And shocking. Not that I haven't seen horrible things before. You know I've worked with the police quite a bit in the last few years, but they mainly use me to help find a missing person or a criminal whose identity is known."

Vicky paused and took a slow breath, the lines on her face softening as she relaxed. "The first time I had a remote viewing, it was completely unexpected, but it involved my husband. He had just had a car accident. It was almost always like that in the beginning. I'd call the person and confirm what I'd seen. But when I started seeing random, intense scenes involving strangers, well, you know that was when I came to you. If you hadn't been able to train me to control the psychic curtain, well, I don't know how I would have coped. This was the first time in nine years that I saw something completely different from what I was looking for."

"So what had you thought of just now before you pulled the curtain aside?"

Vicky clucked her tongue. "It really doesn't make sense. I focused on a friend who moved away a few months ago and I hadn't heard from her recently. I knew she wouldn't object to my mentally checking on her or having you confirm what I saw."

Erin vaguely recalled what a quick study Vicky had

been and how upset she had been over unintentionally "peeping" on strangers. She had trained Vicky to command her subconscious mind to only allow in images when specifically requested by her conscious mind. Since Vicky was certain the victims in the store were unknown to her, there had to be another reason she saw the scene. "It is possible your friend was there but not visible, or that one of those people have a connection to her. Where did she move to?"

"Katy. A little west of Houston."

As the good doctor searched for recent criminal activity in Katy, Roman went over all he'd just heard. He couldn't help but wonder if the incident Vicky described had any unusual psychic energy attached to it, since that could have pulled her attention to it in spite of where she had intended to look. If he had Falcon's gifts, he would probably know immediately, but as it was, he would have to wait to find out if the Innerworld emissary in Houston picked anything up. Of course, that agent wasn't as skilled as Falcon—no one he knew was—but after Roman's first report, they were all on high alert for unusual energy signals.

Thinking of his trainer made him recall Prince's suggestion that Erin might have Falcon's ability to sense energy signals. Being able to follow someone's residue energy trail was just one of the things that made Falcon such a phenomenal tracker. Being half-felan also enhanced his sense of smell and night vision. Roman was fairly certain Erin's sense of smell was stronger than that of an average Terran and, perhaps, even that of an average Noronian.

Roman's gaze shifted to Erin's eyes and considered the luminous gold-brown color. Falcon's eye color was distinctly gold, and glowed in the dark, but his black pupils were marquis-shaped. Erin's were round.

Full-blooded felans had very thin bodies with arched spines and were covered in fine hair. Falcon's Noronian genes had dominated his physical appearance with the exception of his pupils and the thick mane of long, gold-streaked hair. Erin's body was—

No! He slashed off that thought as though his life depended on it.

Erin's dark red hair appeared to be long and thick but since she always kept it tightly restrained at her nape, Roman couldn't be sure if it was like Falcon's. Although, he had noticed how a few stray, curly hairs around her face regularly fought her efforts to control them, especially following one of her episodes of flushed cheeks and upper-lip perspiration.

Roman suddenly realized how far his mind had drifted from his true purpose and forced his thoughts away from Erin's physical appearance. His instincts, which *were* highly developed, insisted Vicky had revealed a piece of information important to him personally. But whatever the piece was, it hadn't been obvious.

He wanted to look at Erin's notes but he didn't dare move from his squat-spot behind a large plant in the corner of her office. At least he wasn't bored. Seven days ago he'd transmigrated from Innerworld to Erin's office in a northeastern suburb of San Antonio and had spent every day there since. Her efficient assistant, Nola, had potential task force members marching in and out non-stop and, even when they weren't team material, the interviews were interesting to observe. Roman had come to two conclusions—Dr. Breswell was an exceptionally good interviewer and, although he had never personally enjoyed voyeurism in a general sense, he really liked watching *her*.

Numerous times over the past week, he had tried to

get closer, but she somehow detected his slightest movement. Sometimes she glanced in his direction, sometimes her nose twitched or she simply frowned, but there was no longer any question in his mind that she sensed his presence.

Because she began her search with homicides in Katy, Texas, Erin had little difficulty verifying the crime Vicky had remotely viewed. "It happened six months ago," Erin told her.

"Are you sure?" Vicky countered. "I hardly ever view past events and the few times I have, I was given a specific date and location when a crime occurred. Even then the vision has a dreamlike quality to it. What I just saw was very clear, like it was happening at the moment."

Erin's fingers moved rapidly over her computer screen. "It's definitely the event you described. What's your friend's name?" As Vicky spelled it for her, Erin instructed her computer to search for a commonality between Vicky's friend and any of the victims. She soon had another piece of the picture. "There is a connection to your friend. The elderly woman was an aunt of her mother's."

"Oh, that's terrible. But I'm pretty sure they didn't have a close enough relationship to explain my tuning into that woman instead of my friend. Like I said, ever since you helped me, my viewings are limited to what I choose to see."

Erin tapped her index finger against her lips while keeping her gazed fixed to Vicky's. It was something Roman had seen her do whenever she needed the other person to stop talking for a moment while her brain sorted through information. He wasn't sure why it worked but it always seemed to.

"I've worked with others whose gifts have occasionally altered or expanded over time. That could be the case here. Or there could be something you missed because you were surprised by the violent crime. Why don't you give your friend a call tonight and see what you can find out. Maybe she was waiting outside and you just couldn't see her."

The moment Erin walked Vicky out of her office, Roman grabbed the opportunity to stretch.

As the women passed the assistant's desk, he heard Erin say, "Nola will let you know when the first group meeting will be held."

Roman continued to eavesdrop as Erin gave Nola the list of team members she'd confirmed so far. She instructed her to assist with travel arrangements to get them here as soon as possible and suggested they be put up at the Faust Hotel in downtown New Braunfels. Then Erin insisted Nola call it a day. Roman was back in his corner by the time Erin returned to her desk.

"Call Chief Friedrich's hotline," she instructed her computer.

Seconds later, the Chief's deep voice filled the office. "Hello darlin'. Do Ah dare hope this is a social call?"

Erin's soft smile was evident in her voice. "Afraid not, Chief. I just had something disturbing occur during an appointment with a long-time patient of mine. I have a strong hunch it may be connected."

As she related the scene her patient had viewed remotely, Roman found himself wondering about the nature of Erin's relationship with the Chief. Unless he was mistaken, "Darlin'" was a personal endearment. He told himself it didn't matter, since he was determined not to interact with her personally. He was just...*curious*.

"You know Ah trust your hunches more than hard evidence sometimes. Hold on a sec while Ah pull up the case file," Friedrich said without a hint of his initial pleasantry. "We've been goin' on the premise that all the weird incidents started around four months ago, when the computer picked up the repeated usage of phrases like 'odd behavior'. And you know all those reports were in the annoyance or misdemeanor categories, so Ah'm not surprised a triple homicide plus suicide wouldn't have been added in with the others."

"Of course not. There was another reason why I felt it might be connected though. My patient doesn't normally pick up on past events unless specifically guided to it on a conscious level, but she did this time. Or at least we thought so at the time. But then I realized that, before her vision started, I was telling her about the psych team and why I was forming it, so if that incident was somehow connected to the rest, I may have unintentionally directed her to that place and time."

"Ah think Ah actually follow that," Chief said with a chuckle. "Ah must be gettin' better at this parapsychology stuff. Now, give me a minute to skim the reports."

Erin remained silent as she waited for Chief to finish going through the file.

"Okay," he finally said. "Here's somethin' that suggests a connection. The officer was a loner, no family or close friends, which seemed to support the theory that he simply cracked under pressure of some kind. Also, there were no drugs or chemicals in his system to account for his erratic behavior. But another officer was ridin' with him that day. His statement says they were on a regular route, talkin' about Friday night's game, and only stopped at the store to use the facilities. He saw no hint of agitation or depression when the shooter got out of the vehicle. Ah'm watchin' the security video now and what Ah see is a desperate, furious man with a specific goal. Kinda like a completely different personality took over when he stepped through the doors and into the store."

Erin rubbed her forehead and sighed. "That could definitely support my feeling that whoever is behind the misdemeanors may have started with a big event then scaled back for some reason. Maybe to stay below your radar while he was working on his plan, whatever that might be."

"Agreed. How soon will you have your team assembled and tunin' in, or whatever you're callin' it?"

"Vicky was my last interview and I'll have decided on the final members of the team tonight. Then Nola will be correlating schedules tomorrow. Hopefully we can get everyone here and ready to work in a day or two."

Roman watched her prepare to leave after she ended that call. He was growing more and more anxious to review her notes, but another call came in before she could depart. This one was accompanied by a holographic image of a woman who bore a resemblance to Erin.

"Hey, Mom. Everything okay?"

"Everything's great on my end. I'm calling to see how *you* are feeling. Have the herbs I suggested helped at all?"

"Quite a bit actually. I'm still getting sporadic flashes of heat but they've been a lot milder. At least I don't feel like I'm going to spontaneously combust all the time."

Her mother chuckled. "Sorry, I know it's not funny but that's how menopause felt for me. You're just too young for that to be the answer."

"That's what the doctor said. All my hormone levels

are normal. She suggested I go in and be monitored for a day, but I can't afford the time right now."

"Honestly, sweetheart, my feeling is it would be a waste of time. Whatever is going on, you'll have the answer very soon. And speaking of strange phenomena, still think you have a ghost haunting you?"

Erin sighed. "I don't know. Maybe my imagination is just working overtime. I am under some stress."

"Have you done a reading on it?"

"Actually, I'm planning to do one tonight, though not about my phantom stalker."

"It will only take another minute to ask about it. If a disembodied spirit is hanging around your office, he or she might be trying to tell you something. Okay, that's all the mothering I have time for today but I wanted to remind you that game night is at my place this weekend. And I was thinking it's been a long time since the girls have seen you. Any chance you're free?"

"Sorry. I have plans."

"Plans?" her mother said brightly. "Anyone interesting?"

It took Erin a beat or two to respond and, when she did, it was with a slightly forced smile. "No. It's work. I swear, if I ever invite anyone *interesting* into my life, you will be the first to know."

Roman felt irrationally pleased by her answer…not that it mattered to him.

Erin said goodbye to her mother then put some papers and items into a carrying case. At the door, she turned around and declared, "Attention please, whoever or whatever you are, I'm going home now." She let her gaze cover the entire room before speaking more directly to the plant stand in the corner. "And you may as well know, my house is shielded with white light, so don't bother following me. If I sense you anywhere around my property, I swear, I won't just do a reading about you, I will exorcise you whether you are ready to go or not!"

Roman had to fight the urge to laugh out loud and prove to her how wrong she was. Actually, he *was* more than a little tempted to follow her home just to see what sort of information she might glean from her "reading" about him. He was familiar enough with the metaphysical tools she used in her practice, but he'd never seen them being used. Would her cards show he was a living man? Perhaps he could just—

The instant he thought of being alone with Erin, in her personal space, he knew there was a chance he'd be tempted to reveal himself to her, and once he did that, he might be tempted to find out if her lips were as soft as they appeared...

Drek! This mission would have been a lot easier if he didn't find her so attractive. Or better yet, if she were a man. He had never been distracted by a man. His train of thought was enough to remind him of why he needed to stay invisible to her. As he'd told Prince, he never mixed work and play and he never played with Outerworld Terran females.

Ordering himself to get back to that work, he sat down behind Erin's desk. Using the programming capability of his Innerworld ring, he circumvented the security walls in Erin's computer and was able to access all her files rather quickly. The only ones he cared about, however, were the ones in the folder labeled "Psych Team".

She used a lot of abbreviations in her notes, but since he had been present during most of her interviews, Roman managed to interpret most of them. She had already divided the interviewed candidates into "Definites", "Possibles" and "Passes". How like her to refrain from using the word *rejects*, he thought with a grin. He assumed the reading she'd be doing tonight would determine the fate of the Possibles.

All twenty-five of those interviewed practiced transcendental meditation and visualization, were highly intuitive and sensitive to positive and negative energy in their immediate environment and were able to shield themselves from that energy at will. But beyond that, their expanded abilities varied.

He began with the notes on Vicky Trumble, hoping he could quickly figure out what she'd said that was important to him. No such luck.

Next he reviewed the notes from Erin's meeting with the other parapsychologist, Dr. Kanji Cho. He resided in Tokyo and was considered to be one of the most respected experts in their field. His work was quite different from Erin's however. Where she assisted the Texas Rangers in criminal matters and personally helped patients deal with their very real life problems, Cho was occupied almost completely with scholarly theories and research connected with those ideas. Also, he had gained celebrity status due to his books and seminars, while Erin maintained a very humble profile.

Nothing in the notes about Cho's background or credentials triggered anything for Roman. However, the information regarding the specialist Cho had brought with him made a light flicker in Roman's brain. Haruko Zhang, who preferred to be called Hari, was able to remote view, like Vicky, but could also move lightweight objects with her mind. Though she had always had a well-developed intuitive sense, the specific abilities listed did not manifest until around nine years ago.

Vicky's first remote viewing occurred nine years ago.

Roman hurriedly skimmed the other three Definites.

As the psychic recommended by CIA Director Najinski, Wendy Santana had been automatically accepted for the task force as the representative from the North American States. Her gift was the use of psychometry to profile a person. Erin had noted that she sensed Santana had additional talent but either she didn't know she had it or she was keeping it a secret for some reason. There was no mention of when her skill had awakened.

The pretty, blond, fraternal twins, Jamie and Ryan McCraig, were accustomed to sensing things about each other from early childhood, but on their twelfth birthday, *nine years ago*, they were suddenly able to clearly communicate telepathically, even at great distances. And when they both, simultaneously, made physical contact with a third person, Jamie could read his or her thoughts as well. Their foster parents had brought the twins to Dr. Breswell for analysis shortly after their abilities expanded. Once they were told parapsychology could not be used to "make children more normal", they did not return.

According to Dr. Breswell's notes, when she began choosing her team, Jamie and Ryan were on her list but it took some searching to locate them. The couple who had initially brought them to her office had subsequently returned the twins to the foster system. They were unsuccessfully placed in other homes over the next four years until they were granted emancipation. The twins weren't simply difficult adolescents, they were referred to as abnormally connected, strange and, in one case, evil. Breswell's final note stated that she believed Jamie and/or Ryan also had considerably more skill than they had acknowledged in their interview.

Once Roman found several more mentions of *nine*

years ago among the Possibles, he was certain the time period was what had personal meaning to him.

Approximately nine years ago, while he was still attending the academy, he awoke as he normally did and went to the dining area to have breakfast with his parents. At first they each thought the other was pulling a prank, but it was soon confirmed that they couldn't see him despite his standing right in front of them. He was completely invisible, with no explanation as to how that had happened. He remembered the minutes of panic before he realized he could mentally *will* his body to reappear. There were several weeks of accidental disappearances before he learned how to control it.

The timing could not be a coincidence. Using the twins' birthday, he searched for anything unusual that had happened on or about that date, on Earth or in the surrounding galaxy. Nothing out of the ordinary had been recorded, but something *must* have happened to simultaneously trigger the transformations.

Dr. Cho had insisted Erin create a team of nine, including herself. He had said something about it being a lucky number in his ancestral culture. Was there an importance to the number of years that had passed as well?

As he closed the digital folder and turned off the computer, Roman decided to skim some of Cho's publications before the first gathering of Erin's psych team. He hoped the scholar might already have figured out a few answers to the questions suddenly running through his head.

"*Peaceful Soul*," Erin stated clearly as she entered her home. The voice-reactive entertainment system complied with her favorite relaxation music.

She had chosen to live outside the historical town of

New Braunfels because it was fairly close to the north-south expressway and about midway between Austin and San Antonio. The small, two-story farmhouse seemed to have welcomed her as soon as she stepped onto the land around it. She remembered the feeling of peace that had risen from the earth and embraced her. The bonus was that there was a bit of distance between her living space and that of her neighbors. After dealing with people all day, some of whom required her to expend considerable mental energy, she relished her alone time.

The house itself was over a hundred years old and had required major renovations. Erin wasn't so concerned with preserving the original design elements as making adjustments to suit her taste. Although she liked the *idea* of being in an old house, she had no intention of giving up any contemporary amenities, particularly in the kitchen or bathroom. Décor-wise, she preferred her furnishings to be modern as well—minimalistic, with clean lines. Her biggest concessions to comfort over simplicity were plush wall-to-wall carpeting, so she could walk around barefoot, and her large bed. And though most of the walls and furnishings were in neutral shades, she brightened every room of her environment with happy yellow and green accents.

As the calming melody filled the air, she went upstairs to her bedroom suite. Shedding the constricting day clothes released a good deal of the tension inside her and a long massaging shower did the rest. Knowing she would not have any unexpected visitors, she donned a thin, white, sleeveless shift.

Although she had mentally cleared the field around her body before entering the front door, she took another moment to make certain she was not bringing anything negative into the room she reserved as her sacred space.

In the center of the room was a square table with a comfortable chair on the side facing the door. A purple silk scarf covered the table top. In the center sat a well-used deck of tarot cards. She rubbed the chunk of smoky quartz crystal and piece of green fluorite on the north side of the table. A yellow feather and a cone of lavender incense sat in the east. In the south was a white candle in a red holder and in the west, a blue glass.

As she poured some fresh river water into the glass and lit the candle and incense, she called in the Spirits of the North, East, South and West. Settling into the chair on the south side of the table, she picked up the deck and moved the candle to the center of the table.

"I perform this reading for only beneficial reasons and ask my spirit guides and Guardians to protect me as I pull back the curtain between what is seen and unseen."

Kanji wanted there to be nine team members for luck. Erin was agreeable based on numerology, within which nine was a number for endings and closures. Since the goal was to put an end to whatever dark force was in motion, nine seemed fitting. Including herself and Dr. Cho, she had seven members selected. She needed to pick two more adepts out of the Possibles.

Focusing on her desire to find two more team members who had the basic requirements plus an additional gift that would be useful in locating and stopping the psychic criminal, she drew three cards for each of the twelve Possibles. She studied the images of each set of cards for several minutes then made her choices.

Without the reading, she would not have selected Tripper, who possessed a semi-dependable ability to dream future events. Through her work with the Texas Rangers, she had successfully interacted with him on two occasions after he had dreamed about an impending crime. He was a handsome young man with a dancer's body and long, light brown hair, but his green eyes held secrets and his single nickname usage suggested he wanted no part of his past. To his detriment, he had bluntly stated that his sexual prowess was one of his special gifts and she feared his overblown ego could one day get the best of him. But the cards clearly told her he would be an asset.

On the contrary, she had been fairly fixed on choosing Peace One-Feather, a local, elderly woman who devoted herself to maintaining the traditions of her Navajo ancestors. Her primary psychic skill was the ability to communicate with animals and trees, but she also claimed to be a healer. Erin hadn't imagined how either skill would enhance the team, which is why Peace was categorized as a Possible instead of a Definite, but the cards told her to have faith in the woman's gifts, that they would be helpful in unexpected ways.

That settled, she gathered up the cards, reshuffled and spread them across the purple silk for her next question.

She took a cleansing breath and spoke aloud. "I know I have asked this before, but I would appreciate a confirmation or update. Please tell me about whoever is behind the incidents the team will be investigating." Her gaze darted to one card and she turned it over.

The Devil. Not a simple troublemaker. True darkness was involved.

"Male or female?"

Prince of Wands. Man under forty with medium coloring, with both business and creative skills, uses a combination of intelligence and imagination to achieve his goal.

"What is his goal?"

The World. Again. She had now asked that question three times and drew the same card each time. Since it usually meant reaching a goal, it wasn't really a helpful answer. On the other hand, if she was meant to interpret it literally—

"Is he working alone?"

The Tower. A big negative, plus a warning of sudden, impending upheaval and/or danger.

"Terrific."

She blew a soft breath over the cards, visualizing the negative messages being cleared away.

Remembering her mother's suggestion, she again gathered all the cards, shuffled and spread them again. "Okay, tell me something about the energy I keep sensing but cannot see."

Prince of Swords. Male under forty. Dark. Possibly a soldier or police officer.

Seven of Swords. Deception, lies, betrayal, something hidden from sight.

Judgment. Could involve a legal matter...*no, not that interpretation*...something or someone raised from the dead.

Erin was actually surprised to have been given such a clear answer so easily. Based on just three cards, she interpreted that her phantom stalker was in fact a disembodied spirit, perhaps killed in the line of duty by someone he trusted but who betrayed him.

"Is there a connection between his stalking me and my search for the Prince of Wands?"

Ace of Cups. Absolutely, and in a very positive, loving way.

She hadn't sensed anything dark or negative about her ghost but she was relieved to have that confirmed.

"Does he want to help me find the Devil and stop him?"

Three of Coins. Yes, using his expert skills.

It was almost *too* clear, *too* easy. Erin considered calling her mother to get her thoughts but the infernal heat inside her body had started building again. She had been honest with her mother about the herbs helping but the help tended to be short-term. To keep the heat under control in the office, she had consumed more tea in the past week than she had in the last year.

At least in the privacy of her home she could deal with the demanding sexual arousal that accompanied the heat and the action required to cool it, even if it was only for a few hours.

Erin awoke the next morning feeling wonderfully calm, cool and completely confident in her card reading. She had called Nola with the final two names last night and was anxious to find out how far she'd gotten with bringing the full psych team together. She could hardly wait to see what they were capable of once they all began pooling their gifts.

However, her upbeat mood took a sharp downturn as she walked out her front door and saw her car in the driveway. The shatter-proof windshield had not only been shattered, shards of glass covered the whole interior. She couldn't imagine the force necessary to do such damage.

Part of the answer came to her as she made a closer inspection of the front passenger seat and saw a cantaloupe-sized, jagged hole that went all the way through the bottom of the vehicle and into the packed-dirt driveway beneath. It looked like her car had been the victim of a meteor.

CHAPTER 5

After skimming volumes of Dr. Cho's written words, Roman felt he understood the general appeal of the man's work. Dr. Cho believed humans were on the brink of a major evolutionary advancement that would involve the awakening of dormant parts of the brain, resulting in expanded mental and psychic abilities. It was hardly a new thought, but his research in recent years served to prove his hypothesis in ways the average Terran could comprehend and anticipate in a positive way.

Unfortunately Roman found nothing to suggest the man believed there had been a distinct trigger of any kind or that the awakenings among his research subjects had all occurred precisely nine years ago.

Knowing Erin had completed her interviews and that the first gathering of her team had not yet been scheduled, Roman decided to use the day to file a report to his handler in person and visit his parents. Perhaps they could shed some light on the timing of his ability to disappear.

"Falcon!" Roman practically shot out of his chair when his trainer abruptly materialized in his parents' sitting room. "You must have picked up on my thoughts."

Innerworld's most gifted tracker grinned as they shook hands. "I am here in answer to your mother's call but I am most pleased to see you as well." Falcon had two distinct voices—the strong, professional one and this softer, personal one that had the low rumbling quality of a cat's purr.

Roman had never been told the specifics, but he knew that something had happened between Falcon and his mother before she joined with his father. And ever since, all she had to do was think his name and he would show up to help.

"Thank you so much for coming," Aster said, giving him a firm hug. "I hope we didn't pull you away from anything too important. How's the family? I do wish we could get together more often, but you know better than anyone how hard it is for us to get out there for a—" Her gaze darted to Romulus and back to Falcon. "It has just been suggested that I should take a breath and allow you to catch yours. I apologize."

Falcon's grin broadened to a full smile. "There is no need. Residing in Outerworld has accustomed me to emotional responses. Steve is quite well. She is deeply involved in a new case but can manage without me for a few hours this afternoon. The children and grandchildren are all flourishing, but perhaps details of their progress could wait until you tell me what is pressing."

Romulus motioned for everyone to be seated then said, "Roman was given a routine observation assignment in Outerworld. Not the kind of thing we would normally bring to your attention, but we'd like your input."

For the next half hour, Roman updated Falcon on everything he'd seen and heard, including his conclusion that something important had happened nine years ago that had triggered his ability to alter his body's cells and gifted some Outerworld Terrans with psychic abilities.

Falcon remained silent for nearly a full minute after Roman stopped talking. When he finally spoke, his words were far from what they all expected.

"I am aware that all Outerworld emissaries have been instructed to be vigilante with regard to any type of unusual energy surge, psychic or otherwise. I remember well what I felt when the Illusians were using their abilities on the surface, so I have taken time each day since I received the advisory to scan for such emissions. I have noticed nothing of the kind. However, it is possible they are using a wavelength that does not register as unusual."

"Are you thinking they might be piggybacking off a communication satellite?" Aster asked.

"Precisely," Falcon replied with an admiring expression. "The other possibility is that the perpetrator is in fact a telepathic manipulator, in which case he may have the ability to block other psychics' awareness of what he is doing."

Roman abruptly rose and paced back and forth. "If that's the case, Erin's team might not come up with anything."

"But that might not be the case," Aster said quickly. "Or one of her team might have an ability that sees through a block like that."

"Your mother is correct, Roman. Have faith in your lady."

"She's not my *lady*, Falcon. She's my assignment. And I don't mix work with pleasure."

Falcon chuckled. "I once believed the same thing...until I was proven wrong."

"What about the nine-year timing?" Roman asked,

neatly changing the subject.

Falcon shook his head. "It is most curious, but I am not aware of anything that could have caused the expanded mental abilities you spoke of. Perhaps, when time allows, you should investigate whether any Innerworlders, besides yourself, experienced an enhancement at that time."

"I thought of that too," added Romulus. "It's certainly possible that others woke up with a new or improved talent but, as Noronians, only something as extreme as Roman's vanishing act would have been noteworthy and no one else has reported experiencing anything of that nature."

Before they could discuss the possibilities further, a high priority message came in for the Co-Governors from Outerworld Monitor Control.

"It may be nothing," the OMC agent said. "But under the current orders—"

"Anything could be significant," Romulus interjected. "What have you got?"

"An energy disruption followed by a weak communication signal was picked up by the International Space Station early this morning. Then the source of the signal shot to the surface."

"Shot?" Aster and Rom asked together.

"The speed of its descent suggests it was propelled in some way. We have no idea what it was. If it wasn't for the propulsion and the signal, we would have assumed it was simply a meteorite. The signal stopped as abruptly as it started, but we do have the coordinates where the last tone occurred."

"Has an emissary been sent to investigate?"

"Not yet, sir. There is a considerable amount of official activity at the site. At any rate, the closest agent in place is currently your son, who we've been told is visiting you today."

"That's correct. Transmit the coordinates to his ring and I'll send him out immediately. Thank you."

Romulus turned back to Falcon and asked, "How would you feel about making a small detour with Roman before heading back to California?"

Falcon teased Roman about his cowboy attire from hat to boots, until he saw for himself how the outfit and the words *Texas Ranger* commanded respect among the people milling around the site. Some appeared to be quite official, taking measurements and images, while others simply gawked.

Roman walked up to a man who seemed to have some authority. "Can you tell me what happened here?"

"Can't rightly tell," the man replied, rubbing his chin. "It's a real mystery so far. The woman who lives here reported that she came out of her house this morning to go to work and saw her car's windshield smashed in. Seems that there rock hit the windshield and tore right through the passenger seat and the bottom of the car. Guessin' it could be a meteor. And, in case you were wonderin' she backed the car up before we got here, not realizin' it shoulda been left alone for the experts to examine."

"Good to know." Roman glanced over the automobile then squinted at the pink and gray chunk of rock partially buried in the dirt driveway leading up to the house. Tiny metallic bits embedded in the rock captured the sunlight. The part he could see was rough and about six inches in diameter. It didn't look like any meteor chunk he'd seen before.

"I am a geologist working with the Rangers," Falcon told the man. "Would you mind if I give the rock a cursory examination?"

"You can look all you want. There's no

radioactivity coming from it, but don't touch it or move it. There's a geologist from the university coming by any minute now to take it to his lab and he gave very explicit instructions about leaving it alone."

Roman watched Falcon place his hand just above the rock and realized he was using its resonant energy to *see* exactly what had happened here. His part was to distract the official.

"Is the owner around? Ah'd like to ask her a question or two." He hoped his attempt at imitating Chief Friedrich's accent was passable.

"She's inside. Nice lady. Brought us all some sweet tea a while ago. Name's Breswell. Doctor Erin Breswell."

Roman had already taken a step toward the house when the name stopped him cold. He instantly pretended to receive a call, thanked the official for his help and signaled Falcon to get moving.

"It's her house," he told Falcon as soon as they were away from the onlookers. "Doctor Breswell lives at the coordinates that just received a signal-emitting rock from space. That can't be a coincidence."

"I can assure you it is not a coincidence. That rock is also not the object that tore through her vehicle. Your lady may have more psychic ability than she admits. She is definitely intuitive and quite inventive."

Before Roman could ask what he meant by that, he noticed the official they'd spoken to pointing them out to someone else, possibly the scientist he'd mentioned. "I think we need to make ourselves less obvious." He quickly led Falcon behind a truck, closed his hand over Falcon's shoulder and, a heartbeat later, they were both invisible.

"I wondered what that might feel like," Falcon murmured. "But if you have the need to do that again, I would appreciate a warning."

"Sorry. Are you okay?"

Falcon took an audible breath. "Yes. It was somewhat similar to the sensation during transmigration, like a strong shiver but with a slight electrical charge."

"That's about how Shara described it when I once grabbed her without thinking. And if you multiply that by a million, you might be able to imagine what it feels like when every cell in my body breaks down to nothingness in order for me to walk through a wall. Believe me, I only use that trick as an absolute last resort."

"Have you ever taken anyone with you?" Falcon asked.

"No. Since I have no clue how it works, I have no way of knowing what would happen to someone else. So tell me. What did you see back there?"

"Your lady came out and saw the damaged car, just as she reported. But then she backed it up, got a shovel and dug down several feet to get to the object. She used the shovel to carry it into the house—she took care not to touch it—and came out with the rock you saw. She refilled the hole and planted her rock into the dirt. That rock is metamorphic and contains quartz, feldspar and several other crystals. It is native to this planet and not at all rare, though not commonly found in this area, which seemed to be why she chose it. As I said, she was being inventive, as though she knew the object should not be turned over to local officials."

"And that brings us to what actually *did* crash into her vehicle?"

"It would be more efficient to show you, if I may?" Falcon raised his hand toward Roman's temple and awaited permission to touch his mind.

A second after he nodded, Falcon made contact and

Roman received a mental image of the object. It was a decahedron, made of a black, matte-finish metal, with symbols etched into each of the three sides he could see clearly.

"I don't think this sort of thing has been used in a millennium," Roman ventured. "If I'm not mistaken, that's a cryptodrone, a type of communication device once used by the Confederation of Planets to transmit secret messages. And those symbols might be from an ancient Noronian alphabet. I learned about both in my cryptology class at the academy but I don't remember enough to translate the markings."

"If that is what this is, it could have been floating around in space for a very long time and would not contain any currently relevant information," Falcon replied as he lifted his fingers from Roman's temple.

"Or it's something else entirely."

"Obviously, you will need to retrieve the drone to discover which it is."

"Obviously," Roman said with reluctance.

"But you are not moving. Could you not simply remain invisible and enter the house? Since she removed it from the hole, she could hardly claim that it disappeared from her home without admitting what she did."

Roman knew there was no way to hide the truth from his mentor. "There's a slight complication with that plan. Even though I've never been visible around her, Doctor Breswell seems to know when I'm nearby. In fact, she thinks I'm a ghost and threatened to *exorcise* me if I stepped onto her property. I'm not sure what that would entail but I gathered it wouldn't be pleasant."

Falcon chuckled. "And yet you insist she is not your lady. Since you must postpone the retrieval, may I suggest we go back to Innerworld and have someone translate the markings we saw on the drone."

Minutes later, Falcon was drawing an image of the drone and its markings while Roman updated Romulus and Aster. And a few minutes after that, they called Shara's mate, historian Gabriel Drumayne, for his opinion and, hopefully, a translation.

"Of course, without my handling it personally, I can't authenticate it as a genuine antique, but from the drawing, it does appear to be a cryptodrone. They were used to transmit secret information through space using atomic propulsion, astronomical guidance and an indestructible casing. Various devices were implemented to prevent an enemy from being able to open the drone. The markings on the outside usually identified a specific recipient. Even if someone else figured out how to get it open, the message was imprinted with the DNA coding of the intended recipient. Contact with the wrong DNA code would cause the message inside to incinerate."

"Can you translate the symbols?" Roman asked impatiently.

"I'll need to do some research. Give me an hour and I should have something for you."

It took Gabriel closer to two hours and, when he called back, he looked more perplexed than pleased with himself. "You were right about one thing, brother. The symbols are from an ancient Noronian alphabet. Unfortunately, you only sent me images from three sides of the drone and two of them appear to be part of the encrypted instructions on how to open it. As I understand it, one side normally has the key to the rest but I would need all ten to figure out which it is and come up with a translation."

He paused, frowning at the drawing for several seconds before continuing. "However, if you're certain these are the exact markings, what the third side spelled eliminates the possibility that the object has just been floating around in space for a thousand years."

Falcon answered without hesitation. "Although I could not see what was on each side, I am completely certain of the precision of the symbols I drew."

"Gabriel, just tell us what it says," Aster said firmly.

He paused another moment then said, "Roman Locke. It's definitely his name, which probably indicates the message inside the cryptodrone is addressed to him. In which case, he may be the only one who can open it."

Cattar's heart thumped in her chest when Johann abruptly appeared in front of her desk.

"Pardon the interruption, Madam, but you did request that I notify you—"

"Yes, yes, of course. Have you found something?"

"My continuous scan of Innerworld's historical records has revealed a notation regarding the discovery of an alien object, possibly the cryptodrone, landing on the planet's surface."

Cattar exhaled heavily. "Thank the heavens. Anything more? What about the time and place?"

"It landed very close to the coordinates and time you had intended. However, there was nothing more to the entry and Terra's sun is still dying."

Cattar smiled. "But at least we know the message arrived and Innerworld would not ignore it. That's enough to give me hope."

CHAPTER 6

"It's all set."

Adam was so relieved to receive Eve's call, he held back the severe reprimand he'd intended to deliver. "Any problems?"

"Of course not."

"When is the first gathering of Doctor Breswell's team?"

"Tomorrow afternoon."

"Remember what I told you. It is imperative that you raise no suspicions."

"My memory is excellent. But speaking of raises, I need you to make another deposit to my account tomorrow. The same amount as last time will be fine."

Adam's stomach churned. "That's not what we agreed to. You'll be paid in increments of—"

"That agreement was made before I became your partner. I know that's what you have planned for me eventually. I'm just moving up the timing of my promotion. You'll pay me what I request when I tell you to. Don't worry, cookie, I won't ask for more than you can afford."

He was furious with her and, at the same time, impressed by her leap into a dominant position. She was turning out to be everything he wanted his Eve to be. But he was still in charge and she needed to know that. "I'll consider it. In the meantime, I had expected this call days ago. If you want favors from me, it would be in your best interest to provide me with daily reports."

"I'll consider it."

CHAPTER 7

Roman stared at the door to Erin's townhouse as though the answer to his dilemma were written across it. Since the last light had been turned off an hour ago, he had no doubt she was asleep by now. He could slip in, locate the cryptodrone and be gone without leaving a trace of his visit.

After learning that the drone was addressed to him, he had returned to Erin's property, only to discover there were still a number of people milling around outside and she was still inside. He had no choice but to wait for an opening. Only twice was he distracted from boredom—when Erin came out of the house with sweet tea for everyone and when Chief Friedrich paid her a visit. The rest of the day, Roman battled the temptation to take a nap.

But now it was after midnight, everyone was gone, the curious rock had been carefully taken away in a secure vehicle by men garbed in unnecessarily protective gear. Erin's vehicle had been towed away and a replacement was brought to her.

And yet, Roman was still standing on the porch, staring at Erin's front door. Imagining Falcon's frown of disapproval, he stopped wasting time. Bracing for the discomfort, he switched from invisible to incorporeal long enough to pass through the wooden door into Erin's unlit foyer. It was times like this when he wished he had Falcon's gift of night-vision, or even Shara's telepathic abilities, but he had to work with the one unique gift he had.

As soon as his eyes adjusted to the near-darkness, Roman quickly searched the downstairs, not really expecting to find the drone so easily. As he started up the stairs, he heard muffled cursing then the sounds of rushing water. Panic gripped his heart but he quickly relaxed and grinned when he realized she was taking a shower. This was even better than her being asleep. At the doorway to the master bedroom, he hesitated a moment to make sure his assumption that she was in the shower was accurate.

As soon as he stepped inside her room, his gaze was caught by the rumpled sheets on the large bed. Then he noticed the distinct scent of sexual activity. He had seen her go in and out of the house alone and the Chief had only stayed about a half hour. He hadn't considered the possibility of her having a lover arrive for an overnight stay while he was in Innerworld. The professional part of his brain both scolded him for the oversight and acknowledged how her being distracted, along with the noise of the shower, would give him an advantage in his search. Unfortunately, the only things of interest he discovered were a recently-used, electronic phallus on her nightstand and a collection of other sexual aids in the drawer. Though the search for the drone turned out to be futile, the personal part of his brain demanded he hang around to see what sort of individual earned Erin's intimate attentions.

Roman held his breath as she came out of the bathroom dripping wet and stood in front of the air conditioning vent. He could make out the curves of her silhouette and confirm that no one else had shared the shower with her.

She was alone after all…and obviously very, very hot.

Hands behind her head, she raised the mass of tangled hair and turned around to let the air cool her neck and back. He ordered himself to leave immediately. Not only was he invading her privacy, the shadowed vision before him was as erotic as anything he'd ever seen in full light.

He started to turn away, but then her arms moved and he could tell she was running her hands down her body, caressing her breasts and skimming down her stomach. She moaned softly and he knew without clearly seeing what part of herself she had just stroked. His sex swelled in response and he failed to withhold a sharp intake of breath.

Instantly Erin's eyes opened wide and she yanked a sheet off the bed. *"Who the hell are you? How'd you get in here?"*

Roman's head was filled with possible responses but two thoughts took precedence. First, his unexpected arousal had somehow made him fully visible to her. And second, her eyes were glowing…just like Falcon's did in the dark.

"You don't need to hurt me. Just tell me what you want."

He noted that once the sheet was wrapped around her, she was able to speak in her normally calm, confident voice. Her experience as a profiler had kicked shock and fear right out the window.

"Ah would never hurt you, Erin," he said sincerely. "And Ah'm very sorry for the intrusion. Ah only came to retrieve somethin' that belongs to me."

"Don't move," she ordered flatly and kept her golden gaze fixed on him as she turned on a lamp. In a heartbeat she reached beneath the mattress and had a handgun pointed at him.

Roman considered dramatically pushing aside the edges of his duster to show off his two holstered laser pistols. Instead, he sighed and made himself invisible.

"What the—" She jerked her head from side to side.

In a millisecond, the gun had been snatched from her hand and it disappeared also.

"Where are you? How did you do that?"

Retreating to a spot beyond her reach, he replied, "If you'll refrain from pointing any more weapons at me, Ah will explain."

She huffed and arranged the sheet more securely around her. "Fine. But I want to see who's talking to me."

Roman became visible, took off his cowboy hat and gave her his friendliest smile. "Howdy, ma'am. The name's Roman Locke and Ah'm a Texas Ranger Specialist—"

"Hold it right there." She glided slowly toward him, wrinkling her nose while sniffing the air. When she was within inches of him, she gasped. "It's *you*!" Backing away too quickly, she tripped on the sheet and landed on her bottom.

Rather than helping her up, he sat down. In an effort to gain a little trust, he set the gun down on the carpet where she could see but not easily grab it. "It appears Ah'm not the only one in this room with a secret identity."

"That's ridiculous," she retorted with a smirk. "My identity is public knowledge. Which reminds me, you called me Erin but I'm sure we've never met. I also realize you're the ghost who's been stalking me. And now I know why I could never see you!"

"But you recognized my scent, right?"

"I admit to a keen sense of smell."

"You also have exceptional night vision. Ah saw the reflective glow in your eyes."

She let out another huff then clucked her tongue. "How is it that *you* broke into *my* house but *I'm* the one being interrogated?"

"It's okay, Erin. My trainer is half felan. Are you a healer as well? Is that why you became a doctor?"

"I have no idea what you're talking about. Or why I'm sitting here, wearing only a sheet, while some lunatic holds me hostage in my own bedroom." She swiped perspiration off her upper lip. "And why the hell is it so damn hot in here?" She tried to rise but he grasped her hand.

And she went completely still.

He quickly released her but it was already too late. He should never have touched her. The sexual heat radiating from her body was nearly impossible to block but the bewilderment in her eyes kept him from melting into it. She began rocking back and forth, her breathing altered to short pants and her hands clenched into fists between her thighs.

A long strand of damp, curly hair hung over her face and Roman tucked it behind her ear. Despite the lamplight, there was still a faint golden glow emanating from her eyes. "You really don't understand, do you?"

"*No!* I don't understand any of this. Not you or your intoxicating smell or your disappearing act or why my eyes glow. But most of all I don't understand why the hell I've turned into some damn alley cat in heat!"

Roman almost managed to hide the smile he was feeling. With the lightest touch of his finger under her chin, he got her to meet his gaze. "Well, ma'am, Ah do believe Ah can help you with *all* of that."

The instant he relaxed, she dove for the gun, but the twisted sheet slowed her down just enough for Roman to counteract. As her fingers closed around the handle, he clamped his hand around her forearm. With strength fueled by fury, fear and the fire inside her body, she squirmed and turned, punched and kicked. Roman had no choice but to defend himself before she managed to seriously injure one of them.

Despite his superior size and skill, it took a while to completely immobilize her. Though the weapon remained in her grip, she was on her back with her arms pinned to the floor above her head and the weight of his torso and legs reduced the rest of her resistance to futile squirming.

"Damn you! Damn you to hell!"

He certainly didn't mean to laugh aloud, but the sound escaped his throat, which, naturally, made her wriggle more ferociously beneath him.

"Give up, Erin," he murmured in a low voice. "Please. You've lost. But, like I said, I'm not here to hurt you. And if you'll promise to stay calm, I'll let you up, and then I'll explain why I'm here." He waited for her to reply, or at least stop struggling, but she merely groaned, as though she were in pain. Suddenly he became aware of a change in her movement...a totally unexpected, but quite familiar, movement.

With her eyes tightly shut and her head turning from side to side, her hips rhythmically pushed up, lowered, pushed up and lowered again. A heartbeat later, the arousal that had caused him to become visible returned with a vengeance and she acknowledged his response by pumping her core harder and faster against his. He knew he should stop what was happening before he gave into it also, but instead, he shifted his legs to align between hers and she immediately wrapped her legs around his back.

Her blazing need radiated through his denim pants

as though he were as naked as she was. However, despite his own ignited lust, awareness came to him like a splash of icy water—she was using him as inhumanly as she would one of the implements next to her bed. Similar to the effect of the Noronian mating fever, her need was clearly clouding her mind. He could hold himself back from taking pleasure from her pain, but she was beyond his stopping her.

He forced his mind to wander to asexual territory—a history class at the academy, playing catch with Prince, Falcon's hand-to-hand combat training—until her body trembled in climactic relief. He remained motionless until she unclenched her legs and tossed the gun from her hand.

"I would consider it a favor," she murmured in a husky voice, "if you would take that gun and put me out of my misery now."

Rather than answer, Roman rose, picked up the weapon and slipped it back into its hiding place under her mattress. Out of the corner of his eye, he saw her curl up into a ball and pull the sheet over her entire body, including her head. He wanted to lie down beside her, hold her close and take away the shame or frustration or whatever she was hiding from. But, although he felt very well acquainted with her, he was still a complete stranger to her. He picked up his hat, walked to the bedroom door and said, "I'm pretty sure some conversation over a cup of tea would be a much more sensible choice. I'll fix it while you get dressed."

Erin used the sheet to wipe away the ridiculous, girly tears. *How could I have done that? What the hell is wrong with me?*

The stranger's words had suggested he had the answer to that, but after what she had done, she wasn't anxious to talk to *him* about anything.

She gave her guides a moment to give her any sort of comprehensible explanation and, when nothing popped into her mind, she took a shaky breath and got up off the floor. For several seconds, she simply stood still, ordering her mind to quiet itself. Since she couldn't change the events of the last fifteen minutes and she couldn't just disappear—as her intruder obviously could—she needed to figure out what to do next.

Obviously, if he'd wanted to hurt her, he could have done so easily. And if he'd had any interest in raping her—She cut off that sentence before she reverted to curling up in a ball on the floor. Better that she concentrate on what he had done *wrong*. Obviously, he had broken into her home. She had intended to call for help once she had him at gunpoint, but then he vanished, or at least she couldn't see him, and the surprise had cost her the advantage.

How had he done that? Stealth technology? She had heard of it, of course, but didn't believe it was perfected for human use. And she was fairly sure the Rangers didn't possess anything like that.

So was he a criminal? A secret agent? A psychopathic scientist?

Logic told her she had to listen to whatever her *ghost* had to say, while her intuition warned her she wasn't going to like it. She heard a noise downstairs and wondered if he was actually making her tea in her own kitchen.

His audacity was enough to push her into action. Dropping the sheet to the floor, she stretched her arms outward, visualized a gigantic ball of white and gold light overhead and, inhaling deeply, she drew the light down into and around her body. She gathered all the sensations, emotions and thoughts connected with her humiliating behavior and locked them in a memory box to be reviewed later. For now, she needed to at least *pretend* nothing out of the ordinary had occurred and she was in complete control of her actions. A few focused breaths later, she felt calm enough to put on loose-fitting pajamas and go downstairs.

She paused before the archway to the kitchen and readied herself for a verbal confrontation. His Stetson, duster and gun belt were draped over a stool. His claim of being a Ranger was confirmed by the badge hooked to the belt. The items were appropriate yet something was wrong. Her gaze skimmed over the man's back from head to toe. His clothing looked new...maybe *too* new. He might have recently bought the jeans and shirt but Texans tended to be proud of how well-worn their boots were. His weren't even scuffed.

Somehow, the man himself looked right though. He was tall, broad-shouldered and narrow-hipped, with a well-muscled frame. Even filled with panic, she noticed what an attractive specimen he was...in a dark, untrustworthy sort of way. Perhaps he was new to the Rangers but experienced in another branch of law enforcement or the military. That would go along with part of what she'd gotten about her *ghost* from the tarot reading. The cards had told her he was there to help her find the devil in a positive, *loving* way. He wasn't there to harm her. Her interpretation of the cards may have been faulty, but she felt certain of that much.

Deception and lies had also been indicated. Was that about his invisibility trick or would she be hearing verbal lies from him as well?

Another anomaly tapped at her brain's door. When he first spoke, he had a distinctive drawl, yet he seemed to have lost it by the time he'd left the bedroom.

Her perusal ended as he turned around holding two steaming mugs and set them on her kitchen table. *Stay calm. Don't let him see your insecurity.* "I see you've found your way around another room of my house," she said, sitting down. "Or have you been here before? Perhaps when I was at my office? Oh, wait, no that couldn't be, since you were there too, skulking in corners if I'm not mistaken. Unless, of course, besides making yourself invisible, you can also be in two places at the same time."

He frowned slightly as he sat down across from her. "No, I was never here before. And no, I'm not able to be in two places at the same time. I apologize for being in your office like I was, but it was part of my assignment…making sure you remained…safe. I've never had anyone notice my presence like you did. And finally, I apologize again for trespassing tonight, but I had no choice."

Erin slowly took a sip of her tea. His speech pattern had definitely changed. She wanted to shout at him, demand answers to her long list of questions, but she had years of experience at being quiet and waiting for the other person to fill the silence.

"My assignment was to get in and out without…botherin' you."

She took another sip and met his gaze over the mug's rim.

"Let me start again. My name is Roman Locke and Ah'm a Texas Ranger, here on a temporary special assignment from Houston. Ah'd explain more, ma'am, but it involves a highly classified matter."

The drawl had returned. A definite lie there. She resisted the urge to smirk. "I understand. How long have you been a Ranger?" She noted how his shoulders slightly relaxed with the thought that he had fooled her.

"It'll be seven years comin' up."

Seven days is more like it. Another lie. "I'm just surprised Chief Friedrich didn't mention your assignment to me...considering I obviously play some part in it. He and I often work quite closely together and, since you've been eavesdropping, you know we are currently in the midst of a very highly classified matter ourselves. In fact, I'm quite sure he considers it *the* top priority on the Rangers' action list." She watched him take a swallow of his tea and deduced it was a delaying tactic for him as well.

After several seconds, he said, "It's a, uh, another matter entirely. One he's not actively involved in."

Since that was highly improbable, she chalked that up to his third lie. She would give him only one more chance to say something truthful. "How strange. I didn't realize there were such matters. But I guess that's the point." She gave him a disarming smile. "Although...I think you already let something slip. You said you were here to retrieve something that belongs to you. Not the Rangers or the government, but *you*."

"A figure of speech only. Ah certainly didn't mean to imply—"

"Enough!" She slapped the table for emphasis. "You are lying. About everything! In fact, I am absolutely certain that *you* are a walking, talking lie. And, either you never expected to have to explain yourself or you're just not very good at it. I insist you tell me the truth, the whole truth, or I will call Chief Friedrich to come haul you away. The Rangers have a certain reputation when it comes to their interrogation techniques. And please drop the phony Texas drawl. It's a travesty."

He let out an audible sigh and combed his fingers

through his hair. "You can tell truth from lies, can't you? Any other gifts you're keeping a secret?"

She smiled slowly. Her confidence that he was a liar through and through had more to do with deductive reasoning than psychic ability, but it was to her advantage to have him believe she was a human lie detector. "You first."

He sighed again and raised his gaze upward as though asking for help from above. "I assure you, the explanation I had prepared is a lot easier to believe."

"Try me. I've heard a lot of strange-but-true things in my profession. I bet your story isn't even extraordinary."

"All right. Here's the truth." He rose from his chair and meandered around the room, touching this and that, as he spoke. "This morning, your car was damaged by a ten-sided metal object. The strange markings on it were in an ancient language. It was addressed to me, Roman Locke. I know you brought it inside this house and put a rock in its place. That object is what I came here to retrieve and if you'll give it to me, I will leave and never bother you again."

His words felt completely truthful, yet they raised so many more questions, she barely knew where to begin. "Since you said you haven't been in my house before, I guess that means you've been loitering outside?"

He shook his head. "This morning was the first time, I swear. It was just a coincidence. I didn't know this was *your* home."

"But if that's true and the thing was meant for you, why did it land on my car?"

"I don't know."

"What's it for?"

"I don't know."

She arched an eyebrow at him.

"I mean, I don't know for sure. Such objects are used to send highly sensitive, secret messages."

Narrowing her eyes at him, she waited to see if he would say more. It felt like he was being honest while leaving out very important information. "Let me see if I understand this. Someone has sent you, *personally*, a secret message by dropping it out of the sky onto a random location, which just *coincidentally* happened to be my driveway."

"It looks that way, but I won't know for sure until I open it."

"Do you have any idea how ridiculous that sounds?" He shrugged and Erin forced herself to stay on a direct line of questioning, rather than jump around like the thoughts flying through her brain. "You make it sound like the message could be something official. So, why you? Why not Chief Friedrich, our President Garcia or President Callahan?"

Roman returned to his seat at her table and purposefully met her gaze. "They would have no way of recognizing the language. And if someone other than the addressee tries to open it, the message will instantly disintegrate. At least that's what the historical records state."

"Yet you recognized the language," Erin concluded. "I'm getting the distinct feeling there's one question I could ask that would fill in all the blanks at once. But unless I ask it, you'll keep skipping around it. I'll tell you what. It's very late and I'm very tired of this game. You want your message box. I want the whole story. Starting with the truth about why you've been playing the invisible man around me for the last week or so."

"I told you the truth about my assignment. I was to observe but not interfere. The message box is called a cryptodrone. Other than that, I've already told you more than I'm permitted—"

"No more stalling. Your *cryptodrone* is not in this house. In fact, I sent it to a location where someone could try to open it, which according to your *historical records*, would destroy the message you're so anxious to get your hands on. I'd say you have no more time to waste." The strained look on his face let her know she had chosen the right threat.

"Will you at least agree not to relate anything I am about to tell you to anyone else, including Chief Friedrich?"

She clucked her tongue. "I seriously doubt there's anything you can tell me that he doesn't already know. So, yes, I swear I will repeat nothing you tell me to anyone."

An hour later, she truly regretted making that promise.

CHAPTER 8

Roman now understood how a particular female could have the power to make a man *want* to reveal his deepest secrets to her, regardless of the potential repercussions. His politically-minded Noronian father, the barbaric Gallant, even Falcon, with his unemotional felan breeding, had all been vulnerable when it came to the women who were to be their mates. And now it seemed he had joined their ranks...except for the part about all the women being fated mates.

Erin had not triggered the Noronian mating fever in him, leaving him with no control over his actions. And yet, he had told Erin all about Innerworld, Norona, his ability and his mission. Without a second thought, he had given in to the urge to reveal much more than she had demanded.

In his own defense, *her* burning definitely played a huge part in his getting flustered and losing his ability to efficiently maintain his cover story. The subject of her uncontrollable lust had yet to be broached but, like an octoman in the room, it could not be ignored for long.

A lesser excuse for his giving into her demand so

easily was how her appearance had affected him when he'd turned around and saw her standing there, scanning him. She was wearing oddly unflattering clothing, her face was clean of enhancements and her wild mane of hair was barely controlled by an off-center clip on top of her head. And yet he thought she was the most beautiful female he'd ever seen.

He chalked up that irrational notion to the fact that in his mind he could still see the sensual vision of her nude silhouette, simmering with unquenched need.

At least Erin had accepted his revelations as acceptable explanations for his ability to disappear and his stalking her. Then again, as soon as he had told her everything she wanted to know, she had excused herself and left the room. That was fifteen minutes ago and she had yet to return. Although he wanted to allow her some privacy, he was sincerely concerned that she might be having a breakdown after everything she'd heard. With only her welfare in mind, he went looking for her.

The house wasn't that large, yet she was nowhere to be seen. There was only one place left to search and that was behind a closed door upstairs. Had he driven her to hide in a closet?

He tapped gently on the door. "Erin? Are you in there? Are you all right?" Several seconds passed before the door was opened.

"You may as well come in," she said. "It's not like I have anything left to hide from you."

To his surprise, he entered a cozy, incense-scented, candle-lit room. His gaze fell on the cards spread out on the table, some of which were picture-side up. "Your home office, I presume?"

"I think of it as my safe room. I needed to know for sure whether you can be trusted."

"And what did your cards tell you?" He stepped

closer to the table to get a better look.

Quickly, she gathered up all the cards into a neat pile. "I got a confirmation that you are indeed an alien."

"Half alien," he corrected gently. "And which half depends on who's qualifying me. What else?"

"That I can, and should, depend on your assistance in the upcoming hunt."

He nodded. "That's good. It will certainly make my mission easier."

"But you have to stop pretending to be a Ranger."

"Fine with me. These boots are wrecking my feet." She almost smiled at that. Perhaps he was already making progress with her. "Anything else?"

"How would you feel about giving up the invisible mode and joining my team openly?"

"I have no problem with that but, like I told you, I don't have any extrasensory perception to throw into the pot."

"Maybe not, but I got that your professional experience will be of use. We're hunting a very dangerous man and I may need protection. I'll introduce you as my personal bodyguard and team security officer."

He grinned. "I like the sound of that. As long as I can keep the gun belt and laser pistols. After what happened in Katy, it seems like a good precaution to be armed."

She narrowed her eyes at him and twisted her mouth from side to side but finely relented. "Fine. I'll get Chief's permission for you to carry the pistols but, unless you want to tell Chief everything you told me—"

"No. I realize adding a manufactured background file into the Ranger system isn't enough to fool Friedrich. I'll have it deleted and have something less noteworthy made up in case he wants to check my credentials."

"Better that you have nothing on file anywhere. After the realignment, plenty of people in the New Republic went off-grid completely. Believe me, my endorsement is all he needs. The first meeting of the entire team is tomorrow—"

She glanced at the clock on the stove and made a face. "Today. Two o'clock in my office. I know you've been there before but please pretend like it's your first time. And even though you have your own agenda, would you *please* remember to behave as though you work for me."

He forced a serious expression. "Yes ma'am. I'm good with being your hired gun."

"And don't let anyone see your disappearing act."

"Yes, ma'am." He fought the grin trying to break through. "I swear, I'm very good at controlling…the *disappearing act*…when I'm not distracted by a beautiful, naked—"

Erin pressed her fingers to his lips. "Please don't. I'm not ready to talk about that yet."

The bewildered look in her eyes completely erased his urge to smile. "Whenever you're ready. I really do think I can help you." She immediately took a step back from him. "I mean, I can help you *understand*. At least I'm pretty sure I know what's happening to you."

"Thank you. Now, is there any chance you could go away and let me get a few hours' sleep before I have to be in my *public* office?"

"Of course," he said, but remained where he was. "Right after you get me the cryptodrone."

Her eyes widened. "Oh. I was telling you the truth about it not being here. I gave it to Chief when he came by. He mentioned having it couriered to ISA, the International Space Agency, in Houston. I'll send him a message right now. If he still has it, I'll tell him to hold it until we can pick it up tomorrow. If he already sent it off, I'll warn him to make sure no one tries to open it."

Roman followed her downstairs, allowing himself a moment to feel encouraged by his improved circumstances. She had invited him to openly sit in on a gathering he needed to observe as part of his current assignment...and as her *bodyguard*, no one would question his staying close or keeping his eyes on her when she moved around. But his good feeling had more to do with her saying "we" would get the cryptodrone. She was already thinking of him as a partner.

On a professional level, he knew he should not be pleased about that. He should return to Innerworld, confess that he'd been compromised and request a substitute be sent to complete his assignment.

But he couldn't make himself do that. What he *could* do was take advantage of the professional courtesy she'd offered, *not* take advantage of her vulnerable physical condition and reinforce his guard against the strong attraction he felt toward her. It would take incredible willpower, but he believed he could handle it.

"You know," she said when they were back in the kitchen. "If you're supposed to be my bodyguard, you really should be staying here and escorting me everywhere I have to go. Where are your belongings?"

"At a motel. I don't have much."

"Good. Go get whatever you need and come back...but not for at least six hours. I'm serious about needing sleep and I really have to be alert for the meeting. And wipe that grin off your face. You'll have your own room."

He hadn't even realized he was smiling again. Apparently his willpower needed some work. "Yes ma'am." Looking away from her, he grabbed his hat, coat and gun belt and headed for the front door. "I'll be back in six hours," he said firmly. "And I expect you to have news of the cryptodrone's status by then."

As he walked away from her house, he took the ring out of his pocket and programmed it to transmigrate him back to the motel. At the last second he turned around and caught her watching him through the front window. He grinned, touched his ring...and vanished.

Tripper's heart pounded, his legs kicked and his arms flailed. As though he were drowning in deep water, he fought with all his strength to get to the surface. Finally he awoke from the frighteningly lucid dream. As was his habit, he recorded every detail before any of it faded. His pulse was still racing when he finished.

Before going to sleep, he had called for a dream about the project he was about to be involved in with the sexy doctor. He had understood the psych team would be "looking" for a bad guy. He never considered he might personally end up in real danger.

There was a time when his life was consumed by danger and death. He had worked very hard to rise out of that darkness, to ensure it would never control him again. He could tell Breswell about the dream and walk away. He didn't have to join her team.

On the other hand, as much as he abhorred that other life, he couldn't deny that he hadn't felt completely alive in years. The possibility of danger called to him like an ex-lover and he needed to answer that call. He rationalized that, considering his dream, the psych team might actually need someone like him.

* * *

Erin was usually very self-aware. As part of her routine to stay balanced, she meditated every morning before heading out the door. If something felt amiss, she used that time to identify the problem, review it, analyze it and deal with it in a matter of minutes. Maintaining a calm demeanor regardless of what she saw or heard required constant vigilance. It was a necessary requirement for any practicing parapsychologist.

She had just never imagined sitting in her kitchen having tea with an alien. She still had plenty of doubts about his explanation and watching him disappear from her front yard hadn't helped her clarity.

She desperately needed to calm her mind and prepare for the afternoon gathering in her office. But a brief meditation was hardly going to sort out the jumble of thoughts and feelings darting through her mind. If only she'd been able to fall into a deep sleep for a few hours, she might have had the mental energy to process everything, but that escape had eluded her.

The only remedy was to temporarily shelve the confusion and polish her exterior as best as possible. Though it took the remaining time she had, a hot shower, prim hairdo, touch of makeup and getting dressed in one of her favorite suits went a long way toward reinforcing her confidence.

The alien would return any minute…to stay in her home…*at her suggestion.*

Until the suggestion had thoughtlessly slipped out of her mouth, she really had never considered the possibility that this project might put her or the team in danger of any kind. It certainly hadn't occurred to her that she might need, let alone *want*, a bodyguard.

Yet, with barely a pause, she'd gone from pointing a gun at an intruder to granting him access to her entire life.

Curiosity was a plausible reason. He had insinuated that he knew why her eyes glowed and her senses were enhanced and why she felt like a cat in heat. The first two oddities had become noticeable nine years ago, but they hadn't worried her enough to seek a medical opinion that could possibly call attention to anything unusual about her. The uncontrollable heat and sexual frustration, however, were new and exceedingly aggravating. If he could help with that, it would be worth giving up her solitude for a short time.

She felt herself blush at the memory of how he'd already helped, then realized that she hadn't felt the heat rise again since the use of his body had given her some relief. Perhaps his being an alien had something to do with that. She wondered if his people engaged in intercourse or if giving and receiving pleasure took place on a higher, mental level. On the other hand, he'd said he was only half alien. In that case, she wondered which half was responsible for the impressive erection she'd—

She should have switched topics right then, but her thoughts continued down the orgasm track. What if his alien half was responsible for the heat and intense arousals she'd been experiencing? Now that she thought about it, the symptoms started in the Oval Office, which was also the first time she had picked up his scent. If that was actually the first time he began spying on her, there really could be a connection. In which case, she should be very, very angry with him.

However, as an alien, maybe he wasn't doing it intentionally. Maybe his kind simply had that effect on human females. Or maybe, she had stepped into an old science fiction movie where the aliens were here looking to breed with easy Earth girls.

She burst out laughing. Geez, she needed that. By allowing her thoughts to run free for a change, she had released the wildest explanation her brain could concoct and felt quite a bit lighter for it. Perhaps she needed to do that more often. Before she could move on to the next question on her mental list, the doorbell rang.

Her alien was back. She had not yet been able to think of him by the name he'd given her. Somehow that would make him completely real, which would make everything he'd told her completely real as well. And no matter how intelligent and open-minded she was, she wasn't entirely ready to have her view of the world rewritten.

Something her mother had told her more than once popped into her head. *If you aren't ready to hear answers, you shouldn't ask questions.*

Erin checked her video monitor to confirm that the person at the door was in fact her alien. The sight of him brought back the jumble of feelings in a rush. He was still dressed in black and wearing the gun belt and hat, but the badge and long coat were gone. He'd also added dark sunglasses and exchanged the boots for plain black slip-ons. Alien or human, he was one sexy specimen. The satchel in his hand sharply reminded her of why he was standing outside her home.

She had to take several calming breaths before opening the door. Without fully meeting his gaze, she greeted him politely. "Thank you for being punctual. I forgot to mention that I need to get to the office a little early to set up the room." She stepped aside and motioned for him to enter, but left the door ajar. "If you don't mind, you can leave your bag right here for now and get settled when we get back." She picked up her briefcase, stepped outside and, as soon as he joined her, she locked the door.

The instant after she stepped off her front porch, she stopped and asked, "Where's your car?"

"I don't have one. Can't we use that one?" He pointed to the vehicle in her driveway.

She made a face at the rental car the insurance company had provided. It felt as though the accident had happened a lifetime ago. Although her vehicle preference had wheels to the ground and manual control, the replacement was a hybrid that could be switched to a computer-controlled hovercar. Like most of the people in her neighborhood, if she couldn't take a commuter train, she preferred to do her own driving. "Of course. But how did you get here?"

He shrugged. "I have my own means of transportation."

Don't ask questions if you aren't prepared for the answers.

"Of course you do." When he walked straight to the passenger's side, she added, "I don't suppose you have a license to drive either."

"I have a license...for identification purposes. I've never had the need to learn how to drive one of these. I don't believe it would appear strange for you to drive. As your bodyguard, my attention should be on you, not the traffic."

As they drove off, she realized how very formally he was behaving and how he'd only spoken in response to her questions. "By the way, I spoke to Chief Friedrich after you left. He still has the cryptodrone and he assured me he will keep it safe until we come to pick it up later on. I promised him an explanation, so maybe you can help me create one."

A nod was his only response.

"I also told him I hired a trusted friend to protect me

and the psych team and he said he'd take care of the permit for you to carry the laser pistols. I hope you know how lucky you are to have him in our corner."

Again he just nodded. When he remained silent during the short trip to her office, she was certain his formality was intentional. She told herself she was very relieved that he'd made that choice without her having to request such behavior.

Then she called herself a liar.

CHAPTER 9

"I'm so glad you were all able to rearrange your schedules to be here on such short notice." Erin took the one empty chair in the circle she'd set up in her office. "As I explained when I first spoke with each of you individually, the reason for our coming together is to assist the Texas Rangers in solving a series of unexplained crimes, one of which now appears to have been murder."

Roman had remained standing in order to walk around behind everyone. Erin had yet to introduce him but each person in the circle had shown a varying degree of curiosity about his presence. Her mention of murder yanked their attention away from him and caused a mixture of surprise and dismay from all but two people in the group—Vicky, who had glimpsed the murders during her remote viewing session, and a man about his age, with very long, light brown hair. That one had entered the office looking worried and that expression didn't alter now. Had he already picked up on the homicide connection?

"What we are attempting is relatively unproven in the area of law enforcement," Erin continued. "There's no guarantee of success. However, the hope is that, by joining all our efforts and focusing on one goal, we will be more successful than any one person might have been alone.

"Before we begin, I need to advise you that our sessions are being videographed for internal review purposes. Nothing said or done in this room will be disseminated to the public in any form."

Roman noted how she sent a quick, meaningful glance to Dr. Cho, who gave her a nod of agreement in return.

"Next, I would like to cover etiquette. Every one of you is extremely talented, intelligent, intuitive and trustworthy. No one person's ability is more valuable than another's. Likewise, no one person is more useful to this team than anyone else. Although the intention is for us to enhance each other's gifts, no one may use any of their special abilities to invade the privacy of another. If one of you accidentally acquires personal information that was not freely offered, keep it to yourself. In other words, there is just one rule— do unto others as you would have them do unto you.

"That said, I think we should start by having each of you introduce yourselves to the team. Please give your name and a brief description of your ability." She nodded at the woman on her left to go first.

Roman took a few steps to get a better look at the female as she spoke. She was an attractive, well-dressed brunette in her late thirties or early forties, with a well-muscled physique.

"Hello. I'm Wendy Santana and my ability involves psychometry. If I'm holding something that a person's energy is strongly connected to, like a ring they regularly wear, I gain an understanding of what makes them tick, like a personality profile, sometimes including facts about their past that made them that way. Also, Doctor Breswell, it wasn't in my resumé because it's been very random, but a few times, when I'm holding an object, I've picked up what the owner is thinking about at that moment. I've been trying to improve that skill."

So, thought Roman, the CIA's rep did have an additional skill as Erin's notes had suggested.

Erin smiled at Wendy. "Thank you for letting us know what you're working on. Let's add that to our introductions. And please, everyone, call me Erin."

The elderly woman sitting next to Wendy was dressed in what Roman recognized as a type of Native American attire. She had steel-gray hair woven into two long braids, brown skin and a youthful twinkle in her eyes.

"My name is Peace One-Feather and I am so very pleased to be part of this team. My gift is that of healing. Among my people, what I do comes so naturally, I don't usually think of it as a special ability, but I trust that I've been included here for a reason."

"Peace is being modest. She also has the ability to communicate with animals and read signs from Mother Nature," Erin added, then nodded at Vicky.

"Hi. I'm Vicky Trumble. I remote view, usually in present time and with a specific trigger, though occasionally I see things I'd rather not. Erin, you mentioned murder. Was it connected to what I saw when I was here last week?"

"It looks that way. In fact, I believe it was the connection to the case rather than to you personally that pulled your view toward it. Did you check with your friend?"

Vicky bobbed her head. "She wasn't there. And although that was her mother's aunt, I remembered correctly about them not being at all close. Her presence seemed to be a true coincidence."

Erin took a moment to briefly relate to the rest of the group the scene Vicky had viewed then quickly introduced the Japanese gentleman next in the circle. "I'm sure you are all familiar with the work of Dr. Cho. He has kindly agreed to assist me in guiding this team and has generously offered his experience and expertise to any member who requests his counsel, whether in session or out."

To his credit, the celebrated author and speaker did not feel the need to add anything to Erin's summary, merely saying, "Please call me Kanji. And this is my most honorable student, Haruko Zhang."

"Hari," she corrected in a very subdued voice and, rather than speaking to the group in general, she directed her introduction toward Roman. He noted that her English was perfectly anglicized. "I'm also able to remote view in present time. I've never experienced a viewing in past or future time. As to an ability I'm attempting to improve upon, that would be telekinesis. I'm able to move most lightweight objects with my mind, but denser objects are still beyond me. Kanji believes it is lack of faith rather than ability."

Roman thought Hari could be very young in age but her face had a hardened edge to it. It occurred to him that a smile could make her much more attractive, so he gave her one first. It only made her look away.

The worried-looking fellow was next but he asked to go last, turning the floor over to the blond twins.

"I'm Jamie McCraig," stated the stunning, barely adult female with a smile that could turn a man to a puddle of drool.

"And I'm Ryan," her brother added then one corner of his mouth lifted slightly, creating a very likable, cockeyed grin. There was no doubt he had a line of young ladies begging for his attention. Roman didn't think either one needed any special powers to get whatever they wanted.

"We can communicate telepathically with each other…" she began.

"No matter how far apart we are," he finished. "And when we both touch a person at the same time…"

"We can read that person's thoughts." Jamie's head jerked toward Ryan and they had a brief exchange that no one else could hear. "Fine. There's something else that I can do but he can't. Sorry Doc, I mean Erin, we should have mentioned this in the interview but we really wanted you to accept us—" Again she turned toward Ryan. "Stop pushing me."

"She can make people do something and think it was their idea," Ryan blurted out.

"Do you mean Jamie can plant suggestions into someone's mind without them knowing?" Erin asked without judgment.

Jamie nodded. "But I only do it now when it's for their own good…like to get them to stop a bad habit. And let me assure you all…" She made sure she met every person's gaze as she swore, "I will never do anything like that here."

"We believe you, Jamie," Erin said reassuringly. "That's really very interesting news though and I'm glad you told us. You see, I'm fairly certain that the ability to plant suggestions is how our perpetrator has done what he has. It would definitely explain why individuals have behaved out of character, even to the point of a law-abiding citizen committing a major crime."

Kanji added, "It could also explain the burglaries where there was no sign of illegal entry. The villain may have simply instructed the owner to unlock the door for him and then forget about it, as well as whatever he might have seen the stranger doing."

"Plus, he might have put a different story in the

person's head about what he had really been doing during that time," Jamie suggested. "If he was just told to forget it, he might wonder why he had lost an hour of time."

Erin's smile broadened. "This is excellent. You're all here because of your special abilities, but brainstorming is just as important. Before we get any further into why's and how's, we have one more member who needs to tell us about himself."

The man forced a half-smile for Erin then shared it with everyone else. "I go by Tripper. I'm a lucid, predictive dreamer and the dream I had last night still has me shaking inside." He returned his gaze to Erin. "You know I can't always tell what a dream means exactly, but I know when it involves a crime. This time I actually asked to have a dream about the criminal we'd be meeting about. And if the real thing is half as sick as the dream, we may be getting into some seriously dangerous territory. I thought, maybe if I could tell it to you—"

Erin stopped him from continuing by holding up her index finger. "I believe Tripper has set up our first group exercise. Dream interpretation usually involves a combination of logic, intuition and personal symbolisms. So it will be interesting to hear what each of you comes up with. Also, please understand, I have no idea if this is going to work, but there is no more talented group of people to test it with. If everyone would rearrange your positions so that Jamie and Ryan are on each side of Tripper then move your chairs close enough for everyone to join hands. Rather than melding our energies, however, Tripper will mentally recall his dream in detail, our twins will use their combined abilities to read his thoughts and send them to everyone else in the circle."

She looked directly at each of their faces then,

satisfied they understood, she began the exercise. "If everyone would please join hands, close your eyes, take a deep breath and block out everything except Tripper's dream. Let the images and words enter your mind, but think of it like a movie. Be aware that you're only watching, not participating. When he's finished, we'll each give our impressions and possible interpretations, particularly its relevance to the person or people we're looking for." She gave everyone a few seconds to get comfortable in their space then said, "Tripper, if you would please remember your dream in as much detail as possible and don't concern yourself with whether or not anyone else can see it the way you do. Trust Jamie and Ryan to take care of that part."

A man and woman walked side by side through a tropical jungle, both naked except for a large leaf over their genitals. The woman had a small bag attached to a string around her neck. He looked happy. She did not. They were both scanning the area in search of something.

A few steps later, the man stuck his hand into a bush and yanked out a man half his size. There was no objection or resistance from the little man. He stood perfectly still as the woman bent at the waist beside him. She appeared to be about to whisper something in his ear.

Suddenly a long, serpentine tongue slithered out of her mouth, bored into the little man's ear and extracted a piece of his brain. When she stood upright, she too looked pleased. She spat the piece of brain into the bag and said, "Welcome to the family."

As the couple continued on their path, the little man was surrounded by an army of little people, all trudging mindlessly behind the man and woman.

Tripper saw them heading toward the bush where he was hiding. He now understood there was no hiding place nearby where they could not easily find him. He had to run. He had to warn the others to run also. Run as fast as they could because their lives depended on it.

Roman watched the faces of the team change from passive to uncomfortable to horror to concern. He completely understood why he couldn't be part of this circle but he hoped Erin would fill him in on the details when they were alone again. Less than five minutes later, without anyone saying a word, everyone opened their eyes.

"Thoughts?" Erin asked.

Kanji spoke first. "I've done extensive research in dream interpretation and, as Erin mentioned, the symbols can sometimes be very personal to the dreamer. Are you a Christian, Tripper?"

He shrugged. "Not in practice. I think of myself as spiritual in general rather than a follower of any organized religion. Why do you ask?"

"The scene had a few distinct similarities to the Garden of Eden creation mythology…Adam and Eve wearing only fig leaves and the snake tongue for instance."

"I had the same thought," Wendy said and several more heads nodded in agreement.

Kanji continued. "If the backdrop of the dream wasn't rooted in Tripper's own ideology, then it would seem to suggest that the setting has meaning. They could actually be hiding in a dense jungle location or other primitive setting. I also think the size of the couple versus the little people gives a hint into their attitude toward the natives, or, perhaps, general populace. They clearly see themselves as superiors, possibly even gods of a sort."

"Each time I've done a reading," Erin said, "I've asked for a description of who was behind the incidents and I've gotten a male presence with truly evil intent. But I also got that he's not working alone and the dream did indicate there is a woman at his side."

"It seemed to me," Wendy offered, "that the man was happy because he believed he was in charge but the woman was the one with the real power. If there's an evil presence out there planting suggestions in someone's mind, I'd say it was the chick stealing pieces of peoples' brains with her forked tongue."

Jamie and Ryan both giggled over Wendy's description, which helped the entire group relax a little. Inserting an occasional question, Erin kept the group speculating about the relationship of the couple to each other and their victims until everyone either offered an impression or agreed with someone else's...except Hari, who seemed to be more interested in studying the others than participating.

After a time, Erin summarized their conclusions so far. "We seem to be in agreement on the idea that we are actually looking for a man *and* a woman, that they see themselves as superior beings, and that it is the woman who has the ability to effectively plant suggestions or control a person's behavior. Also, they have done this to a number of people already and are still looking for victims, but the way they are searching the bushes in the dream may suggest that their choices aren't random. They might have a list of qualities or characteristics that attract their attention.

"On the other hand, we're divided on why the dream was set in the jungle. So I have one more question. Did anyone get a sense of a goal or why they have been manipulating innocent people into committing crimes?"

There was some head shaking and shoulder shrugging, but no responses to her question. Then Roman saw Hari's lips move and whispered in Erin's ear to call on her.

"Hari? You've been quiet. Did you have an idea?"

Her Asian features barely moved, even when she murmured the word, "Slaves."

"For what purpose?" Kanji asked his pupil.

"I don't know," she said quietly, keeping her gaze lowered. "That's just what came to me when I saw all those little people whose freedom had been stolen from them."

"Thank you, Hari." Erin said sincerely. "That could be very relevant considering our conclusion that this couple sees themselves above ordinary people. But your intuition also supports something I picked up. I wanted to hear all of your ideas before telling you another hint I got from several readings. I had asked what the person's goal was and I repeatedly got *The World* card. The interpretation usually refers to a final step in a journey or the accomplishment of a goal, so I thought I wasn't getting a helpful answer. But when I heard Hari say 'slaves', I realized in this case, the interpretation of the card could be completely literal. The man's goal could be to set up his own world."

Ryan's eyes widened. "You mean like he could buy an island or take over a small country?"

"If that's the case," Jamie added, "they could be planning to use the ability to make sure the natives are compliant."

"*She* could do that," Ryan told everyone somewhat proudly as he pointed his thumb at Jamie.

"Very credible," Wendy said. "Another possibility could be he's setting up a cult, like the one that was in Waco in the last century. That could explain why

Texas has been the center of activity as well as the religious connection in Tripper's dream."

"Anyone else?" Erin asked. No one spoke up but Kanji and Peace stifled yawns. "Then I will call this session to an end. Tripper, your dream gave us the perfect tool to expand on my preliminary profile. We now have a few leads for our remote viewers to start searching in tomorrow's session. All of you deserve congratulations. This was really good work for any group let alone one so new. Now, I know some of you are still exhausted from your travels, but I have one more assignment for you today."

Erin paused to make sure she had all their attention. "I've reserved a private dining room at the Faust Hotel for this evening. Since you're all staying there, I thought it would be the easiest location but it's also an interesting and fun place. The reason I'm making it an assignment is because it's really important that you get to know each other well enough to be at ease when we start melding our energy tomorrow. And, by the way, dinner and brews are on the Texas Rangers."

Tripper slapped his thigh. "Now that's my kind of homework."

Erin passed out the hotel's promotional cards. "Our reservations are for seven, so that should give you some time to rest or do some sightseeing in town. So, unless someone has a question, I'll see you then."

Jamie and Ryan both raised their hands. Jamie did the talking. "We have a question."

"Yes?"

"Has anyone else noticed a gorgeous, armed man in black, skulking around the room or is he a figment of our imagination?" Wendy and Vicky laughed. Peace smiled. Hari's face remained unreadable.

Roman winked at Jamie and got a bright smile in return.

Erin blushed but accepted the teasing with a smile of her own. "I do apologize. I hadn't wanted to draw extra attention to any potential danger we might be facing but since Tripper's dream suggested we needed to be aware of it, I should have introduced my...friend. I've hired him as my bodyguard and security for the team. Mind you it's only a precaution, but if any of us need protection, he is immensely qualified."

"Does our immensely qualified protector have a name?" Jamie asked sweetly, though the way she slowly raked her gaze down his body was a far cry from innocence.

Roman could have introduced himself but he was enjoying Erin's obvious discomfort over being questioned about him. Besides, he was curious as to whether she remembered what his name was.

Erin tilted her head at him and asked, "How would you prefer to be addressed by the team?"

The possibility that she really didn't remember bothered him more than a little. "Roman will be fine."

"Works for me," Jamie said with another appraising look.

Erin rose and smoothed her skirt. "Please don't be offended if he keeps himself apart from the group tonight. In his profession, he can't afford to become friendly with his charges."

Jamie pouted prettily, Ryan gave her a nudge and Wendy chuckled at all of them.

A few minutes later, everyone filed out of the office and Erin told Nola she could head home. "I need to record my notes while they're fresh," Erin told Roman as she sat down behind her desk and turned on her monitor.

He sat on the sofa a few feet away from her desk.

Erin typed a little, stopped, straightened her spine,

typed a little more, stopped again and rubbed her neck. After several more starts and stops, she sighed. Without looking at Roman, she asked, "Would you please go sit in the reception area? I'm not used to anyone being in here while I'm working."

He arched a brow at her even though she was making an effort to keep her eyes on her notes. Satisfied that he had paid her back for not remembering his name, he rose, bowed his head and said, "Yes ma'am."

"Y'all don't seem to be the type to be at a woman's beck and call."

Roman snapped his attention toward the voice and was surprised to see Nola still sitting at her post. He grinned at her conjecture and his own lack of awareness. "I've heard that before, but, believe it or not, being a personal bodyguard actually makes me the authority figure in the relationship."

She gave him a soft smile for his effort at humor. "I seriously doubt Erin would agree with you. She's a great boss but she can be pretty tough when it comes to how she wants things done. I'm actually kind of stunned that she agreed to a bodyguard. I gather Chief Friedrich insisted on it though. Are you staying at her house?"

Under the circumstances, her question wasn't *that* strange, but there was something in the intensity of her expression that suggested it wasn't a simple question of his duties. Rather than respond at all, he asked, "How long have you worked for Doctor Breswell?"

"We're going on three years together," Nola said cheerfully and proceeded to tidy up her desk. "I'd stay and keep y'all company but I have a dinner date. Erin could be a while so feel free to use my computer to play a game if you'd like."

Roman gave her a nod and, after she left the office, he sat in the chair at her desk. It seemed odd that she would offer him access to her computer, so his curiosity was aroused enough to check it out. He was barely surprised when he realized all her files were locked except the gaming folder. Nola was the stereotypical perfect assistant—neatly dressed in pants and blouse, well-groomed from her short brown hair to her sensible flat shoes, and efficient in her work while remaining unobtrusive. He could certainly understand Erin being happy with her assistance for three years.

And yet, that one question, about whether he was staying at Erin's house, and especially the way she tensed waiting for his answer, seemed to be out of character. He shook off his uncertainty by rationalizing that he wasn't a client or patient of Erin's and therefore Nola wasn't restricted in her conversation with him. Since he had no interest in playing a game, he moved to one of the more comfortable guest chairs and picked up a magazine.

A half hour later, Erin came out of her office carrying her case. "I just got a note from Chief. He's in his office right now if you want to go pick up your package. The bullet-rail can get us up there and back in time for dinner. Unless your method of transport would be faster?"

Roman set down the magazine and stood. "The rail will be fine."

He considered treating her to his "method of transport", but that would involve holding her against him and he wasn't sure his willpower would hold up under such a direct hit.

On their way to the station, Erin brought up the question of what they were going to tell Chief. "I really haven't come up with a reasonable explanation for why I want the thing back rather than letting him send it to ISA. Have you got any ideas?"

"No. At least not a *reasonable* one. You said he trusts you. Maybe you need to have faith in that trust." When she made no comment, he changed the subject. "The team's discussion about the dream was interesting but I'd like to hear what you saw."

For the remainder of the short trip to the station, Erin related an overview of the dream without asking for his opinion, so he didn't offer any. And when she made no attempt to converse with him during the train trip, Roman supposed she might be deep in thoughts about the afternoon's session. However, it felt like she was making a point of keeping their relationship strictly professional, as though he really was her bodyguard and she really believed what she had told the team members about his needing to remain apart. Whatever her reasoning, it played into his determination to block his attraction to her.

So why was her silence annoying him?

As it turned out, it took longer to get from Erin's office to the rail station than the trip to Ranger headquarters in Austin. When they arrived, Chief Friedrich was in his office staring into a shipping box on his desk. He quickly rose to greet them, giving Erin a peck on the forehead. "You're lookin' a bit peaked, darlin'…and Ah can't help but wonder if this here fella might be to blame." He grinned at Erin's dismayed reaction to his unusually suggestive comment then held out his hand to Roman, saying, "Mike Friedrich."

"Roman Locke," he returned, shaking the man's larger hand.

"So, Erin says you're a *trusted friend* and you'll be protectin' her and her team while they look into whatever's goin' on."

"Yes, sir. That's correct." Roman glanced at Erin, urging her to take control of the conversation.

"The psych team had an excellent first session," she told Chief. "I have high expectations for rapid progress. Did you want to see the videograph or my notes?"

"A summary of any conclusions should be good enough. Today Ah'm more interested in what made y'all decide to hire a bodyguard after refusin' my offer of a Ranger guard. Or maybe we can just jump right into the strange thing in that box and your change of mind about havin' Houston check it out." He turned back toward his desk, opened the box and stared inside. "A hell of a thing. That's for sure. Don't think Ah've ever seen anythin' quite like it. And Ah know Ah've never seen writin' like that. Kinda foreign-like. Or maybe...*alien*?"

Erin's eyes widened and Roman held his breath as he waited for her to give the man an explanation.

"Chief, I can explain...just not right now. I know it's a lot to ask but if you could trust me—"

Chief waved a hand at her. "Ah trust you, darlin', y'all know that. Ah'm just not sure Ah trust *him*." He and Roman stared at each other for several long seconds. "Ah'm gonna play a hunch here and see where it takes us. After the meetin' in the White House, President Callahan read me in on a top secret file involving a man named Romulus Locke. An' Ah'm thinkin' that's awfully close to your name, Roman. Any chance y'all know that man?"

Roman fought a grin that threatened his sincerity. "Yes, sir. That would be my father."

"Ah see. In that case, Ah'm sure y'all wouldn't mind provin' that by tellin' me the name of the woman who was with him when he...paid us a visit in...what year was that?"

The grin couldn't be held back. "Terran year 2013. And that woman's name was, *is*, Aster Mackenzie Locke, formerly of San Francisco, California. She's my mother."

"And your father's birthplace?"

"Norona. They are the current Co-Governors of Innerworld."

Chief smiled broadly and slapped Roman's shoulder. "Well, Ah'll be damned. It's a pleasure to meet you, son. Glad you're here to help out with this one. Ah assume y'all had to tell her?"

Roman's mouth turned down. "She insisted on the truth. But I don't think she believed any of it."

"Hmmm. That doesn't sound like the Doctor Breswell Ah know. Must be the way y'all told it." He handed Roman the box. "Ah gather this belongs to you?"

"That's what I've been told."

Erin cleared her throat. "I'm not sure what just happened here, but I do need to cut this short. We're due to have dinner with the team in less than an hour."

"Right. Right." Chief placed an arm over each of their shoulders. "Ah'll take you out through my private entrance. Otherwise that thing is sure to set off an alarm."

Erin felt as though her world had just tipped sideways. She barely managed to hold her questions until they were alone in her car on the way to the hotel. "What was that all about? What file was Chief talking about? How does President Callahan have a file on your father? How does Chief know to ask your mother's name or about Norona? And does this mean everything you told me really is true? That you're an alien?" A need to breathe forced her to pause.

"*Half* alien. Like I said, my mother was born and

raised in California. I'm confused. I thought you *knew* what I told you was true. Don't you have the ability to tell truth from lies?"

She looked away. "Not the way you mean it. I'm just very…observant…and a little perceptive."

"But you said your cards confirmed it. And as to the file, there was a situation with an asteroid, decades ago, before I was born. It was necessary to reveal Innerworld's existence to a handful of Terrans in order to save the planet. I didn't mention it last night because I didn't really think it was relevant. Now, if you don't mind, I'd really like to take a look at this." He opened the box and lifted out the cryptodrone.

Her gaze shot to him then back to the cars ahead of her. No matter what her perception or the cards had told her, she had still been holding out for an alternative answer, like it had all been a hoax or she was on some sort of game show. But Chief would never be part of anything like that.

There really was a being from another world sitting next to her.

And he'd be sleeping across the hall from her tonight.

He was real and at least half alien. What had he called the people of Earth? *Terrans.* She could no longer deny it. The only thing left to make it all real was to acknowledge his name. "Roman."

He responded by glancing at her curiously but quickly returned his attention to his own mystery. "I don't see any way to open this, but Gabe thought it could be programmed to my DNA." He turned the black decahedron in his hands, stroked every side, rubbed it like a magic lamp and blew on it, but nothing happened. "There's no seam anywhere, like it's been carved out of a solid piece of ore. I thought maybe there'd be raised nodes, like on my ring, but it's completely smooth on every side. Even the writing appears to be within the metal itself."

Erin realized he was talking to himself and not expecting dialogue from her. What could she say anyway? If it was a mystery to him with his advanced technology and superpowers, she certainly wasn't going to be of help. Then again, she'd never been able to resist a good puzzle. "Maybe the markings are instructions." When he didn't reply, she remained quiet until she'd parked the car at the hotel.

"We're here," she said quietly, no longer sure what tone to take with him. "I'll understand if you don't want to—"

"What? Oh, sorry. I was trying to remember some of the alphabet, but it's no use. I'll have to get help." He put the drone back in the box and tucked it behind the seat with his hat on top of it. Present again, he looked outside and nodded. "I like the building. Do you have any instructions for me?"

"Um, no, not really. I guess just continue acting like you did this afternoon or like you would as our professional security."

"Particularly the part about not fraternizing with my charges, right?"

He seemed to be teasing her, but she didn't know for sure. She had never been very good at that sort of exchange with the opposite sex. "Right."

CHAPTER 10

"It's one thing to remain aloof. It's quite another to be off on a private excursion."

Roman turned his head as Wendy sat down beside him. "I beg your pardon?"

"I don't need to be holding anything of yours to tell your mind isn't on your job...at least not the one I'm part of."

Her tone of voice and smile was completely friendly but Roman reminded himself she was the CIA's representative, possibly an agent herself. He offered a sheepish smile in return. "You're right. I received some information—totally unrelated—right before we got here, and I'm afraid it's had me distracted. Terribly unprofessional, I know."

Wendy chuckled. "It happens to the best of us. You know what I do when I'm presented with a problem I can't figure out? I have a *totally unrelated* conversation with someone who has no connection to the problem. Would you like to try?"

Before answering, Roman scanned the room. Erin was deep in her own conversation with Kanji. Hari, Vicky and Peace seemed to be bonding over their appreciation for chocolate cake and Tripper was entertaining Jamie and Ryan. Wendy could have easily joined any of their after-dinner conversations but she chose to chat with him. "Sure," he told her with another smile. "What would you like to talk about?"

She leaned toward him. "Which do you think Tripper is hoping to seduce?"

He was expecting a more personal question, or at least a topic more worthy of a spy. He certainly didn't expect gossip. Rubbing his chin and frowning, he pretended to study the threesome then murmured, "Both."

Wendy laughed loudly enough to have everyone glance toward them. "I think his original target was Erin but she sent him off with one warning shot. How long have you two been together?"

Roman angled his head. "I beg your pardon?"

Wendy laughed again. "You and Erin. How long?"

He froze his pleasant expression in place, as he said, "You're mistaken. We just met."

"Really? I apologize for the assumption. She said you were her friend and the way you were watching her—"

"I'm just a hired gun. Nothing else."

Wendy shrugged. "Too bad. I think that lady needs someone to protect her on more of a long-term basis."

Roman's smile vanished. "Why would you say that?"

She shrugged again. "I don't know. Just a feeling I got when I first met her and she shook my hand, like there's a frightened little girl inside that strong woman. I try not to touch people, but sometimes it happens when I'm not prepared. Subject change. Have you ever been around psychics before?"

He made his shoulders relax and lied as convincingly as possible. "Nope. At least I never met anyone who admitted to having any special abilities like you and the others. I think it's going to be interesting though." He made a mental note to avoid physical contact with her and to warn Erin that the CIA's rep may have downplayed her mind-reading skills.

Before Wendy could pose another question, Tripper and the twins appeared and pulled chairs up to join them. They wanted to hear some exciting bodyguard stories but when Roman declined for "reasons of confidentiality", the conversation shifted to people and places Roman had no interest in. Wendy soon excused herself to visit with the chocolate-loving females. Unfortunately, there was no polite way he could follow her.

After a half hour of feeling trapped, he stared at Erin's back and willed her to turn around and save him. Since he didn't expect that to work, he was shocked when she abruptly whirled around and noted his predicament. Within minutes, she had said good night to everyone and gently reminded them that they'd need to be alert and punctual for tomorrow's session. Shortly afterward, she'd paid the bill and they were in her car.

"That went—"

"How did you do that?" Erin demanded rather than letting him finish his sentence.

Roman shifted toward her on the seat. "Are you angry with me? I swear I tried to keep to myself all evening. They came up to me—"

"I'm not upset about that. I was actually surprised it took them that long." She took a deep breath. "You told me you had no psychic abilities—"

"I don't. I have no reason to lie about that."

"Then tell me how you whispered my name in my ear and said 'Save me', like you were standing right next to me, but you were on the other side of the room?"

"Could it have been someone else? You know they haven't all admitted to everything they can do."

She gave him a quick frown of disbelief. "It was you. I...recognized your scent...like you were...close."

He ran his fingers through his hair and shook his head. She had heard the exact thought he'd directed toward her. Almost as if they were—No. That wasn't possible. "I was...frustrated and feeling trapped and I wished you would turn around and save me. It's hardly the first time I've wished for something in my head, but believe me, it's the first time someone has heard me. So it must be *your* ability."

"And I've told you, I have no enhanced mental gifts either! Believe me, if I could choose one, being a telepath would not be it."

They were both quiet for a moment then Roman muttered, "Too bad. I'd love to know what Wendy had going on in her head tonight."

"Did she proposition you?"

"What?" Roman hadn't expected her to go there. "Why would you think *that*?"

She shrugged without looking at him. "All the women found you attractive. I just thought Jamie would be the first one to approach you."

He smothered a laugh. "Tripper kept her occupied tonight."

She gave in to a smirk. "So what happened with Wendy?"

"Did you know she can read someone's thoughts, or at least get impressions, by touching the person?"

Her expression tightened instantly. "No. All I was aware of before today was the psychometry, which involves handling an object...although...logically, a person's body could work at least as well."

"You shook hands with her."

"Hmmm, if I remember correctly, I had expected her to have a very firm grip, but it was barely a touch of fingers."

"It was long enough for her to get the feeling that you needed someone in your life to protect you."

It took her a moment to respond. "That's ridiculous. Maybe she just wanted you to feel needed. Or she may have wanted you to think she had that ability for some reason."

"Maybe. But I'm going to make sure I keep out of her reach just in case." He anticipated a retort, but when none came, he tried to get a better look at her face. The interior of her vehicle was too dimly lit for him to see her expression but he could see a subtle glow coming from her eyes. Then he saw her dab her upper lip. He touched her cheek and she swatted his hand away.

"You're getting hot again, aren't you?"

"We'll be at the house in a minute. I'll be fine. It was probably the glass of wine plus the coffee and the chocolate cake. Lots of histamines and then you frightened me…"

"I didn't mean to," Roman said softly. "How long has it been since the last flush?"

She swiped her forehead. "Um, I, uh, haven't felt this way since, um…" She exhaled heavily. "*You know*." The last two words were barely audible.

Roman wished he hadn't asked. Or that she hadn't been honest. By itself it could be meaningless. Added to her hearing the thought he'd directed at her earlier, he could not ignore it. As she pulled into her driveway, he noticed how tightly she was gripping the steering wheel. "Erin, I have a very important question to ask."

"It'll have to wait." She hurried toward the house without closing the car door behind her.

Roman was torn between giving her the privacy to deal with her discomfort and insisting she let him help her. The decision was made when he saw her fumbling with the front door lock and heard her growl in frustration. In a few strides, he caught up with her but, rather than let him have the keys, she fought to hold onto them. "*No!* This is all your fault. Just get away from me!"

As soon as he took a step back from her, she got the door unlocked, slipped inside and slammed the door in his face. He remained calm until he heard the click of the lock. That was one step too far for his patience. In an instant he made his body shift to incorporeal, passed through the closed door and shifted back. "*Erin!*" he called at her retreating form. "Stop. I might be able to help."

"I don't want your help," she shouted from the kitchen.

"You may not want it, but I'm pretty sure you need it." As he entered the kitchen, she was frantically opening cupboard doors.

"I just need some tea. What the hell did you do with my tea?"

He picked up a small glass jar filled with crushed leaves on the counter. "*This* tea?" She tried to grab the jar but he held it high above his head. "If you will just sit down, I'll make you a cup."

She let out a huff of exasperation, but she sat.

He watched her tightly cross her legs and clench and unclench her fists and recalled Wendy's advice about unrelated topics. Rather than ask Erin the big question on his mind, he opened the jar of tea and sniffed. "This is different from what I brewed last night. What is it?"

It took her a moment to reply. "It's…herbal. For menopausal symptoms…like hot flashes."

There were several retorts on the tip of his tongue but, since that would hardly distract her from the current problem, he held them all back and prepared the tea. "Aren't you curious about how I got past your locked door?"

"No." She squeezed her eyes shut and took a slow deep breath. "Yes. Wait. You told me something about that. Incorporeal was the word you used."

"Right."

"I'm sorry I tried to lock you out. It was…childish."

"Apology accepted." He sifted through the day's activities for another subject. "I found today's session very interesting. Especially about Tripper's dream. Of course, now that I know the details of it, the team's comments make a lot more sense. I don't know anything about dream interpretation, but the conclusions seemed rational." When all he got in response was a nod, he set the mug of steaming tea in front of her. "I'll leave you alone now. I assume you'd prefer me to sleep down here. I can use the couch. If you'll just tell me where I might get a sheet and pillow…"

She made a face at him. "Like you'd fit on that couch. No. You'll stay in the guest bedroom upstairs. It's all set up for you. But mine is the only bathroom upstairs, so you'll have to use the one down here…between the laundry and mud room."

"Thank you. And you can trust me not to enter your bedroom again." This time she just shrugged. "Good night then." He left the kitchen, picked up his bag from the foyer and went slowly up the stairs. With each step he felt a twinge of disappointment that she didn't stop him but he didn't blame her for being upset. The past two days had hardly been tranquil for her.

By the time he'd unpacked his few belongings and went back downstairs to use the bathroom, she had already retired to her room. He could hear the shower going and ordered himself not to think about what she was undoubtedly doing to deal with the burning. Not wanting to accidentally overhear anything private coming from her room, he took his time getting cleaned up and had a glass of sweet tea before going up to bed.

Nothing he did, however, stopped him from wondering if he had guessed correctly about what was happening to Erin. Since he wasn't experiencing any of the symptoms he'd been told to expect, he could be completely wrong about the problem. If he was correct about her having felan genes, it could have nothing to do with him at all. Her answer to one question could be all he needed to know, but since she wasn't in the mood for another conversation about aliens, he willed himself to sleep.

"Erin?"

She opened her eyes. "You promised not to come into my room."

"But I heard you call for me. I just wanted to make sure you were all right. I'll go."

"No. Please stay. I want to know what the important question was."

"It can wait."

She could feel the lust rising in her body and her mind. She knew he had what she wanted, what she desperately needed. "You said you could explain."

"That can wait too."

He stood at the foot of her bed, naked and beautiful. Available for her use. "One thing then. Just tell me one thing."

"Which thing?"

"Are you responsible for my feeling like a cat in heat?"

"Yes."

"Can you make it stop?"

"Yes."

"Then do it. Help me." She opened her legs and he crawled between, bending her knees against her shoulders to better accommodate his entry. With eyes closed, she waited expectantly for the ultimate penetration, waited on the brink of orgasm to feel him thrust into her body.

After a moment, she opened her eyes to see why she was still waiting. The look on his face suggested he was in pleasure paradise. Her gaze zipped down his body for a confirmation. Where she expected to see a sizable, erect penis, there was a hole and the heat radiating from her vagina was being vacuumed into it.

"Roman," Erin whispered. "Roman," she murmured a little louder, then poked his shoulder. "Are you really sleeping or are you pretending?"

"Huh? What?" Roman was fully alert an instant later and pushed himself into a sitting position. "Are you all right? What's the matter?"

"Have you been in my room?"

He blinked several times and his eyes adjusted to the semi-darkness. The light from her bedroom across the hall allowed him to see Erin clearly enough to know she was wearing a robe. He was not. He pulled the sheet up over his lap. "No, I promised I wouldn't. I've been asleep. For a while, I think."

"Were you dreaming about me?"

He scratched his head. "I don't think so." When she continued to stand a few feet away, with her arms stiffly crossed, he patted the bed. "Sit. Tell me what's wrong."

Instead, she strode to the door, stopped and came back to his bedside. "Swear. Swear on your mother's name that you had nothing to do with the dream I just had."

He carefully formed his answer in his mind before saying it aloud. "I swear I did not consciously manipulate your dreamtime. But unless you tell me about the dream, I can't be sure I had nothing to do with it."

She huffed, walked to the door and came right back. "I think I need your help."

Roman patted the bed again and, although she sat, it was as far from him as she could get. "Tell me the dream."

She took a deep breath and hugged the robe more snugly around her. "Could we start with something easier? You said you had an important question for me. I'd like to hear that first."

It took him a moment to recall how he was going to approach his question. "Do you remember the first time you felt your body heat rising without an obvious reason?"

She nodded. "In the Oval Office. I thought it was the room but no one else appeared to be overly warm. Then I felt…" Her gaze roamed the room and settled on a spot on the floor. "It started like a pulse…throbbing, growing more insistent…as though I was being…expertly aroused. I could barely think about what was being said. Two days later, it happened again, in the middle of an inter—Wait a second. I remember something else. Both those times I distinctly caught your scent, right before…"

"You called it intoxicating."

"Yes. But also somehow…seductive, like I wanted to rub it all over myself and roll around in it."

"Like catnip?"

Her wide-eyed gaze met his. "*Yes.* Exactly. And that's another cat reference. Oh my gawd. You said your mother is human. Is your father a cat?"

He grinned. "No. He's humanoid also. But my trainer, Falcon, is half-felan. His eyes have a golden glow and his senses are very enhanced. And he told me about a time when he felt like a cat in heat. It's possible that somewhere in your ancestry, some felan genes got mixed in."

"But then, wouldn't those qualities have been present from birth?"

"I assume so."

"But my eyes only started glowing in the dark about nine years ago."

Roman grabbed her shoulders. "Are you sure about that timing?"

"Yes. What's wrong?"

He noted the panic in her eyes and eased his grip. But now that he had touched her, he couldn't make himself let go. His hands slowly moved down her arms, found her fingers and interlocked them with his own.

He felt her go from rigid to wary to pliant.

He felt himself getting hard.

"What are you doing?" she asked with more curiosity than concern.

"Testing a theory. How do you feel? Warm?"

"A little." Her nose twitched. "I should be okay for a while."

"Because you took a cold shower, relieved the need and had some of your mother's special tea?"

She only hesitated a moment then admitted, "Yes to all of that." She sniffed the air and frowned.

He inched his body closer to hers. "Close your eyes,

Erin. Stop thinking and just breathe." He watched her inhale slowly, deeply, taking in his scent that he guessed was now boosted by his arousal.

"Catnip," she whispered then leaned forward and slowly ran her tongue up the side of his neck.

"*Erin*—" She nipped his earlobe and an intense shiver ran through his body. She freed her hands from his and ran them up his arms and over his shoulders. As she rubbed her face against his chest, the last bit of temperance left his mind. His fingers threaded into her thick hair and urged her head up to his. She took a quick breath and pressed her mouth to his with an aggression that stunned more than excited him. Her tongue pushed into his mouth, stroking, stabbing and challenging him to retaliate or submit, but she lost interest in his mouth before he could attempt to satisfy her demand.

The next instant, she tore off her robe and the annoying sheet that was keeping her from rubbing all of her skin against his. Wherever she touched, he felt a spark of heat and was soon unable to tell if he was being consumed by her fire or his own. He rolled her beneath him, wanting only to slow her frenetic movement, but her legs locked around his waist, clamping his hips to hers as she rubbed her wetness against his engorged shaft.

She cried out an instant later, making him feel oddly used and unsatisfied for the second time. Only she wasn't yet finished with him. Effortlessly, she flipped him onto his back and mounted him without preliminaries. As she wantonly rode his erection, she brought his hands to her breasts, showing him what else she needed from him.

Her demand for strength over gentility pushed him over his wall of restraint. As he squeezed her nipples, her pace picked up to a hard gallop. He could only withstand a half dozen of her clenched rises up his shaft, before his body took its release, whether she was finished with him or not. Seconds later, she went limp on top of him.

As soon as the fire burned itself out, their bodies cooled...and clarity returned.

Roman eased her to his side and covered them both with the sheet. She started to rise but he tucked her into the curve of his body. "Sh-h-h. Just go to sleep now." She didn't put up a fight, which was a relief since he had never felt so weak in his entire life.

CHAPTER 11

The light making its way through her eyelids let Erin know she had slept well past her usual wake-up time. She took a deep breath, stretching her body and thanking her guides for an exceptionally good night's rest.

Her sense of wellbeing only lasted until she opened her eyes, realized which room she was in and remembered why she was not in her own bed. She started to rise when she heard a floor board creak in the hallway, followed by the smell of coffee and warm bread...*and Roman*. It was already too late to hide or even find her robe and pretending to still be asleep would only postpone the inevitable morning-after conversation. And geez, she really needed to pee and brush her—

"Good morning," Roman said quietly as he entered and set a small tray on the nightstand. He hesitated for a second, as though he had something else to say then changed his mind and left the room.

Erin's heart gave a little flutter, reminding her to take a breath. Even though he was obviously freshly showered and the coffee and toast enticed her with their aroma, she could still detect his irresistible scent.

She lifted the edge of the sheet to her nose and inhaled. The pillow he'd slept on was next. Then she sniffed her hand. There was no escaping it. She was literally covered in *him*.

To her dismay, the smell of him triggered a memory of the feel of him on her fingertips, the taste of him in her mouth, how she'd mindlessly taken what her body demanded from his…*Damn!* Grabbing the hot coffee mug, she hurried to her bathroom before the flashbacks tempted her into a reenactment.

Although it all had a dreamlike quality to it, she knew which part had actually been a dream and which part was real. She also knew she had experienced incredibly satisfying sex, with a man, without having a care as to whether he had enjoyed it as well.

What she didn't know was how her body had completely taken over her mind. *Again.* She supposed she should be grateful that, so far at least, it had only happened with one man and in the privacy of her home.

But now that it had happened twice, would it happen again and again, perhaps on the street, with a random passerby?

The good news was, she felt cool. And, by the time she had showered, dressed for the office and headed downstairs with the tray, she had quieted her anxious thoughts.

She found Roman sitting at the kitchen table, having a bowl of cereal and squinting at the cryptodrone. Whatever had been on his mind earlier, he didn't seem to be fretting over their encounter. She did a quick internal check and was relieved to note that his proximity didn't instantly cause any unwelcome response in her body.

Taking his demeanor as her cue, she greeted him cordially. "Good morning. Thank you for the coffee.

You certainly didn't have to do that." She poured herself a refill and sat down.

He tore his gaze from his puzzle box and returned her smile. "I took a guess that you'd prefer it to tea in the morning."

She wondered if he was making a veiled reference to her *special* tea but let it go and pointed at the cryptodrone. "What are you going to do about that?"

"My sister's mate, Gabriel, is coming to pick it up. He's an expert on antiquities and he should be able to interpret the symbols. I was going to send him a video of it, but he said he needed to study it in person. I gave him these coordinates. I hope you don't mind."

"Of course not. Can he disappear as well?"

Roman shook his head. "No. I'm the only one I know who can do that. Gabe is a universal receiver. He can hear everything everyone is thinking around him. But don't worry, as long as he's wearing a gold earcuff, he can't hear what you're thinking. It's a jammer."

"I wonder if that would work on Wendy," Erin said with a smirk. "Does your sister have an ability as well?"

"Shara is telepathic and has a few other talents, like the power of suggestion. The two of you would probably get on very well. She's a distinguished genetic researcher."

A blurry image appeared in the kitchen and, a few seconds later, a beautiful man with curly blond hair stood where the blur had been. If he had wings, Erin thought, he could have passed for an angel.

"Hello," he said as he stepped toward her and held out his hand. "You must be the enigmatic Doctor Breswell. I'm Gabriel Drumayne, Professor of History and Procurer of Antiquities for Norona."

She noted the gold earcuff on his left lobe, rose and

shook his hand with a welcoming smile. "It's just Erin and I'm hardly enigmatic. Would you like some coffee or tea?"

"No, thank you. I can't stay. I've agreed to give a lecture this afternoon and I haven't gathered all the exhibits yet." He turned toward Roman and gave him a brief hug. "It's good to see you too of course. *She's lovely.*"

The last two words were whispered but Erin still heard them. So, the brother-in-law gives his manly approval and someone told him she was *enigmatic*. Roman must have mentioned her. But what could he possibly have said that would suggest she was mysterious? Since she was part of his "mission", she supposed mentioning her wasn't so odd, but the adjective didn't seem to be a professional description. And professionally speaking, what would her appearance matter?

"Would that be all right with you, Erin?" Roman asked.

She blinked. "Of course. That would be fine." She had no clue what she had agreed to, but both men grinned at her answer.

A few minutes later Gabriel and the cryptodrone were gone and, letting out a sigh of resignation, she asked, "What did I agree to?"

Roman chuckled. "Gabe asked if he and Shara could come have dinner with us one evening. They would be pleased to host us but it's against the law for me to take you there."

"Of course it is." What she didn't understand was how they had gone from being two strangers with a similar goal to being a couple having a dinner party. "Umm, Roman, I, uh, think we need to talk."

"All right. What would you like to talk about?"

His tone claimed innocent curiosity but the glint in

his eye revealed the truth. He knew exactly what they needed to discuss but he wanted her to be the one to bring it up.

"Fine. Let's start with the dream that woke me up last night. It was very, very weird and, in the light of day, I can see why it played out the way it did, especially following Tripper's dream. But in my dream I asked if you were responsible for my *cat-in-heat* dilemma and you said, yes. Then I asked if you could stop it and again you said, yes. Is that true or was it my looking to blame you?"

He chuckled. "Maybe a little of both. When Falcon told me about the one and only time he was 'in heat', the symptoms weren't triggered by a particular female. It was just a matter of his reaching reproductive maturity. Apparently, with purebred felans, their mating time is more animal instinct than passion. It urges them to take a mate, though usually only long enough to breed. If I guessed right, and you have some felan DNA—which is possible by the way—last night's...activities could be the end of it."

She felt her cheeks warm and ignored it. "I do feel much better this morning."

"Good. But there could be something else going on with you. You seemed certain that your...discomfort began only after you picked up my scent, so there's a chance that I actually triggered your time, which is closer to what happens to Noronians. We even refer to it as the mating fever."

"Okay," she said slowly, though she wasn't actually okay with anything he had said so far. "So tell me how *that* works."

Roman ate another spoonful of cereal before continuing. "Do you believe your soul has a mate?"

She was momentarily thrown by his question. "Are you talking love and romance, or Plato's philosophical explanation that each human is only half of a whole being and only by finding the other half are we complete?"

"Mostly the second but the first is definitely a big part of it for Noronians. When two soulmates meet as children, they are drawn to be together as close friends. As adults, soulmates are both stricken by the mating fever. It's how a couple can be certain they're meant to be together."

"Forever and happily ever after?" Erin said with more than a bit of sarcasm.

"Yes." He paused for a beat, as though he had something else to add to that but, again, changed his mind. "Once the mating fever starts, only two things cool it. You've experienced the one that's temporary."

She felt a flush of nervous warmth but she had to know more. "Temporary?"

He nodded. "At first, sexual relief brought on by intimate contact with the mate's body can cool the fever for days at a time."

"And then?"

"The comfortable periods grow shorter and shorter."

Erin felt her chest tighten and sat forward. "Until?"

"Until the two people are joined, which is the only permanent way to cure the fever. Under normal circumstances, the formal joining ceremony takes place shortly after the fever is apparent in both people."

"Joining? Is that like our *marriage*?" She heard the caustic edge she attached to that word and scolded herself for it.

Roman arched a brow at her but didn't make her explain. "Joining isn't a legal arrangement. It's the metaphysical bonding of two souls and two minds. Together they elevate higher than either ever could individually."

"But that shouldn't happen to me, right? I was born here on Earth, not Norona."

"So was my mother. But it turned out she had a Noronian ancestor in the far-distant past. Because of her mixed DNA however, she wasn't affected by the fever until weeks after she and my father met."

"Wait a minute. You said I might have a *felan* ancestor."

He shrugged. "It's possible you also had one from Norona. Or maybe not. Like I said, after last night you may be completely back to normal."

"And if I'm not? If I start burning up again? Then what?"

Rather than answer, he ate the last spoonful of cereal in the bowl and carried it to the sink.

"Oh," she murmured with understanding. "I'll turn into the wildcat again. And would I be correct in assuming you're the keeper of my catnip?"

He turned around but remained by the sink. "If it's the Noronian mating fever, only one person, the soulmate, can help."

She sighed and nodded her head. "Well then, nothing against you personally, but I'll be rooting for the felan heat over the Noronian fever. I'm not keen on the idea of my freedom of choice being taken away. But just in case I need a fix in the middle of the night, I suppose I should be grateful that we already decided you'd be staying here."

"I am sorry, Erin. I swear I've done nothing to cause this, at least not consciously or intentionally."

She tilted her head and frowned thoughtfully. "I believe you. And if I find it necessary to avail myself of your personal service, I hope you'll get some pleasure out of it. Speaking of which, I suppose I should have asked, did you—"

"Yes," he said, cutting her off with a grin. "I did.

Although it wasn't—Not important. I would have paid you a compliment with your coffee this morning if I'd known you were going to handle this so well."

"I can't really say how I'm handling any of it. I think it's more that I'm shocked into numbness. I reserve the right to get completely hysterical later. But there's something jangling around in my brain…" She closed her eyes, massaged her right earlobe and ordered her mind to quiet everything except what needed to be examined.

Gabriel's oddly personal comments.

Her mind flashed back to the cards she had pulled to determine if Roman was telling her the truth…the cards she had quickly scooped up before he could see them. One of them was the Ace of Cups, which she had also drawn the other night with regard to her "ghost" and had thought it meant he would be assisting her in a loving way.

But it also represented new love.

The other card was the Two of Cups, representing the ideal partnership.

But it could also be interpreted as the soulmates card.

She took a calming breath and met Roman's gaze. "If you triggered the Noronian mating fever in me and having sex with you cools it, that would seem to imply you and I are soulmates. But you said *both* people are stricken. Have you had symptoms that I haven't noticed?"

He hesitated long enough for her to glare at him. "No. Please understand, I am extremely attracted to you. But have I been burning up when I'm away from you for a few hours? Feeling like insects are tearing at my flesh? Have I succumbed to sanity-blocking sexual cravings? No, I have not."

"Insects tearing at your flesh?" She made a face and

shivered. "I haven't had that one. Anyway, maybe that's because we aren't soulmates and I'm just having a sort of mutated felan heat because...I, uh, also have some Noronian and Terran all mixed together. That makes some sense doesn't it?"

He gave it enough thought for her to believe his answer. "Yes. I think it does. So unless you feel the need to drag me back upstairs for a precautionary cooling down..."

Her mouth dropped open and she felt her face get warm again.

"Erin, I was just teasing. I can *see* when your temperature starts to rise."

"Oh. Okay. I have some difficulty recognizing when I'm being teased."

"Then I'll have to do it more often," he said with a wink.

That was exactly the opposite of what she'd hoped he would say. As to Gabriel's comments, it now seemed that she might be premature in worrying about any of it. "Okay, new topic. Did Gabriel mention how long it would take him to figure out how to open the cryptodrone?"

"He'll let me know when he's done. What's on the agenda for today?"

"The only thing scheduled is the psych team gathering at two, but I need to go in and get some work done before that."

"Anything I can help with?"

Figuring she would get more accomplished if he were busy as well, Erin assured him there was a task he could do. And by the time they reached her office, she had in fact come up with something.

Assigning him a comfortable chair next to the plant in the corner—where she was certain he'd already spent many hours—she handed him a computer. "I assume you know how to use this, or can figure it out. I've opened the file I'd like you to review. It contains all the Rangers' reports and interviews that have been deemed relevant to the people we're looking for. The investigators concluded the victims were chosen randomly. But in yesterday's session, the team felt there was a search and selection process."

"So maybe I'll pick up something they didn't," Roman finished for her.

She gave a little shrug. "You're definitely coming from a different mindset. You'll see in the Rangers' analysis that they found a few similarities or connections but nothing that painted a clear picture."

"Sounds like fun. But I need you to leave me alone. None of your chattering or ogling me from across the room."

Her eyes widened and her mouth opened to protest...and then he grinned. "Oh. You're teasing me again."

"Maybe, maybe not. I'm not going to tell you anymore. Now go to your own corner." He waved her away and gave his full attention to the monitor in his hand.

She held back her smile until she turned around and walked to her desk.

Two hours later, Nola interrupted the silence. "I'm running out to grab some lunch. Do y'all want me to bring you back something? If it's anything like yesterday, your group might show up early."

"That would be very helpful, thank you. Grilled chicken sandwich for me. Roman?"

He glanced up curiously. "Yes?"

"Nola's taking lunch orders."

"No meat. Dairy's fine." He instantly returned his attention to his task.

Nola gave Erin a look that seemed to ask how that

body could have been built on veggies. Erin shrugged and went back to her research.

What had Roman eaten for dinner last night? She hadn't noticed. *Are all his people vegetarians? Whatever will I make for dinner with Shara and Gabriel?*

Those questions sent her mind right back to the morning's lecture on the mating habits of aliens. She slammed and locked a mental door on that issue and the plethora of questions related to it. She needed all her wits and intuition for the meditation she would be guiding that afternoon.

Roman noted the arrival of each member of the group but remained in his seat by the potted plant. He was interested in observing whatever exercise Erin had planned for them today, but the files he'd been reviewing had him in full tracker mode and he was reluctant to stop. He hadn't found a specific quality that connected all the victims and yet, his instincts told him there was one. A thought popped into his mind that yesterday's session held the answer but before he could consider that, Erin locked the office door and started the session.

"As you can see," Erin began, "we're using floor cushions instead of chairs today. Hari and Vicky, please sit down on the two in the center, touching back to back. Kanji, if you'll take a spot opposite me. Everyone else, please form the rest of the circle around them, close enough to comfortably join hands."

Erin gave everyone time to get situated then continued. "The intention today is for our remote viewers to use the images we got yesterday from Tripper's dream to search for the man. We all had the sense that the woman was the more dangerous and possibly had stronger psychic abilities, so do *not* look for her. Also, be careful not to make any attempt to read his thoughts. He could possibly sense an invasion and we don't want to do anything to tip him off. Remember, our job is only to find him and turn his location over to the Rangers.

"Kanji and I will concentrate on holding a protective shield in place to block any incoming interference or other sort of negativity. The rest of you will focus only on merging your individual psychic energies and sending the combined strength to Hari and Vicky for their use. I will guide you into the meditation but then turn it over to them. Does everyone understand and accept the limitations?"

Again Erin paused until everyone voiced their agreement. "Hari, I understand you don't normally speak while viewing but we need to know if and when you have seen something of importance. Vicky is accustomed to narrating what she's viewing. I'm afraid you'll both have to make adjustments along the way."

"I've never done anything like this," Hari interjected. "But I'm willing to try."

"I think it helped that we got acquainted last night," Vicky added.

"Wonderful," Erin said, glancing around the circle. "I think we're ready to get started. Roman?"

She had given him one assignment and he had almost missed his cue. He picked up the tuning fork and redwood stick she'd given him. Erin had instructed him to strike the fork each time she paused and nodded, for a total of ten sonic vibrations.

"Please join hands and close your eyes." With each of her guiding phrases, followed by his strike, she led the team deeper and deeper into their subconscious space.

As Roman watched their faces and shoulders relaxing, he felt the temperature of the room rising. Rather than having his mind expanded, however, he just felt like taking a nap.

To remain alert without causing any distractions, he mentally reviewed the case files he'd just read. The Rangers had already evaluated all the usual commonalities such as gender, age, physical appearance, ethnicity, religion, class and careers. No one characteristic popped up more than what might be expected among any random group. He was certain the Rangers had already thought of every piece of a person's profile that could be compared with another.

The few things they'd deduced as consistent had to do with what was missing from the group. There were no very old or very young victims. No one had a criminal record. Though they varied in physical condition and levels of intelligence, no one was physically or mentally challenged or seriously ill. It really wasn't enough to draw any conclusions about the targets or profile the perpetrator, but it was enough to suggest the victims had not been selected completely at random.

As one hour stretched into two without anyone in the circle making a sound, Roman's thoughts detoured to the group in front of him and how Erin had chosen each person for what they could individually contribute to the whole. It was their different abilities rather than their similarities that were important to her.

What if the perpetrator was also selecting people based on *different* strengths or abilities? What if Hari's intuitive reaction to Tripper's dream, that the crowd of little people were "slaves", was taken literally? Historically speaking, a slave might be chosen for how he or she might best serve the master and different characteristics would be sought for different positions. There could be house slaves, field slaves, warriors, breeders...

Roman stopped looking for a definitive type of individual and looked at the victims as separate parts of a group with a common goal to serve someone or something in particular. Once he got on that path, Roman's mind raced with possible conclusions but Vicky's voice reeled him back into the present.

"I'm seeing a man...he looks like the one I saw when Tripper described his dream...Caucasian, mid-to-late-twenties, short brown hair, rounded face, full lips..." Vicky gave a shiver. "He looks...normal...harmless...but he feels...dangerous."

"Yes," Hari confirmed. "I'm sure I'm seeing the same man. He's radiating darkness, suppressing tremendous anger. He's behind a large desk...very fancy office..."

"I don't see any name plate...but there are photographs on the walls...different kinds of buildings and houses...a few have plaques beneath them, like awards..."

"One wall...it's all glass...there's a large city outside..."

"He's a few stories up...from his chair...he can see a park. I know that park," Vicky said in a more normal tone of voice. "It's near The Alamo. He's in downtown San Antonio."

"It's gone," Hari said flatly.

"Like the video went black the instant I recognized the city," Vicky added.

"Okay everyone. Slowly now," Erin said. "Take a deep breath and consciously separate your minds. Pull back all that is yours and release anything that is not. Then release hands and open eyes. Take your time getting up. We were out-of-body for quite a while."

Roman saw a pained expression pass over Peace's face and was on his feet in a heartbeat. He helped her rise and poured her a glass of water, then made sure everyone else was up and moving before pouring a glass for himself.

Within seconds everyone agreed that they had sensed a distinct interruption in their concentration the instant Vicky had said *San Antonio.*

"The man could have sensed he was being watched and threw up a wall," Kanji offered.

"I don't think so," Hari said quietly. "He seemed to be completely unaware."

Tripper looked worried. "Maybe the wicked snake woman was somehow tuned in on our session and put a stop to it."

Roman thought Hari had something else to add but she kept it to herself. He felt the mood in the room shift to wariness. Erin's next words confirmed it.

"Let's not ruin a great day's work with negative conjectures. We have enough to give the Rangers a refined location. And even though we didn't get a name, we have a general physical description and an indication of the kind of business he's in. Hari and Vicky, if you could both come in tomorrow morning at nine, I'll have a sketch artist here for you to give your descriptions to. Everyone else, you have a free day. After I speak with Chief Friedrich, I'll let you all know if the group needs to meet again or if we're finished helping with this case."

Jamie and Ryan looked the most disappointed. "But we didn't get to do anything special," Jamie said.

"That's not true," Erin countered. "I think we, as a group, achieved something remarkable in a very short time. And, even if we're done with this one, I have faith that we'll be called upon again." That assurance brought the smiles back.

Another half hour passed before everyone, including Nola, had left the office.

"You're worried one of them did it," Roman said as soon as they were alone.

She didn't deny it. "Why do you say that?"

"I've watched you work. The way you ended the session was too abrupt. You usually encourage discussion and I'm sure you planned to have another session tomorrow. What changed?"

Before answering, she sat in her desk chair, so he took the sofa. "Extended meditations tend to disintegrate slowly. In a group session, some people will naturally tire and fade out before others. All nine of us had our concentration disrupted at the same moment, like a lightning bolt of negative energy. Hari confided that it seemed to her like the source of negativity was *very* nearby, probably within the protective shield Kanji and I established. If so, that means we've been compromised. But I believe, and *feel,* with absolute certainty, that no one on the team would work against us, at least not consciously. For all I know, Tripper could have been onto something. The woman might not have been able to cause a disruption from outside the shield, but what if she was controlling the mind of someone on the team?"

Roman frowned. "That doesn't make sense. Every person recognized the disruption and negative energy. Surely they would notice someone manipulating their mind."

"I would think so. But we don't actually know the extent of that woman's abilities. At any rate, I felt it was necessary to disburse the group for everyone's safety. At least Chief might be able to deduce the man's identity with what we've come up with. Speaking of whom, I'm sure he's waiting impatiently for my update and I need to arrange for a sketch artist, and..."

"Take your time," Roman said getting to his feet. "I was coming to some conclusions of my own before the session started. I'd like to spend a little more time on those files."

As he grabbed the computer and went out to the reception area to work, her determined expression let him know she wasn't even close to ready to walk away from this case.

CHAPTER 12

"They found you. I stopped them before they got your name and exact address, but they got enough."

Adam felt the fury rise in his throat. "*You intervened? I specifically instructed you—*"

"To be your spy. But I also agreed to be your Eve, which made me your partner. If you get caught, we both lose. By this time tomorrow, the Rangers could have you locked up and I'd have to go back to telling fortunes in Cassadaga. The good news is, Breswell cancelled tomorrow's group session, so if you leave immediately, you should be able to get to Eden without anyone picking up on your departure."

"I'll call you when I'm settled," he told her in a more agreeable tone.

"Don't bother," she replied. "I know how to find you."

That statement was clearly meant to make him believe she had possession of something of his. Though he hadn't seen her take anything, it's what he would have done had their positions been reversed. Once again, rather than be annoyed at her refusal to acknowledge him as her superior, her dictatorial attitude left him strangely exhilarated. Repeatedly over the past months she had enticed him with hints of how she would soon be his Eve in the biblical sense, that their relationship would become physical once The Eden Experiment was up and running. Although he was fairly sure she could not read his specific thoughts, she seemed to know that his sexual needs were not...*ordinary*.

For a simple release of energy, he had his choice of willing women. His success and wealth ensured that. But Eve promised to satisfy his secret desires, to introduce him to a level of pleasure he'd only fantasized about. As anxious as he was to discover whether her titillating promises were worth the wait, he had no intention of altering his master plan for a prurient need.

That plan called for more organizational time, and he would have had it, if it wasn't for Breswell's team of psychic vigilantes. They were the serpents in his garden. And soon, he would make them pay for causing him this inconvenience. It was insulting enough that several of them had rejected his recruitment efforts but to have them use their gifts to oppose him was unforgiveable.

The one who'd been the greatest disappointment was Dr. Kanji Cho. He'd read the man's books and traveled the world to attend his seminars. He had been certain the esteemed parapsychologist would understand the value of his experiment. However, not only had Cho neglected to respond to his letters, Adam had been swiftly dismissed as a candidate for Cho's clinical experiments. After only three standardized tests given by a bored technician, Adam was bluntly informed that he had no extrasensory perception. That his visions were simply caused by years of powerful medications. And that those medications were solely responsible for the recovery he called a miracle.

He knew with absolute conviction that was not the case.

From birth, an incurable strain of osteogenesis had rendered him severely physically handicapped. Under his mother's justifiably constant observation, he'd never had the chance to experience being a boy. Her wealth afforded him the best care and protection available and thus, he was kept alive far beyond the initial prognosis. But with bones that broke with the merest hug and lungs that could not function without mechanical assistance, he was unable to have anything close to a normal life. His mental capacity, however, almost made up for his physical inadequacy and with the knowledge of the ages at his fingertips, he found ways to have a semblance of life inside his imagination.

Then, nine years ago, his imaginary world of normalcy became reality. The transformation began with an amazing physical recovery as his body corrected itself to a state of perfect health in a matter of weeks.

The doctors and pharmaceutical companies took full credit for his miraculous healing, but they were wrong. He had read and wholeheartedly accepted Dr. Cho's prediction about an upcoming evolutionary human development that would involve mental expansion. Unlike *normal* humans, he had spent two decades exercising his brain. Believing the day would come when his mind would be capable of wondrous things, he had constantly imagined himself with a strong, healthy body. When the change finally occurred, he was the only one not shocked.

He was somewhat surprised though when, months later, he accidentally cut his finger and watched his skin repair itself within minutes. Having had his fill of being examined by doctors and imprisoned in hospitals, he kept his recuperative ability a secret from everyone.

Somehow, he had mutated from an ineffectual invalid to an immortal. *A god among men.* But he had no clue how he was meant to use such an incredible gift.

The answer started to formulate when the self-healing was followed by visual and audio flashes—small, insignificant previews of something that was about to occur, like *hearing* a particular song that would come on his music channel seconds later or *seeing* which outfit his mother was wearing moments before she'd entered his room. That trait was interesting but had yet to be of any practical use.

His final surprise came with the third development—the clear visions of his future. Because of the accuracy of his little flashes, he had no doubt the long-term visions were equally valid. He just couldn't prove that to anyone else. No matter how hard he tried, he had no control over the content of what he foresaw or when the visions occurred. Also, because the brief flashes only happened seconds in advance and the longer visions always involved his own future—something that was arguably within his control—no one on Dr. Cho's staff believed he had acquired a special gift.

The money and time he'd spent attempting to gain Dr. Cho's attention had not been a total waste however. The seminars put him in contact with other people who had suddenly acquired new mental skills, some of whom were intrigued by The Eden Experiment. More importantly, a few of those were willing to sell their talent to him without ethics entering the bargain. In the case of Cain, his parents were in dire financial straits and happily believed that

The Eden Institute—something he had seen himself establishing in one of his visions—would give their son a better future than they ever could.

Adam had hoped to recruit a few more shepherds before launching his project but, after Eve's warning, he knew he would have to manage with just the seven he'd already enlisted. Considering what each was capable of, he wasn't the least bit worried about them being outnumbered by his flock. And once news of his successful experiment leaked out, other enhanced humans would be begging to be let into Eden.

CHAPTER 13

Erin's nose told her Roman was there, in the reception area, but she couldn't see him. "Roman?"

"Hmmm? What? Sorry, I guess I dozed off. Are you ready to go?"

She stared at the spot on the sofa where his voice seemed to come from and slowly he became translucent. "Why are you doing that?" She watched him hold up his hands, wiggle his fingers and feel his chest and face. A moment later he was fully visible to her.

"That's new," Roman said, studying his hands again.

"You mean you didn't purposefully disappear?"

"No. At least I don't think so. I suppose I could have dreamed it, but I—" He glanced at her face and looked away.

"What?"

He shook his head and shrugged. "It's gone."

She sat in a chair opposite him, crossed her legs and folded her hands on her lap.

He arched a brow. "That's your waiting-for-the-patient-to-speak pose. But I really don't have a better explanation. As far as I know, except for when it first manifested, I've always controlled the on and off switch."

"Are you hungry?" she asked casually without moving.

The corner of his mouth lifted. "Absolutely. I have a payment card we can use to go to a restaurant." He started to rise then stopped when she didn't move. "We'll get there faster if you just tell me what you're waiting for me to say."

"You were about to say something and you lied about it slipping away. Under the circumstances, I think we need to be completely honest with each other. I'd like to hear what you were about to say. In other words, you satisfy my curiosity and *then* we can satisfy your hunger."

He exhaled heavily, stood up and walked toward her. "I dozed off and I was having a dream. But it wasn't about making myself invisible." He held out his hand and when she accepted it, he drew her to her feet in front of him.

She tilted her head back to meet his gaze. The intensity in his dark eyes stole her next breath away. Only their hands were touching but she felt him in every cell of her body. When he didn't move or speak, she made herself ask, "What were you dreaming about?"

He took a step closer. "Are you sure you want to know?"

His voice was low, his words suggestive and warning. She felt her heart beat a little faster and whispered, "Yes."

"I was dreaming about this." He released her hand, removed the clip holding her hair in place at the back of her neck then ran his fingers through her hair.

The sound she made was something between a sigh and a whimper.

"And this," he murmured, running his hands down her back and up her arms.

Her skin tingled wherever he touched. She felt dizzy and warm and...*desired*.

"And this."

As he lowered his head, she closed her eyes and parted her lips in invitation. She felt a feathery-light touch on the tip of her nose, a peck on her forehead and ticklish brushes against her eyelashes. She smiled and he placed tiny kisses on the corners of her mouth.

His mouth grazed her cheek on its way to her ear. "I was dreaming of showing you how I could be tender and soft and how nice it could be to go slowly. I was dreaming of feeling your pulse...here." His lips pressed a spot below her ear. "Feeling your heartbeat...here." His hand eased down between her breasts and nestled there.

She inhaled slowly and drifted into the intoxication that accompanied his enticing scent. A whisper was all she could manage. "And then?"

He eased back and withdrew his hands. "And then you woke me."

For a moment she felt as though she had just stepped off a crazy whirling ride. Though her mental clarity returned with her equilibrium, she had to blink at him several times before he came into focus. "I know. I insisted." She took a deep breath. "Did I respond like that because I'm in heat or because I have the fever for you?"

"Do you feel the need to analyze everything or is it just your way of keeping everyone at a distance?" He touched her cheek with the back of his hand. "You're warm but not burning up."

"So, basically, you're just that good at seduction?" She watched him struggle not to grin but his answer was tactful with a sprinkle of flattery.

"A good seduction is never one-sided, Erin. Watching you melt was very...seductive to me as well. You're welcome to examine my body if you need proof."

She started to smirk then gave into a chuckle instead. "Thank you, but I'll take your word for it."

Eve watched Erin and her so-called bodyguard leave the office. She congratulated herself on getting her marionette to install a hidden camera into the reception area so she could continue to monitor the goings-on even when the dummy was absent.

Dear Nola—so efficient, so trusted...so *normal*. She was the perfect instrument for Eve's use. Nola had no idea that a few of her hairs had been salvaged from her desk chair months ago. Neither did she retain any memory of depositing a copy of the videographs of every interview and session into a cyberspace lockbox for Eve to download. Nor was she aware that, at Eve's mental command, she had turned on the intercom into Breswell's office during the remote viewing session, so that even with a psychic shield in place, Eve had heard everything said aloud.

Eve fingered the three little black velvet pouches, representing Nola, Vicky Trumble and Adam Sirilovich. She had hoped to have a memento from each member of the task force, but everything progressed too swiftly and she'd only had the opportunity to get a strand of hair from Vicky. Not that she had intended to try anything while it might risk exposure. But afterward...it might have been interesting to test their abilities against her own.

As it turned out, she had only needed the one team member connection to disrupt their viewing session before they got Adam's name.

She glanced back at the monitor and the empty

reception area. She had never expected the backup camera to win her a jackpot.

She wasn't surprised that the doc was having a fling with such a gorgeous hunk of man. Hell, she got wet just watching his little tease. But discovering that he was more than security, that he was one of the elevated, filled her with a different kind of excitement. Why would they keep something as unusual as invisibility a secret? Why the masquerade, even from Breswell's handpicked team?

She had no doubt Adam would be thrilled to hear what she had discovered. However, if he wasn't already on his way to Eden, this could tempt him to stay and try to recruit the bodyguard, and that could be detrimental to them both. It was imperative that he be securely protected under Eden's dome when the Rangers go looking for him, which they undoubtedly would. It was only a matter of how many hours it would take for them to figure out who he was.

There was no reason for her to stay any longer. The assignment Adam had given her was finished. And yet she wasn't quite ready to join him in his Garden, where there were others with her abilities. The best she could hope for under the present circumstances was some extra privileges earned by being the leader's bedmate.

Her intuition insisted Roman's secret was more than the ability to disappear. Adam didn't want her acting alone, but if she used her gift to uncover something helpful to his precious experiment, she'd not only be forgiven, she might raise herself to the superior position she was aiming for.

She watched the scene again, hoping to see or hear some clue she'd missed the first time. There was no additional hint to the invisible man's identity but there was something much, much better. Distracted by his own seduction, he had left his hat behind. Eve hadn't intended to risk using Nola's help again, but if even one of the man's hairs was in his hat, he would soon be hers, to use however she wished. And *that* would definitely be worth the risk.

"I'm sorry you didn't like your dinner," Erin said as they walked to her car. "There is a vegetarian restaurant in downtown Austin we could try next time. Unfortunately, most Texans are confirmed carnivores."

"It was fine," Roman insisted. "If I need to be out here much longer, I can always order some meals from home."

Erin chuckled. "That certainly puts a new spin on home delivery." Her smile faded as the first part of his sentence replayed in her head. "You never really said how long you'll be staying."

"It depends on the assignment."

She stopped before getting into the car. "You already got the cryptodrone. And the Rangers will probably have the perp in custody tomorrow. So, your assignment will be over, right?"

"Erin, don't—"

"No, no. It's okay. I completely understand. It's not like there's anything going on between us." She quickly got behind the wheel and turned on the car.

He slipped into the passenger seat a second later. "I'm not going anywhere until we are *both* certain you're back to normal. I would never abandon you while you still need me."

Erin's fingers clenched around the steering wheel. "Look, I haven't needed anyone in my life for a long time. And I'm certainly not going to allow a few hot flashes to turn me into a simpering female who can't survive without a man to lean on. I saw too many female patients make personal concessions for the sake of a husband." She hadn't meant to say any of that out loud and now Roman was looking at her like she had sprouted a second head. "Sorry. Sometimes all the psychoanalysis in the world goes out the window when a certain button is pressed."

"Psychoanalysis? You mean your studies?"

"I mean, I spent as much time with head doctors as I did studying the human mind."

"Why? When? I'm not just being intrusive. I have a reason for asking."

She sighed and made herself give him the short version. "I was extremely hyperactive as a child, couldn't sit still or focus on anything. Then when other girls were getting their period, I started having confusing dreams in which I was different people in different times and places, as though they were past-life memories. And, you may as well know, in some of those dreams I, uh..." She exhaled heavily. "I was sort of...*a cat*."

Roman refrained from vocally congratulating himself on his guess about her felan heritage. Instead, he asked, "And when you were awake?"

Erin's expression contorted with the memory. "I heard voices no one else did. I was diagnosed as schizophrenic with a side of multiple personality disorder, and was heavily medicated through most of my teens. I never went out on dates like the other girls. No boy wants a nut-case for a girlfriend, no matter how pretty she is. The strange thing was, their disinterest never really bothered me. Somehow I knew I would be better off alone, looking out for myself."

Roman felt a tightening in his chest and recalled Wendy's impression that there was a frightened child beneath Erin's strong exterior. "I can't imagine how awful that must have been for you. How did you finally manage to control it?"

She shrugged. "Something changed. I just woke up one morning and knew how to shut out what I didn't want to hear or see. That was when my eyes started glowing in the dark and all my senses got an upgrade."

"Nine years ago?"

"Yes."

"That was when I could suddenly go invisible. And I know several of your psych team's mental enhancements occurred around the same time."

She nodded. "I know. I think I've been afraid to give that too much thought. I put it on a shelf to analyze when I have more time...or less stress, but that never seems to happen. So tell me, what happened nine years ago that caused the upgrades?"

"I wish I could tell you, but I don't know. And neither does anyone I've talked to, although Kanji is of the opinion that all of humanity was due for an evolutionary bump." He smiled at her look of curiosity. "I skimmed one of his books."

"But you don't think that's the answer."

"No, but I haven't come up with anything better."

"Thank you."

"For what?"

"Instead of getting annoyed over my little rant, you distracted me."

The grin and wink he gave her made her want to pull the car off the road and thank him in a more physical way. The veered conversation also distracted her from thoughts of his leaving. If he really would be gone in a day or two, it might have been very nice to experience the *going slowly* he had teased her with in the office.

But as soon as they were back at her house, they bid each other good night and headed to their separate bathrooms. Erin waited until she heard the downstairs shower turn off before stepping into her own. By the time she was combing through her wet tangles, she'd convinced herself that she would be much better off *not* knowing what it would be like to have Roman make slow love to her. Having him leave after that could be much, much worse.

It had been a very long, eventful day and, in spite of the multitude of thoughts buzzing around her brain, she felt herself starting to drift off seconds after her head settled on the pillow. But she wasn't to be so lucky.

She was getting warmer.

A subtle pulsing in her core let her know what was coming. She pressed a fist against her sex and tried to smother a frustrated moan by turning her face into the pillow.

She heard a knock on her door and ignored it.

He knocked again. "Erin? You couldn't be asleep already. I think we need to finish the discussion about my being here for you. I want to make sure you're not upset."

Erin sat up and tried to speak normally. "I'm not upset. I'm just tired. Please go to bed. We can talk in the morning."

Abruptly, the door swung open and, as Roman strode to the side of her bed, she buried her face in the pillow again.

"Look at me," he ordered.

She shook her head, no.

He moved her hair and placed his hand on the back of her neck. "You're hot. And you know I can help. There's no reason to wait until your mind goes dark with need. But if you really want me to leave you to deal with it alone, I will. However, I may lock my door to protect myself from another assault."

She groaned in protest but sat up and looked at him. He was the most beautifully formed man she'd ever seen, dressed or nude...as he was now. The sight of his shaft thickening and rising on her behalf instantly turned her heat up a notch. Unable to admit she needed him, she simply said, "I'm a mess."

He grinned down at her. "You're exquisite."

As he continued to stand next to the bed, ready to serve but only by invitation, she decided giving in now rather than blindly attacking him later was the more logical option.

She removed her nightshirt and tossed it aside. "I would have liked to have you show me the slow way, but..." She leaned forward, took the length of him into her mouth and grazed his rigid flesh with her teeth as she eased away again. "I think it's already too late."

"Next time," he murmured and swiftly repositioned her on her knees facing away from him.

There was no seduction, no foreplay, just one deep, hard thrust into her slick channel and she cried out in relief. His fingers massaged her sex as he pulled back and thrust forward again and again, keeping her on an orgasmic plateau until he enjoyed his own completion.

Just as he began to relax inside her, she felt an electrical sensation zip through her body. Turning her head back to him, she received another sort of shock. He had gone invisible. And so had she!

She jerked away from him and instantly became visible again, but it took him several seconds to become translucent and another second to be back to normal.

"I...need to..." Without finishing his sentence, Roman collapsed on her bed.

Erin's concern for him erased her questions. She

gave his shoulder a firm shake. "*Roman!* Talk to me. Should I do something? Call someone?"

"No. I'll be fine," he mumbled. "Just need to rest a minute."

It took some effort to get his legs up on the bed and make sure he looked comfortable. She would have covered him with a sheet but she couldn't help but notice how very warm his skin felt. *Almost like he had a low-grade fever.*

Which was rather ironic since she was now as cool as she could be.

CHAPTER 14

"This is Shepherd Leader."

"Come in Shepherd Leader. What's your ETA?"

"I'm about five minutes out. You can open the Garden Gate anytime now."

"Roger that."

"Have the shepherds been notified of my arrival?"

"Yes, sir. They'll be waiting to greet you in the Planning Room. Except for Eve of course."

"Right. She's still needed elsewhere. Over and out." Adam switched off the helicopter's intracom with the touch of a button. Learning to fly the baby bird was one of the first things he did when his body healed. Fulfilling his greater dream took much longer and a sizable chunk of his inheritance.

He chose West Texas for his Eden Experiment primarily because it was so easy to buy up miles of land without anyone caring, particularly after the realignment. It only mattered that his payment was liquid. He let it be known that he had plans to build a totally self-sufficient, prototype town in the harsh environment. His reputation as a daring and successful architect, as well as the holder of patents for dozens of engineering advancements, made the explanation believable. Where others had tried and failed, the brilliant Adam Sirilovich just might succeed.

Besides, it was a version of the truth. For several years, Eden served as a testing site for Adam's inventions. Only when he was certain the Garden and its intended inhabitants could be continuously maintained and supported without the need for any external interaction did he move on to the real experiment.

Adam's mother had believed The Bible contained all the answers one needed to get to heaven, and life on Earth was merely the series of challenges and hardships one had to endure along the way. Her disabled son was never a burden. Rather, he was a test to her faith. Because she believed so deeply, Adam wanted to accept her truths as his own. But no matter how many times he read her holy book, he always had questions. Some of those were answered as his mind developed, others became irrelevant as he expanded his knowledge through scholarly readings.

One conclusion that came out of all his reading was that God's cruelest act was in granting free will to all mankind then sitting back and watching the debacle play out. For Adam, it raised the question of how humanity might have developed if free will was only granted to a superior few, who would be given the task of keeping the rest of the population on positive and productive paths until they experienced their own elevations. He likened it to a shepherd tending his flock and the flock, in turn, providing the shepherd with sustenance. However, until he experienced his personal miracle and learned that others had been simultaneously elevated, it hadn't occurred to him that he could get the answer to that question through an experiment.

Six months ago, the foundation for the town of Eden was finally ready and, with Eve on board, he began selecting the men and women who would become his flock. Although, out of necessity, he selected a few professionals in medical and technological careers, most were only moderately educated, simple folk. There were artisans, tradesmen, mechanics, farmers, and others who would normally be found in a mid-western town in the early-twentieth century. None were married or had children, but were of an age to form family units. All had answered the ads he'd placed, signed confidentiality agreements and willingly relocated to Eden.

And then, through the talents of Eve, Seth and Sarah, their free will and behavior was subtly managed by the power of suggestion. His two telepaths, Cain and Rebekah, were charged with monitoring the wholesomeness of everyone's thoughts.

Abel's talents had been tested and proven, but to date, the only one Adam had taken advantage of was his exceptional ability to observe and later recall minute details. However, that alone was sufficient to justify Adam's naming him Second Leader, which basically meant Abel was Adam's eyes and ears when he was absent from Eden.

The only shepherd, besides himself, whose skill was not used to control the test subjects, was Noah. He was the sole person Adam had encountered with such a high-level of innate and learned technological ability that he seemed to be part computer himself.

The residents of Eden were spared an awareness of the horrors of war or the stress of poverty. They had no reason to lock their doors or fear their neighbors because any hint of sinful activity was countered by altering the sinner's thoughts. If that didn't work, he or she was cast out of the Garden with a substituted memory. Their daily news was created and distributed within the domed town and all of it was oriented toward positive attitudes and serving the communal good…which was generally whatever the shepherds needed to make their lives comfortable.

In the past three months, the population of Eden had grown from a few dozen to nearly five hundred, due in great part to the spreading discontentment over how the world had changed following the China Compromise. In Eden, they were all well cared for, sublimely happy…and completely controlled.

As Adam approached Eden, the grid for the electromagnetic dome covering the entire project showed up on his monitor and he noted that the Garden Gate had already been opened. Normally, anyone flying over the property would only see the holographic image he wanted them to see—an uninteresting panorama of unimproved, nearly uninhabitable mountains and plains.

And soon, another of his inventions might be tested. The dome's construction was meant to be impregnable. However, even if it failed and the Texas Rangers figured out where he was and how to break through the dome, they would never get past his gifted shepherds…at least not with their minds intact.

CHAPTER 15

Erin woke up alone.

She knew that for a fact because she had passed her hand over every inch of the king-size bed to make sure Roman wasn't there in his invisible mode. A search of her house confirmed he wasn't there in any mode. Before she had a chance to worry or wonder, she found a scribbled note under her coffee mug.

Good morning. I hope you slept well. Sorry about last night and leaving so early this morning. Got a message from Gabe saying he has news, so I figured I'd pay him a visit and check in with Medical while I'm there. Maybe they can tell what's going on with me. Also figured you could manage your morning appointments without my oversight, though I did send a message to Chief to send over a watchdog or two.

See you tonight. I'll bring dinner.

Oh, one last thing—I recall promising you something about "next time" and I want to assure you that I always keep my promises…

Erin brought the piece of paper to her nose. His

scent was faint but recognizable. At least he had taken a moment to leave a note.

With a promise.

Did his mentioning "next time" mean he knew she would need him again? Or was he just being a horny man? And if she did need him again, did that mean she was in the throes of the Noronian mating fever after all? He certainly had the ability to cool her down, but he'd said it affected both people.

With a loud, frustrated moan, she banished all the questions to a far corner of her mind and poured her coffee. She had more urgent matters to deal with this morning and she actually glad Roman would be absent for a while.

An hour later, she entered her office and was pleased to see Hari, Vicky and the sketch artist already working together.

"No shadow today?" Nola asked.

"He had a personal matter to attend to," Erin ad-libbed. "Chief Friedrich has already assigned several Rangers to keep an eye on all of us…just in case."

"But he'll be back, right? I mean, the Rangers are good but you hired *him* to protect you and the team, right?"

Erin smiled despite the little pang of jealousy her assistant's words caused. "He'll be back if he's needed. We'll know soon enough."

Did Nola have a personal interest in Roman? Had he found her attractive?

She ordered herself to grow up and get to work.

"Good morning, everyone," she said brightly as she sat behind her desk. "Making progress?"

"Just finished," the artist said, handing his sketchpad to Vicky. "Is that him?"

"Absolutely," Vicky said and passed the pad to Hari.

"Let's conference in Chief Friedrich," Erin said, quickly making the call. "They may already have a lead—"

"I've seen this man," Hari said in her soft voice. "I couldn't tell from our remote viewing but I'm certain. It's been awhile. Maybe a year or more. I've often assisted at Kanji's seminars and this man attended enough of them to be called a regular." She closed her eyes and rubbed her temples. "He was more than a follower. In fact, I remember the security guards had put him on the fanatic watch list. It turned out he was a successful businessman and very wealthy, so he was never banned, but he just stopped showing up. I might remember the name if I saw it on the list."

As Hari used Erin's computer to contact someone for a copy of the watch list, Erin reached the Chief. His hologram joined them at almost the same time as Hari received the list.

"Adam Sirilovich!" she announced. "That's his name."

"Adam?" repeated Vicky. "As in Adam and Eve, maybe? Tripper's dream is turning out to be more lucid than he thought."

"Yep," Chief chimed in. "That name's on our list too. Based on the details y'all came up with yesterday, we pulled our own list of architects, realtors, contractors and designers who have offices around The Alamo. Send me that sketch and Ah'll have a couple Rangers go pick him up for questioning. Do Ah recall that y'all had someone on the team with a knack for readin' minds or encouragin' a suspect to tell the truth?"

Erin chuckled. "You recall correctly, and the twins were quite disappointed when they thought their talent wasn't required. I'll let them know to stand by."

"And Ah'll give y'all a call the minute we have this

guy in custody."

Two hours passed before Chief Friedrich called back and, by then, the others had left.

"It's not good," he told Erin. "His assistant was packing up her desk when our team got there. She'd been told he had an emergency out of the country and would be away for several months. The Rangers believed she was legitimately shocked and upset to be let go so suddenly. They went by his condo also. Nothing unusual there. No sign that anyone had packed in a hurry, or packed at all for that matter. But the concierge said he caught a cab to the airport around eight last night. A team is following up on that lead, but we'll run surveillance on both buildings as well."

"It sounds like someone alerted him," ventured Erin.

"Agreed."

"Add that to how yesterday's session was disrupted and I'm afraid the *someone* is part of my team."

"Well, that would be one possibility. But they were all thoroughly vetted. Your office might be bugged or your video feed hacked. Ah'll send a tech over to run some scans."

"Thanks," she said, but she had little hope of them finding anything. Her intuition told her that, either consciously or through mental manipulation, the spy was one of her team members.

Roman took his time walking from Medical to the Advanced Learning Academy where he was to meet Gabriel. He needed time to process what he'd just been told.

Unintentionally fading to invisibility, then having to put effort into returning, was abnormal for him. Passing out after a sexual release was a sign that something was very wrong. He recalled how weak he'd felt after his orgasm the night before, even though he'd barely participated in the build-up. It was more than enough to convince him to get an immediate checkup.

Leaving Erin a note rather than waiting for her to awaken was a little cowardly but he couldn't explain something to her that he didn't understand himself. After what he had just been told, he was even less inclined to talk to her about it.

The one thing he was clinging to was the word "possibly". The doctor had used it no less than a dozen times during the exam and consultation.

His cellular walls showed signs of weakening. It was *possibly* just a nasty virus he'd picked up in Outerworld. For that possibility, he'd been given a precautionary antiviral injection.

But it could *possibly* be as serious as the beginning of another stage of his personal mutation, one that could leave him permanently invisible, or worse, incorporeal—alive but without a physical body.

Adding to that, his hormone levels were dangerously elevated, which could be related to the cell damage, but *possibly* the spike was due to the onset of the Noronian mating fever. This prognosis seemed to be supported by Erin's condition beginning when she first picked up his scent, though his instincts still suggested her felan ancestry was to blame. The fact that none of the regular symptoms had manifested in Roman could *possibly* be due to his not being pure Noronian.

Or *possibly*, everything was due to the mutation in his DNA that allowed him to go invisible and incorporeal. Since there were no previous such cases to refer to, the doctor couldn't make an educated guess one way or another.

There was no question as to whether he was

attracted to Erin, only to what extent. He'd always been told that when his mate appeared, he would know…instinctively. But his instincts, as finely tuned as they were, could be clouded by whatever was happening to him. So, his *not* instantly knowing she was the one destined to be his mate wasn't a clear indicator. On the other hand, he didn't feel as though he might die if he never saw her again. At the moment, all he knew for sure was that he wanted to spend more time with her and have a sexual encounter that lasted more than sixty seconds.

The doctor had instructed him to make notes of anything he considered unusual and report back to Medical for a follow-up exam in a week.

As he neared the enormous crystal prism structure that housed the Academy, Roman consciously switched his thoughts to the more grounded mystery in his life. Whatever secret message was inside the cryptodrone, he counted on it taking his mind off his personal dilemma.

"Patience, brother," Gabe told Roman. "This next one could do it." From the symbols in the surface, Gabriel had figured out that opening the drone required specific placements of all ten of Roman's fingers. Which fingertips had to be pressed onto which of the ten segments turned out to be a game of chance. For over an hour, they'd been sitting side by side on a sofa in Gabe's office. Roman had been turning the drone as Gabe instructed, while Gabe had been noting which combinations did *not* open the drone.

Although the correct combination wasn't "the next one", it was the one three tries later. A barely audible click had them both holding their breath. A *whoosh* followed as a seam appeared around the entire drone between Roman's right and left hands.

"Easy now," Gabe said in a hushed voice. "Without moving your fingertips, gently twist the two halves in opposite directions."

Roman did exactly as directed, the two halves came apart and a thick wad of folded papers fell onto his lap. "I'll be drekked," he said, handing Gabe the drone halves so he could focus on what had been hidden inside. "I was half expecting there to be another puzzle box inside."

"*Hmmph.* I was just hoping it wasn't empty. Well? Is there a message? Is it really addressed to you? Can you read it?"

Roman smirked and tossed Gabe's words back at him. "Patience, brother." He unfolded the sheets of paper—there were four—and spread them out on the table in front of them. Other than a waxy coating, they appeared to be blank. "Great," Roman said sarcastically.

"Wait a second. Another DNA confirmation may be needed." He went over to his desk, rooted through a drawer and came back holding a needle. "Hold out your hand."

Roman frowned but allowed Gabe to prick his index finger.

"Now, squeeze out a drop of blood onto each corner of each page."

Seconds later, hand-printed words were revealed on every sheet.

"Everything about this is antiquated," Gabe said. "But it's dated two hundred eighty-nine years in the future. My interpretation was accurate though. It's definitely addressed to you."

Roman held up one sheet to have light show through it. "The paper bears the official seal of the Ruling Tribunal of Norona. Why would it be sent to me instead of my parents?"

Gabriel shrugged. "Only one way to find out."

Both men leaned forward as Roman read aloud...

To Roman Locke, son of Innerworld Co-Governors Romulus Locke and Aster Mackenzie Locke:

I am Catastrophic Science Director Cattar, of Norona, and your immediate assistance is required to save the people of Terra.

I have no doubt you are wondering why such a dire message was addressed to you personally. Essentially, I had a previous encounter with your family and know that loyalty to the Terrans runs deep within you all, as does the courage to push established restrictions when there is no other way to do the right thing. Also, historical records indicate that you are currently in a most opportune position to make a difference.

As you must realize, I took numerous precautions to avoid this information reaching anyone besides you, while still confirming that it originated on Norona. If you found it necessary to request the expert assistance of your sister's mate, Professor Gabriel Drumayne, I hope he will not interfere in what needs to be done. Unfortunately, I have no choice but to implore you not to share the contents of this missive with your parents or any other authority figure. What I have done to get this message to you, as well as what I'm suggesting you do, is against very explicit time travel and non-interference laws.

With regard to my meeting your family, because an illegal time-hop by a Noronian resulted in altering Terra's primary time line,

I was given special permission to travel back to your time to correct the damage. Though none in your family will remember my visit or what happened at that time, my memory of it remains due to my simultaneously moving between time-space continuums. For purposes of expediency, I will summarize rather than detail the event.

Nine years ago, a very disturbed Noronian citizen hopped from our time to yours in order to give his time-travel device to your sister, Shara. She and Gabriel used that device, which turned out to be faulty, and, in doing so, caused the Terran time line to deviate. On the new time line, you, Roman, were never born. I was able to go back and forth and counteract to restore the primary time line. Unfortunately, there were still multiple repercussions and, from that moment on, we were not permitted to travel through time again for any reason.

In the current situation, the Tribunal was convinced that what was happening on Terra was its natural progression, albeit many millennia sooner than predicted. They decreed that the event, no matter how catastrophic, would not be tampered with. I, and a small assembly of scientists, secretly persisted in hopes of finding a way to save the planet. Eventually we uncovered evidence indicating that, once again, Terra's future had been altered by a non-Terran device, but it was too late to safely rectify the situation in present time. The only solution was the one I have illegally performed—sending a warning back in time to you.

One aftereffect from the use of time travel nine years ago involved a mutation of sorts in a small percentage of Terrans and even fewer Innerworld Noronians. Some called it an evolutionary leap, but it was actually a reawakening of ancient abilities connected to individual, pre-Terran ancestries. In your case, it was your ability to alter the density of your body's cells. In most, it involved extrasensory abilities. If this letter has reached you in the time period intended, you are, or soon will be, working with a woman named Erin Breswell to stop a mysterious abuse of extrasensory power.

I offer this additional piece of evidence to convince you of my credibility. According to the account of your missions, you will be tracking a criminal involved in that abuse of power. His name is Adam Sirilovich. According to the reports, when his capture was imminent, he orchestrated the fatal poisoning of nearly five hundred innocent people whom he had lured into a community for something he called The Eden Experiment. Then every law enforcement officer involved in the attempted capture was killed by a fellow officer or obliterated by a powerful weapon that was never found. You can begin saving the Terran population with this group. They do not need to die.

Although Sirilovich was identified as one of the dead, he actually escaped and altered his appearance. In the decade that followed, under the name Damien, he built upon what he started at Eden. Through mind manipulation, he and his band of mentally enhanced beings easily rose to a position of great power in a vulnerable world. The majority of Terrans were forced into another dark age and made to suffer under his rule. Again, the Tribunal had forbidden interference, despite Noronian interference being the cause, or at least a contributor to that tragedy. This too may be prevented if he is stopped before he becomes Damien, though it is still not the most important task I put before you.

Other than what I have written thus far, you need only trust your instincts to know the truth of what I now assure you is coming.

Two hundred eighty-nine years in your future, Terra's sun will implode. It will come about too suddenly to save anyone on the surface and Innerworlders will be trapped...unless you prevent it in your time, well in advance of the disaster. Here are the facts we've uncovered and the conclusion we have drawn.

Unbeknownst to anyone in your time frame, Terra has a mirror planet known as Heart. It is located in an alternate dimension that, at one time could only be reached through a gateway between the northeastern hemisphere of Terra and the northwestern hemisphere of Heart. In the past, that gateway was closed and undetectable except on the rare occasion when a violent electrical storm was raging simultaneously on both sides. In those instances, a powerful, one-way magnetic field was created...and accidental passages from Terra to Heart sometimes occurred.

One such accident involved Tarla Yan, a

Noronian emissary who once worked for your father. The military aircraft she was on vanished without leaving a trace. The disappearance is a matter of record; the cause is not.

On that same craft was a Terran engineer named Geoffrey Cookson. What little we learned about Heart came from a scientific journal article in which Cookson described his use of reverse magnetic polarity to travel through a wormhole in space. He had written it in the latter part of the twenty-first century, after he and several others claimed to have used his system to return to Terra from Heart. The only comments he included about the mirror planet was that it was inhabited by violent, primitive creatures and the environment was not conducive to human life. For those reasons, he strongly objected to anyone trying to find the gateway.

Once the existence of the wormhole was confirmed, all air and sea traffic was barred from those coordinates. But it was never considered to have anything to do with the deterioration of Terra's sun until we began looking for an un-natural cause for the cataclysm. What we found was that the erratic, minimally problematic gateway had become a stationary portal through space. It had gone from only being opened by massive electrical storms to being held open by a sonic signal of some sort. The signal, which emanated from Heart, had slowly but steadily strengthened from magnetically attracting a passing plane or boat to extracting core energy from Terra's sun.

We can only assume the solar energy was being absorbed by Heart's sun and as it became hotter, the speed of the extraction increased exponentially, thus explaining the suddenness of the implosion of Terra's sun. Obviously, if our assumptions are correct, the transference of solar power would be as disastrous to Heart as it has been to Terra.

Roman, should you accept what I have written and choose to act on it, you will need to go to Heart, find the source of the signal and destroy it before it obliterates both planets. However, if the brief description in Cookson's article is true, you will need to be prepared for an arduous journey.

I leave you with a phrase that I believe has meaning to you:

Desperate times call for desperate measures.

Wishing you good fortune and illumination,
Cattar

CHAPTER 16

The two men stared at the pages for quite a while after Roman finished reading.

Gabe finally broke the silence. "It doesn't say how you're supposed to get to this *mirror planet* without alerting any authorities."

"If we weren't positive the drone came from outer space with Noronian tech, I'd assume the whole thing was a hoax."

"But it did," Gabe countered quickly. "We also know you were suddenly able to go invisible nine years ago, but no one ever knew why."

Roman picked up the first sheet of the letter and scanned it again. "And I can confirm that there are a number of Terrans who suddenly acquired very special abilities at the same time."

"But isn't it too convenient that neither the story from the past nor the warning about the future can be proven. I certainly don't have any recollection of time-traveling with Shara. I'd never agree to doing something that could accidentally alter history."

Roman twisted his mouth from side to side. "Maybe not, but Shara might...if she had the opportunity to prove one of her genetic theories. When we were kids, we had a secret motto that was supposed to have explained anything stupid we ever got caught doing."

"Don't tell me. *Desperate times call for desperate measures.* I've heard her say it."

"Exactly. But I can't remember the last time *I* used it."

"Maybe you just haven't felt desperate about anything lately. Or maybe Cattar got it from something you do in the future."

Roman chuckled. "And we're back to things that can't be proven."

"Not completely. The phrase does have meaning to you. And it's very possible that Shara used it in front of Catttar when she visited your family."

"It sounds like you're leaning toward believing the warning."

Gabriel slowly nodded then shrugged. "Let's just say, I'm not automatically rejecting it. You are working with Erin. That's another confirmation."

"But her name is already in my filed reports, which means it would appear in the historical records."

Gabriel stroked his chin. "What about your tracking Adam Sirilovich? Or his experimental community?"

Roman quickly gave him an overview of the case he was involved in. "Erin's team got close to locating whoever is behind the possible mind manipulations, but no one came up with a name. Nor did anyone mention a community…although there was a mention of the Garden of *Eden*…maybe that's what *the family* referred to…or what the slaves were for…"

"Slaves?"

Roman waved the question away. "It was part of a lucid dream interpretation. But if it turns out to be on target, I can warn the Texas Rangers to come up with a plan that doesn't involve a blatant attack force. According to this letter, Sirilovich is responsible for collecting and then murdering five hundred people.

The Rangers only have case files for about twenty three people who were apparently mentally manipulated and all of them are accounted for."

"You really should turn this over to your parents."

"And that's what I would have done if Cattar hadn't gone to such extremes to get it to me personally. Or if my instincts weren't insisting it was all true. Cattar was right. If I turn it over, nothing will be done except a note in the records to censure Cattar and her scientist pals in the future. So I'll give it a week or so. If there's no Sirilovich or a community named Eden that the Rangers intend to invade, I'll turn it over. But if it turns out the perpetrator's name is Adam Sirilovich and he happens to be holding a couple hundred people in a place called Eden, I'm going to take the rest of this letter as fact. And as Cattar reminded me, desperate times call for desperate measures."

Gabriel frowned. "I don't like it, but I won't stop you...which Cattar apparently knew I would say. Will you at least keep me updated?"

"Yes. But I need to ask a big favor of you. Until I decide what I'm going to do, could you refrain from telling anyone that we got the drone open?"

"Shara already knows."

Roman nodded. As Gabe's mate, Shara's mind was constantly connected to his and she would have been too curious not to eavesdrop. "And I know she'll agree with me. I meant anyone else."

"You want me to lie to your parents?" Gabe asked, raising one brow.

Roman shrugged. "I'm sure you can figure out a way to avoid telling the truth for a very good cause." They shook hands on the agreed delay then Roman asked to use the vidcom.

Roman instructed the Outerworld Monitor Control

agent to connect him to Chief Friedrich with high-level security protection. The instant he saw Chief's face on the monitor, he didn't waste any time with preliminaries. "I need to know if you have a name for the man Erin's team homed in on."

"Sure do. Adam Sirilovich, kind of a big—"

"Does he have a community somewhere, big enough for at least five hundred residents, maybe named Eden?"

Chief narrowed his eyes. "Ah just got a list of his real estate holdings thirty seconds ago. How did you—"

"I'll fill you in when I get back there…in about two hours. It would help if you and Erin would wait for me at her home. I'll feel better handling what I need to if I know she's with you. For right now, it's imperative that no authorities go near any property of Sirilovich. He should be considered armed, well-protected and extremely dangerous. And tell Erin to make sure none of her team is doing anything psychically about this guy or any of his associates. He might have the ability to foresee an attack and it would end very badly for everyone. You know I wouldn't interfere if there was another way."

As soon as Roman disconnected from Chief Friedrich, Gabe said, "So much for giving it a week or two."

An hour later, a copy of the pages had been made for Gabriel's safekeeping and Roman had paid his parents a brief visit to save Gabe the angst of lying to them about the cryptodrone or its contents. It wasn't that he felt comfortable keeping the truth from his parents, but Roman's mind kept replaying the final words of the message: *Desperate times call for desperate measures.*

He could not imagine a time more desperate, or

more worthy of taking whatever risk became necessary, than the end of all life on and within Terra.

By the time Roman left his parents, he had an inkling of a plan in mind. It required a pilot who wasn't put off by wormholes. After a pleasant chat with Prince, the inkling had grown into a strong possibility.

CHAPTER 17

"What time did he say he'd get here?"

Chief's gaze followed Erin as she paced back and forth in her living room. "Around ten."

She whirled back at him, eyes wide. "*Ten?* You said five. I'm sure you said five."

He shook his head and smirked at her.

"Oh, you were teasing me. Well, in case you haven't noticed, I'm not in a giggling sort of mood." She marched across the room and spun back toward him. "It's two minutes after five. What if something happened to him? What if they wouldn't let him come back out? What if—"

"Honestly, Erin, if Ah didn't know you better, Ah'd think you were a might smitten with the alien fella."

She opened and closed her mouth several times before plopping down in an armchair across from him. "I know. I'm being ridiculous. He's as much of a professional in his world as you are here. I'm sure he'll get here when he can. I'm just anxious to hear what he found out today that had him asking you those questions."

"So, you're *not* smitten?"

She felt her cheeks warm. "Of course not. I mean he

is perfectly…nice, but you said it. He's an alien, here on a mission, not to stay. It's not like he came out here to find a mate or anything like that." She sighed. "Let's talk about something else. Anything else."

Chief did his best, but nothing distracted Erin from counting the passing minutes. When Roman finally arrived at a quarter after five, it took all her willpower not to show how worried she'd been. "What's that," she asked instead, pointing at the bags in his hands.

"Dinner," he said as he set the bags down on the dining room table. "I did say I'd take care of it…and believe me, with everything that happened today, I'm surprised at myself. Just one condition—don't ask me to relate any part of my day until after we've eaten. Nothing about the situation is going to change in the next half hour but what I brought won't taste as good reheated."

Erin forced herself to silence all the questions buzzing around her head and sniffed the air instead. "It smells wonderful. I'll get the utensils. Chief, what do you say to some wine?"

"Ah'd say, we could all use a glass. Let me help."

"Roman?"

"Just water for me, thanks."

When they sat down, Chief was served a thick steak, sweet potato fries and coleslaw. Erin and Roman both had shrimp and vegetables in a pink sauce over pasta and a loaf of garlic bread was set out to share.

"I don't understand," Erin said. "I thought your people didn't eat meat."

"We don't. Everything on the table came from plants, but with a little magic, it can be made to look, taste and smell like any Outerworld food you choose."

Chief cut a piece of steak, placed it in his mouth then grinned. "Ah'll be damned. That's as tasty as anythin' Ah could grill up in the back yard!" He held up his wine glass in a toast. "Here's to alien magic."

Erin tried a forkful of her entrée and nodded her approval as well. Nevertheless, anticipation of Roman's news had them consuming their dinners in silence and too quickly to fully appreciate the excellent meal.

"Thank you so much for dinner, Roman," Erin said as soon as she saw Chief set down his fork. "We respected your wish to delay the update, but it's time to fill us in."

Roman took a sip of water then addressed Chief. "Have you put a hold on the Adam Sirilovich case?"

Leaning forward, Chief met Roman's gaze. "All the personnel involved in the search have been ordered to cease all activity related to him or his properties. They've been instructed to treat the entire case as a class-one security issue—top secret and so on. But it's impossible to lock a barn door that big once it's been opened. It's only a matter of time before the man gets wind of our lookin' for him. But based on his abrupt departure, Ah'd say he already knows." He took a swallow of wine before continuing.

"Before Ah shut down the search, a bit more came in on him. You were right about him havin' a chunk of land big enough to keep a whole passel of people. It's out in West Texas. But he bought it openly about five years ago. There were a few news items right after the purchase about his havin' plans to establish a self-sustaining community in the desert, but nothin' since then, and satellite imagery shows there's nothin' there. No community, no buildings, no people, not even a road. Just desert, rocks and some cactus."

"Tell him what he called it," Erin prodded.

"Let me guess," Roman interjected. "The Eden Experiment."

Chief frowned. "Well, those words were in one of

the old news articles, but the registered name of the planned development is Garden of Eden. So what put the notion in your head that we may be lookin' at another Waco out there?"

"There was a message about it in the cryptodrone."

Erin's eyes widened. "You got it open? Who was it from? Was it just about a massacre at Eden or were there other warnings?"

Roman couldn't help but grin at her enthusiastic interest. "Yes, Gabe figured it out. As best we could tell, it came from a Noronian official in the future and the information about Sirilovich and Eden was given to convince me of other things in the message. According to historical records, the Rangers showed up at that property and everyone ended up dead. Except Sirilovich and some of his followers. If he is not stopped *now*, before any attempted capture, he goes on to—" Roman stopped himself from revealing too many details. "I can only say, it will be very, *very* bad."

Erin narrowed her gaze in a way that reminded him of his inability to keep a secret from her.

Roman's gaze darted to Chief. "At any rate, it is possible that the experimental community is somehow hidden from view, maybe even underground. But my instincts say Sirilovich is there, and so are about five hundred innocent people who've probably had their minds stolen…like in Tripper's dream."

Chief shook his head. "Almost hate to say it, but my gut agrees with your instincts, Roman. It's a good thing Ah don't have to explain my orders to have them obeyed. Ah could send a few scouts out there with some tech equipment to case the area on the ground. They could pretend to be surveyors. But if this guy is using psychic powers, won't he know we're onto him and his community in the desert?"

Erin had an answer to that. "Not necessarily. There are a lot of different extrasensory abilities. He could just have the power of suggestion. When we did our group remote viewing, he seemed oblivious to our watching him. Perhaps a few of my team could go with—"

"No!" Roman snapped.

"Absolutely not," Chief seconded.

"But—"

"No one goes near that place!" Roman commanded. "Remember what the message said—*everyone* ends up dead! The Rangers *and* the captives. Even if you send a few scouts, it could tip off Sirilovich and he's apt to escalate. He *has* to be stopped before that happens."

Roman took a breath and spoke to Chief in a less agitated voice. "I'm the only scout you need. I have a way of getting in, observing the entire situation, and getting out, without anyone being the wiser." He shot Erin a *don't-say-a-word* glance, and she held her tongue. "I need to get some sleep tonight but I'll go tomorrow, check everything out and we can meet back here at five again. At least that way you'll have enough information to come up with a viable plan of action. I just need the coordinates of the property."

Although Chief tried and failed to convince Roman to explain his "way", he grudgingly agreed to hold off taking any action for twenty-four more hours.

As soon as Erin closed the door behind Chief, she turned on Roman with fists on hips. "Don't you *ever* do that again."

"Okay," Roman replied and began gathering up dishes.

Quickly picking up the glasses, she followed him to the kitchen. "Do you have any idea what you're saying 'okay' to?"

"Not precisely," he replied in a pleasant tone as he headed back to the table to finish clearing. "But whatever I did, I clearly upset you, which was not my intent, and I'm proving that by agreeing even before you tell me what it was I did."

"Interesting tactic."

He grinned. "Did it work?"

She rolled her eyes. "I'm going to say yes, only because I have a whole list of questions to go through, starting with—did you visit one of your doctors today?"

He blinked in surprise. He'd expected her first question to be about the other warnings in the cryptodrone's message. His appointment at Medical had been pushed to the bottom of his own priority list. "Yes, but I need that to be the last question rather than the first. How did I upset you?"

She straightened her spine. "I am not helpless, nor am I without common sense. If you explain why you do not want me to do something, I will probably accept your reasoning."

"You didn't like that I said you couldn't go with the scouts."

"I didn't like that you *barked* at me!"

Roman slowly nodded. "I think I understand. But you should understand that the tone I used was triggered by sheer panic at the thought of you putting yourself in a dangerous situation."

She walked up to him, drew his head down to hers and gave him a light kiss on the mouth. "You're forgiven."

When their eyes met, he realized it was the first calm moment he'd had all day. With what he had to tell her, he decided to extend the moment a bit longer. His fingers combed into the hair on the sides of her face and he held her still for a deeper kiss. As his tongue stroked hers, he felt her soft moan of submission all the way down to his toes and all thoughts but one were abruptly erased from his mind.

He wanted…no, he *needed* to be inside her, as deeply as she could take him. Suddenly there was nothing in the universe more important than satisfying that need.

And just as suddenly, he instinctively knew there was only one female in the universe who could give him what he needed. That awareness sparked a burning in his brain that compounded the tension in his genitals.

He wanted to warn her but no words would form. He felt himself losing control, but he lacked the ability to stop. Against his will, he saw himself shoving her to the floor, yanking open his slacks, tearing at her clothing, thrusting into her body, and still relief was beyond his grasp. Violent spasms overtook his entire body and his mind went dark.

Erin gaped at the body on the floor. One second they were sharing a slowly arousing kiss. The next, Roman shuddered and collapsed at her feet.

And now he'd begun to fade.

Kneeling beside him, she touched his cheek and realized he was burning up. She thought to fetch a cold compress but his hand clamped over hers and pressed it to his crotch. She moved her fingers and he cried out. He wasn't simply aroused, he was fully rigid…and in pain.

Horny. Hot. Mindless. The only thing she wasn't personally familiar with was the translucence. But three symptoms out of four told her what she had to do to help him.

Within seconds, she freed his erection from its confinement, shed the panties beneath her skirt and quickly mounted him. She barely took in his length when he twitched, trembled from head to toe, relaxed and went invisible…and so did she.

This time, however, she was content to let their bodies stay connected. This time, she'd been the one to stay cool and conscious. She remained still, her thighs straddling his hips and her palms pressed against his chest. As his heartbeat and temperature returned to normal, their bodies became visible again. Yet she waited for him to assure her that he was okay before moving.

Roman opened his eyes and focused on the exquisite woman who had just saved his life. He didn't need a doctor to confirm that fact. He instinctively knew it. He was now also quite certain which of the many "possible" causes was behind his symptoms.

Though he hadn't experienced the traditional signs of the Noronian mating fever, he was definitely in the throes of it. His human half and cellular deviations had obviously added some complications, and the trigger of his fever had complications of her own…like having some felan *and* Noronian ancestry. "Are you all right?" he asked her. "Did I hurt you?"

She exhaled and visibly relaxed. "I'm fine. You're the one who crashed and burned. Is it the fever?"

He looked away. "I'm not sure."

"Liar." She squeezed her vaginal muscles around his erection. "At least one part of you says otherwise." She separated their bodies and sat beside him. "Did your doctor confirm it? Is that why you wanted to postpone that question?"

He shook his head. "No. I actually have something more important to tell you." He tried to pull up his pants, but between the tangle of material around his knees, his overheated body and his swollen member, he ended up stripping instead.

Erin remained quiet until he was done fighting with his clothing and sat up in front of her. Her gaze skittered from his well-muscled arms and legs to his sculpted chest and abs, and down to his incredibly full erection. "You were saying you had something more important to tell me."

He slipped his hand beneath her hair and cupped the back of her neck. "You're warm."

She moved his hand away. "I'm fine." She picked up his shirt and laid it over his lap. "Talk."

He looked down at the tent she'd made and smirked. "Are you sure? I'm more than ready to help you cool down."

Erin wiped the hint of perspiration from her upper lip. "Talk fast."

"The doctor said my cell walls are showing signs of deterioration but he couldn't pinpoint the cause or the cure. If I told him what just happened, he wouldn't be so undecided."

"Then it is the fever."

He nodded. "And if you hadn't done what you did, I could have ended up…in bad shape."

"Elaborate."

"The fever could burn out my brain."

"Or?"

"I could become permanently invisible."

"Or?"

"I could have died. You saved my life, Erin."

"I believe you've already done the same for me."

Roman sighed. "Not quite. You were burning, but not close to dying. You never reached a point of no return."

"But I would eventually, right?"

He hesitated, searching for the best answer without lying. "Not necessarily. Because of your felan ancestry, there's still a chance that if I stayed away from you, your symptoms would stop."

"But if you stayed away, something tragic would definitely happen to you. You said only one's mate can cool the fever. Since that appears to be me, you need to stay close. So forget that option. And, if I remember correctly, having intercourse several times a day is only a temporary solution, besides not always being convenient." His silence and serious expression confirmed her recollection. "And the permanent cure is…"

"Joining."

Erin rose and paced back and forth several times. "You said joining wasn't a legal arrangement like marriage. That it's a mental and spiritual bonding. Is there a way to break that bond after the fever is cured?"

Roman frowned. "I've never heard of any couple breaking the bond but it is possible to construct barriers under certain circumstances."

"What about living arrangements? Does the couple have to live under the same roof forever…or is it possible to have separate lives?"

Roman finally guessed where she was headed with her questions. He just wasn't sure how he felt about it. "Again, I've never heard of anything like that, but I suppose, under certain circumstances, it would be possible. Now, would you like to get to your real question?" He saw a faint flush rise on her cheeks. Was she embarrassed or getting hotter?

She sat back down in front of him and took his hands in hers. "Roman, just a few days ago you admitted that you didn't have any feverish attraction to me. And as sexy and interesting as you are, even if you were of my world, I would never marry you or make any other kind of eternal commitment. I don't believe in passion lasting forever. And I consider marriage the fastest way to ruin a good relationship. Mind you, that's not a biased opinion because someone once broke my heart. It's my scientific conclusion after observing thousands of people. One mystical soulmate per person is a cruel fairy tale that prevents too many people from enjoying their lives while they conduct a futile search for *the one*."

"I can't argue with that, but—"

She squeezed his hands. "Wait. Let me finish. As strongly as I *don't* believe in marriage and happily ever after romances, I *do* believe in the concept of everything happening for a reason. Whatever is really going on with us, we do seem to have been pushed together, presumably to accomplish something. And if joining is the only way we can both remain alive to do that something, then I will agree to it."

His brows raised in surprise.

"But," she said before he could speak. "I want the barriers you mentioned. I do not want you to have constant access to my mind or my spirit, or vice versa. Nor will I promise to stay with you forever. Are those terms acceptable?"

Roman could hardly believe his ears. Although he had never heard of a joined couple leading separate lives, in their case, it was the most logical solution. "Completely acceptable to me...with one addition. We continue living together for one month after the joining. You'll need at least that much time to get used to the mental bond and to learn how to put up your own barriers without my help. After that, we openly and honestly review the situation and, if either one wants the separation, we do it quickly and with no guilt."

Without hesitation, Erin agreed. "So how is it done?"

"There's a book that each person must read and understand in advance, then there's the day of preparation with the parents, and that night the formal joining ritual takes place with..." He noticed the dismayed look on her face and jumped ahead. "But there's also the shortcut version which can be used in case of an emergency."

She chuckled. "An emergency mating? Well, I'm pretty sure we can consider our situation an emergency. And definitely no parents. Not for something we're both looking at as short-term. Considering what you just experienced, I'm guessing we should do it soon."

"That would be best. From here on, there's no way to tell which one of us might, uh...*lose control*...in a public place."

Erin's eyes widened. "Oh. You're right. That wouldn't be good."

"Plus," he continued reluctantly. "There's something else. I have a vital, possibly dangerous mission coming up that will require all my attention."

"Does this mission have something to do with the cryptodrone message?"

He nodded. "I couldn't tell Chief, but you should know—"

"Is it urgent? Do you have to go tonight?"

"No. Not tonight. And I promise to tell you everything before I go anywhere."

"Okay, it's settled. We may as well do it right now. Is this room okay? Do I need to do something or just stand here and be willing? Should I take a shower?"

Roman grinned and stroked her cheek. "I appreciate your cooperative attitude, but at least one of us needs to be in the throes of the fever. You're getting warmer, but you're not desperate enough for it to be an emergency. Besides, I need to look up the exact procedure so, if you'd like, you can take a shower while I do that." As she headed for the stairs, he added, "Just put on a robe or loose nightshirt, white if you have one."

Using his ring and Erin's computer monitor, Roman made a connection with an Innerworld reference source. By the time Erin came downstairs, he was able to hand her a printed copy of the emergency ritual requirements. He smiled at her choice of a thin white, sleeveless shift. But as soon as their hands touched, he noticed how much hotter she was. "Do you feel like you have five or ten more minutes?"

She nodded. "This is familiar. I should be coherent for a while yet."

"Good. You need to read through this. If you can memorize it, great. If the fever blocks it out, I'm permitted to prompt you. I'm going to take a quick shower while you read." He noticed the way her features tightened over whatever line had caught her attention. "Erin, there's one other thing…"

She dragged her narrow-eyed gaze back up to his eyes. "Yes?"

"I know some of the phrases may seem strange, or you might be tempted to change them to suit the agreement we just made, but that's not an option. I'm sorry, either we do this exactly as written or we don't do it at all."

Erin sighed. "I'm pretty sure we don't have a choice." She wiped the back of her hand across her perspiring forehead. "On second thought, you'd better make it a *very* quick shower after all." He turned to leave but she stopped him. "What's this word?" She pointed to it.

"*Shalla*. Noronian for…" He paused then gave up. "It's the feminine for soul's mate. *Shallar* is the masculine form. We have to use those terms."

In spite of all the comments and questions that came to mind, when he turned away this time, she let him go.

Although Roman was barely gone ten minutes, to Erin, it seemed like hours. There was no question about what she was feeling—the "throes" Roman had said was a requirement for the emergency joining were close. The insistent throbbing in her vagina had raised her need to the point where her concentration was disintegrating. But she was still clearheaded enough to know she was going to have a difficult time stating the vows that went against her basic beliefs about relationships. She was going to have to be completely mindless and Roman was going to have to do more than simply *prompt* her.

At the same time, she understood the reason for Roman's warning. In the metaphysical world, spoken words have tremendous power. Changing a phrase to suit her personal opinions could negate the joining. Then where would they be?

"Are you still willing?" Roman asked as soon as he saw her taut expression.

Erin took a deep breath and rose. "Yes. I see we need a drink of some sort."

"The wine from dinner will work. We just need one large glass."

Glad to have something specific to do, she hurried to the kitchen and filled a water goblet with red wine. Only when she returned and handed him the glass did she notice he was naked except for a white towel around his hips. Obviously her mind was foggier than she realized.

With the glass in his left hand, he stood directly in front of her and took her right hand in his.

A tiny electrical shock almost made her jerk away but he held fast. She had felt something unusual every time he'd touched her before, but this was different, strange…*ominous.*

"I can't tell you what you're going to experience," he told her quietly. "I don't even know for sure what will happen to me. But if you're full of fear, it will affect me. You know I won't let harm come to you. I need you to trust me."

She met his gaze and forced her shoulders to relax. "I trust you. I'm just not sure I can trust myself to do what's required. It's…the heat…it's building. *Fast.*"

He gave her hand a squeeze. "Try to keep looking right into my eyes." He took a sip of the wine then passed her the glass. "Take a good swallow."

She did so and handed back the glass. Several seconds passed before he spoke and when he did, she latched onto the strength she heard in his voice and the promise of safety she saw in his eyes.

"I, Roman Locke and my shalla, Erin Breswell, call to the Supreme Being to hear our plea. We have an emergency that supersedes traditional rituals. Thus, we request your blessing of our urgent joining."

Another few seconds passed then, very gradually, a feeling of calm filled Erin. A faint humming sound drifted to her, grew louder then faded to near silence before increasing once again. She became overly aware of the pounding of her heart, of her lungs filling and emptying. A fire was raging in her body but her mind seemed to have separated from the heat. All that mattered were the words.

"Erin Breswell…"

Roman's voice seemed far away and inside her head at the same time. She'd heard that voice in her mind before. She knew it as well as if it were her own.

"Only you can satisfy my thirst and my desire. You are all the nourishment I shall ever need." He took a swallow of the wine and handed her the glass.

Her response came forth effortlessly. "Roman Locke, only you can provide my wants and needs. You are the only solace I shall ever need." Erin drank and returned the glass to Roman.

"Your happiness and comfort is my greatest desire. I choose to spend all my days and nights with you in my life, my heart and my mind." He drank half of the remaining wine.

Erin made the same vow to him then drained the glass.

"That entity which is the soul within Roman Locke speaks now to the soul within Erin Breswell to fulfill their destiny. Are you willing to be joined with us, Erin?"

"That entity which is the soul within Erin Breswell recognizes its shallar. It is our destiny to be joined with you and I am willing."

"There can be nothing between us ever again. Your flesh will be my flesh," Roman said.

"Your blood will be my blood," Erin responded.

"Our minds will be as one," they voiced together.

Erin pulled the towel away from Roman, and dropped it and the glass on the carpeted floor. Roman eased the shift off Erin's shoulders and let it slip to the floor.

Roman held up his hands, palms facing Erin. She raised her hands to meet his, palms to palms, fingers to fingers.

A heartbeat later, a tingling sensation began in their toes and moved upward like an electrical current coursing through their bodies. It finally settled in their fingertips, where a golden glow appeared. The light spread over their hands and retraced the path the tingling had taken, coiling snakelike, round and round their arms, spinning around their heads then down their bodies until they were bathed in a golden iridescence. The distant, rhythmic humming suddenly became a deafening crescendo making further speech impossible. Each slid their hands up the other's arms and over shoulders. Their fingertips trailed upward to the other's temples and pressed there.

As they stared into each other's eyes, a torrential collage of remembered images and sounds passed from one to the other. Together they revisited the days since they'd met, seeing their encounters from the other's perspective.

And from that moment on, their individual minds were as one.

Roman eased Erin onto the floor and leaned over her. There was only one step left and she was in control of it.

Without hesitation, she blinked and thought her invitation. *As I welcomed you into my mind, I now welcome you into my body.*

As soon as he physically joined their bodies, a violent, head-to-toe shudder rocked her, as though every cell was experiencing an intense orgasm. Instantly she realized he was feeling the exact same, powerful sensation, not because she observed or sensed it, but because she *knew* it and was experiencing both of their climactic surges simultaneously.

The aftershocks rolled over them again and again, like the ebb and flow of the ocean tide. It was impossible to tell if the waves of pleasure went on for seconds, minutes or hours. But eventually their bodies relaxed and with that, the humming sound faded then disappeared altogether.

Roman shifted to Erin's side but continued to hold her close. *Please be unharmed*, he prayed silently.

I think I'm fine. Better than fine actually. You?

Incredible. But—

She felt him struggling to erect a barrier between their minds and took the responsibility away from him. Almost effortlessly she created a solid wall that cut off their thought flow and allowed them to keep their memories to themselves. All she'd had to do was visualize it. "I gather that's not something you've ever done before."

He chuckled. "You gather correctly. I've never had any telepathic abilities. I just thought it was supposed to come naturally after the joining. How did you— Wait, you told me…the voices you heard as a child…you had to learn how to shut them out."

She propped herself up on her elbow to see if he looked as worried as he sounded. "That's right. Although it usually required a lot more concentration than it did just now. Then again, I've had quite a bit of experience teaching gifted clients how to block out what they don't want to hear or see."

"Like Vicky."

"Right. I'm sure I can teach it to you if you don't pick it up naturally."

"And here I thought *you* were the one who would need an adjustment period. Well, I'm just glad one of us has some skill."

"Hey, I'm just glad I survived that ritual with my sanity intact. Does the mind-meld mean it worked? We're cured?"

He drew her head down for a soft kiss. "We'll know soon enough. In the meantime, what would you say to a post-joining celebration upstairs?"

Erin rose to her feet and gave his hand a tug. "Why, Roman Locke, I believe you've been reading my mind."

CHAPTER 18

Eve wished she had thought of putting a camera in Breswell's living room. Holding one of Roman's hairs had allowed her to witness what had just transpired between them but without sound, it made no sense. If only she'd had his hair earlier, she would have been able to see what he'd been up to all day, but she hadn't been able to meet up with Nola until after Breswell had left her office.

Even without sound however, she knew something paranormal had occurred between the couple. She'd dabbled in witchcraft enough to recognize a ritualistic casting of a spell but she'd never seen anything like the swirling golden light they'd manifested. How had they done that? What sort of spell had they cast? Regardless of what they wanted to bring about, the fact that it was sealed with a sexual exchange gave it extra power.

More than likely, it had something to do with Adam and his Eden Experiment. That thought cinched it for Eve. She knew what she had to do.

Two hours later, her suitcase of essentials was in the trunk of her hovercar and she was parked a block away from Breswell's house. She extracted the little black pouch she'd tucked in her bra and fingered the strand of hair inside. As Eve had hoped, Roman was in a deep sleep. Before he took another breath, Eve had full control of his mind.

Roman Locke. Open your eyes and look around the room. You have been held in this prison against your will but your guard has fallen asleep and the cell door was left open. The love of your life, Erin Breswell, has been kidnapped and you must escape to rescue her. Be careful not to wake the guard. Slowly get out of bed, take the clothes on the chair and go downstairs. Get dressed and go out the front door.

As Roman obeyed, Eve felt a wave of relief. She'd been afraid that the spell had been one of protection or that he might have sensed her intrusion. But he put up no resistance whatsoever. She tucked the pouch back in her bra where she could easily touch his hair again if the connection weakened. With her car's headlights off, she pulled into the driveway as he was exiting the house.

Get in the car, Roman. The driver is Eve, a kidnapping specialist for the Texas Rangers. She knows where Erin is being held. She will take you to her. You trust her with your life and all your secrets. You will answer her questions truthfully. You know it is the only way to save Erin.

"Do you know why I am here?" Eve asked her new puppet as soon as he was in the passenger seat.

"You're going to help me rescue Erin," Roman replied without hesitation. "Is she close?"

"It's a long drive, but we have plenty to talk about along the way." She smiled and he gave her a tight-lipped nod in return. It would be a long drive—almost three hours, using the ultraspeed drive unit Adam had installed in her car. Without it, the trip would have taken more than twice that time.

Eve noticed that Roman's expression was a mixture of concern and battle-readiness. She had obviously chosen the right scenario to manipulate him. He would do whatever he was told in order to save Erin.

And she would do whatever was needed to become Adam's second in command in the perfect society he had envisioned.

With that in mind, she backed out of the driveway and headed toward Eden.

A stab of terror awakened Erin. Her heart racing, she gasped for air as though she had been holding it. A nightmare? She didn't think so. She opened one eye just enough to see the time—4:15. She'd only been asleep about four hours. Something had jarred her awake. She listened intently, but the house was quiet. She turned her head to see if Roman had also been awakened but he wasn't next to her. Just to make sure he hadn't gone invisible, she ran her hand over the space he had been in when she fell asleep.

"Roman?" she said toward the dark bathroom. When she received no answer, she turned on a light, got out of bed and peeked into the other upstairs rooms. "*Roman?*" she called a little louder, but again there was no response. Wondering if he was investigating the cause of whatever had woken them, she quickly donned a robe and went downstairs, turning lights on along the way.

Her concern rose when she noticed the front door was slightly ajar. Her mind leapt to the worst case scenario. *Someone had tried to break in. Roman ran after the intruder. Did he take a weapon?*

She ran back upstairs. His gun belt was still hanging on the arm of the chair and the pistols were still holstered. But the clothes he'd been wearing were no longer there. For a moment she just stared at the chair.

If he'd heard a noise and went to check it out, he may have pulled on a pair of pants, but the whole outfit, including his shoes and socks, were gone. Getting fully dressed to chase off a possible burglar made as little sense as leaving his pistols behind.

Even if there were no intruder and he had to leave for some other reason, he still would have taken his weapons. She had never seen him go anywhere unarmed. Also, wouldn't he have left her an explanatory note, as he had yesterday morning? She hurried back downstairs to be sure she hadn't overlooked one. Then she put on a pair of boots, switched on all the outdoor lights, grabbed a flashlight and did a slow search of her property.

Absolutely nothing was amiss...except for the door not being closed.

As she stood in her front yard, staring at the door, panic crept in and Erin's mind raced to an entirely different scenario. Roman had needed to join with her to cure the fever, remain sane, *survive*. Once the deed was done, he no longer needed her to—

Quiet, she ordered the near-hysterical voice in her head. *He did not leave me. Not like this. Not after last night.* She took a calming breath, erased all the negative thoughts and let her intuition take over.

The moment of panic wasn't unfounded. Something was definitely wrong. But what? What else could she—

The answer came to her before she finished working out the question. *Their minds had been joined!* She should be able to reach out to him telepathically. Consciously she lowered the barrier she had constructed and all of Roman's memories, experiences and stored impressions were available to her. Though she had no idea how she was doing it, she realized she could keep all his information separate from her own.

Roman? Where are you?

She waited but nothing came to her. Based on what Jamie and Ryan had said about being able to communicate with each other no matter how far apart they were, she eliminated distance as the reason he wasn't answering.

But if he was asleep...or unconscious...or—*No! Don't even think that. Roman was still alive.* She was absolutely certain of that much.

Roman! She envisioned herself giving him a hard shake. *Why can't I hear you? What happened after I fell asleep?*

Her peripheral vision caught a movement in her driveway, but when she turned her head, there was nothing there. She took a step toward her front door and sensed it again. This time, however, instead of abruptly turning and trying to focus, she relaxed her gaze.

There, in her driveway, was a barely visible outline of a hovercar. She closed her eyes and the image became somewhat clearer in her mind.

Suddenly Roman was crossing the lawn in front of her. It was surprising enough to make her open her eyes, but when she realized he wasn't actually there, she returned to letting her mind's eye do the observing. She watched Roman get into the passenger seat and, a few seconds later, the car drove off...which meant *someone* was in the driver's seat.

Erin concluded that she was seeing the scene in answer to her question. Even if he was unconscious, it seemed probable that she was accessing Roman's memory of what had occurred.

She could not get a sense of the time of his departure, but she did note that he walked to the car on his own, without hesitation or caution. He had been awake at that point and seemed to be aware of what he was doing.

But who was driving that car? Where was he being driven? And, perhaps most important, why?

She hurried back up to her bedroom, sat on the side of the bed Roman had been on and closed her eyes. As soon as she asked to see what happened to make him leave the house, she saw him rise, get dressed and leave the room. Erin followed the path he'd taken all the way to the hovercar. From what she could perceive, absolutely nothing had occurred to prompt his leaving.

Discounting the possibility that he had expected someone to pick him up in the middle of the night, she walked through the scene again. What she noticed this time was that, although his eyes were open and he moved steadily, he never glanced back toward her before heading downstairs. It was almost as if he were unaware of her presence.

When a logical explanation failed to come to her, she knew it was time to let her spirit guides do some talking. A minute later she was in her reading room, had lit a white candle and spread her tarot deck out across the table.

The first three cards she drew seemed to be the answer to all her questions—the Prince of Swords, *Roman*, the Hanged Man, *trapped and turned upside down*, and The Devil, *Adam Sirilovich and/or his female partner*.

In a flash she understood how Roman could appear to be awake and aware and yet doing something he would not normally do.

The Devil had taken control of Roman's mind!

Her first thought was to call Chief Friedrich, but Roman had been very clear that any openly aggressive action would result in the death of all the officers as well as the innocents at Eden. At the moment, Chief had agreed to stand down because Roman would be secretly infiltrating Eden to safely assess the situation. If he learned that his spy had been kidnapped and mentally incapacitated by the suspects, she was certain he would take action regardless of Roman's warning.

She slumped back in the chair and stared at the cards. It was solely up to her to rescue Roman. But how? She had no skills that would help her break into a hidden compound protected by someone with extrasensory abilities. She could put up a shield to protect herself from a psychic invasion, but that was about it.

The instant after that thought occurred to her, she created the shield...just in case.

If only there was a way to contact Gabriel. She knew she could count on his help and was certain he or another Innerworlder could take care of everything. But it wasn't like she could just pick up the phone and—

The ring. Roman used it to travel and to interface with Innerworld technology. In a flash, she thought she'd seen it on the nightstand and quickly went to check.

He hadn't put it on before he left! Absolute proof that he'd been unaware of his actions.

Erin snatched up the heavy ring and held it tightly in her hand. Even more so than his weapons, he would never go anywhere without having that ring on his finger. It was his mainline to home. He had only taken it off last night when they'd gotten into bed and it had caught in her hair...

A deliciously warm feeling flooded through her body as she felt his and her memories of the sensual minutes that took place in that room. They had every intention of having sex—*normal* sex, without the mind-stealing heat or any supernatural side effects, where they would both remain conscious and visible and it would last more than a few seconds. After he'd removed the ring, they'd kissed and he'd gently stroked her skin, but instead of enjoying their first *normal* sexual experience, they'd drifted into a peaceful sleep in each other's arms. They were supposed to finish what they'd started when they awoke.

She shook her head to turn off the memory and get back to her immediate dilemma. She peered closely at the ring. It was a gaudy, gold piece with a center gem similar to a fire opal and, when she turned it toward the lamp light, she could see a geometric design within the opalescence. There were markings and raised nodules of gold on both sides of the setting and around the band, but she had no idea how to turn it into a communication device.

"Hello?" she said, holding the ring close to her mouth. "Is anyone there? If you can hear me, I'm trying to reach Gabriel—" She had no idea what his last name was. "Umm, the mate of Shara Locke. I need his help. Oh, this is Erin Breswell in Texas, er, Outerworld. He met me through Roman Locke, who I just happen to be—"

She stopped herself from rambling so she could listen for a response. But none came. Just in case someone had heard her call for help and tried to respond, she put the ring on her thumb.

For several minutes, she tried to retrieve instructions on using the ring from Roman's memories but she didn't know what any of the terms meant. Then she sought a rescue plan but nothing in his previous missions had any relevance to the current situation. Besides, he tended to rely on his ability to go invisible or incorporeal to perform his tasks.

Eventually she came to the only possible solution. Her new ability to *see* where he had gone would allow her to follow his trail. And if it led her into the Devil's den, so be it. She would keep her mind open to his in the event he regained his independence, but she couldn't count on that. And she would keep her psychic shield up against an intrusion by the Devil and his fork-tongued disciple.

That decided, she dressed in black jeans and a black t-shirt, put on her boots and cowgirl hat, and strapped on Roman's holster. Not knowing what she might encounter along the way, she attached Roman's Texas Ranger's badge to the belt. She felt confident Chief wouldn't be too angry with her if he knew why she was impersonating one of his people. Thinking of contingency plans, she packed a small bag with a change of clothes, basic toiletries, bottled water and snacks.

She was less than a mile from her house when her phone buzzed inside her bag. It was barely six a.m. and the caller's identification was concealed, but considering the situation, she answered it. "Hello?"

"Good morning, Erin. I hope I didn't wake you."

Erin shivered as a chill of warning slithered up her spine. "Who is this?" she asked as she pulled the car into a vacant parking lot and stopped.

"You can call me Eve."

"As in *Adam* and Eve and the Garden of Eden?"

"Oh, you are a smart one. Just not quite as smart as we are. But we'll have plenty of time to get to know each other much better later. For now, there's someone here who wants to talk to you."

Erin heard Eve speaking to someone else but she couldn't make out the words.

"Erin? Is it really you? Did they hurt you? I've been

so worried—"

"Roman! Where are you? What has she done to you?"

"Eve has been wonderful. She's the one who brought me to where the kidnappers were holding you. We were going to rescue you but when we got there, you had already escaped on your own. Eve said it would be best to wait for you here at Ranger headquarters. When do you think you'll get here?"

Erin's brain analyzed Roman's narrative at ultraspeed. He sounded sincerely relieved to hear her voice, which suggested he fully believed she'd been kidnapped. He also seemed to believe he was in a Ranger's field office, which was highly improbable. On the other hand, the speech sounded slightly stilted as though he'd been told exactly what to say. Obviously Eve had planted a full scenario in Roman's mind, but why? What was her goal in taking him? "I'm not sure how long it will take. Very soon I hope. I'll have to get the exact directions from Eve. Put her back on the phone." He complied immediately.

"Hello again," Eve said cheerfully, as though they were old friends.

"What have you done to him?"

"I just gave him something to think about that made him extremely…cooperative."

Erin felt the icy tendrils again. "What did you make him do?"

"Why Erin, you sounded downright lethal just then. Fortunately, I know you aren't actually capable of harming me. Don't worry. The only thing I made him do was answer a few questions. And because he is such a devoted…*bodyguard*, he didn't hesitate to spill his secrets in order to save you. And now *you* are going to follow my orders to save *him*."

Erin had a whole list of profane orders she wanted

to shout at the woman but managed to restrain herself. It wasn't in Roman's or her best interest to anger his captor. "Why don't you just take over my mind and make me do whatever it is you want me to do. Why threaten Roman's life?"

"Like I said, we'll have time to learn all about each other later. But first, you have an assignment and not much time to complete it."

"I'm listening."

"Adam would like you to extend an invitation to all the members of your psych team to be his guest for the weekend at his Garden of Eden."

"For what purpose?" Eden asked bluntly.

Eve chuckled. "He has something very interesting to discuss with you, a presentation of sorts. But it really doesn't matter what his purpose is. If you want Roman back, you will come as invited. At precisely noon today, you will all enter Hangar Twelve at Alamo Air Field. You will then board the private plane inside. You will not speak to the pilot. He is merely a drone who believes you are all executives of the corporation he works for. Are you with me so far, Erin?"

"Yes."

"Good. There's just a little more. Under no circumstances will anyone contact the authorities. You'll have to take my word that there's a small army in place here with equal or greater abilities than any of your team possesses. We can hear and see everything you say and do. If anyone tries to contact Chief Friedrich or any other official, we will turn your precious Roman over to people who would pay any price to get their hands on an alien with the ability to disappear."

Erin audibly gasped. Eve had forced him to reveal his greatest secret to her. A second later she realized

Eve had referred to an *army*. She wasn't terribly surprised that there were more people involved than just this woman and Adam Sirilovich, but an *army*? Were there really that many gifted people without morals or had she used her ability to manipulate them to her will?

"Now that I have your full attention, let me be perfectly clear. Referring to it as an invitation was Adam's attempt to be polite, but it isn't extended with an option to decline. Oh, I almost forgot. You are *not* to invite Wendy Santana. She is not to be told about this."

"Why not include Wendy?"

"She's a tool of the CIA and he'd rather not have a representative of the North American States sitting in on this meeting. Do *not* contact her."

"Fine. I will extend Adam's invitation to everyone except Wendy, but I certainly can't promise they'll go along. They barely know Roman and they *do* know Adam Sirilovich is a criminal."

Eve chuckled. "I suppose he could be described that way, but he is also a genius with a master plan that he wants to share with exceptionally gifted people, like yourselves. However, if curiosity isn't sufficient to convince your team to go with you, you should tell them this. For every psych team member who does not attend Adam's presentation, ten ungifted residents of Eden will be committing suicide...in your presence."

"That's insane!" Erin shouted. "How dare he—"

"He *dares* because he can. Every revolution has casualties and we have plenty of...what was it Haruko Zhang called them? Oh yes, *slaves*, though we refer to them as volunteers, since, technically, they consciously signed up for The Eden Experiment. At any rate, we have recruited more than enough little people to allow for some collateral damage. However, I strongly recommend you restrain yourself from expressing your insulting opinions in front of Adam. He's rather sensitive about what others think of him.

"Now, there's one last, but very important, instruction. No one is to use any of their extrasensory abilities against us. I assure you we would know and counteract immediately. As an act of good faith, Adam promises his team will observe equal limitations but will permit everyone to shield themselves from intrusion. You'd better start making calls, Erin. You only have six hours."

CHAPTER 19

"Well?" Adam asked anxiously as soon as Eve disconnected from Breswell. "Will she make them come?"

She turned toward him with narrowed eyes. Surprising him while he was still asleep had been a strategic move to put him at a disadvantage. Sitting on the edge of his huge bed, in boyish pajamas, hair mussed, he didn't look like a master strategist. Instead he looked...insignificant. "I'd be shocked if she didn't...and I am very seldom shocked. Like I told you, that ritual I saw her and the alien perform was some sort of major commitment. She'll cooperate to save him and his secret."

"And the others? We didn't discuss threatening the lives of our test subjects to get Breswell's team here. I'm not sure—"

Eve cut him off by sitting down on his lap and pressing her thumb against his lips. "Sometimes you can be so charmingly naïve. I am going to have so much fun teaching you to enjoy the dark side of power." She continued the pressure as she slid her finger across his cheek and down his carotid artery then tightly pinched the base of his neck long enough for him to pale. Then she kissed him hard on the mouth, stabbing her tongue between his teeth.

His hand found her breast and squeezed. Instantly she bit his lower lip and stood up. "I did not give you permission to touch me. Do not make that mistake again."

She smiled as he touched his lip and saw the blood she'd drawn. Pacing back and forth, she got back to his questioning her methods. "As to the threat, Breswell's team is made up of *good* people. They would never knowingly cause the death of innocents. Besides, you told me yourself that you approached some of that group and they turned you down. Thought you weren't worth their attention. A very strong motivation was needed to get them to listen to your presentation."

"You're right, of course."

She came back to him and straddled his thighs. "So, I take it you're pleased with your gift?"

He tilted his head and arched one brow. "You're absolutely certain he's a being from another planet? He doesn't *look* alien."

"Positive. The situation I implanted in his mind compelled him to honestly answer every question I posed. Like I said before, the only challenge I had was in asking the right questions. His secrets were buried beneath layers of experienced subterfuge. It took most of the drive here to find out what I did."

"Go over it for me again. I want to make sure I have all the facts about him before I decide what to do with this *gift* you brought me."

"He was born in a place called Innerworld, in the center of the Earth—"

"Which is ludicrous."

She ignored his sarcasm. "Which is a colony of a planet named Norona. His job title is transient emissary, which equates to his being a spy for his people. His current mission is to find out about us—I'm paraphrasing there—and to keep Erin Breswell safe from harm."

"And the ritual they performed?"

"He called it joining and, as supernatural as the foreplay was, the sex was very human. I thought they were casting a protection spell of some sort but he said he's unable to perform magic and that the ritual had nothing to do with us."

"Are you certain he said he acquired his ability to go invisible nine years ago?"

"Right."

"Very interesting. No other special talents?"

"I asked about all the ones I'm familiar with. His answer was no to everything. But would you really need more if you could be invisible whenever you wanted?"

"Perhaps not. Anything else?"

She smirked. "You mean like his mother being a human from San Francisco, or that he doesn't eat meat? Believe me, I know more about him than I do about you, but other than him being an alien who can go invisible, it was all pretty boring stuff. Although…" She squeezed her eyes shut.

"What is it?" Adam asked quietly.

She opened her eyes again and shook her head. "I don't know. I just have a feeling there's something else, something bigger, more important, but I didn't ask the right question to find out what it might be." She abruptly rose from his lap and walked to the door.

"Where are you going?"

She turned back to him. "I need a power nap, then maybe I'll have another go at Twenty Questions with the sexy alien."

"What about…*us*?"

Her gaze slid over him, purposefully settling on the bulge in his pajama bottoms. "Have I earned the second-in-command post?"

He sighed. "I told you I would consider it...*after* I see if your plan works. You give me Breswell's team and I *may* give you that promotion."

"Fine. And when I get the promotion I've earned, you'll get what you have coming to you as well."

CHAPTER 20

"I've been ready to go for an hour, just waiting for someone to call and tell me *where* I had to go," Tripper told Erin. "I'm glad it was *you* calling though. I dreamt it was the snake lady."

"Well, your dream wasn't entirely wrong. The command appearance came through her. I'm just relieved I didn't have to talk you into going. Though, considering your first dream, I would have understood if you'd declined."

"No way would I pass. In the dream, she snapped off one of the little people's heads and told me if I didn't obey, the same would happen to me."

"Well, the threat she made to me felt very real. And by the way, she claimed they have an army. However many they have, I believe these people are capable of unthinkable atrocities. Anyway, I suggest you pack an overnight bag. I have a—"

"Already packed. I'll shake Jamie and Ryan and meet you at the hangar a little before noon. Are the Rangers coming too?"

"Unfortunately, no. If they go anywhere near Sirilovich, there will be a blood bath. But once we get in and check things out, we should be able to tell

Chief Friedrich what he needs to know to keep casualties to a minimum."

"So, we're on our own and can't use our extrasensory abilities against them."

"Right."

"Well then, you should know you can count on me if any, uh, physical aggression is needed. I never talk about it, in fact, I try not to think about it, but, my specialty during the war was lethal hand-to-hand combat. I'm not that person any more, but he's still inside me."

Only because she was so accustomed to not reacting to patient confessions, Erin gave no indication of surprise. "Let's hope it doesn't come to that, but it's good to know that Roman will have experienced backup if needed." She had always felt Tripper had a troubling secret, but his outward persona never gave a hint to his being capable of violence.

Erin thanked Tripper again and disconnected. Her other calls had been easy enough. They just hadn't been completely successful. Although Hari didn't hesitate, Kanji had left for Japan last night and couldn't possibly return in time. Since Adam Sirilovich seemed to have his sights set on exceptionally gifted people and Kanji's talent was more academic than practical, she hoped his absence would be forgiven.

And surely, they would not harm anyone because of Vicky's absence once they heard the reason. When Erin had called, Vicky's daughter let her know her mother had been hospitalized with severe chest pains the evening before and was being kept for observation. Erin assured her she was just checking on her and would call back.

She glanced at the clock. She still had over two hours before she needed to pick up Peace and Hari.

She filled five minutes of the time sending her mother a note to let her know she was unexpectedly called out of town to see a patient and would call when she had more time. She was trying to decide what to tell Nola when that woman called her.

"Oh, Erin, I'm so sorry." Nola sobbed and sniffled. "I've done something terrible. But I swear I didn't know."

Erin's heartbeat escalated. *What now?* "Whatever it is, we'll figure it out. Just take a breath and tell me what happened."

Nola audibly gasped for a breath and blew her nose before speaking again. "I've been having nightmares, but I never remember what they're about when I wake up. Last night was different. Not only did I remember the dream, it felt real, like a memory. I was…hiding something from you…something that would hurt you and your team."

"Well, we know that's not true—"

"That's what I told myself but I couldn't let it go. So I came into the office, you know, to check and make sure everything was where it should be. That's when I saw Roman's hat. It was on my desk and when I picked it up, I had a memory flash of holding his hat and taking a hair from inside and giving it to a woman. But I was sure I'd never done anything like that."

"It's okay, Nola."

"*No!* It's not. I found a new program on my computer that I don't remember installing, but who else could have done it? There's also a record of confidential files and all the psych team sessions' videographs being deposited into a cyberspace lockbox where they were downloaded to an address I don't recognize. The time stamp shows these things were done while I was at my desk! It *had* to be me, but I *really* don't remember, and somehow, I didn't notice any of this until this morning."

Erin forced herself to keep her voice calm. "What was the new program you found?"

"It was a live feed of the reception area and someone outside the office has access to it. Copies of some of the video were also deposited to the same lockbox."

Erin formed a conclusion before Nola finished her sentence. "I never had a camera installed there."

"I know, but someone did...maybe I did that too. I skimmed the videos and saw myself listening in on your interviews and taking the hair from the hat, just like the flash I had. I also saw you and Roman—"

"None of it is your fault, Nola. You were being used...by a very skilled mind manipulator. After the last session, we were fairly certain someone in the group was either a spy or being controlled. I'm actually very relieved to know that no one on the team was a plant. The fact that you were able to do what you did this morning suggests the person has released you. But just in case it's only temporary, erect a protective shield of light while you have the chance, the way I taught you. Then you need to immediately contact Chief Friedrich and tell him he needs to assign a full-time guard to you as soon as possible, to make sure you don't do anything else...*unusual*. He'll understand.

"Tell him everything you told me. He's fully aware of the situation and was planning to send someone in to check the office for illegal surveillance equipment, but it sounds like you've already proven at least one surveillance device is there that shouldn't be. I trust Chief implicitly, but there will be others investigating this and I can't be sure how discreet they'll be. So, before anyone gets there, delete all the video files of the reception area and all the deposits you made into that lockbox. Lastly, tell him I have something...*personal* to take care of this weekend...*with Roman*, but I'll call him as soon as I can."

After Erin disconnected from Nola, it took several minutes to quiet the panic bouncing around in her head. She wished she could call Chief herself but didn't dare. Adam and Eve could truly have the ability to observe what she and the psych team were doing. She simply had to hope the innocent-sounding message she'd asked Nola to give Chief would be enough to alert him to a development of some sort but not to take action.

After analyzing Nola's confession, especially about giving one of Roman's hairs to a woman, Erin felt comfortable concluding that Eve required something of the person she wanted to control. She had a hair of Roman and something of Nola's, that much seemed certain. But she must not have something of anyone else in the group or she wouldn't have needed to threaten Erin to convince them to obey. *Unless she didn't have the ability to get through their protective shields.* Either way, Erin felt like she and her team would at least be safe from psychic invasion...if not a straightforward physical assault.

As to those who were vulnerable, Nola was soon going to be protected by a Ranger. And now that she knew how Eve was controlling Roman, she simply had to take the tool away from her. Recalling Tripper's initial dream, she assumed Eve would keep the hair on her person. Once she freed Roman, she had no doubt that, together, they could figure out how to stop them.

Her hands settled on the holsters at her hips. If Eve had been able to watch her remotely, wouldn't she have noticed the weapons and insisted they be left behind? Also, Eve hadn't seemed aware that she was in her car when she answered the call. Those two omissions convinced Erin that her protective shield was effective against Eve, or Eve did not have the ability to remote view without a tool. Either way, her intuition told her she was not being watched, which gave her the confidence to conceal the slim laser pistols and Roman's ring in her boots.

Erin...

She froze, unsure if she had imagined Roman's voice in her mind.

Erin?

Roman! I hear you. Where are you? A jumble of thoughts came through. Slower. Focus on one word at a time.

Don't know where I am. Small room, like at the academy. I don't remember—

Eve made you go with her. She's using one of your hairs to control your mind. Try to fight it but don't do anything that could get you hurt. I'll be there soon.

No! I can—

Erin felt the disruption as clearly as though they'd been cut off during an audible conversation. Eve's control must have been momentarily weakened somehow but it was back. Roman's conscious mind was once again a blank to Erin.

It was hard to believe that, after all this time, she had someone else's voice in her head again. *And a very familiar voice at that.* In a flash, she realized why his mind voice seemed so familiar. It was one of the ones she'd heard as a child. No matter what other voices came and went, his was always there. She remembered Roman telling her how some soulmates meet as children and instantly become best friends for life. But she and Roman had never met, nor would they ever have crossed paths as children. The bond must have always been there but she was told hearing voices meant she was mentally unstable. At least hearing his voice now gave her some comfort.

For the first time since she'd awakened, she was able to take a full breath and, a few seconds later, her stomach informed her that it was ready to take in some food. She did a quick check on her protective shield, gave it a booster shot of light and headed for the kitchen.

She made herself a ham and cheese melt and was about to make a cup of the special herbal tea when she wondered if she still needed it. The morning's crisis had kept her from thinking about her physical condition but now that she was somewhat calmer, she realized how *normal* she felt. The intense heat, the sexual itch and the frayed nerves that had caused constant agitation for weeks had miraculously gone away...just as Roman had said it should after the joining ceremony—something else she hadn't thought about since she'd awakened.

Although she'd never wanted to be married, as of last night, she was bound to another person...*for eternity*. It was still too strange to fully comprehend, but she acknowledged that the timing of the ceremony was fortuitous, if not completely welcomed by either party.

But was it simply luck? Or had their fate been written long ago? Had the Universe and their combined spirit guides escalated their symptoms to ensure they would already be joined before they were physically separated against their wills?

She sighed. Luck versus fate was a debate with no clear winner, and she had much bigger and more important things to be thinking about.

The words *more important things* vibrated in her

mind until she recalled Roman telling her he had something more important to tell her, something about the cryptodrone's message that he didn't want Chief to hear. Concerned that it had something to do with Roman personally, she felt justified in searching the memories she had access to rather than waiting for him to tell her himself.

Remembering how her specific question had triggered images of Roman getting into the hovercar, she opened her mind to Roman's memories and focused on the message in the cryptodrone. She saw Roman sitting next to Gabriel, figuring out the key, unfolding the papers, reading the words aloud…

All the information Roman had not shared with Chief became knowledge to Erin in an instant. And just as quickly, Erin knew that Roman had no doubt about the truth of the message, so she accepted it as well. Earth's sun would die and its system would implode in less than three centuries…unless Roman prevented it in the present. She also knew he had a plan, or at least a semblance of a plan, that relied on a friend named Prince and a *borrowed* spacecraft.

It took all of Erin's mental strength to keep from slamming the door against the deluge of background information that attached itself to the details in Cattar's message, as each bit had her raising other questions. However, she needed to understand as much as she could absorb. As Roman's mate, his concerns were now hers as well. Pretending the dire message had nothing to do with her was not an option. The importance of rescuing Roman had suddenly escalated to a galactic level.

Although she now knew how to use Roman's ring to contact Gabriel for help, she was also aware that making such contact could possibly alert his parents, something Cattar had warned against.

Erin took a moment to sort out all the noise in her mind and calm herself. There was only one way to deal with all the problems that just fell on her shoulders—one at a time, beginning with freeing Roman from Eve's control.

At a quarter to twelve, Erin, Peace and Hari arrived at the airport hangar. Tripper, Jamie and Ryan were barely a minute behind. As Erin had suggested, they each carried an overnight bag, as though they actually had been cordially invited for a weekend stay at the Garden of Eden. The door to the private plane opened and stairs were lowered.

"Before we get on board," Erin said in a hushed voice, "I want to remind everyone to keep your protective shields and psychic antennae up at all times. Trust your intuition and each other. From here on, we will literally be winging it." She quickly filled them in on her conversation with Nola. "Even though no one may be able to invade your mind through your shield, assume you are being watched, and/or heard, at all times, starting when we get on that plane.

"We can also assume that Adam Sirilovich is unbalanced, so, no matter how irrational or insane his so-called presentation sounds, show him respect for his brilliance. If he believes he has won us over, we may be able to convince him there is a way to achieve his goal, whatever it is, without harming anyone. Lastly, we can probably assume Eve keeps the tokens she's collected on her person. Getting those away from her is my number one priority. It's imperative that I free Roman from her control. Once he's free, he'll make sure we all get home safely. He can...do things none of us are capable of. Any questions?"

"I don't have a question," Ryan said. "But I wanted to thank you for including us. We'll help any way we can."

Erin sighed. "Believe me, if it wasn't for Eve threatening her captives' lives, I wouldn't have included any of you. But I am very grateful to each of you for your courage." She checked the time. "Okay, Eve said we had to board the plane at precisely noon and it's that time. Let's show them how obedient we can be."

A half hour later, they felt the aircraft begin its descent and were stunned to see the barren desert vista suddenly peel back to reveal a landing strip. Erin recalled Chief saying there was nothing on this land, so Sirilovich obviously had his development well camouflaged. Minutes later, they were on the ground and being assisted onto a horse-drawn wagon by a silent but smiling, middle-aged man who took them several miles down a hard-packed dirt road. The road ended in front of a one-story, log cabin with a cozy porch, rocking chairs included. A wooden sign bearing the white-painted words *Welcome to the Garden of Eden* hung across the porch eave. A solid wall of very tall, thick hedges extended from each side of the cabin as far as one could see.

Hari touched Erin's arm. "There is terrible darkness here. Going beyond this building feels...hopeless, as though there is no way out."

Tripper picked a pebble up off the ground and threw it at the hedge. The spot where it hit visibly rippled then stabilized. "It's an energy field of some sort. Hari's right. Once we go in, we could be trapped."

Erin nodded, still not quite reconciling the Tripper she thought she knew with the battle-savvy man before her. His entire demeanor had changed with his revelation about his past. "Roman will get us out," she stated more confidently than she felt.

The door to the cabin opened and a petite woman

stepped out onto the porch. She wore a full-length, long-sleeved, cotton print dress covered partially by an apron. A matching scarf demurely held back her brown hair. Her attire seemed to match the dated log cabin.

"Welcome to the Garden of Eden," she said with a pleasant, seemingly genuine smile, then curtsied. "My name is Sarah. If you'll follow me, I'll take you to your lodgings." She turned around, took a step and faced the team again. "Perhaps one of you didn't get the message about not using any special abilities while you're here."

"You tested my shield first," accused Jamie. "I just gave you a tap back."

Sarah's smile remained fixed. "And now that we have taken each other's measure, we can move on."

The interior of the cabin was a single room with four wooden chairs set around a wood-plank table. There was also tiered, wooden shelving that could be used to display trinkets, brochures or maps, if this were truly a welcome center.

"What is this place?" Ryan asked.

The smile Sarah gave Ryan had a distinctly sensual slant. "Adam will explain everything, and he's very anxious to do so, but he had some last minute business to attend to. In the meantime, as I said, I'll take you to your lodgings, where you will remain until he is ready for you. A light lunch has been provided in your suite."

Erin saw Jamie about to question Sarah and shot her a silencing glance. To Sarah she said, "That sounds lovely. We appreciate the hospitality."

The stark log cabin and Sarah's attire were a fair preview of what lay beyond the exit door. If she didn't know better, Erin would have assumed they were stepping onto a movie set or entering a theme park.

The scene before them was absolutely picturesque—the epitome of an American small town's Main Street from long ago, hard-packed dirt road, planked sidewalks swept clean, neat, whitewashed buildings with colorful trim and signage. From where they were standing, it was impossible to tell just how far the town spread out, but it was definitely large enough to have a population of five hundred or more, as Cattar's message had indicated.

Men and women rode bicycles on the road and strolled along the sidewalks, going in and out of doors along the way. They were all dressed in prim clothing befitting the depicted era. As Sarah escorted them to the Texas Bluebell Inn, they were greeted with friendly waves and cap tips. Again Erin was reminded of a theme park, where all the employees were in period costumes and always looked happy to be of service.

Yet no one tried to actually chat with them and Sarah hustled the team directly into the inn and up four flights of stairs to the top floor, where they were shown into a three bedroom suite with the same period style of décor. As Sarah had mentioned, platters of cold meats, cheeses, breads and salads had been set out for them on a long, rough-hewn wooden table in the common area.

As soon as Sarah left, Tripper checked the door. "It's locked."

Jamie and Ryan quickly inspected the windows. "They're all sealed shut," Jamie said when they rejoined the others.

Erin quickly cut off any discussion. "Look at the nice lunch spread they provided. I know I'm hungry. But first let's join hands and say a prayer of thanks." It only took a heartbeat for the team to remember that they were probably being observed and should refrain from airing any derogatory opinions or intentions aloud. With the twins' help everyone could communicate in silence.

As soon as the circle was formed, Ryan shared his thought. *Yeah, we're welcome to look out at the perfect village and see how content the townspeople are but we can't talk to them. Wonder if it's all a set-up for our benefit?*

I don't think so, Hari replied. *I'm quite sure we just saw some of the victims.*

You called them slaves, Tripper reminded her. *And that's how it seemed in my dream. But those people didn't look abused or frightened. They looked damned content.*

The operative word may be damned. I couldn't see any of their eyes to be sure, Erin added. *But I think we can assume they're all being manipulated. I just don't understand why.*

Peace had been quiet up to that moment. *I agree. Despite the pleasant expressions, I sensed that they were ill, perhaps in a mental rather than physical sense. If I could put my hands on one of them, I might be able to help them heal.*

Maybe that's why they don't want us roaming around on our own. They might think we could help free all of them, Tripper thought.

Erin smirked. *I'm sure that's only one of the reasons. Commanding us to appear then making us wait is a typical ploy of an egomaniac. Don't forget what I told you about playing to that ego. There's no telling what he'll do to us or these people if he feels insulted.*

Erin waited a moment to make sure no one had anything else to add, then let go of the hands on each side of her and said aloud, "Amen. Now let's have lunch before we get called to the presentation."

As they began serving themselves, Jamie mentioned a trip she had taken to Brazil and everyone went along with her non-controversial topic choice. To an outside observer, the team would look and sound relaxed.

Erin?

Roman! I'm here. In Eden. With most of the psych team.

What? No! You shouldn't be here.

They gave us no choice. Have you figured out how to break Eve's control?

Not really. I'm just suddenly awake again. And, unfortunately, I have no idea what happened since I got through to you before.

From what she said to me, she's been pumping you for information, and you've revealed quite a bit, like that you're an alien. She felt his anger, concern and dread.

Since our minds are joined, I guess you know…everything.

Yes, but fretting over the end of the world will have to wait until you're free to do something about it. Even if you think you have a chance to escape, don't. Not while she has your hair. Once I get that away from her, I will come for you.

I wish I could give you a hint of where I am, but there are no windows in this room.

That's okay. I seem to have developed the ability to follow your trail.

Ah, more evidence of your felan heritage. But just because you can doesn't mean you should.

I promise not to be overly brave. Meanwhile, take advantage of our minds being connected to catch up with everything I know.

"Erin, are you feeling all right?" Peace asked. "Do you need my help?"

Erin opened her eyes, noticed how they were all

watching her with concern, and smiled. "I'm fine, thank you. Just needed to rest my eyes for a minute."

Shortly after they finished eating, Sarah returned. "Time to meet your host."

"Absolutely," Erin said before anyone else could respond less positively. She rose and the others followed her example, swiftly queueing up behind Sarah.

At the end of the hall, Sarah placed her hand on the wall and a doorway-size section quietly slid away to reveal a mirror-lined elevator. The instant they were all inside, the door closed and only the slightest sensation alerted them to a downward movement. When the door opened again they were in another, much longer hallway, but this one had walls and floor of black glass with copper inlaid geometric designs. A few yards down the hall, Sarah placed her hand on the wall and another section slid silently away, creating an opening into a contemporary board room with comfortable seating for four on each side of the conference table.

"If you would all please be seated, Adam will join you in a moment." Sarah left the room and closed the wall behind her.

Erin, Ryan and Peace sat on the left side. Tripper Jamie and Hari took the right. No one spoke a word but their minds were all busy conjecturing. Several more minutes passed before a man and woman entered the room.

Erin felt the tension increase among her team. Although these two people were physically unimposing, the negativity radiating from them was nearly suffocating. They did not need to be told this was Adam and Eve.

As Adam's gaze quickly scanned the faces around the table, his eyes widened and his cheeks flushed.

"Where are the other two?" he muttered to Eve. "Didn't you tell her what would happen if one of them refused my invitation?"

Erin felt her stomach clench. Surely the explanation was adequate, but before she could say anything, Eve replied.

"I'm afraid the absence of the woman, Vicky Trumble, may have been my fault. When I broke through her shield—to protect you—I may have used more force than she could handle. And as to Doctor Cho, he was hardly Eden material. All show, no substance. Better to weed out the weak ones right away."

So, Erin thought, Eve had used Vicky to disrupt their circle. But that meant Eve still had something of hers also. Erin now had at least three tokens to recover.

Adam's hands balled into fists and he took several steps away from Eve then strode back before replying. When he did, his voice was strained with muffled anger. "Trumble's skill as a remote viewer was of value to me. I will not forget that you took that upon yourself. And *you* do not decide who qualifies for Eden. *I* do. *I* wanted Cho here. Maybe even more than any of them." With that last word, he waved a hand at the psych team.

Erin watched Adam's expression change in an instant, as though he just realized they were there. Erin had told the group he was unbalanced and an egomaniac, now they also knew the relationship between Adam and Eve was far from smooth.

"Excuse me," Hari said into the uneasy silence. "If I may be permitted to speak?" Her soft voice had an unusually melodic quality.

Adam turned his attention to Hari and nodded. "Haruko Zhang. I believe we met at one of Cho's seminars, but I don't believe we ever had a chance to speak."

"I wasn't given much opportunity to socialize," she replied, keeping her tone musical and her gaze fixed on his eyes. "As you know, I am Doctor Cho's apprentice and companion. I know he would have been here if it had been at all possible, but he had already left for Japan when Doctor Breswell called. I can assure you, however, that I have his proxy."

With each word Hari spoke, Adam's expression softened and his body relaxed. Erin had heard of such a vocal gift but had no idea Hari possessed it. She quickly glanced at the others. Despite their shields being up, they all seemed a bit calmer than they had minutes ago.

"In that case," Adam said, "I believe we can begin." He proceeded with the unnecessary formality of introducing Eve and himself and confirming the names of the psych team members and their acknowledged gifts.

When he identified Jamie and Ryan, his pleasant smile faltered. "We also met before. It was Career Day at one of the schools you attended. I had tried to tell you about my social experiment, but you weren't interested."

The twins glanced at one another then Jamie spoke. "You do look a little familiar, but our foster parents were very strict. We were never permitted to talk to anyone about our abilities, not even them. I do hope we weren't rude to you."

Sufficiently appeased by her sweet response, Adam dropped the matter and moved on. In case anyone in the room needed to be reminded of how brilliant he was, he spent several minutes boasting of his many accomplishments.

Roman? Are you listening?

It comes in and out. I need practice.

Erin felt a chill and glanced up to see Eve looking at her curiously. She quickly averted her gaze, but in her peripheral vision she saw Eve slip her fingers into the scoop neck of her loose-fitting blouse, as though she was adjusting it or her bra.

In a blink, Roman's mind was taken from her. It took all Erin's willpower not to jump to her feet and shout *aha!* She now knew for certain where Eve kept Roman's hair and how little it took for the woman to regain total control of him.

Or was Eve testing her? Perhaps she'd already gotten Roman to tell her that their minds were joined and the odd look was because she guessed they were communicating and wanted to send Erin a warning.

"I invited you all to the Garden of Eden so that you could see firsthand what I have been working on here. I call it The Eden Experiment. Not only is my domed Garden completely self-sufficient and safe from the evils of the world, including unwanted intruders, with the support of special, advanced people like yourselves, I am proving that the inferior masses can lead healthy, productive lives."

Erin could tell that Adam completely believed in his right to conduct his social experiment regardless of the fact that he had taken away his subjects' basic human rights. She was relieved to see that her team remembered the warning she'd given them and maintained looks of interest rather than judgment.

For nearly an hour, Adam elaborated on the advantages of his version of an isolationistic society, how free will was the downfall of the average individual, and how careful management of the thoughts and actions of the *little people* was the only way to save humanity.

Despite the radical content of his speech, Erin had

to admit that Adam had the sort of verbal passion and ethereal charisma that drew followers to a cause. Add that to his being a genius and having extrasensory abilities and she didn't doubt for a moment that this man could eventually become one of the worst despots the world has ever known. But whether he *would* become that anti-hero was no longer certain.

Erin felt a shift in Adam's presentation and brought her full attention back to him.

"Each one of you has a valuable gift which would enhance the operation of the Garden of Eden, and ensure the ultimate success of The Eden Experiment. In return, your lives would be enriched beyond your wildest dreams. Without the tedium of everyday survival, you would be free to concentrate on expanding your minds and discovering how best to use your sudden evolutionary elevation. All you have to do is accept my invitation to become part of something revolutionary...to dare to *make* history rather than simply observe it passing you by."

Adam paused and scanned their faces. "But before you make your decision, I have arranged for several of my shepherds to take you on a tour of Eden, including the administrative sector, where you are now, and the facilities where you would reside as a shepherd. Afterward, you will be taken to our dining room for a gourmet feast."

Erin raised her hand and Adam reluctantly nodded to her. "I just wanted you to know that, although we were not...*comfortable* with how we were...*invited* here, we are all looking forward to seeing what you've created. However, at the risk of seeming disrespectable, there is one question on everyone's mind that we would like answered before we go any further."

Adam made her wait a few beats before allowing

the question.

"Thank you," Erin said politely. "Our question is this, if we accept your invitation and become one of your shepherds, would we be required to do anything...*illegal*?"

Adam narrowed his eyes at her. "If you are referring to the laws of the New Republic of Texas, or even the North American States, we do not recognize any governing body beyond Eden's dome. But be assured, you will never be required to do anything against your personal morals...unless absolutely necessary to your survival."

CHAPTER 21

In the three hours between Adam's presentation and the service of dessert in the formal dining room of the underground administrative sector, Erin and her team were never left alone. Using a horse-drawn wagon, shepherds Sarah, Seth and Rebekah escorted them from one end of Eden to the other. When they were on foot, *herded* might have been a more relevant word since one shepherd was always at the front, one off to a side and one brought up the rear. The tour, as extensive as it was, did not permit any straying. Seth and Rebekah, both gingers, were quite a few years younger and far less cordial than Sarah. They were clearly bored with the assignment they'd been given.

There was no question Adam Sirilovich had established a self-sufficient community, all of which was kept humming by contented worker bees. The psych team was even allowed to speak briefly to a few of them. The subjects looked healthy and showed pride in their work. None of them expressed unhappiness with their situations. When prompted by Sarah, they each recalled having willingly signed confidential, exclusive, long-term contracts to be part of The Eden Experiment. If Erin didn't know their behavior was being psychically manipulated, she would have considered Eden a remarkably, or perhaps incredibly, successful commune. At least it did not appear they were being controlled by fear or physical abuse.

And yet, when Erin was able to get a good look at their eyes, she detected a hint of mental vacancy. Worse, although the residents were unaware of it, Adam and Eve clearly considered them easily expendable.

Within her own group, a shift had taken place. Tripper was practically stuck to her side in front. He seemed taller, stronger and definitely more alert to his surroundings. He had obviously decided it was his job to be her protector. Jamie and Ryan stayed close on their heels and Hari and Peace maintained watchful positions behind them. As serene as everything appeared, they could not forget there were deadly snakes in this Garden of Eden.

Thirteen people gathered for dinner, including two shepherds Erin's team had not previously met—a tall, heavy-set young man named Noah, and Abel, a very short, middle-aged man whose head moved back and forth as he constantly scanned the room and whose dinner plate remained empty. Her group was seated at one large, round table; Adam's was at another. Erin heard mention of someone named Cain, but no information about any of the shepherds' specific gifts was shared, nor was there any way to tell how many more of them Adam had recruited. The fact that they all had biblical names suggested they were given aliases to fit in with the Garden of Eden theme. This was the sort of information Roman would have obtained for Chief Friedrich…if he had been able to invisibly infiltrate Eden as he had planned.

She was wondering how much longer it would be

before they could return to their suite and exchange thoughts when Adam rose and tapped his water goblet with a spoon.

"I have a marvelous surprise for everyone. We have a very, *very* special guest with us this evening, someone who can help us take The Eden Experiment to an even higher level."

Adam touched his ear, murmured something and stared expectantly at the entranceway to the dining room. A moment later, Eve entered with her arm entwined with Roman's.

Erin's breath caught in her throat and the gaze of every member of her team darted from Roman to her and back to Roman as he and Eve strolled up to Adam.

"Rest," Eve said to Roman and his eyes closed. She let go of his arm then walked over to where Erin was seated. "As you can see, he is unharmed, just mentally controlled. By me, and only me. Don't be hurt that he didn't say hello, he isn't aware that anyone else is in the room besides me." Eve's gaze skimmed over the other psych team members. "I'm sure you've all wondered about the bodyguard's background and what sort of relationship he has with your prim and proper Doctor Breswell. You may as well know, they are very definitely...*intimate*, no matter what she's told you."

Eve crossed to the table of shepherds. "I apologize for keeping him a secret from all of you, but we had to be sure." Adam loudly cleared his throat and Eve reluctantly stopped talking and took the seat that had been left vacant for her.

While everyone's attention was on Adam and Eve's silent exchange of glares, Tripper took the opportunity to lean toward Erin and whisper, "I've got a really bad feeling."

"Justified," she whispered back. "But no matter what is said in the next few minutes, do not act. Not yet. Not while she has control of Roman's mind. There's no telling what she could make him do." She felt Eve's stare and gave Adam her full attention as he continued his after-dinner speech.

"This fellow—" Adam pointed at the unconscious Roman. "Well, perhaps fellow is not the correct term for him. You see, we have discovered that Roman has at least one super power none of us has. More importantly…" He paused to make sure everyone in the room was looking at him. "He's not one of us. He's actually an alien from a civilization advanced far beyond our own. Doctor Breswell, if you would be so kind as to confirm this to your team."

They all stared at her, waiting for her denial, a response, a sign, anything but a confirmation of Adam's outrageous claim. Suddenly a spark of an idea pushed its way to the front of her thoughts. It felt as though it was borne in Roman's knowledge but blended with her profiling abilities. It greatly depended on Adam's megalomania and partly relied on his and Eve's personal power struggle. If it worked, Roman could be freed and able to proceed with saving the planet, and Adam's dark reign as Damien might never transpire.

With the feeling that she was about to jump out of a plane without knowing if her parachute would open, she slowly got to her feet, walked up to Roman and stroked his cheek. She had hoped her touch might interrupt Eve's control, but it made no difference. She was on her own.

"What Eve said is true. Roman and I are…very close." She then faced Adam and gave him a nod of submission. "And what Adam said is also true. Roman is from another world." From the murmur that passed through the room, it was clear that her confirmation had been needed, even by the shepherds.

"*But*," she said emphatically, hushing the room, then addressing Adam directly. "He's only of minimal use to you like this. I can certainly understand why Eve would want to maintain total control of his mind, but this is *your* project. You should be communicating with him directly, with his mind fully intact."

Eve tried to interrupt but Adam held up his index finger and she held her tongue.

Erin continued with just a bit more confidence. "Roman's people have great respect for genius like yours and under the Noronian Code of Honesty, if you made a deal with him, he would have to abide by it."

Adam's eyes showed interest while Eve's expression turned murderous. Everyone else in the room seemed to be sitting on the edges of their chairs, ready to run or dive for cover if necessary.

After giving Erin's words some thought, Adam asked, "What sort of deal?"

Erin purposely sauntered around the two tables, looking intently into each person's eyes, as though she were deciding who else she should toss onto the fire with Eve. Though she wasn't thinking anything of the sort, it gave her an extra minute to organize her thoughts. She stopped on the opposite side of the room from Adam, physically including everyone in the forthcoming discussion.

"Earlier you said you have no regard for the authority of the various governmental bodies. However, as long as Eden is legally situated within the New Republic of Texas, there remains the possibility of interference, whether you like it or not. Also, you're very proud of Eden's being totally self-sufficient and independent, but the truth is, if something went wrong, you know you have a safety net just beyond the dome. There is no doubt of the value of The Eden Experiment, but wouldn't it be more of an accomplishment without the safety net?"

The look on Adam's face suggested he couldn't tell if he'd just been flattered or insulted. "If you're suggesting I buy an island or stage a military coup in a small country—"

"Certainly not. Anyone with enough money could do that. I'm suggesting you relocate Eden to another *planet*." Erin had to wait a moment for the new wave of murmurs to quiet down. "One that is primitive in nature but capable of supporting human life. A newly discovered and as yet *unclaimed* planet. Your name would go down in history for such a grand endeavor."

She could see he was skeptical. So she paused, dramatically rolled her eyes and shook her head. "I'm sorry. I realize I've overstepped. I've seen what you've accomplished here. Your lives are comfortable, predictable. You've proven your theory. Why would you want to risk failure?"

"I've never failed," Adam said defensively.

"Exactly," Erin replied.

"You said the planet is *unclaimed*. How would one go about claiming an entire planet?"

"The same way the United States claimed the moon. By being the first to plant a flag on it."

"And just how would we get there?"

"Roman would take you."

"On a spaceship?"

"Of course."

Adam grinned. "Would I be able to name the planet Eden?"

She shrugged. "I don't see why not. It would be even more appropriate than what you have here."

"And did you say it's uninhabited?"

"No, I said it is primitive. If the information Roman was given is accurate, there may be a small colony of humans already living there. But that shouldn't be a problem for your shepherds."

Adam paced back and forth in front of the room several times before speaking again. "I will admit to being intrigued. It definitely fits in with my visions. It just never occurred to me—" He stopped talking aloud but the changes on his face and the movement of his hands implied that he continued his thoughts in silence. Apparently coming to a conclusion of some sort, he returned his attention to Erin. "What would Roman want in exchange for passage to this planet?"

"Release him from Eve's control. He has an urgent mission of such great importance to his planet that it would be worth his assisting you to be able to get on with his assignment. Second, his hair and any other tokens that Eve, or any other shepherd has acquired, from any of my people must be returned. Third, you must promise not to harm a single one of the subjects here."

Eve got to her feet so quickly, her chair fell backward. "This is ridiculous, Adam. Don't you see what she's doing? She's using your ego and childhood fantasies to manipulate you. She's making it all up!"

Erin strode up to Adam. "You don't have to take my word for it. Order her to wake up Roman and order him to answer as to whether he could get a spaceship and take you to another planet. Ask him about the Code of Honesty. She's obviously made him tell her other secrets." Erin's intuition pushed her to say more. "I bet she already learned about his mission and the ship and was just keeping it to herself. In fact, I know she hasn't told you everything she's learned. And by the way, when you make her turn over the tokens of my people, you should make sure you get back whatever she has of yours."

Adam inhaled sharply, his hands balled into fists and his cheeks flushed. Despite the physical response, his voice remained eerily calm. "Is that true, Eve? Do you have something of mine that you've been using to control me?"

Eve groaned aloud, dramatically raising her gaze and her outstretched arms to heaven. "As God is my witness, I swear, she's lying! How can you question me, Adam? You know I'm completely loyal. Everything I've done has been to assist you."

He stared at her for several seconds then said, "In that case, you won't mind submitting to a little test to prove that."

"I will if she will." Eve pointed at Erin.

"Doctor Breswell?"

She had no choice but to continue to trust her intuition. "May I ask who will conduct the test?"

Adam's gaze moved from face to face. "Your twins for Eve, Rebekah for you. With a mutual agreement to only seek the truth of what has been said here."

Erin could see the panic rising in Eve's eyes. She had nothing to lose by agreeing. "That's acceptable to me." She motioned for Jamie and Ryan to come forward.

Eve glanced at the doorway and took a step toward it. "All right. I'll admit that I have something of yours but I'll give it back. I swear, I've never used it. It was only a precaution—"

Her next words were cut off, as Abel raised his right hand toward her and a ball of silvery-blue light shot out of his palm. In an instant, Eve was gone, with only a small pile of dust on the floor to mark her former existence.

CHAPTER 22

Roman slowly raised one eyelid then the other. He had no idea where he was, but at least he was out of the windowless cell and once again free of Eve's control. Or was he? The scene he awoke to appeared to be a living tableau in a formal banquet room, a man and woman standing, ten people sitting at two round tables, all frozen in mid-action. His gaze shot back to the woman. *Erin!*

She instantly spun around, realized Roman was awake and ran into his arms. Their movement stirred everyone else to action. Erin's psych team got to their feet but stayed huddled on their side of the room. All but two of the others left the room quickly.

Roman felt Erin's body quivering and held her even tighter. The moment he wondered what was going on, he saw it all in his mind.

Erin let out a shaky sigh of relief. "I took a big chance—"

"And it worked. I have my mind back."

"And you're not upset…about my promising you'd take them to another planet?"

Roman chuckled and lifted her chin so he could see her eyes. They were glowing pure gold. "How could I be upset with a stroke of brilliance? In fact, *shalla*, I might have done the same thing if I had the chance."

"I think it *was* your idea. I just added some icing."

"You see, it's not so bad having two brains to work with." He was relieved to see her almost smile at that. "Tell me about the man Adam's talking to. I have the scene in my head but I can't tell what happened."

She eased away from him to take a look. "That's Abel. All I know is he seems very low-profile but he's second in command here and just reduced Eve to dust in the blink of an eye. Not sure if it was an extrasensory ability or a weapon built into his hand. But either way, I gather one of his jobs is executioner of anyone who defies Adam."

Roman frowned. "Good to know. Any chance you can use some of that special icing of yours to convince Adam to leave his muscle behind when we leave?"

Before Erin could respond, Adam approached and held his hand out toward Roman. "I'm sorry to interrupt this reunion, but I can't wait a minute longer to meet you, Roman. I'm Adam and I apologize for how you were mishandled. Thanks to Doctor Breswell's insight, I now realize Eve may have been manipulating my decisions for some time."

The last thing Roman was expecting from Adam was a gracious apology. He forced himself to smother his anger and reply in kind. "Unpleasant things often happen for beneficial reasons."

Adam smiled broadly. "I agree completely." He turned to Erin. "Perhaps you'd like to reassure your team that Roman is well and send them back to the inn. I'm sure we can trust them not to wander...under the circumstances. Then, the three of us can sit down and take care of the fine strokes of the deal you made on Roman's behalf."

Tell them—

We'll tell them everything together, Erin thought to Roman. *Just keep up the cooperative pretense and we'll all avoid the wrath of Abel.*

In the minutes it took Erin to convince her team to return to the inn, the tables had been cleared, Adam ordered a meal for Roman and hot tea for her.

"You mentioned a deal," Roman said to Adam once they were seated. "I hope Erin promised something I can actually deliver." He kept his tone light and smiled at Erin but he barely breathed as he waited for Adam's response. He had no idea how much he had unconsciously revealed to Eve or what she had passed on to Adam.

His tension ebbed considerably as Adam related the basics of what Erin had promised. It was immediately apparent that Adam was *not* aware that his and Erin's minds were joined and that he already knew everything she had said.

Did you bring my ring? He asked Erin while Adam was talking.

The ring and your pistols are in my boots. No one checked...or they didn't care.

Considering Abel's ability, I'm guessing they weren't worried about our attempting a takeover.

Your phone?

Blocked.

"Did she exaggerate?" Adam asked.

"Not at all," Roman replied. "Because of my mission, I had already arranged for a ship and pilot. I can have it brought here and depart without any Terran awareness. But there are two issues that I have no control over." The arrival of his meal gave him an excuse to pause for effect, but the sight and smell of it made him aware of how hungry he was.

Adam impatiently tapped his fingers on the table as

Roman ate a chunk of bread and some vegetables before continuing.

"The first issue is the ship itself. It's mainly used for cargo transport with minimal accommodations for passengers. Even though we should reach the…I mean *your* planet in a matter of hours, there is only space for about a hundred people. Plus you'll have to limit how much equipment and supplies you want to transport."

Adam had grinned at the reference to his having his own planet but was clearly displeased with having to deal with restrictions. "You said there were two issues."

Roman nodded as he took another mouthful of food, chewed and swallowed. "The second is the bigger problem. Before Eve hijacked my mind, I had met with Chief Friedrich. The Rangers are prepared to launch a full-scale raid on Eden. I had convinced him to wait until I could scout out the situation for him. Even if I contact him immediately, I may only be able to buy you another day. In other words, you have about twenty-four hours to be ready to go."

Adam took a moment to absorb the additional challenge before moving on. "Erin said the planet is primitive but habitable. Have you been there?"

"No, but I know of two people who have and survived," Roman said honestly, thinking of Tarla Yan and the engineer, Geoffrey Cookson. "Unfortunately, it's the only one I'm familiar with that is unclaimed. If we get there and it's not acceptable, I can bring you back here."

Adam smirked. "Where the Rangers will be waiting to wage war. If I just stay inside the dome, they can't get to us."

"Are you absolutely sure about that?" Erin asked. "Chief Friedrich knew about Roman and where he was from. He implied the Rangers have access to some very advanced alien weaponry from—"

"*Erin!*" Roman said harshly.

"I know, top secret and all that, but I think it's too late to worry about revealing secrets. Besides, I gave Adam my word that we would help him if he helped us."

Adam gave Erin a nod of appreciation. "Speaking of which…" He raised his arm, waved and Abel approached carrying a black metal box.

As he handed the box to Adam, Roman noticed the lock had been melted, probably a bit more of Abel's handiwork.

Adam raised the lid and turned the box so that Erin could see its contents. It was packed with tiny, black velvet jeweler's pouches. "You required the return of any of the tokens in Eve's possession that came from your people. Abel, are you certain these are *all* the tokens she had?" Abel whispered something in his ear, then Adam relayed his response. "These are all that were not on her person. Those were destroyed in front of you. However as you can see, there is no quick way to identify who each token belongs to, so unless you have an objection, I will have Abel destroy all of them."

"In front of us, please," Roman requested.

Adam moved the box to the far side of the table and gestured to Abel. The second in command held his right hand over the open box, a pea-size ball of blue light dropped from his palm into the collection of pouches and, in the blink of an eye, nothing but dust was left in the box.

The demonstration allowed Roman to deduce that the man himself was a weapon and he had control over its strength.

Considering one of those was Adam's, I think we

can trust what we just saw, Erin thought to Roman. To Adam, she asked, "Am I correct in assuming most of those tokens belonged to, um, subjects of The Eden Experiment?"

Adam nodded. "Eve directed the behavior of approximately one hundred of the residents. Seth and Sarah were in charge of the remainder."

"Do they keep tokens as well?" Erin asked nonchalantly.

"No, they require proximity and regular physical contact. How does Jamie's gift work?"

Erin blinked and lied. "The same way. Physical contact. I hope you don't mind all my questions, but I'm sure you understand how your experiment has roused my professional curiosity. You said you now feel as though Eve had been manipulating some of your decisions, though obviously you didn't realize it at the time. Once Eve...was gone, did all of her charges wake up, like Roman did?"

"Yes, but remember, they came here willingly and have no idea that time has passed. Abel simply had Seth and Sarah gather them in a barn and put them to sleep, while I decide our next step. From what Roman said, I would be forced to whittle down our numbers considerably..."

"You mustn't hurt any of them," Erin blurted out. "If you want Roman to help you establish a new world, you must release the ones you leave behind, *unharmed.*"

Adam arched a brow at her. "That was not one of your conditions."

"But we're adding it now," Roman said firmly.

"I will consider it...in exchange for a small demonstration of your ability."

Erin sent Roman a quick thought. *I'm pretty sure Eve only knew about your disappearing act, not the walking through walls part.*

Roman got to his feet, took several steps away from the table and vanished.

Adam laughed out loud. "That is amazing. Eve was right about one thing, you would have been a great asset...but only if we remained here." As Roman became visible again, Adam stood. "I understand that time is of the essence, but I need to meet with my shepherds. Go back to the inn and we'll come to you when a decision has been reached."

Adam watched the alien and psych doctor walk away with their arms around each other. Even if Eve had held back some of the information she'd learned, she'd told him enough to know that what was being offered was truly possible. It was the extreme version of the future visions he'd had.

He didn't doubt for a minute that the Rangers were standing by, ready to pounce, but it had never occurred to him that they might have a weapon that could puncture Eden's protective dome. And, assuming that was also true, the vision he'd seen of being a leader of masses would never come to pass. *Unless he was no longer on planet Earth.*

As the alien had said, some things happen for a reason, and now he understood how the future he'd seen, and become totally committed to, was going to come to pass...just in a different way than he'd assumed.

It was too bad about Eve. Despite her ambition and dishonesty, she had valuable skills, and he had really looked forward to the sexual games she had enticed him with. But Abel did what he promised to do as second in command—protect Adam. As long as Abel was at his back, he had no fear of whatever trick his opponents might have in mind.

However, he preferred to know what they were thinking in advance and, without being able to have Cain or Rebekah read their minds, he had to spy the old-fashioned way. He could only hope their little victory would make them less careful. He didn't actually need to meet with his shepherds before announcing his decision. They would never consider defying him after watching Abel eliminate one of their own. Instead, Adam headed for Noah's lab to personally observe the goings-on at the inn.

CHAPTER 23

Erin and Roman entered the suite holding hands and never let go for the next hour as they related the conversation they'd had with Adam and answered the team's questions about Roman's true identity. A signal from Erin reminded everyone that they were probably being observed and, with Abel's retribution in mind, everyone carefully avoided vocalizing any negative comments about their host or his shepherds.

Roman was explaining the Noronian Code of Honesty when Ryan said, "I want to go."

Erin released Roman's hand in order to comfort Ryan. Placing her hand on his shoulder, she used her compassionate voice. "I know. We all do. And if we just keep using our heads, we'll all be home in—"

"Um, Erin," Jamie interrupted. "That's not what he meant."

Erin turned toward Jamie and frowned.

"He meant he wants to go on the spaceship. We all do."

"Absolutely not," Roman replied quickly. "It's too risky. None of you should even be here."

"We came to save you," Peace said gently.

"And I am extremely grateful, but—"

"We took a vote," Tripper cut in. "And we all decided to accept Adam's offer to become shepherds if he decides to claim that planet."

Go along with it, Erin thought to Roman. *If Adam's listening, this could be the bait needed to get him to go for it and agree to free the ones left behind. She gave Tripper a quick wink to let him know they understood what he was doing.*

And what about the ones he takes?

Erin's mouth curved into smile. *I have no doubt you'll figure out how to strand the bad guys and get all of us back here safely. And by the way, don't underestimate Tripper.* She felt him absorb the secret Tripper had shared with her and watched his shoulders relax a tiny bit.

Roman pinched the bridge of his nose, sighed and shook his head. "It could be dangerous, even deadly. The planet is barely habitable."

"We could all go down in history," countered Jamie.

"Besides, you would never simply drop us off without checking things out," added Peace.

Though Hari said nothing, she met Roman's gaze with a look that assured him of her support.

Erin brought the subject to a close by saying, "This isn't worth debating until we hear Adam's decision."

Her assumption that they were being closely watched was confirmed when a very self-satisfied Adam arrived seconds later with Abel at his back.

"I have a follow-up question. How were you planning to get the spaceship here?"

"I would go—"

"No. I don't trust you to leave. I am sure you have a way of contacting your world and requesting the ship be brought to this location. Are you willing to do that?"

Roman's expression turned troubled but then he

shrugged. "Yes. I can manage that."

"How soon?"

"By sunrise at the latest. It depends on my pilot's schedule, but I did alert him to my need to hitch a ride in regard to a mission when I last saw him."

"Good. We will begin choosing the passengers immediately. Besides my shepherds and your team, it sounds like we're limited to taking about eighty-five subjects. Correct?"

"Ninety max," Roman replied.

"And you will also contact Chief Friedrich and advise him to wait another day."

"Agreed."

"We will need a schematic of the storage area to figure out what supplies and equipment we can bring."

Roman got a piece of paper and a pencil from the suite's desk drawer and wrote down an approximation of the measurements. "Don't worry about the weight, just the cubic feet. And remember, think *primitive*. If you don't bring enough food, you may have to hunt until your farm is productive. And there must be water but I would make sure you—"

"Thank you," Adam interrupted and took the paper. "I think I've got the idea."

"And don't forget a flag," Ryan said with a broad smile.

Adam chuckled and gave him a mock salute as he turned to leave.

"Stop!" commanded Erin and Adam turned back to her with a look of surprise. "Before Roman has the ship brought here, we want your guarantee that no one left behind will be harmed in any way."

For a moment it seemed that Adam might refuse but then his expression softened. "Of course. As you have negotiated, those left behind will be unharmed and waiting in the barn for the Rangers to pick them up. Security systems will be disengaged and the dome will be set to remain rolled back after our departure."

"Also," Erin added. "No traps, bombs or anything else to stop or injure the Rangers or the subjects as they leave."

"Agreed," Adam stated firmly. "*No one* will be harmed as long as we depart safely."

"What about residual messages?" asked Jamie, the one who would know about such mental devices.

"Those left behind will remember nothing of the past months in Eden and neither Seth nor Sarah is capable of leaving delayed instructions once they are separated from their charges. I believe we are now in accord on all aspects of the matter and can agree to a truce for the remainder of our time together. Doctor Breswell, is that acceptable to you?"

As she looked at each person in her group, they nodded. "Yes, as long as it is understood we will continue to maintain our personal psychic shields."

Adam almost smirked then smiled. "Of course. As will we. Now, I have a lot to arrange before sunrise, so I bid you all what I will not have—a good night's rest."

Truce or not, they were once again locked in the suite, but this time, anticipation replaced anxiety.

Roman spoke before anyone else had a chance to express their thoughts. "Adam's right. You all need to get some sleep and I need to make arrangements, which I can do right here."

"Don't be ridiculous," Jamie said with a laugh. "You and Erin take that room." She pointed to the bedroom that was separated from the other two by the common area. "Trip and Ryan can take that one and Hari, Peace and I can share the one with the two big beds. Okay, everyone off to your own rooms. *Now.*

Sunrise will be here before you know it."

"She can be so bossy sometimes," Ryan said with a smirk but he and Tripper headed for the room Jamie had assigned them.

Two bedroom doors closed before Roman spoke again. "Well, Doctor Breswell, we better not disobey such a direct order." He held out his hand and Erin placed hers on it. Keeping his gaze on her eyes, he brought the back of her hand up to his lips for a light kiss then led her into the bedroom. He closed the door, switched off the light and drew her into his embrace.

"Never in my worst nightmare did I imagine having a day like today," Erin murmured against his solid chest.

With his mouth close to her ear, he whispered, "I'm sorry I couldn't help. It was my duty to make sure no harm came to you. Instead, you were sucked right into the serpent's garden because of me."

She rose on tiptoes, gave him a soft kiss on his cheek and whispered, "But it was *my* job to find the serpent, so it was because of *me* that you got kidnapped."

Roman tightened his hold on her for a moment. "All right, we can share the blame. This time. Now, as much I appreciate Jamie's thoughtfulness, I think we should assume a lack of privacy." He kissed her ear, her cheek and the curve of her neck.

"I'm sure you're right," Erin murmured, "but…just to help me forget what a horrible day this was, I wouldn't be horribly embarrassed by a kiss or two."

He kissed her forehead, her nose and each eyelid. "I could use a little of that myself, but there's nothing in my experience with you that suggests we could stop after a kiss or two."

Wasn't the fever cured by our joining?

He planted several more pecks on her face and neck. *Hard for me to tell. I've been unconscious most of the time since. How have you been feeling?*

Other than being terrified and angry and worried...I think I'm back to normal. I mean, you're making me want you...

His chest moved with a silent chuckle. *I know. I feel your arousal as if it were my own. Very, very hard to resist.* His hands eased down her back, grasped her rear and brought her hips against his, just to show her how strongly her arousal affected him. *Maybe they can't see in the dark.*

Erin took a deep breath and gently pressed against his chest. *And maybe they can. Even if they weren't interested in voyeurism, I'm sure they're watching to make sure you make those two calls.*

It was Roman's turn to take a slow breath and ease away. "Business first," he said aloud. *Ring, please. Discreetly.*

Erin sat down on the bed, removed her boots and tapped the one with the ring and a laser pistol inside. "Do you need a light?" she asked reaching for the lamp on the nightstand.

"No, thanks." *I'd rather not make it that easy for them to see how I do this.* Sitting down beside her on the bed, he made a show of removing his own shoes while he reached into the boot, palmed the ring and, as smoothly as possible, moved the laser pistol from the boot to the waistband of his pants.

Though Erin knew the ring could be used as a telecommunicator between Innerworld and the Earth's surface, she was still fascinated when she heard a strange, almost warbling voice echo through the room. She knew instantly that it was Roman's pilot friend, Prince.

"Roman?"

"I'm glad I got through to you. Remember the secret mission I told you about?"

"Of course."

"It's on, but I need your help even more than I thought I would."

"Whatever it is, I can do it."

Erin was simultaneously relieved that Roman had such a true friend and awed by the fact that she was listening to him order up a spacecraft as easily as having a pizza delivered. Roman gave him the coordinates and arrival time along with the instruction that he remain in stealth mode the entire time he was in Outerworld's atmosphere. He also repeated twice how important it was that absolutely no one discover where he was actually going.

"Couldn't he get in trouble for this?" Erin asked after Roman disconnected from Prince.

"No. It's all on me." He felt her worry as sharply as a needle prick. "But I don't intend to get into trouble either. Prince has a legitimate flight to Norona already scheduled. The detour should be quick enough to go unnoticed. And if not, I have a plan."

Erin clucked her tongue at him. "That's a lie. You don't even have a hint of a plan. But we do have two brains now so I have to believe we'll figure something out. One thing at a time."

He gave her a hug and a kiss on the temple. "Right. We have a ship coming in the morning. On to calling Chief. Do you want to talk to him?"

She shook her head. "You'll be able to hold things back better than I would. But let him know I am with you. I had Nola give him a rather cryptic message this morning. I'm sure he's fretting."

Despite Chief's fretting and demanding more information, Roman managed to keep the call time down to a minimum. With a guarantee of no resistance from anyone in Eden, Roman got Chief's promise to stand down for twenty-four more hours, then arrive with an airbus or two to transport the residents back to Austin for debriefing. He also had to swear that Erin was perfectly fine and they'd provide him with every minute detail when they returned. What he did not say was *when* they would be returning.

Do you think that will satisfy Adam? he thought to Erin.

I sure hope so because it sure didn't satisfy Chief.

Roman tugged Erin to her feet, pulled down the bed covers and moved the pistol from his waistband to under a pillow. A moment later, he stretched out on the bed and patted the space next to him.

Are you sure? Erin thought even as she nestled against him and pulled a sheet over them.

I'm sure you're exhausted and I have a plan to work out. Despite how much of a distraction you are, I'll be able to think much more clearly as long as I know you're safe.

She sighed and relaxed a little. *I'm sorry I fell asleep last night before—*

Hush. He turned on his side and tucked her more firmly into his curved body. *Forget about what Eve did. You rescued me and she's gone.*

I wasn't thinking about Eve's kidnapping you. I was going to say, I was sorry I fell asleep before you had a chance to show me...the slow way. She felt his sex stir against her bottom. *I suppose we could—*

Uh-uh. Not like that. And especially not here. Now go to sleep or I'll put you on the floor and shut you out of my head.

Can you do that now?

He chuckled. *I can definitely put you on the floor.*

Erin fell asleep with a smile on her face.

Roman's smile kept him awake for several hours. He had barely nodded off when Prince sent the alert that he was on his way.

He gave Erin a kiss on her head and gently shook her shoulder. "Time to get up. Better hurry." As soon as he was certain she was moving, he hurried to the other bedrooms, knocked and ordered, "Everybody up! You don't want to miss this." To the common room in general, he said, "Whoever's listening, it's time to let us out. The ship is about to arrive and I need to be there or it may not land."

By the time the team was gathered with their overnight bags, the door to the suite was opened by Sarah. "Good morning everyone." To Roman she said, "The dome has been rolled back and the field has been marked so the pilot should have no problem seeing where to land. If you're ready to go, I'll take you there now."

An uncharacteristically modern hoverbus awaited them in front of the inn.

"Thank God," Tripper murmured to Erin. "I don't think Roman would have had the patience to ride in the nag-wagon."

Erin smiled. "He is pretty anxious to show off a bit of his world. He always has to keep everything a secret from people he meets out here."

"Out here?" Tripper said with a laugh. "It sounds like you're already thinking like him."

She shrugged lightly and stepped into the bus.

When they reached the field, Adam and the other shepherds were already there. Roman directed everyone to an area he estimated would be safe and, discreetly using his ring, he gave Prince the signal to come in.

Erin neither heard nor saw anything unusual. The only indication that something was happening was a gust of wind that lasted about ten seconds…and a wink from Roman. A dozen more seconds passed with nothing happening.

And then, like a bit of techno-magic, the enormous ship became visible. Although Roman had implied this craft was limited in size, it was at least two stories at its highest point and about two hundred feet long. The shape reminded Erin of a perched hawk. A wide door opened in the tail section that was touching the ground and out came…*a giant, walking octopus.*

That's Prince, Roman thought to her. *You're going to love him.*

She smiled but her response was cut off at the sight of a monstrous, four-legged creature galloping past Prince and straight for Roman.

While everyone quickly backed up, the hairy beast knocked Roman to the ground, caged him between his mighty legs and proceeded to lick his face.

"Prince!" Roman yelled.

"Dog! Heel!" Prince's mouth formed a toothless smile as he extended one arm to help the two-legged Roman to his feet. The four-legged one stood obediently at Prince's side but was barely controlling his desire to pounce again.

"I told him about you so he recognized you right away he is really smart."

Roman grinned. "I thought you named him after me."

"I did but people in Innerworld sometimes got confused so I started calling him Dog and he seemed to like that better he wants you to rub behind his ears now."

As Roman did his best to say hello to the incredibly large dog, Erin stepped toward Prince and held out her hand. "Hello, Prince. I'm Erin. It is truly a pleasure to meet Roman's best friend."

Prince curled the end of one arm around her wrist and lowered his bulbous head far enough to touch the back of her hand to his silky cheek. "And I am very happy to meet Roman's pretty Terran friend who he said he was not going to play with but I did not believe him."

Erin grinned. Prince's voice sounded like he was gargling water while speaking but she had no trouble understanding him...or picking up on the fact that Roman had talked about her to his friend. She couldn't help but wonder when that happened.

Right after the Oval Office meeting.

That long ago, huh? She would have teased him a bit more except for noting the cautious approach of her group.

There was no way to stop any of them from gaping at Prince, but each person politely shook hands with the octoman as Roman introduced them.

Satisfied the animal was subdued, Adam's group stepped forward for their introductions but abruptly backed up again as the mastiff emitted a low, warning growl and the hackles rose down his back. Peace hurried forward, knelt down beside the dog and whispered in his ear as she stroked his broad chest.

"It's all right now," Peace told Adam. "His instincts are highly developed and if one of you is feeling fear, he interprets that as a possible threat. He was just protecting his companion. I've assured him that none of you intend to harm Prince or any of his friends. But I would recommend you approach slowly."

Adam frowned at her, but remained at a distance as Roman introduced the shepherds to Prince.

"You know, Doc," Jamie murmured as she and Ryan inched closer to Erin, "up until this minute, I was still thinking you might've concocted the whole Roman's-an-alien thing."

"I told her it was real," Ryan declared proudly. "But that horse-dog is almost as much of a surprise as our pilot. It's good to know Peace really can talk to animals. Who knows what we're going to run into where we're going."

Erin noted the body language of Adam's huddled group. He may have called a truce but they were not to be trusted. She caught Tripper and Hari's attention and they joined her and the twins. Turning her back on Adam's group, she kept her voice low. "Adam knows you all said you wanted to be shepherds. Maybe you should show your interest to them more directly. Try to insinuate yourselves with them today, maybe help them with their supplies. Hari, Roman and I could use your brain, unless you wanted to practice your telekinesis."

Hari's mouth almost smiled. "Considering how limited my skill is, it would just be embarrassing. I'd rather brainstorm with you."

"You want us to spy on them?" Ryan muttered with his hand over his mouth.

"Carefully," Erin said. "Tripper, I trust you to keep them out of trouble. Speaking of which, there's something in my left boot I want you to have. I'm about to stumble and the four of you will fuss while I make the pass. Ready, set, go."

In the blink of an eye, before anyone else could rush to poor, clumsy Erin's assistance, Tripper was armed.

Nice.

I thought so, Erin told Roman. *Prince's protector gave us a reminder to stay alert, so I've suggested Jamie, Ryan & Tripper show Adam how much they want to be shepherds by offering to help load.*

Another good move. Peace has obviously established who she'll be working with. Now if you, Hari and I could just work on a plan...

Roman walked over to Adam, who was still keeping his distance even though Prince, Dog, Peace and Hari had all gone back inside the ship. "Still want to do this?" he asked Adam bluntly.

Adam huffed. "As long as that beast is controlled."

"How about a look at the cargo hold so you can get started. Prince only has a few hours to spare for this detour, so…"

"Of course. Show us the way."

For the next several hours, Adam, Abel, Noah, Seth and Sarah directed the loading process, while their army of sheep blindly toiled. Rebekah had been assigned to "help" Erin's group inside the ship. However, because Dog was on the bridge with them, Rebekah didn't get close enough to actually tell if they were plotting against Adam. To further convince her they were doing nothing to be concerned about, they played a dice game called cubit…which turned out to be fun *and* the perfect cover while they came up with The Plan.

At one point, Erin took a break and attempted a conversation with Rebekah, who still seemed to be bored in spite of the unusual circumstance.

"Are you looking forward to traveling in space?" Erin began.

"It doesn't matter."

"Well, I'm certainly excited. About the trip *and* seeing another planet. Now *that's* certainly something I never expected to do."

When a shrug was Rebekah's only response, Erin tried a different topic. "I've heard the name Cain a few times, but I haven't met anyone by that name. Is he coming with us?" That got a hint of a reaction.

"Who knows? Ever since you and your people arrived, Adam's confined Cain to his room. Maybe he didn't want you to know about him…or vice-versa."

"That's curious. Is he...*different*?"

Rebekah shrugged again. "Since he's the only kid here, I'd say that makes him different."

Erin tried to hide her surprise. "A kid? How young?"

"Ten. Or eleven. He shouldn't be here."

"Does he also have an extrasensory ability?"

Rebekah's expression tightened. "I'm not supposed to talk to you about that sort of thing. I think you need to get back to your alien boyfriend and stop asking me questions that could get me in trouble."

"Of course," Erin said rising slowly. "I'm sorry. I was just trying to be friendly."

"Don't bother."

Erin returned to the bridge but her thoughts lingered on Rebekah and Cain. Perhaps Eve wasn't the only shepherd whose loyalty to Adam was questionable.

At 11:00 a.m., the spacecraft's cargo hold was solidly packed, ninety Eden subjects were seated in the lower passenger section and everyone else was situated in the upper observation area behind the bridge.

At 11:02 a.m., everyone in the upper area donned breathing helmets "to assist them through the gravitational pull and atmospheric changes".

At 11:04 a.m., the craft shifted into stealth mode and departed the Garden of Eden.

At 11:06 a.m., Prince delivered an odorless, anesthetic gas to the lower passenger section and into the helmets of each of the shepherds.

CHAPTER 24

Roman and Erin stood and removed their helmets. When Peace and Hari also took theirs off, Tripper, Jamie and Ryan followed suit.

"It's all right," Erin told the three who had not been in on The Plan. "We're the only ones awake, besides Prince and Dog."

"Don't we need these to breathe?" asked Ryan.

Roman grinned as he collected their helmets and stored them in a cabinet. "Not inside the ship. They're only on board in case of an emergency landing on a toxic planet. Prince simply rigged them to deliver a powerful anesthesia to the ones Adam's crew put on."

"Geez," Jamie said. "I'm glad I didn't know. I'd have been scared of getting gassed by mistake."

"Prince never makes mistakes," Roman said seriously. "*Never.* The helmets were his suggestion once he understood why Dog had growled at Adam. He'll make sure they stay unconscious for as long as necessary."

"So, where are we really going?" Tripper asked. "Ranger headquarters?"

Roman and Erin glanced at each other and silently confirmed their decision to give the team the full picture, beginning with Cattar's warnings from the future.

When they were caught up, Roman apologized for the multiple deceptions. "Please know, it was never my intention to drag any of you along on my mission. But you should be perfectly safe on the ship for the few hours we'll be there. The way I figure it, a sonic transmission should be easy enough to pick up on a primitive planet. And I promise, as soon as I've found and destroyed the source, you and all Adam's captives will be taken home."

"And the shepherds?" asked Jamie.

Erin took that question. "The only solution we've come up with is to leave them on the planet, as agreed. They just aren't going to get to keep all their slaves...or us. They brought along all they need to survive, but the people of Earth will be spared from the dark age Cattar referred to."

"You have to let us get off the ship," Ryan declared. "Even if it's just to unload all the supplies and equipment while the shepherds and their sheep are still unconscious. You can't risk having them wake up until we're long gone. And hey, it'll give Hari a chance to practice her powers of levitation without worrying about being judged."

When Roman hesitated to agree, Tripper spoke up. "The kid's right. You just told us you have no idea what to expect, so you have to take advantage of everything you have, which in this case, is us."

"Fine, but there will be absolutely *no* wandering off to explore. We have no idea what dangers to look out for."

Tripper's use of the word "kid" jogged Erin's memory. "Did anyone see a young boy get on board?" No one had. "Did anyone hear the name Cain?"

Peace raised a tentative finger. "I overheard the

name mentioned yesterday during our tour, but I couldn't tell what it was about."

Jamie added, "While we were *helping* the shepherds before takeoff, I overheard Seth and Sarah wondering what Adam planned to do about Cain, but they stopped talking when they realized I was listening."

"I'll be right back," Roman said, heading for the lift to the lower section. At least five minutes passed before he returned. "Ninety sheep are peacefully napping. No children, male or female. I also checked every possible hiding place to make sure we didn't have any stowaways. I think it's safe to say Cain was left behind."

Erin frowned. "Hari, could you try to look for him? Maybe he was secured in the barn with the others."

They all remained still and quiet as Hari closed her eyes. When she opened them again, she shook her head. "I couldn't see a child. But if he was one of the shepherds..."

"He could be shielded," Erin finished for her. "Rebekah let me know Adam had purposefully kept Cain away from us, but she wouldn't tell me what the boy's ability was."

Roman, we need to warn Chief—

Already done while I was downstairs. He felt Erin's fear that her friend could be riding into a trap. *They'll keep a special lookout for a young boy who might not be an innocent.*

"Roman!" Prince called out from the bridge and Roman was there in a heartbeat. "I found something in the area you sent me to it is barely a spec with almost no pull but it is definitely a wormhole."

Roman felt his pulse quicken. "To an alternate dimension?"

"We will know when we get there." Prince used one arm to gesture toward the navigator's chair. "Perhaps you could keep your eyes on that screen and alert me if any symbols light up." Roman sat. "It is not always a smooth transition."

Roman turned back toward the observation area and raised his voice to give the order. "Sit down, strap in and try to relax." To Erin he thought, *Prince asked me to...*

I heard. I'll be fine without you holding my hand for a few minutes. See you on the other side... shallar.

CHAPTER 25

"Thank you for coming so quickly, Tarla." Brianne of Acameir touched her cheek to her friend's. The speed of her speech made it clear that her usually calm demeanor was clearly being tested. "It's been nearly a year since Heart had to assimilate new crossovers, and the only time we had so many at once was when your aircraft came through six years ago. But we have *never* had to deal with anything quite like this before."

"If you're concerned, we should alert the Guardians immediately. Logan is—"

"No, no. We don't want to draw more attention than necessary. Just come with me and see for yourself."

Brianne led Tarla through the Imperial Palace at an unusually rapid pace for the reserved young woman. It was also not usual for someone of her status to exit through a service door and hop onto a moving walkway. If Tarla hadn't already gotten the message that something extraordinary had occurred, being taken into the large, windowless building used for recycling was the definitive clue.

And yet, Tarla was even more stunned by what she saw inside.

"I'll be drekked!" she exclaimed. "That's a Noronian cargo ship. What's it doing here?"

"Well, trash isn't the only thing that gets recycled here. When the aircraft you were on first came through the gateway, it was brought here, like this one. This is also where the passengers were initially processed...before being taken to the farm."

Tarla couldn't prevent the unpleasant expression that automatically formed when she thought of that first day six years ago...waking up in the barn with no doors or windows, not knowing how they'd gotten there or how the critically wounded had been miraculously healed, only to step out into a world with green sky, blue grass and two suns...

Tarla gave herself a mental shake. "I'm sorry. Please go on."

"As you well know, since then we adjusted our policies with regard to crossovers, but when I saw two strange beings in the cockpit and noticed that the human man with them wore a ring just like yours—"

Tarla stopped Brianne with a light touch on her forearm. "An Innerworld ring? Where are they?"

"They've all been comfortably secured in the sanatorium."

"Perfect. Let's go."

Brianne led her through a locked door to a corridor, where a tram was waiting for them. Along the way, Brianne continued to explain the anomalies. "The majority of the passengers were unconsciousness before landing and, once I saw the ring, I instructed the medical team to administer a sleep incentive to the few who were awake. However, it had no effect on the one being. Fortunately, he is very cooperative and docile, despite his frightening appearance. He explained that his species is octoman and he is called Prince."

"Prince?" Tarla repeated as a question. "Holy stars, I know him."

Is everything okay?

As always, even though it was only in her mind, Logan's voice made her smile. *I don't know about* everything *but I'm fine, just had a surprise.*

A good one, I hope.

You'll find out as soon as I do. Tarla felt Logan's attention turn from her to one of his trainees. Six years ago, he had hated everything about his life. Now his worst complaint was that there were never enough hours in a day to accomplish everything he wanted to do.

Tarla brought her focus back to Brianne, who had continued to relay her impressions of the crossovers.

"At any rate, the interrogators have been prevented from performing the standard interviews or memory depletions."

"You made the right decision. If one of them is Noronian, and the other is the Prince I met back in Innerworld, you may not want their information becoming part of any record."

"I almost forgot, for some reason, six of the unconscious ones wore helmets, as though they required special head protection or breathing assistance that the others did not. It could also imply they are contagious. Thus, as a precaution, I instructed the medical team to leave the helmets in place and to quarantine those passengers in a separate area."

The tram delivered them to a private entrance of the sanatorium and a short trip on a moving walkway took them to the room where Prince had settled down on the floor. As soon as he saw Tarla smile at him, he rose on his four legs, as high as the ceiling allowed, and grinned back at her. "I remember you Tarla Yan."

"I can hardly believe my eyes," Tarla said taking the

ends of two of his arms in her hands. "When I last saw you, you were applying to flight school. I gather you're a pilot now."

"I have a routine run between Innerworld and Norona."

Tarla angled her head. "And yet you've landed in an alternate dimension." The look Prince gave her could only be described as purposefully blank. "I was told someone was with you who had an Innerworld ring."

"Yes Roman Locke the son of the Co-Governors of Innerworld is with me."

"Oh dear. That's not good." She turned to Brianne. "Seriously, this was no accident. We need to talk to Roman, the one with the ring, as soon as possible."

Brianne gave her a soft smile. "Of course. I will have him awakened and brought here while you catch up with your friend."

"Excuse me," Prince uttered politely. "Where is Dog he needs to be with me."

"Who is Dog?" Tarla asked.

"His name is Roman but I call him Dog."

Tarla squinted. "You call the son of Romulus, *Dog*?"

Prince let out a deep gurgling sound, his form of laughter. "Roman is Roman and Dog is a dog that the Feinsteins gave me for my birthday."

"Oh my. What sort of dog is Dog?"

Prince gurgled again. "A mastiff like the ancient Outerworld Romans used to take into battle."

Tarla rolled her eyes and said to Brianne, "A dog is a four-legged animal that people of Earth adopt to keep them company, much like your kittens. A mastiff is an extremely large, very hairy dog. You'd better have Dog brought here before he wakes up on his own. I can't imagine the terror he could instill if he gets loose and starts looking for his master."

"I am not his master," Prince corrected. "I am his companion and as I said he needs to be with me."

Brianne left with a promise to be back as soon as possible. Rather than start any discussion that would only have to be repeated when Brianne returned with Roman, Tarla asked Prince to tell her all about Dog.

When Brianne finally returned, she was followed by a floating gurney carrying a snoring mass of black and brown hair, a medical tech and a young man who caused Tarla's mouth to drop open.

"Holy stars! You look just like your father!"

"I'm told I have my mother's eyes."

She hurried to Roman and gave him a tight hug then took a step back to stare at him again. "You were still a boy when I last saw you."

"But not so young that I didn't notice that you were the most beautiful female I'd ever seen. When I qualified as a tracker and became an emissary, I promised myself to find out what happened to you. It still makes my father sad that he couldn't find out."

She sensed Logan tuning in and remembered her priorities. "We'll have plenty of time to catch up on the past, but I think we'd better start with why you're here. I don't believe it was an accident, not with an octoman as your pilot."

As Tarla, Brianne and Roman sat on the comfortable chairs provided for sanatorium visitors, Prince squatted on the floor beside Dog. The tech placed a pill into Dog's nostril and swiftly left the room, securely closing the door behind her. A few seconds later, Dog was alert and licking Prince's face.

"You're right about it not being an accident, but the reason is...very sensitive." Roman's gaze shot to Brianne for a split second. "I'm not even sure we are where we were supposed to be. The information I was given stated the planet's name was Heart and that the environment was primitive, not conducive to human habitation. Based on the extremely large, very modern city we saw before we landed, that doesn't come close to being accurate. And yet, your name was specifically mentioned, as well as an engineer named Geoffrey Cookson."

"You are definitely on Heart, the mirror planet to Earth," Tarla confirmed. "And Geoffrey was one of the people on the aircraft with me when we left Manchuria and ended up here. But this planet hasn't been primitive for thousands of years. Maybe the best starting point is with formal introductions. Prince already mentioned that you are the son of the Co-Governors of Innerworld. Brianne is the daughter and First Aide of Parisia, Imperial Prefect of Acameir, which makes her next in line to be the most important person on Heart. Whatever the reason that brings you here, you need to explain it to both Brianne and Parisia."

Count me in on that explanation, Logan thought to Tarla. I can't wait to meet this man who just took your breath away.

Tarla smothered a laugh. *He did not. I was just surprised.*

Big day for surprises. I'll be right over.

"Logan will be here shortly. But, as you suggested, let's hold off on bringing any others in just yet."

Roman recognized the expression of a woman silently communicating with her love and arched one eyebrow with curiosity. "You have a mate now?"

She grinned. "Why yes, I certainly do. But he's Terran, like your mother."

"Then you won't be shocked to learn that I am recently joined with a Terran as well. She's here, with several others that need to be included."

Tarla turned to Brianne. "Would you give your

approval to have Roman point out his people and have them awakened?"

"Certainly. And I'll arrange for mother to join all of us in the meeting room upstairs."

As Brianne gracefully rose and moved toward the door, Roman bluntly stated, "I had a laser pistol."

"Yes, I was told you and two other men had weapons. Were they required for your work on Earth?"

Roman offered the first explanation he could think of. "Tripper is a soldier. He fought in the same war as Tarla did, and I'm law enforcement."

"Oh, I see. Like our Guardians. Don't worry, the weapons are in a safe place." She turned to leave but Roman stopped her again.

"You said *two* other men had weapons. Was the third one wearing a helmet?" Roman glanced at Erin and thought, *Abel, maybe?*

"Yes, he was one of the six with helmets. But his weapon wasn't like yours. It was connected to his body, as an artificial arm. The weaponry was removed."

Roman nodded. "That's good. He wasn't one of us. Please, make sure none of the others wake up until I can explain who, or rather, how dangerous they are."

Roman, Erin and their team had been situated in the meeting room with Tarla and Logan for only a few minutes but the tension in the room made it feel like hours had passed. Although Erin knew her people had plenty of questions, even the twins remained quiet, except for giving their names and places of origin when asked by Tarla.

Despite Tarla's assurance that Roman and Erin were joined, Logan spent more time studying him than any of the others. She also noted the two men had some similar characteristics—both were incredibly handsome, with dark hair and eyes, only Logan was a bit taller, more muscular and had two facial scars. Erin hadn't needed to see the scars to sense that this man had endured a very harsh life, but Erin never found such men appealing. Roman was much more attractive to her.

"Before Parisia gets here," Tarla said, "there are certain facts you all need to understand. Heart is a clean, healthy, peaceful world where manners and behavior are governed by laws and right and wrong are black and white. It is virtually crime-free. But it is *not* a democracy, nor is it a world where everyone has equal rights. This is *not* Norona or Earth. No matter what you see or hear while you are here, do not criticize their way of life. It works."

Tarla paused for a moment then continued with her lecture. "Most important of all, Heart is female-controlled. Women are not simply domineering; they hold *all* the power, politically, socially and privately. Until a few years ago, all males were kept tranquilized and were only used in extremely subservient roles. A small number have since earned limited freedom, but they must still abide by certain restrictions or face punishment. Regardless of why you're here or how long you plan to stay, you will need the cooperation of the women in positions of authority and believe me, they do not grant it easily.

"So, as ludicrous as this may sound, it is imperative that every man in this room obey three primary laws." She accented each number with upheld fingers. "*One*, a man may never speak unless spoken to first by a woman, nor may he look directly at any part of her form. *Two*, a man never makes physical contact with a woman, no matter how slight. There should always be a minimum of one arm's length between a man and a woman, unless he is in the process of performing a requested service, such as styling her hair. And *three*, any request made or order given to a man by a woman, whether or not she is his mistress, must be obeyed quickly and without question or comment."

The stunned looks bouncing back and forth among Erin's team reflected how she and Roman felt about such laws but she touched a finger to her lips and everyone kept their thoughts to themselves.

Roman waited a moment then asked Logan, "Brianne mentioned Guardians. Is that what you are?"

Logan glanced at Tarla and she nodded for him to speak directly. "Tarla and I, and some of the others who landed here with us, were all given the title, Guardian, after we helped fend off an alien army for them. However, even *we* have to be careful of our behavior in public. Someone once caught me touching Tarla's back at the market. We made the evening news and I had to make a public apology. Believe me, only my Guardian status spared me from being sent back to the farm."

"The farm?" Erin asked.

"An explanation for another time," Tarla replied quickly, as three women and a young man entered the room.

Logan instantly rose to his feet, bowed his head and gestured for the others to imitate him. Without hesitation, they did so.

Erin easily guessed that two of the women were related. Besides their tall, slender bodies, pale hair and creamy white complexions, they wore identical, full-length gowns of pleated, white chiffon, except the older woman's braided belt was gold and the younger's was silver. The third woman was quite elderly and wore a dark blue, velvet robe tied at the waist with a triple strand of white pearls. All three carried themselves with great dignity and seemed to glide rather than walk. The young man's dark head was bowed and he remained slouched behind the women.

"Hello," the youngest woman said with a smile. "Please be seated. I am Brianne, First Aide and successor to Imperial Prefect Parisia of Acameir." She made a slight hand movement toward that woman then to the other. "And this is her Domestic Affairs Advisor, Iris of Mergany. We are most anxious to hear what has brought you here. Who speaks for this group?"

As the Heart women moved to the empty chairs at the head of the table and carefully arranged their skirts to cover their feet, Tarla gave Erin a meaningful look at the same time as Roman sent her a mental nudge.

Secure their respect.

Erin took a breath and used her most confident voice. "I am Doctor Erin Breswell, the leader of this team."

"What is your field of medicine?" Iris asked.

"Psychology," Erin replied, sensing that para-anything might not garner respect from these women.

"Interesting. Our experiences with crossovers would suggest that field must be quite a lucrative one on Earth."

When Iris sat back in her chair, Parisia took over. "We are also very interested in why so many of you are here, especially under such unique circumstances."

Erin straightened her spine and made a point of shifting her gaze from one woman to another as she spoke. "There are two separate matters. But first, I want to assure you that we were given a misleading report that Heart was a primitive planet with few, if any, human inhabitants. If we had known there was an advanced civilization in place, we would not have brought the others here. Most of them are innocent victims who we intended to return to their homes, but some are criminals with powerful extrasensory abilities."

Sensing these women would appreciate her opening with a concise overview rather than a long narrative filled with details, Erin related the basic warnings included in the message from the future—the deaths and dark age Adam and his people would bring about if they weren't stopped and the future destruction of both planets if they didn't find and destroy the cause, which was located on Heart.

The facial expressions of the Heart women suggested they understood and accepted the information as truth. They simply didn't appear to be affected by any of it. It felt as though time itself paused as Erin waited for one of them to react or ask for more specific information. And when they did, it wasn't about the dismal predictions for the future as she'd expected.

Again, Iris had the first question. "The criminals with the enhanced mental abilities you spoke of…were they the six wearing helmets?"

"Yes."

"Did the headgear block their abilities?" Parisia asked.

"No. The helmets were just a trick to allow us to administer an anesthetic. The only way to prevent them from causing harm is to keep them unconscious. We—"

"What is the nature of their crimes?" Iris interrupted before Erin could finish answering the previous question.

"To our knowledge, one or more of them have committed murder and robberies, either personally or by forcing innocents to commit crimes by controlling their minds, enslavement of hundreds, some of whom were on our ship, plus kidnapping and a long list of other less violent but still illegal activities. Are the people of Heart able to psychically shield themselves from mental invasion, communicate without speaking or use their minds to manipulate another's behavior?" That question at least triggered slightly raised eyebrows.

"Not that we are aware," Iris replied. "And we would certainly not want to introduce such abilities into our society." She murmured something close to Parisia's ear that stirred the Prefect to rise. Iris stood up much more slowly.

"I'm afraid we must excuse ourselves," Parisia declared unexpectedly. "We have more questions but they will have to wait until tomorrow." She then turned to her daughter. "Brianne, perhaps Tarla can assist you in arranging discreet accommodations and hospitality for our visitors."

"Of course," Brianne said with a slight curtsey. She waited several seconds after Parisia and Iris left the room then smiled and said, "You may all relax now. I have a special relationship with Tarla and Logan and am quite willing to waive the usual proprieties for you as well."

"But only in private," Logan added quickly.

"For instance," Brianne said as she sidestepped, took the hand of the one who had been nearly invisible since he'd entered, and drew him forward. "I am pleased to introduce you to my twin brother, Jason."

The dark-haired young man straightened his back and shoulders, lifted his chin and grinned.

CHAPTER 26

"Oh my gawd," Jamie blurted out with wide eyes and a hand to her chest.

Ryan lightly swatted her arm. "She's just surprised because we're fraternal twins too. I'm Ryan, she's Jamie and we'll be fine with your laws because I'm used to her always bossing me around."

When Brianne's reaction was a giggle, the others were able to relax as she suggested. Erin then introduced Hari, Peace and Tripper but left Roman's introduction up to Tarla since she wasn't certain what Brianne had already been related about him.

"Roman is from my world," Tarla told Jason. "His work involves the security of Earth, though not in the same way as Logan's and mine was. Also, he is Erin's mate."

Erin and Roman were both surprised by her matter-of-fact statement after everything she had told them earlier, but Brianne and Jason weren't at all shocked by it.

"Then I will be certain to arrange a private accommodation for them. Does anyone else have a sleeping partner?" Brianne's gaze met Ryan's for a heartbeat longer than appropriate and her pale cheeks turned pink.

"No other *sleeping* partners," Tripper replied for everyone. "But we can all share a room if necessary."

Brianne's composure returned as she addressed Roman. "Would your pilot be willing to remain on the aircraft with his companion? I could arrange to have anything he needs brought to him, but—"

"No explanation necessary," Roman interjected with a smile. "Prince would prefer to stay on his ship. He has everything he needs there. But it will be best if I walk back to the ship with him and explain why we can't depart as soon as planned."

Erin quit wondering about Parisia's and Iris's abrupt departure when she noticed Logan's taut facial expression. As soon as there was a pause in the conversation, he voiced what was bothering him.

"Before anyone goes anywhere, I have one rather important question. How the hell did you get here *on purpose*? Every crossover has gotten here exactly the same way—electrical storms on both sides, the two suns, being sucked into a black tunnel. Cookson has been working night and day on—"

"Did you just say *two suns*?" Roman asked, sharply cutting Logan off.

"Geoffrey Cookson?" asked Erin at the same time.

"Yes and yes," Logan answered impatiently. "How did you do it?"

Tarla made a face at Logan then said to Roman, "I believe if you fill in the first blank, the rest will fall into place."

"Our pilot, Prince, has a knack for finding wormholes and using them. But the reason he knew where to look for the one that brought us here was because, in thirty years or so, Geoffrey Cookson will write an article about how he and some others—we don't have names or how many—had been to and from a parallel dimension through a gateway. The general coordinates in the article were all Prince needed."

Logan shook his head. "How about that. Geoff eventually figures out how to get back home. How did he—" His expression changed as he realized what Roman's explanation meant. "It doesn't matter what he eventually does or doesn't figure out. You're here, with a ship and a pilot who can navigate through the gateway! Whoever wants to go back can go now…with you."

Uh-oh, Erin thought to Roman.

"Could we set that aside for now? I'm not refusing; there would just be a lot of…complications."

Logan's eyes narrowed and his jaw clenched but Tarla covered his hand with hers and he exhaled.

"Logan mentioned two suns, as though that wasn't normal," Erin reminded, further neutralizing the sudden tension between the men.

"That's right," Tarla said. "From what we learned, Heart revolves around one solar body, like Earth. But every so often, without any discernible pattern, a smaller orb of light would appear close to it for a day or two. Accidental crossovers didn't always occur when there was a second sun, but they *never* occurred when there wasn't. So we concluded that the second sun's appearance may have been what *created* the situation that made the accidents happen. But six years ago, something changed."

Logan picked up the story from there. "That's when Heart was attacked by the Velids, an enemy from Heart's ancient history. Because Heart had no defense system and refused to perform any act of violence, we were able to make a deal with the women in charge. Basically, we did the dirty work for them in exchange for certain freedoms, and they haven't been bothered by the Velids or any other outsider since then."

"*But*," Tarla went on, "the second sun had appeared two weeks before that battle and, although it randomly shrinks and enlarges in appearance, it has never completely disappeared since then. Because the Heart women are positive the second sun never remained continuously visible for more than a few days in all recorded history, it seems possible that there was a connection to the attack, but we've never been able to confirm or refute that."

Roman lurched to his feet and paced as he spoke. "I think we can fill in that blank also. The message from the future stated that the portal between the two dimensions was being held open by a sonic transmission that originated on Heart. As the years go by, the gravitational or magnetic pull of Heart's sun begins to affect that of Earth's, until it implodes and takes the entire system in with it. It stands to reason that the second orb of light you see is Earth's sun."

An instant later, Logan was also on his feet. "And the transmission could have turned on full-time when the Velids got close, maybe because of proximity or like a homing signal for them to follow back here."

Roman completed the conclusion. "You said the Velids were an ancient enemy. Maybe the source was actually planted that long ago, sending out occasional transmissions that created electrical storms and opened the portal!"

Tarla winked at Erin. "They are so cute when they play nice together."

Over the chuckles and chatter, Brianne said, "There's just one flaw in that theory. No one has ever picked up an unexplained transmission."

Tripper had an answer ready. "Just because no one has picked it up doesn't mean it isn't there. We had guys in the war who did nothing but stare at monitors, on thousands of different frequencies, watching for a single blip of heat that didn't belong. And they still missed one or two snipers. If the signal is alien, that could make it even harder to find. But from what I've been hearing today, no one has been looking for it."

"You fought in the war?" Ryan whispered with a look that blended surprise and awe. But an elbow nudge from his sister stopped him from pursuing that story for the moment.

"There was more in the message from the future," Erin said, bringing Brianne's attention to her. "They assumed the sonic transmission itself isn't the direct cause of Earth's sun imploding; it's the open portal. The circumstance that had sporadically drawn air and sea craft through to Heart eventually attracts the energy from Earth's sun to Heart's sun, which suggests that, while one implodes, the other explodes."

"Of course. That's certainly a logical conclusion," Brianne said, making no attempt to hide her concern. "I must pass this information on to mother and Iris immediately. It will go a long way toward influencing a decision to assist you with your missions. I also need to attend to housing, so if you could accompany me, Tarla...and Logan, perhaps you could take Roman back to the guest area to collect his pilot and escort them to their ship...and since I must ask everyone else to remain here for a short while, Jason will bring you a selection of beverages and—" Suddenly she, and everyone else, realized Jason wasn't paying attention to her. "*Jason.*"

Jason stole one more glance at Jamie and Ryan before following his sister out of the room. Tarla, Logan and Roman left right behind him.

"Whew," Jamie sounded, fanning herself. "Did anyone else notice how warm it is in here?" Everyone smiled except Ryan who just rolled his eyes.

Erin inwardly sighed, feeling a little envious of the twins' ability to use humor to diffuse tension in a completely humorless situation. What had she said that caused Parisia and Iris to hurry away before hearing more information? She had just informed them that their planet was facing destruction and yet, their only questions were about the shepherds. Unfortunately, fear of the unknown clouded her mind and her stomach was twisted in a knot and her lungs could barely draw a breath—

Well, ma'am, Ah do believe Ah can help you with all of that.

The warmth Roman sent along with his thought effectively took Erin's mind off her worries, though she was now feeling breathless for an entirely different reason.

Jamie and Ryan managed to keep everyone out of the doldrums by telling outlandish tales about each other until Logan and Roman were back from their errand. Tarla returned shortly thereafter to take everyone to the rooms that had been arranged for their overnight stay.

Again, private, indoor trams and moving walkways carried them along without risk of their being seen. As promised, Roman and Erin were assigned a single room while the others were to be housed two floors above in a three-bedroom apartment.

With everyone gathered in the suite, Tarla pointed out the amenities provided for their basic needs, which included sets of pastel-colored outfits that looked like hospital scrubs. "If you are given permission to go out in public, with or without a Guardian escort, you will be required to wear one of these uniforms. They designate you as a new crossover, one who may accidentally and unintentionally disobey a law of propriety."

Erin felt the surge of questions her team was about to throw at Tarla following her rapid tour but the arrival of Jason distracted them. With him were another man and woman who helped guide in two hovering carts loaded with covered platters and bowls that emitted a variety of mouth-watering aromas.

While Jason started setting up a buffet in the dining area, Tarla drew the couple toward the new arrivals. Pointing toward each, she said, "Roman, Erin, Peace, Hari, Tripper, Jamie and Ryan, I'd like you to meet Geoffrey Cookson and his mate, Robin, who is also my best friend. They were both on the same aircraft that brought me here, and they are Guardians as well. I've already told them about why you're here."

As soon as everyone exchanged handshakes and repeated names, Geoffrey broached the subject Roman had hoped to put off. "Logan said you knew my name because of an article I write in the future. Needless to say, that statement alone raises a myriad of questions, scientific and otherwise, but I'm most interested in hearing the specific details of the article."

Roman grimaced. "And I wish I could give them to you, but I never saw the article. The message I received simply referred to it, saying that in the latter part of the twenty-first century, you claim to have used reverse magnetic polarity to travel through a wormhole in space in order to return to Terra from Heart."

"That is one of the theories I considered, but eliminated. It can't be the answer."

"The only other information shared with me was that the article warned against anyone trying to find the wormhole because the conditions on the mirror planet were primitive and not conducive for human existence. Since that's not the truth, you might have lied to discourage others from looking for Heart. And if *that* was an intentional lie, maybe the method you gave was also untrue."

Geoffrey frowned. "Or perhaps something happens to Heart and it does become uninhabitable and what didn't work before becomes viable. In that case, I may have wanted to share my discovery with others in the field."

"Eenie, meenie, miney, moe," chirped Robin. "The only thing that matters is that we finally get to go home!"

Roman looked to Tarla for help but she didn't intervene. "As I told Logan—"

"I know," Robin interrupted. "It's *complicated*. But it can't be any more complicated than our men having to pretend they're incapable of being anything more than servants, of having to walk hunched over if they're out in public for fear someone thinks they're acting *uppity*! And that's just the men who were lucky enough to be released from the farm—"

"Robin, please…" Geoffrey said quietly.

Ignoring him, she addressed Erin. "Can you imagine never being allowed to show excitement or anger, or run or dance, because if a woman does anything active or passionate, she's breaking the laws of propriety. One of our women—one who had helped save their proper asses—couldn't hack it and got sent back—"

A small skirmish by the dining table cut off Robin's rant and grabbed everyone's attention.

"Everyone's hungry," Jamie was explaining to Jason. "I'm just trying to help move things along."

"It's not proper," Jason insisted. "Serving meals is one of my responsibilities."

Jamie planted her fists on her hips. "Don't you also have to obey any order a woman gives you?"

Jason glanced over at Logan with a silent plea for help, but his mentor simply shrugged. "The pretty lady is a quick learner, Jason. You'd better let her help you."

Tarla shot a warning look at Logan then brought the group's attention back to her. "Obviously, Robin is one of the crossovers who has learned how to follow the rules but has never accepted the idea that Heart is her home. As we told you yesterday, certain concessions were made for the Guardians after our assistance and assurances were given that they would take steps toward giving men more, if not equal, rights. But as the years passed and our wartime skills weren't called into play again, the assurances were forgotten. Nothing we did or might do for them in the future has altered their beliefs about keeping men subjugated or how their society functions. The facts are that Heart has no disease, no poverty, no overpopulation or unwanted or abused children, no crime, no war."

"No surprises," added Robin with a pout.

"That's not what Geoff tells me," Logan said with a crooked grin. Robin punched Logan's arm but gave into a smile.

Tarla reached for Robin's hand and held it as she said to Roman, "Just promise to consider the possibility of taking some of our people home after you've accomplished your mission and we promise not to harass you about it in the meantime."

Roman exhaled heavily. "If there's room on the ship, we'll consider it. For now, I'm starving. And if I'm not mistaken, Jamie's *help* seems to be slowing down the food service."

CHAPTER 27

The moment the door to their assigned, one-room apartment closed, Roman held Erin securely in his arms until her tension ebbed.

"We're still alive and unharmed," Roman reminded her.

"On a strange planet where the only thing primitive about it is that men have to keep their heads bowed in public."

"But we've been fed and treated decently."

"And put in another room we're forbidden to leave."

"But it's a very nice room."

Erin leaned back and made a face at him. "I'm usually the one who tells everyone else to think positively. What has you so optimistic?"

Roman's mouth curved into a cocky grin. "My work requires me to deal with the challenge right in front of me, because worrying about what might happen next is usually distracting and rarely helpful. So I try not to think about it at all. And at this particular moment, the only challenge I need to focus on is how to go slowly."

She arched an eyebrow quizzically…then smiled. "Oh. *That.* Well, I think taking the time to exchange comforting hugs qualifies as a good start." She took his hand and *slowly* led him to the other side of the room…where the bed was located. "Since we share the blame for never going slowly before, how would you suggest we proceed?"

He rubbed his chin and pretended to give her question deep thought. "I suggest…we take turns giving the other person explicit, verbal instructions. No thoughts or images. You first."

"Oh, that's easy. Kiss me." She tilted her head back and closed her eyes.

"I said *explicit* instructions."

She opened her eyes and met his gaze. He was teasing her. "All right. Kiss me like you would…if we just had our first date and you want to make sure I would want a second one."

He gave her an approving nod then tucked an errant curl behind her ear, lightly stroking the velvety edge with his finger as his thumb grazed her cheek. "Thank you for a perfect evening," he murmured in a low voice and dipped his head an inch closer to hers. His fingers slid down her arm and intertwined with hers. He raised her hand then placed a soft kiss on the sensitive flesh just below her palm, lingering long enough to feel her pulse against his lips.

Erin blinked as he released her hand and took a step back from her. His mouth had never touched hers and yet that little peck on her wrist had given her a lovely quivering sensation that made her anxious for more of the same. She almost forgot they were playing a game.

"And now, *you* kiss *me*," Roman directed. "…as if we're about to pleasure each other for the first time."

She slipped two fingers into the waistband of his slacks and brought him closer. Her arms snaked around his neck and drew his head down as she rose on tiptoes. Her body aligned with his, her lips brushed softly over his mouth, teasing, nibbling, then firmer as her hips shifted just enough to test his response. She left his mouth, sighed and returned with lips parted. Her tongue eased between his lips, sweetly begging entry until it was granted. She stroked his tongue with her own and he reciprocated. With his full participation, the kiss deepened and soon the joining of their mouths was not nearly enough.

It took considerable willpower, but she ended the kiss. Her voice was husky with desire as she delivered her next instruction. "Stand perfectly still."

His curiosity was satisfied as soon as she unbuttoned his shirt and removed it. For a moment she merely circled him, admiring his well-toned upper body, but he was far too tempting not to touch. Her fingers grazed and petted and felt the strength of every muscled inch of his chest, arms and back. When his nipples puckered beneath her touch, she licked the tips and released a puff of warm breath over each one. Then she stepped back.

It took him a beat to remember it was his turn, and when he did, it was obvious the *slow way* was going a little too slowly. "Undress...*completely*...for my enjoyment."

The first item she removed was the tie holding back her hair, which she then tossed to him. She took her time shaking her curls loose and thoroughly mussing her long hair, so she looked more than a little wild, before she progressed to her boots, socks and belt, each of which she tossed to Roman and he dropped them to the floor behind him. For the rest of her stripping she turned around. The t-shirt came off first, followed by a good amount of wiggling and bending over to get out of her jeans.

His sharp intake of breath let her know she had

fulfilled the enjoyment part so she smiled at him over her shoulder and removed the last two bits of clothing. But instead of facing him, she said, "Turn around and stand perfectly still."

She peeked over her shoulder again to make sure he had obeyed before going to him. From behind, she reached around to his front, undid the closure on his slacks and knelt at his heels. Removing his shoes and socks was easy; pulling his pants down past his rising interest in their game took a bit more effort.

As she had explored his upper body, she now discovered the feel of his buttocks, thighs and calves. Then she rose and, fitting her nude body to his back, her hands crept around to his belly and found their way down to his sex.

Although a deep-throated groan suggested he was in pain, he remained perfectly still while she caressed, tickled and stretched his shaft to its full extension. When he could tolerate no more of her teasing, he removed her hands from his body, turned around and ordered, "Lay down on the bed, hands over your head, legs parted."

As she willingly complied, he told her, "I was going to have you touch yourself, like you did that first night in your bedroom." He got onto the bed, kneeling between her spread thighs. His palms slid up her thighs, pausing for his thumbs to rub over her exposed core before continuing up her abdomen and cupping her breasts. As he molded her flesh and toyed with the peaks, he murmured, "I know you were pretty distracted, being in heat and all, but you squeezed and massaged your breasts...*like this*. Then you ran your hands down...*like this*." His hands demonstrated what she had done. "All the while, I watched you in the dark, thinking I should look away, but you were so beautiful, and what you were doing was just too erotic."

He eased forward, hovering over her with his sex heavy against hers, sliding over her dampness as he kissed her forehead, her nose, her lips, her throat.

Erin couldn't stop the moan of need as his mouth closed over one nipple, sucked, and moved to the other. With each kiss and nibble his erection taunted her with an elusive promise of satisfaction. "*Roman*, please. You're making me crazy." She squeezed her hand between their bodies and tried to take him where he belonged but that only made him withdraw to the triangle between her legs.

"Sorry. I've seen you completely crazy and you're not quite there yet." He retreated a bit more, his head dipped down and his mouth covered her core.

As his lips and teeth and tongue probed her sensitized folds, she wanted to praise his expertise but all she could manage was to repeatedly gasp as he took her to higher and higher levels of pleasure. When she was positive her body could take no more of his oral foreplay, he slid two fingers into her opening, pressed upward and scissored back and forth.

Erin cried out as the orgasm shook through her only to be shocked when his fingers again found and pressed a vulnerable spot, giving her a second release before the first one had completely subsided.

Roman didn't move again until her body began to relax and she was able to take a deep breath. Then he smoothly repositioned himself above her and very, very slowly, one millimeter at a time, he joined their bodies.

Erin grasped his bottom and tried to hurry him along and when that didn't work, she wrapped her legs around his waist and lifted her hips, taking what she wanted whether he was ready or not.

If the growling sound he made didn't let her know

he was more than ready to be done with the prolonged game, his partial withdrawal and powerful thrust forward was undeniable proof. She lowered and raised her hips to meet his in-and-out rhythm and match his rapidly increasing pace. Her hands were no longer needed to drive him deeper but to simply hold on.

She felt another climax building and prepared for the burst of sensation only to have him withdraw completely, roll onto his back and pull her on top of him. Perching astride his hips, she took the reins, rising and lowering, rotating her hips, shifting back and forth. She could tell he was holding back, waiting for her to reach her peak once again, but she wasn't quite there.

Roman closed one hand over her breast and squeezed as the thumb of his other hand found the tiny bundle of nerves at her base and pressed hard against it.

Erin felt the spear of pleasure shoot from his thumb into every cell of her body, making her feel as though she'd exploded into millions of tiny pieces then recombined as a totally different, totally sensual being. Clenching her muscles around his pulsing shaft, she absorbed his release and kept him within her as she lay down on top of him.

And then she *purred*.

He felt the vibration of the telling sound against his chest and grinned.

Too drained to speak aloud, she thought, *I have never—*

Neither have I, not like that. I'd heard it was incredible after joining, but I couldn't have imagined—

I meant that sound I made. I guess you really are my catnip. But I agree with how amazing it was. Phenomenal in fact.

I guess that means you wouldn't mind if we tried it again, just to make sure it wasn't a one-time thing.

She tightened her vaginal muscles around him. *From what I can tell, a repetition is absolutely necessary. But I don't think the test has to be* exactly *the same to be sure. There are one or two things we haven't tried yet.* She sent him a flash of her mouth enveloping his erection.

Actually, the number is more like one or two hundred. He sent her a montage of sexual positions to give her something to anticipate.

She smiled and gave him another squeeze. *Unfortunately, we only have about six hours before we have to leave this room.*

Uh-uh-uh. Remember, no thinking about what might happen next. Just meet the challenge directly in front of you. He rolled them onto their sides, still joined and facing each other then, bending her top leg at the knee, he brought it up onto his hip.

Challenge accepted.

CHAPTER 28

Although Erin and Roman had given in to a few hours of sleep, their minds were still wrapped in a fog of sensuality when Tarla arrived to escort them upstairs for the follow-up meeting with Parisia. *Going slowly* had been even more magical than Erin had imagined…and she was hoping she didn't have to wait long to experience it again.

They had just sat down with steaming mugs of coffee when Parisia, Iris, Brianne and Jason entered the suite.

"Good morning everyone," Parisia said brightly. "Please be seated. I would prefer to keep this discussion informal. In fact, I wouldn't mind a cup of tea."

The request was not directed at anyone in particular but Geoffrey hurried to comply.

And Robin bit her lip.

Iris began immediately. "We apologize for our abrupt departure yesterday but it was…unavoidable. Brianne has since filled us in on the additional details of your mission. We discussed the matter of the sonic transmission with the Planetary Security Council and they have given approval for a preliminary scan to be performed by the Guardians, from within a secure facility here in Acameir. If evidence is found to support the claim that such a device exists, its disposition will be determined at that time."

"You may as well know," Parisia added. "There is suspicion regarding your arrival. You see, the enemy who attacked six years ago was a metamorph. According to legend, the Velid's natural form is similar to a multi-segmented insect with a hundred legs and a hard exoskeleton, but it's not insect-like in size. An adult can be as large as a human youth. They're power, however, is the ability to instantly transform into any lifeform they see…including humans."

"So you're thinking one of us could be one of *them*?" Tripper asked before realizing his mistake in speaking. He quickly lowered his gaze and bowed his head. "Pardon me. I meant no disrespect."

Parisia gave him a small nod and continued. "When accidents occur, certain measures are taken to ensure that no crossover might jeopardize the safety of Heart's citizens. Those measures include a test that verifies a crossover's humanity. Because of the unusual circumstances regarding your arrival and Tarla's recognition of Roman, those measures were temporarily set aside. But after our initial discussion with you, it was clear that at least some of your passengers presented a clear danger."

As soon as Parisia paused, Iris continued in her more direct manner. "The shepherds and their sheep were dealt with yesterday and have been certified as human. If you would each willingly submit to an examination, it would satisfy the Security Council's concerns and expedite their approvals."

Erin hesitantly raised her hand a few inches and waited for Parisia's nod of acknowledgement.

"Excuse me, but you just referred to the passengers as shepherds and sheep. I don't believe I used those terms yesterday."

"That is correct," Iris replied. "We learned those title words from the criminals during the standard interrogation process."

Erin felt Roman's stab of panic and spoke quickly. "You woke them? After we told you how dangerous they are? Did you not understand that they could be manipulating your behavior right now and you wouldn't even know it?"

Iris's expression never altered as she waited for Erin to take a breath then responded stiffly. "We understood you perfectly. That is why we left so suddenly. The danger you brought to the citizens of Heart was imminent and thus our preventive measures had to be immediate. Because we expend no skills or funds on war or aggression, we were able to develop the technology to repair the human body and radically accelerate the healing process. Crossovers often suffer physical damage of some sort. Tarla can testify that many of her patients had severe burns before they arrived and our medics were able to return them to perfect health."

"That's right," Tarla said. "But these people weren't suffering from battle injuries or being yanked through a violent electrical storm."

"Yet a number of them were carrying diseases or had been damaged in some way and had to be repaired before release. Even exposing our citizens to the mildest infection could have a devastating result. Once the repairs were completed, they were interrogated as usual, memories of the last decade were depleted and they were relocated to the farm."

Questions whirled around Erin's mind so fast, she had a hard time deciding what to ask first. "I'm sorry.

I still don't understand how you've protected your people from the criminals' mental abilities."

Parisia gave Iris a nearly imperceptible signal then said, "Very simply, the six passengers who were wearing the helmets had lethal growths in their brain tissue and abnormalities in their neurological circuitry. Those problems have been corrected and they no longer possess any abhorrent mental deviations. However, the interrogations revealed that, even without exceptional mental abilities, their natures are still too violent to allow them to come into contact with our citizenry."

This could get really bad, really fast, Roman thought to Erin. *If they find out about our abilities…*

Erin glanced at the faces of her team and saw Ryan grasp Jamie's hand. *It looks like we all just came to the same scary conclusion.*

"What about the others?" Hari asked quietly. "We believe they were good people whose minds were overtaken against their will."

"Those interrogations are not yet completed," Iris replied in a tone that closed the door on further questions.

Parisia offered the group a soft smile, perhaps to counter Iris's cold demeanor. "More information will be forthcoming but we are running short of time this morning. In order to proceed in any direction, we must insist that each of you submit to the standard physical examination and interrogation."

Tarla raised a finger. "May I offer a suggestion?"

"Of course," Parisia told her. There was a hint of relief in her voice.

Tarla rose and slowly walked behind Erin's team. As she moved along, she touched each person's back and sent the thought, *Trust me.* "These people, who I have vouched for, claim they have come here to save your planet. If they had not taken the risk, you would probably never know of the catastrophe awaiting you. Plus, if the transmission is of Velid origin, another, better planned attack on Heart would be in your future as well." She paused for a moment before continuing.

"But, instead of being courteous, you just let them know you have the ability to operate on their brains and wipe out their memories. Needless to say, you've made them uneasy. The Security Council is obviously willing to give them leeway to search for the signal, but has simply asked for a confirmation that they are not Velid spies. I propose that they be given the single test to determine their humanity and that Logan and I, *as Guardians*, be present. In return for that concession, they will not question your laws or decisions regarding the others."

Iris and Parisia exchanged whispers then Parisia said, "Agreed. But Brianne will be in attendance as well." She rose and everyone else in the room stood as well. "Please have everyone remain here until a medical technician arrives with mobile equipment to run the tests."

As Tarla accompanied the Heart leaders to the door, Parisia added more quietly, "We will also leave it to you and Brianne to make whatever arrangements are necessary to begin the search. I trust you to keep in mind the delicate nature of this situation and what it would mean if word of it was leaked to the citizenry."

"Of course," Tarla said with a bow. "But I trust you will leave it to my discretion to bring in other Guardians as needed for their expertise."

"Also agreed." With Iris already out the door, Parisia clasped Tarla's hand and murmured, "Thank you. For everything."

Very interesting, thought Roman to Erin.

I didn't know you could read lips.

I can't, but I'm pretty good with body language.

You certainly are. Erin added a wink for good measure.

Once the team's internal organs had all been photo-imaged and everyone's humanity was certified, they were escorted to the laboratory Geoffrey had been using for his experiments. Again they traveled through passages that kept them out of the public eye. It was a fairly large room on the top floor of a nearby building, but it was crowded with all sorts of equipment. With considerable rearranging the team cleared enough table space for a dozen people to sit in front of monitors.

The bonus was that windows ran along one entire wall. At least they now had a view of the bright, shiny metropolis they'd caught a glimpse of on the way in.

"I'm calling a two-minute break," Erin announced. "You all need to take a look outside." The buildings looked like massive pieces of pastel-colored metal art shaped like cylinders, spheres, corkscrews and pyramids. Bubble-shaped objects with tails floated along silvery ribbons that wound between and through the buildings.

"Oh," exclaimed Jamie. "I see the second sun! That's weird but I don't think I'd ever get used to seeing a green sky and blue leaves on trees."

"What are those?" Ryan asked pointing toward the moving bubbles.

"Transports," Brianne replied with a smile. "They travel on a system of magnets, so they are completely quiet as well as energy-efficient."

"And what's that building over there," Jamie asked. "The one with the golden dome."

"The Imperial Palace." She was answering Jamie but her next sentence seemed to be directed toward

Ryan. "I hope to be able to show it to you now that we know you're not Velid spies."

As though she suddenly realized how improper she was being, she abruptly turned toward Tarla. "There is something I must attend to...at the Palace. Jason can remain here to assist you with whatever you need to get this project launched as soon as possible."

Tarla passed control to Geoffrey. "This is your playground. Any big requests before she leaves?"

"My computer system should be adequate but I'd like to bring in Ray and Kara to help me reconfigure it to scan for unusual sonic transmissions rather than incoming objects or heat sources. In fact, once we get set up, I think we're going to have to bring in all the Guardians and borrow some monitors from the Control Tower if we want to be able to scan the entire surface of the planet in our lifetime."

"We can work around the clock, in shifts," Tarla said. "Like we did six years ago." She smiled at Logan and he gave her a salute.

Erin added, "And count all of us as part of your staff, however we can help."

Roman had been staring out the window, as though he was appreciating the view, but his thoughts were elsewhere and he wasn't letting Erin hear them.

What's wrong? she asked.

I don't know yet. Instincts are twitching, he told her. Aloud he said, "I have equipment on board the ship that could help, but all the known transmissions would have to be blocked out first. Plus, we'd need to get permission to cruise the planet inside your protective shield."

Brianne frowned. "I'm afraid that would not fall under the Security Council's order that the search be conducted discreetly, within a secure facility. But if all else fails, we'll propose it. Otherwise, it sounds like you'll be able to arrange for everything yourselves, but just have Jason contact me if you need my help." Her exit from the lab was quite a bit faster than propriety dictated.

As soon as Brianne was gone, Erin pulled Tarla aside. "Thank you for intervening. You should know, the helmeted ones weren't the only ones on the ship with extrasensory abilities." She gave Tarla a keyword version of each person's skills. "If you think any of that will help, just tell us."

Tarla smiled. "I knew I was picking something up when I touched each of you. But invisibility? How the drek did Roman end up with *that*?"

"It's a story he can tell better than me. Does anyone else know you're telepathic or that you and Logan can share thoughts?" She glanced over at Jason who was busy entering notes into a handheld computer as Geoffrey, Logan and Roman brainstormed over what was needed.

Tarla grimaced. "Only Robin and Geoff know for sure. And we've always been extremely careful around Heart natives. If they ever suspected…" Her sentence trailed off and she shook her head again.

"What is it?" Erin asked. "Would they operate on your brain? Take away your memories?"

Tarla shrugged. "At the very least."

Erin frowned. "Something about the *farm*? You mentioned it before. Is that a prison?"

"Yes, but not like anything you've ever seen on Earth."

Logan crossed the room and stroked Tarla's back. "Geoff, Robin, Jason and I are going to run out and get things moving. Luckily, no one pays any attention to Geoff scrounging for things for one of his crazy experiments. We should be back in an hour."

"Lunch?"

"It's on the list," Logan said with a grin. "Any special requests?"

Tarla touched her stomach and her eyes widened. "Peppermint pie."

"You got it." Logan placed his hand over hers and kissed the top of her head.

As he left the room, Erin held back the question that popped into her mind but Tarla answered it anyway.

"Yes," she whispered. "We're expecting a baby girl in four months."

"Congratulations. I'm guessing that wasn't an easy decision for you."

Tarla sighed. "You guess correctly. We both wanted a child but we kept putting it off because there was no way to be certain we'd have a girl. Neither genetic manipulation nor non-emergency abortions are legal here and you heard how males are forced to behave. Basically we took a chance and got lucky."

"But what if you hadn't gotten lucky?" Erin asked. "What if you were having a boy? I've worked with enough teenage boys to know how rebellious they can be. I can't imagine one of them being submissive just because their told—" Erin stopped when she noticed the taut expression on Tarla's face. "What?"

"They aren't just told to behave a certain way. As soon as puberty hits a male child, his testosterone is chemically suppressed by what they call the antidote. From what we could tell, the antidote contains a combination of ingredients including a fairly strong tranquilizer and mood elevator. It was originally only meant to control natural male aggression, but it has been used on disobedient females as well. It may sound inhumane but the end result is hard to refute. I've seen it turn the nastiest barbarian into a functioning marshmallow."

"Oh. I see." Erin was both appalled and

professionally intrigued. "Logan and Geoffrey don't seem to be tranquilized."

"They're not. Neither is Jason. It was part of the bargain we made when the Heart women needed our help six years ago. But like we explained yesterday, if our men don't behave properly in public, they are subject to punishment."

"Which seems to bring us back to the farm," Erin stated.

"Rather than try to explain, let me show you." Tarla glanced around the room then walked over to one of Geoffrey's monitors and sat down. To the rest of Erin's team, she said, "Would everyone please come over here for a moment?" As they gathered behind her, she said. "What you are looking at is referred to as the farm."

On the screen was an overhead view of a flourishing orchard with neat rows of trees laden with pink fruit. Tarla moved the view to scan other fields, a pasture with horses and cows, and an area of white buildings with red roofs. There was a big barn and a long, single-story building with smoke rising from four chimneys. Behind those were a large number of very compact houses, also painted white with red trim.

"It's an actual, old-style farm," Roman said with some surprise. "But considering the technology I've seen here, why would they need a farm like that to produce food?"

Tarla zoomed in closer so they could see the people working in the orchard and moving in and out of the buildings. "The women don't *need* to produce food this way, though they do consume a portion of it and use another portion as a trade commodity. The real reason they keep the farm going is that it's their way of keeping the unfit busy. This is where the crossovers, almost all of whom were men, lived out their lives…until we shook things up."

"Is it in slow motion?" Tripper asked.

"The video isn't; the people are," Tarla replied. "Everyone is medicated into a state of complacency. What you're looking at is a prison that costs nothing to maintain, requires no guards and is full of inmates who are content and productive. Guardians are permitted to access this feed to check on our people, but we can't do anything to change their circumstances."

She touched a few numbers across the bottom of the screen and the picture shifted to a close-up of a dark-skinned man and a woman of Asian descent unloading baskets of fruit from a horse-drawn wagon. "Those are former soldiers, Lee Tang and T.J. Jones. They were granted their freedom and Guardian status like us, but they just couldn't bend to the rules of Heart's society. After several warnings, they were both returned to the farm. Like we said, some of us adjusted, but many simply couldn't. That's why Geoff spends every minute in this lab, trying to find a way home."

Everyone was quiet for several seconds, then Hari asked, "What about you and Logan? If given the opportunity to return to Earth, will you?"

Tarla turned toward Hari and smiled softly. "No. Both of us have seen too much war and brutality to want to go back. Heart may not be perfect, but it's close enough for us. We're happy here and appreciated for doing work we enjoy. Obeying a few odd laws is worth the price of a peaceful life."

"And do the free women have a choice of career?" Hari asked in a slightly louder voice than usual.

"Absolutely," Tarla replied.

By the time Hari asked a third question, everyone eyed her curiously. "And what about servants? Are they kept under the influence of the drug like the men at the farm? Does the woman get to choose her own?"

Erin wasn't entirely surprised that life on Heart would be of interest to Hari, but she was surprised to see the extent of interest revealed in the woman's eyes. She could tell Tarla had picked up on it as well and was trying to give a careful, unbiased response.

"All non-Guardian males of Heart, whether house servants, child caretakers or business labor, are under the influence of the antidote. Their aptitude for work is determined before they are made available for service. Once a woman can prove she's earning a regular income, sufficient to properly maintain a servant, she is permitted to...*interview* up to three prospects. Once she makes a choice, the man is placed in her home. She is required by law to treat him fairly and with consideration, but if he proves to be incompetent, she may...exchange him."

"This may be crass but I've gotta ask," Tripper said. "Does the service include the, uh, intimate type?" Jamie and Ryan failed to stifle their snickers.

"Absolutely not," Tarla replied. "First, the law prohibits *all* physical contact and second, the antidote eliminates sexual desire and ability. And before you ask, the Guardians are conditionally exempt. In other words, they are permitted to have sexual relationships as long as there is no public display of affection."

"That seems very civilized," Hari said with a smile.

Roman caught Erin's eye. *Are you thinking what I'm thinking?*

If you're thinking there might be an empty seat on the ship home, then yes.

How about you? he asked her. *Feeling the lure of a female-dominant society?*

Her mouth curved into a half-smile. *And give up the right to be inappropriately touched by you in a public place? I don't think so.*

I don't think I've ever done that.

The month's not over yet. Though she meant it as a joke, the reminder of their agreement to live separately at the end of one month abruptly cut off the flirtation.

"And this is Ray and Kara, our computer geniuses," Tarla said in the same supportive tone as she introduced Nathan, Alicia, Sunny, Edward, Trish, Jeremy, Darcy, Hal, Greg, Mandy, Kevin and Charlene.

Erin made certain she sounded equally proud while introducing her team. The room that had seemed so large at first now held twenty-seven people, including Brianne and Jason, ten monitor stations and even more equipment than there was to begin with. But everyone was there to get a job done and Geoffrey was quick to explain what they would each be doing.

As Tarla and Robin started dividing the work force into three, eight-hour daily shifts, Erin approached them and quietly said, "I have a suggestion. Hopefully, this is an unnecessary precaution, but considering all the, uh, *unknown factors* we're dealing with, maybe we should separate the pairs who are able to mentally communicate with one another…in case a problem arises here or at the apartment building."

It took Robin only a moment longer than Tarla to get Erin's meaning. Tarla and Logan, Erin and Roman and Jamie and Ryan would be split up so that nothing could occur in one location that the others would not know about.

Tarla kept her voice very low as she confided, "It's a good idea. We learned years ago that none of the Heart women should be completely trusted when it comes to political power."

CHAPTER 29

"Should we talk about—"

"No," Roman told Erin firmly, but then softened his response with a gentle kiss.

"You don't even know what—"

He pressed two fingers to her lips. "I heard you thinking about ten different things just now and not one of them is important enough to waste the little bit of private time we have."

He kissed her again, more urgently, and she opened her mouth to him. In a blink, the kiss became the center of their desperate need to discard their clothes, grasping and groping each other's bare flesh as they tumbled onto the bed.

For three days and nights, the Guardians and Erin's team had scanned the planet's surface without finding a hint of an alien transmission. Also during that time, there wasn't a single incident to support the need for the pairs to work separate shifts, but they held to the original plan. However, from the first day, the intended eight-hour shifts turned into ten and twelve, which resulted in Roman and Erin repeatedly crossing paths...until that moment.

A hurried romp wasn't what either would have

chosen but a quick climax was better than none at all.

"Remind you of old times?" Roman asked her with a chuckle.

She snuggled into him. "At least we both remained conscious."

"And visible," he added. "I'd suggest we start over but you need to get some sleep while you can. Just close your eyes." He pulled the sheet up over the both of them, tucked her body into the curve of his and gently stroked her temple.

Instead of dozing off in his embrace, she exhaled heavily and sat up. "I can't. I mean, I know I need to sleep but my muscles are stiff and cramped from sitting in one position for so long and staring at a grid on a monitor and straining to hear something in the earmuffs. If I could just go outside and take a walk…"

Neither said anything for a few seconds then Roman abruptly got out of bed and pulled her to her feet. "That's exactly what we need. We should probably get dressed, though it's not entirely necessary." His clothes were back on as quickly as they'd come off.

Erin stared at him as though he'd grown a second head. Even more curious was that he was managing to shield her from his thoughts.

"Hurry up now, we've only got about an hour before I'm supposed to be back at the lab."

She got dressed despite her bewilderment.

He took her hand in his and squeezed. "Ready?"

"I suppose, but—"

In a blink, they were both invisible.

She giggled as the tingling sensation ran its course through her limbs and he let her back into his mind.

From this moment on, you cannot make a sound. Let's just hope no one we pass has your sense of smell.

She smiled then realized he couldn't see her delight

so she sent an image of her giving him a huge hug.

A minute later, they were out of the apartment building and taking quiet yet deep breaths of the outside world. The two suns had dropped below the cityscape but there was still plenty of light to let them see the unique architecture and transportation system at closer range.

Which way, shallah?

Erin was getting accustomed to the sensations of warmth and safety that endearment gave her and she let him know that. *I would love to get a better look at the Imperial Palace.*

Looks like a bit of a hike but there are hardly any people around so we can fast-walk. Just don't let go of my hand.

I wouldn't dare.

The view of the palace they'd had from the lab barely prepared Erin for the magnificent craftsmanship and golden glow of the structure's dome. They had just begun a walk around the perimeter when Roman yanked Erin aside and halted. Four older women in dark robes, similar to the usual attire of Domestic Affairs Advisor Iris, were marching directly into their path.

What's that you're feeling? Erin asked.

My instincts are twitching again. That group is not taking a leisurely walk. They watched the women climb the stone stairs that led to a side entrance of the palace.

They definitely appeared to be on a mission. But it probably has nothing to do with us.

Probably. But that's not what my instincts are telling me.

Then let's follow them inside. She tried to pull him toward the steps but he held still.

It's not like we can just open the door and enter.

*Guards could be on the other side and there's no
telling how they would react to a door seeming to
open and close on its own.*

*But you can do that other thing...go incorporeal,
right?*

If I let go of your hand, you'll be visible.

So don't let go. Take me with you.

*I've never done that with another person. It's too
dangerous.*

*I'm not a random person. We're joined. That makes
us one. You're wasting time. Do it!* She wrapped her
arms around his waist and he held her tightly.

They climbed the stairs quickly then everything
went black around Erin. She couldn't hear or see
anything and, for several long seconds, she couldn't
feel Roman holding her. Then it was over. Her senses
came back and they were standing in an opulent
rotunda.

And so were the four women.

Don't move. Our footsteps might echo in this spot.

They only had to wait a few minutes before a slow-
moving man in a crisp white outfit trimmed with gold
braid approached the women. He stopped several feet
away and his head remained bowed as he said, "The
Prefect has asked that you make yourselves
comfortable in the Blue Salon. She will join you
momentarily." He turned to leave when the youngest-
looking woman called his name.

"Delbert, would you happen to have any of your
special trukberry tarts in the kitchen?"

"Certainly, Secretary Koballa. I will bring a tray
with the tea."

She almost smiled. "That would be lovely. Come
along ladies. We wouldn't want Parisia to be waiting
on us after we requested this meeting."

Oh my heavens, Erin thought. *Who does Delbert*

remind you of?

As the man passed, Roman took in the dark hair, green eyes, distinct cheekbones and jawline. *An older Jason. They may not allow physical contact between the sexes but I'd bet my pistols Delbert is the biological father of the royal twins.*

They followed the foursome into the Blue Salon without anyone being the wiser, mainly because each of the women was focused on getting the others to hear her point of view.

Since no one seemed able to complete a sentence without being interrupted, the subject of their debate was unclear to Erin and Roman. However, they were able to deduce that these women held positions important enough to demand that the Prefect explain her actions. The one Delbert addressed as Secretary seemed to rank somewhat higher than the others.

Before any sort of accord was reached, Delbert entered with the tea service, which immediately quieted the women.

As soon as the Imperial Prefect entered, the women rose and made partial curtseys. Two of the women's expressions noticeably tightened as Iris walked in behind Parisia.

"Please be seated," Parisia said in a formal tone. "Secretary Koballa, since you requested this urgent meeting without providing an agenda, I would appreciate your explanation now."

Koballa nodded. "We are very appreciative of the adjustment your schedule for us. As Secretary of Protocol, it has come to my attention that there may have been...a breach. Perhaps the esteemed Minister of Health Gardenia failed to remember—"

"I did not *fail* to remember anything. The Prefect's First Aide instructed me to temporarily hold my official report until certain determinations—"

"*And*, as Minister of Public Information," the eldest woman declared, "it is my responsibility to make sure Heart's citizens are fully apprised of unusual events regardless of secret instructions from—"

"*Unless*," Iris interrupted with a somewhat threatening glare, "news of an event or situation *before* all the facts are known could cause an unnecessary panic among the citizens. My dear Syracuse, *you* of all people should know the ramifications of releasing inaccurate information."

The Minister of Public Information tightly closed her mouth.

"Koballa, I am still waiting to hear what breach of protocol you referred to," reminded Parisia.

That woman cleared her throat. "Of course. Apparently Heart received a new group of crossovers but some of them were not processed in the usual way. In fact, there is a rumor that they have already been assimilated into the Imperial City's population."

Your instincts were right, Erin thought.

The fourth woman finally spoke. "I heard they were not crossovers but travelers from a distant planet and that their ship landed completely intact. As Minister of Trade, I should have been consulted before any processing was done. The repercussions of insulting a potential new trade source—"

"Enough," Parisia said firmly.

This should be interesting, Roman thought.

"Minister Jinis, the ship *is* from a distant planet but they did not come here to set up a trade agreement. Secretary Koballa, there were crossovers on board, almost all of whom have been properly processed and are now on the farm. However, due to the extenuating factors presented by others who were on board, we could not release any information. Minister Gardenia, I am sorry you were put in a tenuous position by our request for confidentiality, but I assure you, all members of Parliament will be provided with the facts very soon."

Parisia is quite the politician, thought Roman.

And according to Tarla, she isn't above twisting the truth to her advantage.

"Meanwhile," Parisia continued, "the Planetary Security Council has been fully informed and we are abiding by their ruling in this matter. In other words, we are actually following *their* orders, the most important of which is ultimate discretionary tactics until further notice."

Iris walked toward the salon door and opened it. "And now, the Prefect and I still have work to do this evening."

The foursome politely thanked Parisia for her time but they were far from satisfied with the meeting.

Should we follow them? Erin asked.

No. Let's stick around these two a bit longer.

"We knew this situation would leak out," Iris said matter-of-factly. "Between those who were present when the ship landed and those who were part of the medical team, someone was bound to say something that would get back to Syracuse and the rumor circuit would take it from there. But I feel certain your mention of Planetary Security will hold their tongues for a few more days at least."

"Brianne is completely convinced that the people working with the Guardians have told the truth. She said they are obeying all our laws, staying out of sight and putting in very long hours searching for the transmission."

Iris gave that some thought before speaking. "Assuming there is an alien transmission and they locate and destroy it, what then?"

Parisia angled her head at her advisor. "I'm not sure

what you're asking."

"Now that we know it is possible for a ship to intentionally navigate through the gateway, we cannot allow anyone to leave Heart. Once news of their journey is shared, we could be overrun with any number of beings looking for a new world to conquer. You *know* that was the intention of the ones who called themselves shepherds. And despite the Guardians' success fending off the Velids, we are woefully vulnerable to a takeover from an aggressive society."

Parisia rubbed her temples. "You're right of course. We could certainly use a few more Guardians, particularly the two who have relevant training...if they were willing."

"And if not?"

"We'll have no choice but to send them to the farm with the other dissidents. But what about the ship and the octoman? He isn't susceptible to the antidote and he certainly would not be welcome into the citizenry."

Iris answered so quickly it seemed clear she had been thinking of this solution all along. "The ship can be dismantled for parts or refitted for our use. But the octoman and his companion will have to be transported to another, less *sophisticated* planet."

Erin gasped.

Iris jerked her head from side to side. "Did you hear that?"

Parisia shrugged. "Delbert's probably hovering outside the door. I told him I might require his help after the ministers left." She rose and opened the door to the rotunda. As she'd guessed, Delbert was patiently standing a few feet away.

Roman and Erin waited for Parisia and Iris to go their separate ways then they hurried out of the Palace and back to the lab as though they were being chased.

Erin had too many questions in her head to hold all of them in. *Did you hear what they said? They've already incarcerated all the Eden people and they have no intention of letting us leave. And you're responsible for Prince and Dog. You can't let anything happen to them. We need an escape plan. As soon as we destroy the transmitter, we need to get out of here. What should we do? Who should we tell? I don't want to keep our people in the dark but I don't want them to panic either.*

Sh-sh-sh. He squeezed her hand and sent her a wave of calm. *We'll figure everything out. But I can give you one answer immediately. Tarla and Logan are the only two we should talk with for now. They're familiar with the inner workings of this world and we can trust them. As to our people, I don't want to panic them either...until we have to.*

Once they were inside the building that housed the lab and were certain no one was around, Roman released Erin's hand and they both became visible again. However, the intention to speak to Tarla and Logan about what they'd heard was postponed the instant they entered the lab.

"Thank the stars. You're both alright," Tarla gushed as she rushed up to them and gave each a hug. "We tried your apartment but there was no answer."

As several others gathered around them, Roman and Erin glanced at each other then he apologized. "We nodded off. It won't happen again."

Erin noticed that everyone was present, not just those scheduled to work that shift. "Oh my. Is that why you're all here?"

Geoff grinned. "We were concerned when Roman was late but that's not the reason we called everyone in." Robin nudged him and he got to the point. "We found something. Or rather, Ray did. Show them,

Ray."

Ray Higgs led them to his monitor station and handed Roman his earmuffs. "There's a faint sonic pulse coming from this area." He pointed to the highlighted grid on the screen. "The timing's sporadic though, so you might not hear anything even if you kept your ears on that spot for your whole shift. It was just a lucky accident that I picked it up twice in an hour. Here's the replay of the second one." Ray touched a key and for a millisecond a spot on the screen lit up.

"I definitely heard a *ping*," Roman declared to the room in general.

Ray continued. "And it's *definitely* being beamed out into space but there's no way to tell what or where the target might be...if it even has one. What we can be sure of is that it's not on any of Heart's current or discarded frequencies, so there's a very strong possibility this is the signal you were hoping to find. Unfortunately, the two transmissions only allowed us to narrow down the source to about a ten-square mile sector. We'd need at least a dozen more to pinpoint it exactly."

Roman mentally skimmed through Cattar's message until he found something relevant. "This thing is old, possibly ancient, and very probably malfunctioning. I was told the transmission gained power over time. Is it possible that it is continuously transmitting but extremely weak most of the time?"

"Anything's possible," Geoffrey said. "But if that's the case, our equipment might not be able to pick up anything but the sporadic surges."

"Unless we were inside that sector," Ray suggested.

Geoffrey pulled up several maps of the area. "We might have caught a break here. It's part of a dry, rocky area, like a desert, with some underground caves. No marked towns either. But it is within the geographic boundaries of Acameir, so getting permission to perform a ground search will be easier than if it was in a city or on one of the outer islands."

Roman took a closer look at the maps. "The location would have been chosen because of the topography. Less likelihood of it being disturbed, especially if it's in one of the caves."

"We sent Jason to personally give the news to Brianne, rather than calling." Geoffrey advised. "Hopefully we can get the permission process started tonight."

We probably passed him on the way back, Roman thought.

Well, at least we know Parisia will be relieved to hear her breach of protocol can be defended.

"In the meantime," Geoffrey continued. "I suggest we continue scanning as we have been…just in case that's not the only alien thing pinging out there."

Roman thought to Erin, *Looks like I'm still on duty now. But you and Tarla are both off. Might not be a better time to fill her in…*

Erin gave him a mock salute and said, "Okay then, I'll see you in the morning."

Then she caught Tarla's eye and signaled the desire to speak privately. Tarla met her in the hallway seconds later.

Erin quickly told her, "I have something very important to talk to you about but I don't want anyone else to hear. Could you manage dinner in our room?"

"I'd like that. I'll let Logan know where I am and Robin's on duty, so right now is good."

As soon as the door to the apartment was closed, Erin gave Tarla a complete replay of everything she and Roman had heard. For efficiency, Logan and Roman stayed tuned in to the women's conversation from their work stations.

"So they're back to their old tricks," Tarla said with a frown. "Can't say I'm surprised though. Okay, the number one priority is still to destroy the source of the sonic transmission, so you can't simply take off. However, you can take some precautions against not being able to take off at all." She paused for a moment then held her index finger up while she mentally communicated with Logan.

What's going on? Roman asked Erin.

Tarla and Logan are brainstorming.

Tarla's attention returned to Erin. "All right. Logan and Roman will head over to the ship and make sure Prince puts up its shields. That should be enough to protect him and your ride off this planet. The women of Heart will not perform a violent act against any of you. And they will not do anything suspicious while you are trying to save their planet. *But,* they would not hesitate to drug or anesthetize you after your mission is complete."

"Unless we agree to stay on as Guardians," Erin countered. "I sensed that would be Parisia's first choice."

"Would anyone in your group stay behind willingly?"

Erin shrugged. "You saw Hari's reaction. She'd be a possible. But I doubt if anyone else would."

"Not even the twins?" Tarla asked with a half-smile.

"Jamie and Ryan?" Erin looked at her curiously. "Why would you ask about them?"

Tarla raised her brows. "You haven't noticed?"

"I don't think I've noticed anything but the monitor I've been staring at for the past three days."

"I'll admit, living in a world where men and women are not permitted to fraternize has heightened my awareness to any nuance of familiarity. But I'd say those four passed the nuance stage the first day they met."

"Four? Okay, no more hints. I haven't slept in twenty-four hours. Just fill me in."

Tarla chuckled. "When Jamie has been on duty, Jason is present. And when Ryan's on, Brianne is the liaison. Now, that could be coincidence, unless you notice how the shy glances have graduated into lingering gazes. Or how they take their breaks at the same times and have conversations of more than one or two words. Or how Ryan touched Brianne's hand earlier today and, rather than scold him, she blushed and smiled. I'd say those four have more in common than simply being beautiful, fraternal twins."

I was going to say the same thing, Roman thought to Erin, *but when we finally had more than a minute together, I was more interested in our relationship than theirs.*

"Well," Erin said to Tarla. "Apparently Roman noticed also. But Ryan and Jamie are used to flirting. I doubt if either has serious intentions and that would be very unkind to Jason and Brianne, who have no experience at all." She sighed and pinched the bridge of her nose. "I'll have a talk with them, make sure they abide by the laws for the rest of the time we're here."

Tarla shrugged. "That can't hurt. But from my point of view, the laws are being bent by both sets of twins." She watched Erin try to hide a yawn and stood up. "Get some sleep and try not to worry about anything for a few hours. Whenever I fret over something, Logan says that things seldom turn out the way they seem to be heading. By this time tomorrow, we could have a whole new set of worries."

Erin smiled. "Roman says he never thinks about what might happen tomorrow, that it distracts him from focusing on the challenge directly in front of him."

Tarla smiled back and they simultaneously said the one word that summed up their thoughts about not worrying. *"Men."*

CHAPTER 30

Erin awoke five hours later to a very insistent knocking. "Okay, I'm coming, I'm coming." As soon as she opened the apartment door, Tripper, Ryan and Hari rushed in.

"We all had a dream," Tripper reported.

"The same dream," Hari amended.

"Except mine included Dog," Ryan corrected.

"Tell me while I make coffee."

Tripper started the explanation while Ryan found cups and spoons. "It seemed like a typical lucid dream for me but somehow they were copied on it."

"We've formed a very strong bond in our time together," Hari said. "But I believe the dream sharing had more to do with us sleeping in such close proximity."

Tripper sat on a stool at the kitchen counter. "I was alone in the lab, looking at a monitor. And a dot of light appeared. I touched my index finger to the dot and instantly I was in another place, not on Earth though."

"So the trigger was the events in the lab," Erin said as she set the four cups of hot coffee on the counter then sat down on the unoccupied stool. "Describe the immediate environment."

"It was hot and dry. The ground was hard and nearly black, like asphalt. There weren't any plants. Just a lot of jagged black rocks that came to points, like old arrowheads, ranging from a couple inches to hundreds of feet tall. Somehow I knew they were alive and this was their forest. The biggest reminded me of redwood trees in circumference."

Erin held up a finger to stop Tripper. "Hari, does this match with what you saw?"

"Everything except that it was me there, not Tripper. After I awoke, I did a remote view search for the images I saw in the dream. The rock forest exists. Also, I saw the texture of the rocks more clearly. They reminded me of tourmaline, and the taller they were the more they looked dark blue rather than black."

"I noticed that too," Ryan said.

Tripper bobbed his head. "Now that you said it, I'm sure I saw the color difference but I was distracted by really high-pitched whining like an old-fashioned dentist's drill."

"It made me think of a slowly opening door with ungreased hinges," said Hari.

"Sounded like Jamie squealing when she sees a bug."

"Where was the sound coming from?" Erin asked.

"Inside one of the biggest rocks," all three answered at once.

"What was causing it?"

Tripper shook his head. "I woke up in a cold sweat. Almost like when I had the dream about that snake woman, Eve. Something bad was in that rock. Something I really didn't want to see."

"I was also upset when I awoke," Hari said.

"Did either of you see Dog?" Ryan asked.

When neither Tripper nor Hari recalled seeing Dog

or any additional details, Ryan told his extra piece of the dream.

"I didn't wake up right then. I knew there was something out there but I wasn't afraid because Dog was suddenly at my side and I knew he could protect me from whatever it was. Then he started growling and baring his teeth. The hackles down his back stood straight up and he took off toward one particular rock growth barking so loud it woke me up."

"Possible interpretations?" Erin prompted.

Tripper went first. "You know my dreams tend to have some literal and some symbolic images, but there was something different about this one. It felt completely literal. Like that rock forest exists and we need to go there to find the source of that godawful noise. It could be the signal we're here to find and it's very probably inside that specific rock growth, or very close to it. But maybe something else is there too. Something deadly…like a booby-trap."

"My intuition tells me the same thing," Hari said. "The sonic signal is coming from there and it would be logical for whoever put it there to also have protected it in some way."

"And I'm positive Dog has to come along," Ryan added. "Either for protection or because he'll be able to hear something we can't."

"Very possible," Erin agreed. "But Dog only obeys Prince and getting permission for an octoman to go exploring could be a problem."

"Peace can communicate with Dog," Hari reminded her. "Maybe even better than Prince."

Roman? Have you been listening?

With one ear only. The other's been busy listening to nothing. But it sounds like you four should come on over and talk to Geoffrey. I'll tell Logan to get Tarla here also.

How are your instincts? Still twitching? Erin asked.
Upped to high alert.
That makes five of us.

Geoffrey and Robin barely reacted to the news that Erin's group had special abilities but agreed that it was best not to share that with any of the other Guardians. It only took a minute to confirm that there was an area within the subject sector that matched Tripper's dream and Hari's remote view. And since most of the rest of the sector consisted of rugged terrain, choosing the rock forest as a search starting point was rational.

When the next shift of Guardians arrived to relieve others at the monitor stations, Erin instructed each of her team to stay so she could bring them up to date. Brianne and Jason arrived a short while later with the news they'd been hoping for.

Permission to do a ground search had been granted.

"There are a few stipulations though," Brianne announced before the group had a chance to be relieved. "First, the permission is for that specific sector only. Second, although the sector in question is basically uninhabited, there is still a strong need for discretion. We can only allow a small transport to take you there. It's one Geoffrey has been seen using to locate materials for his experiments. It is the only way not to raise suspicion about an unscheduled departure from the city."

"How small?" Logan asked bluntly.

"Ten seats, one of which is for me, and a luggage area."

"We've heard about dangerous creatures that might live in that zone. We need our weapons," Tarla stated.

"And the dog has to come," Erin said quickly. "He has a very keen sense of hearing and can cover an area in a fraction of the time we can on foot carrying mobile equipment...which apparently is the best way to search that terrain."

Brianne was clearly not expecting that demand. "The animal is much too large."

"He should be fine in the luggage area," Roman countered then noted the expression on her face suggested fear rather than practicality. "Peace will take responsibility for him and keep him well away from you."

Peace gave Brianne a reassuring smile.

"I cannot get to the weapons you had when you arrived without raising questions, but I should be able to bring you a stun pistol and some paralyzer spray from the Guardian security room. Will that suffice?"

Roman looked at Logan, who gave him a distinct nod. "Yes, thank you. And since we won't have room for Jason, perhaps you would allow me to assign Ryan as your personal servant on this excursion." The instant flushing of Brianne's cheekbones said more than any words could.

Ryan stepped forward and bowed his head. "I would consider it an honor."

What in the world are you thinking? Erin asked Roman.

We may need to distract her and he's been doing a good job of that so far.

She had wanted to talk to Ryan about his misleading Brianne but Roman had a good point. *Fine,* was all she thought back.

Rather than respond to either Roman or Ryan, she got back to business. "The third stipulation may be the most important. The permit is for twenty-four hours only. There will be consequences if you do not all return in that time. I suggest you make a quick decision as to who else will be going, gather the

equipment that is definitely needed and go to the
building where your ship is docked. I'll meet you
there as soon as I've secured the weapons and made
arrangements for the transport. You needn't bring
anything else. The transport is normally stocked with
a small supply of food and water." She gave the group
a moment to add other concerns and, when they
didn't, she left the lab.

Less than an hour later, Erin's seven, plus Logan
and Geoffrey, took the private passageways to the
recycling facility. Tarla and Robin remained behind.
To everyone's surprise, Brianne was already waiting
for them next to a vehicle that reminded Erin of a
compact hoverbus.

Roman waved at Prince in the cockpit and he
opened the door and lowered the steps. "You're up,
Peace. Let's go get our four-legged helper."

Dog met them at the door, tail wagging and mouth
drooling. Peace knelt down to hug him and whisper in
his ear as Roman headed for the cockpit.

"Are you doing alright, Prince? I'm sorry this hasn't
turned out to be the quick detour I said it would be—"

Prince laughed. "Do not worry I will make up the
time when we leave which will be when?"

"Depends on what happens in the next few hours. It
may be necessary to take off in a hurry."

"Problem?"

"Possibly. Just keep the shields up against
everybody except me or Erin. And do not leave this
ship for *any* reason. Consider this a *very* unfriendly
planet."

"I will stay here and you will protect Dog he likes
Peace she is a kind human."

"Yes, she is." Roman patted Prince's shoulder.
"Hopefully, we'll be back before you have a chance to
miss us."

CHAPTER 31

"Now *this* is the kind of thing I was expecting to see on an alien planet," Ryan declared as he stepped off the transport and onto ground that looked like lava flow and felt like rubber.

"The formations are called kragmar," Brianne explained once everyone had disembarked. "They're unique to this area and quite valuable. A small sliver contains sufficient electromagnetic energy to power the Imperial City's transport system for a month. But it takes great care to harvest them properly in order not to cause harm to the kragmar or the harvester. Be very careful not to touch it. The vertical striations are razor-sharp and the smallest cut requires immediate medical attention."

Geoffrey let out a groan of frustration. "Electromagnetism explains why my equipment is telling me there's a sonic signal close by, but the source indicator is bouncing all over the screen. It could be in, under or around any one of the rock formations. Even if we only search the tallest ones, it could take more than the day we've been given. And, in case you haven't already realized it, the pistols aren't going to be of any use here either."

"If a deterrent is actually needed, the paralyzer spray should work," Brianne said. "Though I've never heard a report about the dangerous creatures Tarla mentioned." She gave Logan a half-smile.

"Well, Ryan," Erin said. "It sounds like your insistence that we bring Dog could save the whole mission. Peace, can you tell him what we're looking for?"

Peace turned to Geoffrey. "When I bring Dog out, you'll need to replay the recording Ray made of the sound you want him to locate. And Brianne, no matter how excited he gets, you have nothing to fear. He understands the need to give you space."

"Thank you, Peace."

Ryan stepped in front of Brianne. "Just in case, you can stay behind me." To which Jamie did a dramatic eye roll.

Peace was back in the ship for over a minute before she and Dog returned to the group. Dog clearly wanted to stretch his legs but while Peace rubbed the tip of his ear, he remained immobile. Geoffrey played the recording several times in a row and Peace released Dog.

Dog bounded into the kragmar forest, trotted left, right, back and forth, sniffing the air and the ground in one spot after another before moving on. Suddenly he stopped short in front of one of the largest growths, let out a loud bark and began pawing at the ground.

Roman, Logan and Tripper each grabbed a shovel from the transport's hold and ran toward Dog, only to have to wait for Peace to catch up and instruct Dog to stand back.

"Be careful with those shovels. You don't want to damage the transmitter before I figure out how long the gateway will remain open once it's destroyed."

Roman arched one brow at Geoffrey. "That sounds

like something you might have mentioned earlier." To Tripper and Logan he said, "You heard the man, go easy. And remember what Brianne said about not touching the kragma!"

To everyone's astonishment, the first careful attempt to break through the spongy surface created a grating sound. A few more hesitant probes revealed that a section of the surface, about three feet by three feet, was attached to a rusty square of metal. For the next several minutes, the four men strained to remove the piece, using the shovels as levers, to no avail.

"It's a hatch cover," Hari said with her eyes closed. "And it appears to be locked from beneath."

Erin moved next to her and quietly asked, "Can you unlock it?"

Hari opened her eyes and gave her a doubtful look.

"There's no punishment if you fail, but we need you to try."

Jamie and Ryan drew close and each took one of her hands. "We believe you can do it on your own," Jamie said, "but we'll give you our strength just in case."

"Same here," Tripper said moving around them and placing his hand on Hari's back.

Hari closed her eyes and took a slow, deep breath. For several seconds, nothing seemed to be happening. Then Hari tightly squeezed her eyes and a grinding sound followed by a *clunk* came from the hatch cover. Hari lifted the hand Jamie was holding and the square of metal rose a few inches, moved to the side and settled down again.

"It looks like a tunnel," Logan exclaimed.

Hari's eyes opened wide and they all rushed to the opening.

The instant Dog caught a whiff of the trapped air, he howled so loudly an echo of the sound reverberated throughout the rocky forest. Ignoring Peace's command, he loped to the opening, barked several times, then wiggled in. A moment later no one could see him but they certainly heard his ferocious growling.

"He found the transmitter," Peace said calmly. "He says it's not far."

"Sounds more like he cornered one of Tarla's dangerous creatures," Tripper said.

"The signal could be at a pitch that hurts his ears," Logan ventured.

"He's not in pain," Peace assured them. "He's warning you to approach with caution."

Roman took a step toward the opening but Erin grasped his arm. "Watch out for a booby-trap." He squeezed her hand and she released her hold.

"Wait!" Geoffrey commanded as he ran back to the transport. He returned with a lighted miner's helmet and handed it to Roman. "I believe in being prepared for any eventuality," he said in answer to Roman's unspoken question.

Roman donned the helmet, sat down and scooched into the tunnel. A few seconds later, the unmoving reflection of light let the others know he'd reached bottom.

"Roman?" Erin called down.

"I'm fine," he returned. "No booby-traps so far. The tunnel goes down at a slant for about ten feet then levels out into a cave. Going to check out what Dog—*ah drek!*"

His expletive, followed by silence had Logan heading down the slope in a heartbeat. *"Son-of-bitch!"* was his verbal reaction seconds later.

Tripper was about to go next when Jamie physically blocked him with her smaller body. "Nobody else goes down there until we know the situation."

"You heard the lady, guys," Tripper called. "What's

got Dog so riled up?"

"Peace was right," Roman replied loudly enough to be heard over Dog's rumbling growl. "Looks like Dog found the source of the transmission."

Logan added, "And it's being protected by the biggest, ugliest insect in the universe."

"Oh my stars," Brianne gasped and clutched Ryan's arm. "It's a Velid! Tell them to paralyze it quickly before it morphs into something they can't control!"

"Already done," Roman assured them as soon as Tripper passed on Brianne's order. "But I don't know if it was necessary. Dog seems to have sufficiently terrified it. Besides, it looks weak. When it saw me, it could barely move its one arm over what must be the transmitter. In fact, now I wish I hadn't been so quick. I get the feeling it understands what I'm saying but can't speak because of the spray. It would certainly help to know if there are other transmitters or more of his kind planted around Heart."

"I have an idea," Erin told him. "Are you sure he poses no danger?"

"As sure as I can be."

She glanced at Jamie then Ryan. "Are you willing to go down there?"

Jamie lifted her chin. "Absolutely."

"It's about time you gave us something to do," Ryan said with a grin. Gently disengaging his arm from Brianne's grasp, he murmured, "I've gotta go take care of your enemy, then I'll be right back. Tripper and Geoffrey will keep you safe."

As the twins scooted into the tunnel, Erin turned to Peace. "I'm going down and create a shield for them. I assume you won't mind staying up here?"

Peace smiled. "My days of sliding down tunnels are behind me. But I'll stay connected to Dog to keep him calm."

By the time Erin reached the cave, Jamie and Ryan had gotten over their initial amazement over seeing a real-life alien and were ready to work.

Jamie explained, "We can't be sure this will work on it, or him, or her...I feel like it's a him...but, assuming he's an intelligent being, it's worth a try. Once we both have our hands on him, I should be able to read his thoughts...and I should be able to force him to think in our language and be open and honest."

"Hell of a party trick," Logan muttered with a dry laugh.

"We'll be glad to give you a demonstration when we're done here," Jamie said with a wicked smile.

"No thanks. I was just thinking how you kids could have helped me out some years back. Not important any more. So, can we ask questions or do you have to?"

"You can ask what you want to know out loud, one specific question at a time. I'm the control and Ryan will verbalize the responses as he hears them."

"And I'll maintain their psychic shield," Erin told Logan. She took a deep breath. "I'm ready whenever you are."

Jamie and Ryan took their places on each side of the Velid. They joined hands around the alien, touching the chest and back of his head. They both closed their eyes.

"Ask how long he's been here," Logan said.

A few seconds later, Ryan spoke in a low monotone with a momentary break between each word. "Six of your years. After the failed invasion, I was left with others to learn the ways of this planet."

"How many others are there?" Roman asked.

Ryan's pause was a bit shorter this time. "I am the last. There were thirteen, in different locations. We were ordered to learn the languages and customs of the humans to better prepare our leader for a victorious assault. But it was impossible to remain in human form for extended periods and Heart's atmosphere was lethal to our kind. I am the last, but I will not survive much longer."

Logan went next. "What's the purpose of the box he's touching?"

"It is a sonic emitter, left here by the ancestors. Commander Xytoc used it as a guiding beacon and directed me to make sure the signal continued to send until he could return with a greater army. It requires a regular infusion of energy, which this location has."

Roman noticed the sliver of kragma sitting on top of the emitter. "Are there other such devices?"

"This is the only one Commander Xytoc knew of. That is why it was so important for someone of my elevated rank to safeguard it."

Logan spoke the question that concerned him most. "Is there another attack planned?"

"That was Commander Xytoc's intention. But no one ever came back, not even to retrieve the information we'd gathered. Are you soldiers?"

Logan glanced at Roman, who shrugged, then said, "Yes."

"Is it your intention to stop the beacon?"

"Yes," Roman replied.

"Then there will be no more reason for prolonging my existence. As one soldier to another who was doing the duty assigned him, I ask for a consideration."

Again the men glanced at each other and shrugged before Logan said, "What do you want from us?"

"I have answered your questions honestly. There is nothing more to be gained by taking me prisoner on a planet that is slowly draining the life force from my body. There is a yellow capsule in the pouch at my side. It will allow me to pass on quickly and with dignity. Since you have immobilized me, I ask that you put it in my mouth."

What does your lie detector say? Roman asked Erin.

It feels like everything he said is the truth, but if we didn't ask the right question, maybe he was able to hold something back.

"One final question," Roman said. "What information would be beneficial for us to know that you have withheld?"

Many seconds elapsed before Ryan had a response to pass on. "Very quickly after the capsule is placed in my mouth, the casing will dissolve and there will be an explosion. Every part of my body will fragment into ricocheting splinters of poison. The essence of any being inside this chamber will move on with mine."

"Now *that's* what I call a booby-trap," Logan said. "How do you want to play it?"

"Dog, go to Peace. She has a treat for you." Dog cocked his head at Roman, looked at the Velid and whimpered. "You did a good job, boy. Prince will be proud." Roman gave Dog a head rub and a nudge on his butt and he reluctantly headed away. "Erin, Jamie, Ryan, get out now. No arguments," he added when he saw Erin's readiness to protest.

"Same goes to you, Logan. This is *my* mission. You take the transmitter. And that kragma sliver. Once you're out, I'll give him another shot of paralyzer, stick the capsule in his mouth and get out as fast as I can. If the tunnel collapses, I'll count on you to dig me out."

The explosion occurred before Roman was halfway up the tunnel. He heard the initial deafening burst, then heard nothing at all. But he could still feel, and the sharp pain in his calf let him know he'd been hit by one of the deadly shards from the Velid's body. The pain shot up his leg and through his back making it impossible to crawl any farther.

Suddenly strong hands clamped onto both his wrists and his body was yanked upward. He could see Tripper and Logan closing the hatch, Peace pressing her hands on his chest, mouths moving but he couldn't make out words. Everyone seemed to be in a great hurry. He looked for Erin but the faces above him blurred and swirled.

Then everything went black.

CHAPTER 32

Erin jackknifed to her feet the instant Tarla and Brianne entered the visitor's room of the sanatorium. Peace rose with considerably more care. "How is he? Can I see him?"

As Tarla gave Erin a brief but firm hug, Brianne announced, "Roman's going to be fine. He's in recuperation now, sleeping off the anesthetic. You'll be able to take him back to the apartment in about an hour."

"Anesthetic?" Erin asked suspiciously. "Please tell me they didn't operate on his brain or pump him full of that male neutralizing concoction, what did you call it—"

"The antidote," Brianne said quietly. "And no, nothing was done to change him in any way. His eardrums had to be repaired and the poison was flushed from his system. The medics were very surprised he survived. And since I didn't see anyone put her hands on him to help his body fight the poison, I couldn't explain it any better than they could."

Erin smiled with gratitude. "Thank you. We never meant for you to have to keep our secrets."

"I can't imagine what you're referring to," Brianne said, smiling in return. "Also, the medics couldn't be sure if it was the explosion or the poison, but they noted that some of Roman's cellular walls had been damaged, so those have been repaired as well."

Erin's mind swiftly sorted through Roman's memories and found a concern about cellular-wall deterioration. Had Heart's medics healed him? Or had they *repaired* something that had allowed him to go invisible or incorporeal?

"Don't look so worried, Erin," Tarla said. "They've had to make a few repairs on Logan over the years and he's always come back as masculine as he went in. But, just so you know, I was permitted to observe the procedures with Brianne, and I assure you, his brain was not worked on."

Erin audibly exhaled to show her relief but she wouldn't completely relax until she and Roman were alone again. "Thank you. But if it's still going to be an hour, I could use a distraction. What's going on with everyone else?"

Peace spoke before Tarla could reply. "As long as Tarla is here now, I hope you don't mind if I return to the apartment for a while. These old bones could use a nap."

Erin gave Peace a warm hug. "Thank you so much for helping Roman...and keeping me calm. When I asked you to be part of this team, it never occurred to me that I would be in need of your healing touch. Hopefully, you'll be able to nap in your own bed very soon."

"I must leave as well," Brianne said. "I have a promise to keep."

"Of course—" Brianne was out the door before Erin could finish her response. She gave Tarla a curious look and got a knowing smirk in return.

"Jamie and Ryan's reward for their assistance in saving Heart from destruction is dinner at the Imperial Palace...with Brianne and Jason. And Jason gets to be served at the table with them...at Jamie's insistence."

"I never got a chance to have that talk with them," Erin said with a frown.

"It wouldn't have made any difference," Tarla assured her. "The young heart rarely listens to the head...or to someone older and wiser. But in this case, I don't think you need to worry about any of them. I have a feeling everything will work out for the best. The attractions seem to be completely mutual, or maybe it's just because they're twins."

Erin sighed. "The first time I saw Roman, I pulled a gun on him."

Tarla laughed. "Well, that's an original way to meet your soul's mate. I gather it was not a case of love at first sight."

That made Erin smile. "Far from it."

"You wanted to be distracted. Tell me the story of Roman and Erin. Then if there's still time, I'll tell you about Logan and Tarla, although my story doesn't have such a dramatic beginning."

Once Erin began, she ended up relating much more than she'd intended but it effectively took her mind off counting the minutes pass. She had just told Tarla about the Garden of Eden when a slightly disoriented Roman was brought into the room by a medic. It was all she could do to restrain herself until the woman left. And when she was finally free to hold him, she had a very hard time letting go.

I was so afraid, she thought.

I'm sorry.

"How's your hearing," Tarla asked, reminding them she was there.

Erin made herself stop squeezing Roman but held

onto his hand.

"I'm hearing better than ever," he said with a crooked grin. "And other than not knowing anything that happened after the explosion, I feel perfectly fine."

"Good. I have some things to tell you but let's wait until we get to your apartment. Logan says he'll meet us there."

As they made their way through the private passageways, Tarla said, "By the way, Robin and I absolutely *love* Hari. The way she meshed with us today, you'd think she'd lived here her whole life."

"Really?" questioned Roman. "She never struck me as the type to make friends easily."

"Maybe you just aren't what she was looking for in a friend," Tarla replied cryptically, then quickly said, "I'm kidding. I think it's Heart that has her opening up. How well do you know her, Erin?"

"Not at all. I invited her mentor, Kanji Cho, to join the Psych Team, and he brought her as his apprentice."

"It's not like she spent the day telling us her life story, but she said enough for me to gather that she was strictly controlled her entire life and her *mentor* was more of a *master*. She was never permitted to form outside relationships of any kind. He made certain she was well treated and received an advanced academic and physical education, but it was all toward developing her gifts for his own purposes. Apparently, her only form of independence was that she never let him know just how mentally gifted she really is. Anyway, she doesn't want to go back and I think she'd fit in here as a Guardian."

"We certainly wouldn't force her to return," Erin said.

"Good. That makes one," Tarla said.

They reached the apartment before they could question Tarla's comment. Logan was already waiting for them.

"You look okay," he said to Roman as they went inside.

"Thanks to you, I assume."

Logan shrugged. "Tripper and I were hanging over the edge of the opening just in case. Thank God you thought to ask that last question or we'd all be dead."

"That was Erin's idea," Roman said bringing her hand up to his lips. "Her intuition is a lot stronger than my instincts."

"Sounds like you make a good pair."

Roman smiled at Erin. "I certainly think so."

"Any chance you'd consider staying on here with us?"

Logan's question was unexpected in spite of what Tarla had said minutes before. Roman and Erin looked into each other's eyes, smiled and simultaneously said, "No, thank you."

"At least not willingly," amended Erin. "Have you had any thoughts as to how we're going to get away?"

"Thoughts, yes," Tarla said. "A plan...maybe. Remember, we got our freedom by saving these women from being overtaken by the Velids. You just saved their planet and took out the last Velid spy while you were at it. That will count for quite a bit with Parisia and the Security Council. Iris is...less flexible. And Parliament falls somewhere in between. But they all understand a good negotiation."

Logan interrupted. "I'm starving, so Roman probably is too. You can keep talking while I throw dinner together." As he opened cabinets and drawers, Tarla, Roman and Erin sat on the stools by the counter.

"While you were all off on your adventure," Tarla

said in a teasing tone, "I polled the Guardians. You already knew Geoff and Robin want to go back and that we intend to stay. It turns out there are only two more Guardians who want to leave—Charlene and Kevin. Hari definitely wants to stay."

"So does Tripper," Logan interjected.

"What?" Erin was shocked.

"I get it," Roman said.

For Erin's sake, Logan explained. "He and I had time to talk over the past few days and our backgrounds aren't that different. Earth doesn't represent a happy home for him any more than it does for me. Here on Heart, he might have to change the way he behaves in public, but he never has to fear someone from the past tracking him down and slitting his throat while he sleeps."

Tarla let that sink in then added, "We would vouch for him as a Guardian so that he would have as many privileges as Logan. And Hari said she would be willing to share a residence with him as her house servant. So you see, that's already two replacements. And if *my* intuition is on target, there are going to be two more by the time dinner at the palace is concluded."

Roman frowned. "Whether or not the numbers match up, I don't remember agreeing to—"

Give it up, Erin warned.

"Heart women aren't the only ones who know how to negotiate. You need our help to get off this planet. And in exchange, you will take six of our people back with you. It's that simple."

"Six?" Roman and Erin questioned at the same time.

"Yes. There are two more. Do you remember me telling you about Lee Tang and T.J., the original Guardians who got sentenced to the farm because they

couldn't follow the rules? Well, Robin and I, um..."
she glanced at Logan and grimaced. "We got them out
today. They're waiting in our apartment."

Logan shook his head and looked away.

"Nobody will find out," Tarla said adamantly.
"With all the new crossovers, the observers' full
attention is focused on them. It's total chaos right
now. You remember how it was. That's how we were
able to sneak them out."

"You're the boss," Logan muttered as he set two
plates with thick sandwiches in front of Tarla and
Erin. "You used the controller?" He brought the other
two plates to the counter and sat down.

"Yes. But I was extremely fast, and used a different
spot going out. The disruptions in the farm's force
field were too minimal to be investigated."

"Excuse me for interrupting," Roman said, "but you
mentioned the new crossovers. Our intention was to
strand the criminals on a primitive planet, but to
return their victims to Earth. How do we go about
getting them back?"

"You don't," Logan said simply.

Tarla took a sip of tea. "Erin told me about the
conversation you overheard between Parisia and Iris.
They may be pushed into letting a handful of you
leave, but if you start messing with their order of
things, not only will you never be permitted to leave,
you'll end up on the farm yourselves. This is Heart,
not Earth. And you are just an uninvited overnight
guest."

Tarla's words hung ominously in the air until she
spoke again. "If it helps ease your consciences at all, I
took a peek into the new crossover files. Other than
beneficial healing, no memory depletion or brain
circuitry adjustments were made on the ones you call
victims. Mind you, the interrogation process is done

using a mild truth inducer before the antidote is administered.

"Every one of them had a similar story. They signed up for The Eden Experiment knowing they were cutting all ties with their previous lives. In most cases, they had no relatives or friends they would miss, which seemed to be why they were selected. They were also anxious to be part of a community that was pre-technology and completely self-sufficient. When asked if they would prefer to live in such a community on an alien planet or return to their home on Earth, every person opted for the community."

While Tarla took a bite of her sandwich, Logan offered his opinion. "I wouldn't even ask Parisia about any of those people. Not about what they'll be doing or how they'll be treated or if they'll ever be offered a chance to leave the farm. *Nothing.*"

"There's one more reason you have to find a way to be okay with leaving all of them behind. Despite what I said first, there is still a chance they will refuse to allow you to leave. You've proven you would all be great additions to the Guardianship…and they don't even know about your special talents. You have to be ready to take off on a moment's notice, and that could only happen if you are traveling super light."

Erin took a breath and accepted what Tarla and Logan had advised as necessary, like it or not. "When you were scanning the crossover files, did you look at the shepherds? Is it true they were all operated on and no longer have any psychic abilities?"

Tarla nodded. "True. And because of their leanings toward negative behavior, they'll be closely monitored and their doses of the antidote will be significantly higher than normal."

"Is there any way to question one of them?" Erin asked.

Logan narrowed his eyes at her. "Why would you want to do that?"

"We were told there was a boy among the shepherds, one with an exceptional ability of some sort. The leader, Adam, named him Cain, which implied he saw him as a son with dark tendencies. He wasn't with us and Hari wasn't able to remote view him among the sheep left behind."

Tarla shook her head. "The last ten years of Adam's memory were erased. He wouldn't remember the boy by Cain or any other name."

"How about dessert?" Logan asked, attempting to put an end to further questioning. "I saw cookies and brownies in your food supplies."

"Not for me, but give Erin one of those brownies," Roman said. "Would anyone care for tea? I know how to make that."

Erin and Tarla both chuckled and accepted his offer.

"I've been wondering," Roman said to Logan. "Since we've been so careful to keep the team's abilities a secret, what was Brianne told we were doing down in the cave to get the Velid to talk?"

It was Logan's turn to chuckle. "Actually, Ryan took care of that. Told her the alien was terrified of Dog so he threatened to let him tear the alien apart unless he spilled his guts. Brianne was so relieved to see him come back out of the hole, I think she would have believed anything he'd said."

"Don't be so sure about that," Erin said. "Brianne is her mother's daughter and will one day be the Imperial Prefect. She saw Hari levitate the hatch cover *and* she knows Peace helped keep Roman alive. My intuition tells me she also knows the two of you communicate telepathically. If she didn't question Ryan's explanation, it was because she decided it was to her benefit to accept it."

* * *

"I like them," Erin declared after Tarla and Logan left. "Not enough to stay here, but if we were forced to, it would have been nice to have another couple we could be open with."

Roman angled his head at her. "What if they wanted to go back with us?"

Erin's eyes widened. "Did Logan tell you that was a possibility?"

"No. I was just wondering if that would make a difference."

Erin knew he was blocking her from his thoughts, which made her glad he could do that on his own, but extremely curious as to why. "I would still like them."

"But you wouldn't *need* them."

"Maybe it's the craziness of this day, or all the crazy days of the past weeks, but I'm not sure what you're really wondering about. And if you don't want me to know your thoughts, I'm afraid you're going to have to come right out and tell me."

He took her hand in his and tugged her toward the bed. "I'm just tired." He pulled the tie from her hair. "And I almost died today." He removed her shirt. "And last night's speed round barely took the edge off my...*tension*." His fingers slipped into the waist of her pants as his lips touched hers.

Erin welcomed his kiss...for two seconds, before she abruptly pushed him away. "Oh no you don't. I'm not in heat any more so you can't just seduce me into forgetting that you're up to something. Talk first."

He pulled her back to him, holding her bottom firmly enough to prove the seduction wasn't all about distracting her. "Talk after."

In a heartbeat, she felt a spear of desire shoot from his body to hers, but it hadn't yet reached her mind. She worked her hand between their bodies and kneaded his erection. "I want this. But not enough to ignore the fact that you're blocking me...for a reason."

He released her and stepped back. "Fine. But can we at least sit? I don't think all the anesthetic is out of my system yet." They sat on the sofa, facing each other, but she gave in to letting him hold her hand. "Logan got me thinking about what it would be like to stay here. It wouldn't be that bad."

She made a face at him. "It wouldn't be that good either. We both have careers we enjoy on Earth. We both have family and friends we care about. I can't believe you'd be *fine* never seeing them again. I know I wouldn't be."

Roman shrugged and his gaze fell to the hand he was holding. "We've made new friends here and we'd have new careers."

Erin squeezed his hand. "And?"

"Even though neither one of us was anxious to be joined, I like how we fit together. And I'm not just talking about sex. I like working with you, and talking with you, and eating meals with you."

"I like all that too. But what does any of it have to do with us staying on Heart?"

He met her gaze. "Because, before we performed the emergency joining ceremony, we made an agreement to maintain separate lives. I figured that agreement would be null and void if we stayed on Heart."

She let the meaning behind his words sink in and tested how she felt about it. Not only wasn't she frightened by the idea of having him as a long-term, live-in life partner, she was positively stimulated by it. "Maybe we could take a clue from the Heart women and renegotiate the agreement."

He arched one eyebrow. "I'm listening."

She inched closer and reached for his other hand. "The agreement made perfect sense when we barely knew each other. But the fact is, we've been on the supersonic track to knowing everything about each other from the night you broke into my house. I've gone from total suspicion to trusting you with my life. And today, when you were nearly killed, I realized how empty my life would be without you in it."

His mouth curved upward. "You love me."

"I did not say that."

"But you were thinking it."

"Maybe I've considered the possibility, but that word is used too easily. It's much more important to me that I *like* you."

"Well, I *like* you too. But I will warn you that when I let down the barrier, you may pick up a thought about my having that other feeling also."

Erin felt her cheeks flush. "One challenge at a time. First we renegotiate the agreement."

For that she got another raised eyebrow and another, "I'm listening."

"I think it would be reasonable if we forget about living apart…for the time being. But we have an open and honest review our situation on a monthly basis."

"Yearly," he countered.

"Bi-monthly."

"Six months and that's my final offer."

The smile she'd been holding back broke free. "Agreed. We will have six month reviews. But they will take place during a special, full-weekend retreat, just the two of us, and no work or secret missions."

"Amend that to every other retreat being at least a week long…and not necessarily on Earth."

Erin's eyes widened. "You mean like Norona?"

He shrugged. "Maybe. There are a lot of planets out

there, but which one we visit will be my surprise to you. So, are we done with the renegotiation?"

"All except for one important detail," she told him as she stood and pulled him to his feet.

"And what might that be?" he asked with a knowing grin as he lowered the barrier between their minds.

"Something that wouldn't be permitted if we stayed on Heart."

He swept her up into his arms and carried her the short distance to the bed. "I'm still listening."

"I get to have my way with you whenever and wherever I choose. Agreed?"

"Yes ma'am. Might this be one of those times and places, ma'am?"

Rather than give him an oral response, she sent him an explicit oral image.

CHAPTER 33

"We stayed up most of the night going over the pros and cons," Jamie informed Erin and Roman.

"And the pros make the cons unimportant," Ryan finished.

"This isn't something you can change your mind about in six months," Erin warned them. "You can't just hop on a plane and go home."

"You know our background," Jamie replied defensively. "There is no home to go back to. We were dumped as newborns. Never found out why or who conceived us. And in all the years after that, we never had anyone to count on but each other."

"You'll have to keep your gifts a secret, even from those you live with."

Jamie shrugged. "Keeping secrets was the only way to survive the foster system. But we both think there's a good possibility—"

"…that eventually," Ryan cut in, "we'll be able to tell Brianne and Jason the truth. They're twins, like us, but with a whole different set of challenges. And they're already agreeable to having, uh, they called it *intimate relations* with us, which is apparently legal if one of the couple is a Guardian and the Heart citizen is willing."

"And Ryan understands how he has to behave in public."

"Which will be harder for Jamie than me."

"And have we mentioned we'd be living in the Imperial Palace?"

"And not just temporarily either. They're like royalty. When Parisia retires, Brianne will take over." Ryan chuckled. "My mistress will be the most powerful woman on the planet. Obviously, that fact was on the pros list."

Roman spoke for the first time since Jamie and Ryan and knocked on their door. "Speaking of the royal line, has Parisia heard about your desire to remain and become part of her family?"

"We met with her first thing this morning," Jamie replied. "Right before we came here. She gave us her blessing...and really seemed genuinely happy about it."

"Which wouldn't make sense except for what we accidentally found out," Ryan mumbled.

Erin sighed. "Oh dear. What did you do?"

The twins glanced at each other, then Jamie explained. "We didn't intentionally *do* anything, we swear. But she touched both our hands at the same time to give us her blessing and we saw what she was thinking about, why she was so happy."

"She and her houseman, Delbert, have one of those intimate relationships," Ryan blurted out. "In secret, of course."

Erin's surprise was evident. Roman had something more important on his mind. "Did Parisia ask about any of the others? If anyone else might consider staying on?"

Jamie and Ryan looked at each other again and both shook their heads, no.

To Erin, Roman said, "Maybe she didn't ask because she still has no intention of letting any of us leave."

"That wouldn't be right," Jamie protested. "Not after what we did for them."

"I'll talk to Brianne," Ryan said.

The communicator buzzed and everyone quieted as Erin quickly answered the call. A few seconds later she disconnected and said, "Actually, we'll all be talking to Brianne and everyone else in about fifteen minutes. That was Tarla. Our presence is requested at the lab."

"I have good news and bad news," Geoffrey announced as soon as Roman, Erin, Jamie and Ryan entered.

Erin's gaze scanned the room. All of her team, and the Guardians who they'd been working with, were already there.

"Good news first," Roman said.

"I spent the night going over all my research and calculations I've compiled over the years and I am ninety-nine percent sure that the transmissions from the Velid's device were the cause of the gateway being opened. I am just as certain that the electromagnet energy from the kragma field had been gradually expanding the beacon's width and range for some time. In a few centuries, it would indeed cause the implosion of Earth's sun and the explosion of Heart's."

"Why only ninety-nine percent?" asked Logan.

Geoffrey shrugged. "I didn't want to sound cocky."

"So what's the bad news?" Roman asked.

"I haven't been able to determine how long the gateway will remain open after the transmitter is destroyed. It could even be instantaneous. Someone on this side will have to take responsibility for destroying it *after* your ship passes through."

"You'll have to trust us to take care of it," Tarla told Roman.

"As much as I'd like to personally take a hammer to the thing after all the trouble it's caused us, I don't mind passing the torch off to you and Logan. Was there anything else?"

It took Geoffrey a moment to recall what else he had to report. "Oh, right. This is neither good news nor bad. I just wanted everyone to know that Ray and Kara are working on a new, fully automated, sonic scan program using the recording of the Velid's beacon. That way they can continue to search the planet to ensure no other devices are making calls to unfriendly planets, without tying up a large staff. And, in case anyone hasn't heard already, I purposely used the pronoun *they* because Robin and I will be departing on Roman's ship."

"As will we," Charlene said for her and Kevin.

"But Tripper and I have decided to stay," announced Hari.

Together, Ryan and Jamie excitedly chimed in. "We're staying too!"

Tarla walked up to Erin and murmured, "Well, that certainly set things up for an interesting conversation."

Erin followed Tarla's gaze and saw that Parisia, Iris, Brianne and Jason were standing quietly in the doorway.

"By the way," Tarla continued in a whisper. "None of the others know yet, but Lee and T.J. are already on your ship with Prince and Dog. Don't worry though, the antidote in their systems will keep them very mellow until you give them one of these." She placed two capsules into Erin's pants pocket. Before Erin could react, Tarla clapped her hands and loudly said, "Attention up front please. We have honored guests."

The group instantly hushed and the men moved to the rear of the room behind the women, and submissively bowed their heads.

"Thank you, Tarla," Parisia said as the four of them entered the lab. "We won't delay your celebrations more than a few minutes but we didn't want an excessive amount of time to pass before we personally extended our extreme gratitude to each and every one of you. Regardless of your role in the recent mission, every one of you has performed an invaluable service to our citizenry." She, Brianne and Iris gifted them with lady-like applause, to which the female recipients responded with partial curtseys.

Brianne delivered the next speech. "To our Guardians, once again you have proven your worth to us. In return, we are rewarding each of you with an upgrade in residence and incidental allowance."

Iris had the final segment. "As to those of you who came uninvited…" Her pause had everyone holding their breath. "We will forever be in your debt. Our reward to all of you is the esteemed position of Guardian, with all the privileges that are accorded that title, including the new upgrades." Again she paused and purposely met the gazes of each member of Erin's team and shot narrow-eyed glances at Robin and Charlene. "We were pleased to hear that four of you have already decided to remain on Heart, but we are equally disheartened to hear that four current Guardians wish to leave."

Tarla stepped forward. "Permission to speak?"

"Of course," Parisia said kindly.

"I mean no disrespect, but six years ago you promised we could leave if we helped you defend the planet from the Velids, only to find out afterward that you didn't have the technology to help us get back. We have once again helped you save Heart, but now we have the means to leave. Even so, most of the Guardians have chosen to stay here and are very appreciative of your acknowledgement of our service. Those who wish to leave are aware of your desire for secrecy and each will swear an honor oath to never reveal where they've been. But you should know that, even if we told every person on Earth, you would not suddenly be overrun with crossovers. Once the transmission device is destroyed, the gateway will be closed and there will never again be a crossover event, accidental or intentional."

Iris's expression remained fixed. "That may be true, but—"

"Excuse me," Jamie gushed and strode quickly toward Iris. "I am so sorry to interrupt but there is something moving on your robe. If I may...?"

The only evidence that Iris had a fear of creepy-crawly things was a widening of her eyes. She held perfectly still as Jamie placed her hand on her shoulder and made a show of capturing something and carrying it outside the lab to release it.

"It was just a little moth," Jamie said as she returned with a bright smile. "I'm sorry if I frightened you, but I couldn't tell what it was and it looked like it was heading for your neck."

Iris visibly relaxed. "Thank you for your concern. As I was saying," she paused, frowning as though she couldn't quite remember *what* she'd been saying. "As I was about to say, even though we may have no reason for concern, our non-negotiable decision is that none of the people who have been transferred to the farm will be allowed to leave. We will miss those of you who decide to leave but our gratitude and positive wishes go with you."

Parisia and Brianne glanced at each other and didn't quite manage to conceal their bewilderment over Iris's declaration.

That was not what she was about to say, Erin thought to Roman.

No kidding. He shifted his gaze toward Jamie who was staring intently at Iris.

She swore she never used that gift—

Unless it was for a person's own good. That was exactly what she swore. And in this case, what Iris was going to say would not have ended well.

Just in case Jamie's influence is only temporary, let's get off this upside-down planet while we can.

After Parisia and Iris left, Brianne handed Roman a package that Jason had been hiding beneath his shirt. Opening it carefully, Roman grinned when he unwrapped his two laser pistols but had to restrain himself from hugging Brianne when he saw his Innerworld ring. "Thank you," he said with a bowed head. "For everything."

Even though it was not discussed, those who wanted to leave Heart moved as though the devil himself was on their heels. Sincere goodbyes and wishes for happiness were shared quickly. Even Tarla and Robin's tearful exchange was understandably brief.

Erin only took one extra minute to give congratulatory hugs to Jamie and Ryan and say two words to Hari and Tripper. "Be happy."

An hour later, the passengers were seated on board the Noronian cargo ship and Roman was in the cockpit with Prince and Dog. Everyone practically held their breath as they waited for the roof door to open. Their silent tension continued as a section of the planet's shield was lowered to allow Prince to take the ship out. But full-fledged relief was held back until Prince got them through the portal and they could see

Earth's northeastern hemisphere below. A second later, Prince switched on stealth mode.

"I knew you could do it!" Roman shouted, giving Prince a strong pat on his back. "You deserve a medal for bravery and being the best friend a human ever had. I just wish we didn't have to keep all of this a secret."

"But it is a very good secret to keep in my mind since I always envied your being able to go on adventures and that is enough of a medal for me."

Roman then vigorously rubbed Dog's head. "And *you*, my four-legged friend, made me proud to have you as my namesake."

Erin entered the cockpit, gave Prince and Dog warm hugs then kissed Roman hard on the mouth. "Do you know what I want to do as soon as we're back home?"

Roman gave her his sexiest smile.

"I meant besides that," she said with a giggle. "Nothing. I want to do absolutely *nothing* for at least a year."

"What about meeting the parents?"

"Oh. You're right, we need to do that." Her eyes slowly widened. "Does that mean we'll be going to Innerworld?"

"Yes, but I'll tell everyone to be as boring as possible."

"Everyone?"

"We did promise to have dinner with Gabe and my sister."

"Right. So a year isn't reasonable. But maybe we could pretend to still be away for an extra day or two."

"I guess that's a possibility. But what about Chief Friedrich? I figured we could call him to pick everyone up and take us home. It's not like Prince can land this thing in downtown Austin."

"Oh, you're right. Then he could update us about what happened at Eden after we left. And we have to help the others get settled. *Shoot.* Maybe we could schedule a few days of doing nothing next week."

Roman drew her onto his lap in the navigator's chair and gave her a light kiss. "Whatever you desire, shallah. As long as your definition of doing nothing is the same as mine." He drew her into a slow, deep kiss just to make sure their agendas matched up.

A half hour later, Prince set the ship down in a barren area well to the west of Austin. He stayed long enough for them to use the ship's communicator to call Chief with coordinates and for the passengers to disembark. Chief arrived with a helicopter shortly after Prince took off.

"Ah was beginnin' to fret a bit," Chief admitted after getting a long hug from Erin and a firm handshake from Roman.

"We had to take a few detours," Erin said. "We'll tell you what we can later, but first let me introduce you to our new friends, Geoffrey, Robin, Charlene, Kevin, Lee and T.J. And I'm not sure you ever met Peace."

Chief greeted each one then said, "Do Ah want to know how it is you left with different people than you came back with?"

Erin grimaced. "Not really, but if you give me a few days to untangle my thoughts, I'll come up with a really good explanation. Meanwhile, they will need your help with new identities and some start-up assistance. Maybe a financial award for helping to save the world, I mean, um…services rendered to the New Republic of Texas."

Chief rolled his eyes. "Ah can't wait to hear that really good explanation, but Ah'll take care of providin' some Texas hospitality to your new friends in the meantime."

On the flight back, Chief told them what they encountered when they arrived at Eden to rescue all the sheep left behind. "All the people were clear-headed but confused about why they'd been locked in a barn. They had no idea that months had passed since they'd arrived at Eden. But here's the kicker. None of them wanted to leave. They insisted they'd signed on for a stab at a new life and it didn't matter to them what happened to the man who'd developed the community. We're still conductin' interviews and dealin' with some legal ownership issues, but no one has been forced to leave."

Roman took a moment to phrase a reply. "Well, we can assure you that all the psychic criminals you were looking for have been dealt with and Adam Sirilovich will never be returning to claim ownership of the property."

Chief nodded. "Ah see. And Ah suppose there'll be a really good explanation to go with that assurance as well."

"Absolutely," Erin promised. "But there's one loose end, we're hoping you have information about. We were told there was a gifted boy among the shepherds, about ten or eleven, but we never saw him. He was called Cain, though that wouldn't be his real name. It was our understanding that he was one of the ones left behind."

Chief shook his head. "Everyone in the barn was an adult. Any idea what sort of ability he had?"

"No. But I'd strongly suggest you search through any records found in Eden. Maybe the boy's real name or home address is in there somewhere."

"Wish Ah could. But what computers were found were wiped clean and no paper files have been located so far. The place is enormous though, so my people are still searchin' for evidence to support that anyone there was connected to the crimes on record. But if the boy was only about ten, he probably had nothing to do with any of that anyway."

Roman exhaled heavily. "We weren't thinking about what he might have done under Adam's supervision. We're concerned about what he might be capable of as an adult."

It was after midnight before Erin and Roman were back in her house. She touched a lamp shade, a table and her favorite comfy chair. "I wasn't all that sure I'd ever see this room again."

Roman stepped behind her and wrapped his arms around her waist. "And I never doubted it for a second."

She turned in his arms and looked up at him. "Not even when you realized Eve had kidnapped you?"

"Nope. I knew you'd rescue me."

"How about when you were hit with the Velid poison dart."

"Nope. That's not the way I'm going to die."

"Oh? Are you telling me you *know* how you're going to die?"

"I know how we're both going to die—of very, very, very old age. If you were impressed with Heart's medical technology, just wait until you see what Innerworld has."

"Hmmm. So what you're saying is there will be an awful lot of semi-annual retreats in our future."

He kissed the tip of her nose. "That's a promise." He lowered his head to kiss her neck.

"Should we talk about how this is going to work?"

"How what's going to work?" He nipped her earlobe.

"Us. Our work. Our living arrangements. Whether we'll—"

He cut off her words with a long, sensuous kiss until he felt her let go of all her questions. "Those are just details. And details are best handled after a good night's sleep...something we haven't had much of since we met."

She took his hand in hers and led him to the stairs. "And you probably shouldn't expect to make up for that tonight either."

As he followed her up to *their* bedroom, he grinned and said, "Yes ma'am."

EPILOGUE

Norona (Terra Date 2353 A.D.)

Catastrophic Science Director Cattar slowly rose from her desk, walked out onto the veranda bordering her spacious office and took a deep breath. A cool breeze lifted and swirled the colorful caftan around her plump figure and she smiled. As often happened at moments like this she thought back to all the time she'd wasted worrying about one thing or another. Even the near catastrophe that old fool Lantana had caused with his faulty tempometer had ended without any residual effects.

She glanced back at her desk with the feeling that there was something she was supposed to check on, but whatever it was no longer seemed important. The day was simply too lovely to stay indoors.

AFTERWORD

Cody, Wyoming, 2079 A.D.

"You are the most beautiful little girl ever born. Yes you are," Soledad baby-talked to the infant suckling at her breast. "And your mama will always keep you safe. But you are a whole month old and I still haven't given you a proper name." She rocked back and forth, considering how she was named for a sadistic commander from the third world war and the baby's father had been named for the first murderer on Earth. No, she didn't want to weigh the babe down with a name that would suggest a personality before she had a chance to develop one of her own.

The pace of Soledad's rocking increased as she sorted through names and words that would suggest strength and intelligence. "Would you like to be called Athena, little one?" The lack of reaction had Soledad moving on. "Maybe something that hints at an extrasensory ability. Your papa could read anyone's mind and use that information for his own advantage. That's how we came to be living in such a grand state. The gift that came to me had very little use on a mundane level. Some might call it supernatural…others might say it was a gift from the devil…if they knew what I could do."

She glanced at the smoldering ashes of the talented young man she'd seduced to impregnate her. Cain had serviced her well enough, but once she was certain the baby was healthy, she had no more reason to put up with his pawing and slovenly habits. Besides, she wanted no one to ever come between her and this precious jewel.

How about a gem, like Sapphire or Ruby? No. Absolutely not. Much too common. The extrasensory ability idea felt the best so far.

"It may be a while before we discover how the combination of your papa's talents and mine will manifest in you, little one. So perhaps your name should leave the door open to any possibility."

Soledad's rocking quickened even more as she hummed the notes of a lullaby once sung to her by…*someone*…another who had served a purpose long ago…She shook off the vague memory and went back to thinking about the perfect name.

"I have it," she exclaimed, coming to an abrupt stop that startled the dozing infant and made her cry. But Soledad ignored the complaint. "I will call you Mysteria. And you will be a mystery to all who meet you."

THE
INNERWORLD AFFAIRS
SERIES

Turn the page for an

excerpt from

BLAZE

Innerworld Affairs Series

Book Seven

Marilyn Campbell

Mysty really didn't want to wake up but she heard the water running in her bathroom and that was enough to evoke the image of the man who spent last night in her bed. She felt her entire body smiling with the memory of how his every touch aroused her in a way she'd never before experienced.

Blaze—a super-sexy name for a super-hot man. She remembered wondering how he earned such a nickname. Now she knew.

She also remembered how strenuously he'd resisted the obvious chemistry between them. But whatever his reason, mutual attraction won out and now the only important question was whether he would rearrange his plans to spend the day in bed with her.

Should she pretend to still be sleeping and see what he might do to awaken her? Or should she take the initiative again and assume a seductive pose that left no question about her desire for another round of play?

Her thoughts took a sharp turn as she stretched and her fingers brushed over something that shouldn't have been on her bed. She jerked upright and stared around her in shock and dismay.

The bedsheets were totally scorched.

Before she could calm the panic, the bathroom door opened and Blaze stepped through a cloud of steam wearing nothing but a grin.

"I can explain," she said quickly, forcing herself to keep her gaze on his eyes rather than where it wanted to go.

"Really? Wouldn't you rather take a shower? You're covered in ash."

She blinked in bewilderment then looked down at her arms and breasts. He was right. She was covered with fire residue. But why wasn't he horrified, or even slightly disturbed? That question suddenly seemed more important than her explanation to him but rather than ask, she simply said, "Please don't leave…at least not until I can explain," and hurried into the bathroom.

Even though she hastily showered and returned to the bedroom wrapped in a light robe, Blaze had already dressed and disposed of the burned sheets. She allowed him to take her hand and lead her to the edge of the bed.

"We need to talk," he said gently and waited for her to sit before taking the spot beside her. "There's no reason to be shy…or afraid."

She angled her head at him. "I assure you, I'm neither. But I am curious. How is it that *you* aren't freaking out on *me*? Have you slept with other women who set the bed on fire?"

He chuckled. "It wasn't the whole bed, only the sheets. And it was very superficial. And no, this was a first for me. But why are you so sure you caused it?"

Mysty frowned. He seemed to be finding this very funny, but she knew from experience that his grin, and his attraction to her, would be erased the instant she explained. However, since she'd never come up with a reasonable lie, she braced herself for his disgust and told the truth. "I can start fires…without matches."

"I know." His amused grin didn't alter.

She stiffened. "What do you mean? How do you know?"

"I saw you light kindling with the snap of your fingers. Don't you remember?"

She struggled to recall the last time or place she might have done that. The scene that popped into her mind was one she chose not to remember. "That's not possible," she murmured.

It was his turn to frown. "Didn't you read my mind last night? I didn't do anything to stop you."

She pressed her temples and shook her head. "Every time you say something, I have more questions. Okay, first of all, I can't just randomly read people's thoughts. I have to have a specific question and be making physical contact. Second, I only use that gift when absolutely necessary."

He smirked. "Like when you're stealing information to commit a crime?"

"I only steal from those who deserve to lose something," she replied defensively.

"A noble thief. I seem to remember that defense being used in the past."

She set aside that discussion in favor of one in which she might have an advantage. "Back to my question. How do you know I can light fires?"

"I saw you do it. In your cave in Wyoming. You were just a little girl."

She abruptly stood and crossed her arms protectively. "You followed me? Spied on me? You're not that much older than I am. What were you, some sort of pervie teenage boy?"

He sighed. "If you gain information by reading my mind, will you believe it?" She slowly nodded. "Then, please, sit back down, hold my hands and focus on when you first met me."

For a few seconds she held a debate with herself then decided to accept his challenge. She sat down facing him and took both his hands in hers. It took her a few more seconds to quiet the noise in her mind and focus on a single question. Gradually, she saw an image of herself as a young girl, moving around in the dark cave, building the fire, lighting the kindling with a snap of her fingers. But it was all from *his* point of view, which was clearly from farther inside the cave. She heard herself telling him how the fire would keep them warm and keep the wild things from bothering them.

Once she recalled that much of the memory, she was able to look at it from her own point of view...and that's when she saw who, or rather *what* she was talking to. He was a huge, monstrous being, with four legs and great wings and a long, snake-like tail, but he seemed weak, possibly dying. Compared to what she was hiding from, the creature didn't frighten her at all. She tried to withdraw her hands but he held tight.

"You weren't afraid of me then, Mysty. Remember that. You were just annoyed that I was trespassing."

She opened her eyes and stared deeply into his. "I thought I'd imagined that beast. How can you be here, like this, and there...like *that*? How is that possible?" The answers to all her questions suddenly filled her mind with a montage of images and words. *Leviatha...a prehistoric planet...colorful reptilian creatures in the air, on the land, in the sea. War...devastation...salvation. Transforming from a magnificent, winged, red and black fire-breather into a duplicate of his human savior...and back again. Middle Ages Earth...dragon hunters. Centuries rolling by...*

"You're immortal?" This time when she pulled, he released her hands.

"It would seem so."

She stood slowly and paced back and forth several times before speaking again. "And not only are you not from Earth, you're not a *real* human."

Blaze was on his feet and towering over her in an instant. Though his voice was quiet, his tone was angry. "There are things you could say that might insult me. However, considering the atrocities I've witnessed humans committing, accusing me of *not* being human might be considered a compliment. But just to be clear, when I am in this form, I am *physically* as human as you are, perhaps more. I don't believe *real* humans are capable of setting bedsheets on fire with their passion."

She glanced at the bed, felt a flash of that passion, and heat rushed to her cheeks. "It could have been your fault," she murmured unconvincingly. "I know you can breathe fire."

He remained within her personal space, making her aware of how much bigger and stronger he was, yet not touching any part of her. "Only when I'm in that form. If I want to set something on fire in this form, I need to use an igniter, just like *real* humans."

More images and thoughts zipped through Mysty's mind too quickly for her to come to any sort of conclusion. "I'm confused."

His expression tightened. "Why? Because you had sex with an alien *beast* and now you're ashamed that you enjoyed it? Try to remember that you were the one who kept pushing me. I tried to discourage—"

"Damn you, shut up!" She huffed. "I'm very aware of who seduced whom. What I'm confused about is this—after a night of incredible sex then the burned sheets then finding out you're my imaginary dragon—why is it that all I can think about is what it would be like to ride you."

BLAZE

available in print and ebook

MARILYN CAMPBELL has been published in the genres of suspense, erotic thrillers, futuristic, time-travel, paranormal, erotic and lighthearted contemporary romances, non-fiction metaphysical works and has had a screenplay produced. A true thrill-junkie, she has jumped out of an airplane, raced around the Indy 500 track, driven solo throughout the United States and believes a great roller coaster ride can cure whatever ails her. She currently resides in Massachusetts with her daughter and their four-legged companions, Milk-Dud and Sweetie.